I0761942

THE TRIALS OF ASCENSION

Eight-One-Five Publishing
Brendan@Brendan-Noble.com

Cover Illustration by Mariia Lytovchenko

Interior art by Mariia Lytovchenko

Cover design by Deranged Doctor Design
www.derangeddoctordesign.com

Books by Brendan Noble

The Frostmarked Chronicles:
A Dagger in the Winds
The Trials of Ascension
The Daughters of the Earth

Frostmarked Tales:
The Rider in the Night
The Lady of Rolika

The Prism Files:
The Fractured Prism
Crimson Reigns
Pridefall
White Crown

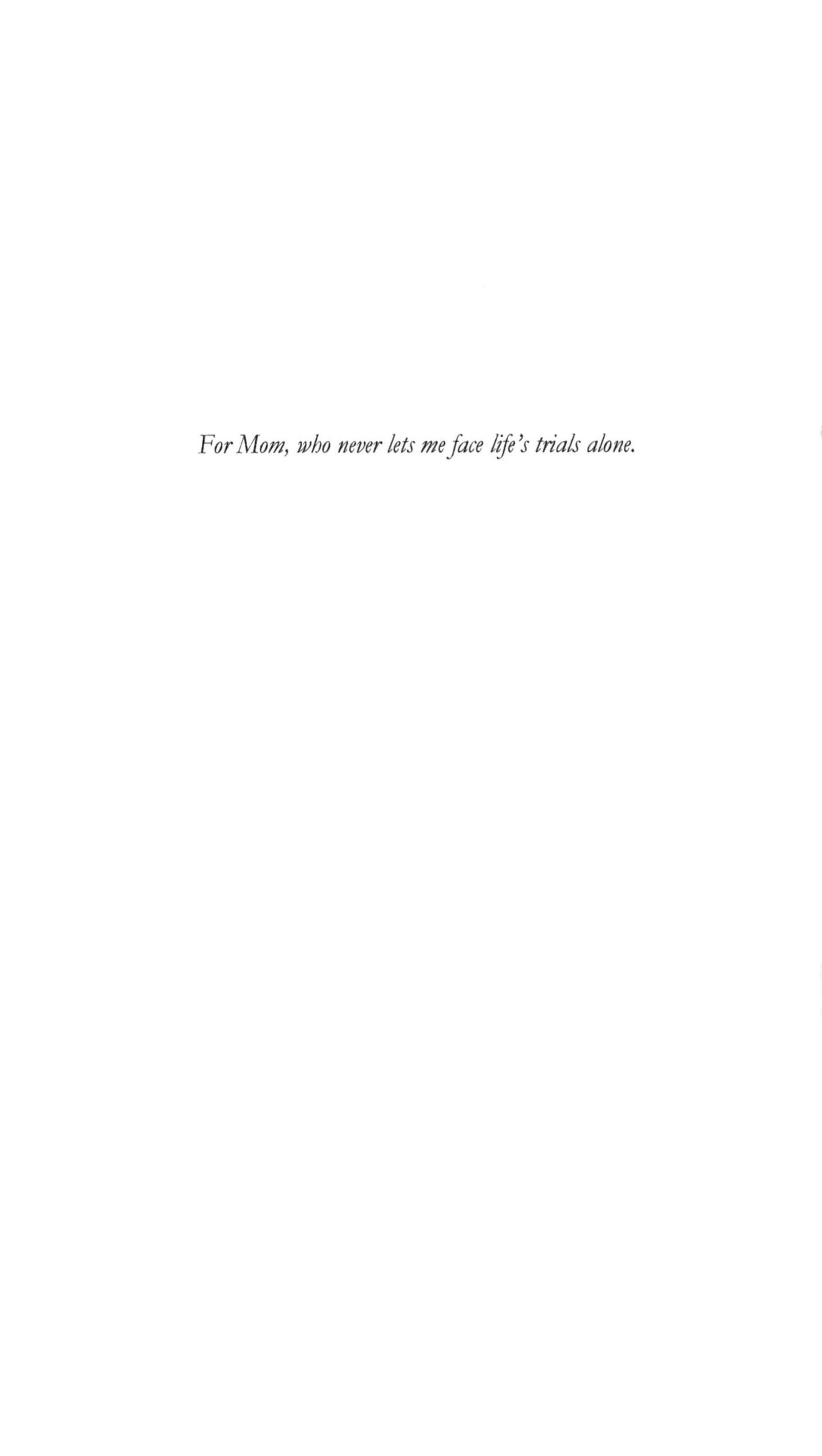

For Mom, who never lets me face life's trials alone.

Godly and Demonic Marks

Marzanna - Frostmark
Winter, Disease, and Death

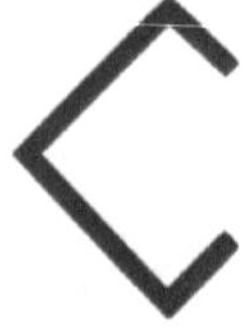

Dziewanna - Bowmark
Wilds, Hunt, and Spring

Jaryło - Springmark
Spring, Agriculture, and War

Mokosz - Mothermark
Women and Divination

Perun - Thundermark
Thunder, Justice, and War

Weles - Serpentmark
Underworld and Lowlands

Swaróg - Forgemark
Celestial Fire and Smithing

Dadźbóg - Sunmark
The Sun

Rod - Wheelmark
Creation and Balance

Wacław - Eclipsemark
Storm Demon (Płanetnik)

Pronunciation Guide

Characters

Wacław Lubiewicz: Vahtswahv Luubeeayvihch

(Little Name) - Wašek: Vahshehk

Otylia Welesiakówna: Ohtihleeah Vehlehseeahkohvnah

(Little Name) - Otylka: Ohtihlkah

Xobas: Kohbahs

Narcyz: Nahrsihz

Andrij: Ahndrey

Kyustendil: Kyuustehndihl

Gods

Marzanna: Mahrzahnah

Weles: Vehlehs

Dziewanna: Djehvahnah

Jaryło: Yahrihwoh

Mokosz: Mohkohsh

Perun: Pehruun

Dadźbóg: Dahdzbohg

Strzybóg: Strihbohg

Other Terms

Žityje: Zhihtyeh

Dwie Rzeki: Dvee Zehkee

Krowik(ie): Krohvihk(ee)

Astiw(ie): Ahstihv(ee)

Szeptucha: Shehptuuhah

Płanetnik: Pwahnehtnihk

Wilkołak: Vihlkohwahk

Żmij: Zmee

Kwiecień: Kvihehchehn

Jawia: Yahveeah

Nawia: Nahveeah

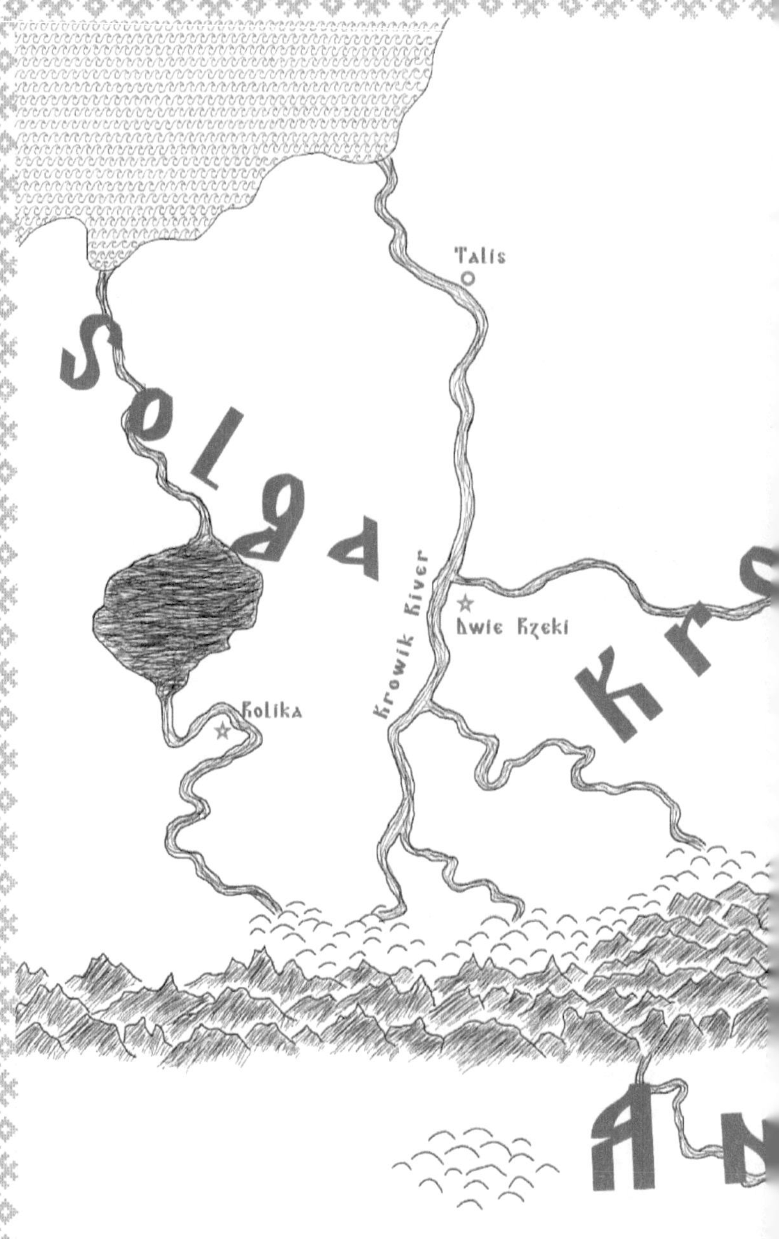
Talis
Solga
Krowik River
Dwie Rzeki
Kolika

Klist
Mangled Woods
Simuk
wik
Clan Encampment
Narrow Pass
Wyzra River
Kynnytsia
Zurgow
ałe Wzgórze
Astiw
uthern Hills
Vastroth
Huchia
vora
Télem

THE FROSTMARKED CHRONICLES 2

THE TRIALS OF ASCENSION

BRENDAN NOBLE

Prologue

Ara

Why must boys always argue?

"THAT'S A LIE!" NARCYZ SHOUTED across the tent in his typical morning spat. Over the course of our journey, his hair had grown oddly long for a Krowikie warrior and its brown curls contrasted with his reddened face.

Bidaês huffed and crossed his arms as he lounged in Narcyz's cot, infuriating him on purpose. "If it were, you'd be dead."

Ever since we'd reached the camp where Bidaês's Simukie clan had joined with the Zurgowie—the nomadic people my family had left four years before—the two boys had been at each other's throats. Our group had traveled with the clans for only a week, but it had seemed an eternity of them trying to size each other up.

I wished Otylia was there instead of trapped in the underworld of Nawia. She would've ended their quarrels or ended them. It was hard to know which I preferred.

Having heard enough of the boys' arguing, I leaped up from my cot and snatched my bow and quiver from the edge of the rounded tent. There was no real reason for me to carry my weapons when the two clans had guards everywhere, but after our trip through the Mangled Woods and witnessing my best friend's death, it was the only thing that gave me some semblance of control.

"If you two are going to spend the whole day arguing again,

maybe use swords and spears," I said, pushing open the flap at the tent's entrance and allowing the late morning light to spew through the gap. "Neither of your tongues are persuasive."

Bidaês grinned—the smile of a prince, or as close to it as a nomadic clan could ever get. He was the eldest grandson of Marzban Katiôn of Simuk, the kinder of the two clan leaders who had greeted us near the border of the Mangled Woods. Unlike most tribes, the Simukie appointed the youngest male in the bloodline as the heir. That was his brother, Zakir, and Bidaês stunk of jealousy.

"If Narcyz was any good with his spear, then he wouldn't already be shunned by every girl in both of the clans," Bidaês said as he ran his hand through his curled black hair. He was paler than my, and most clansmen's, earthen skin, and his hair formed a striking contrast that *most* Simukie girls fawned over.

I had no desire to watch them brawl, so I stepped outside as the sound of Narcyz smacking Bidaês slipped through the tent's flap. I sighed. *Boys.*

The sun's heat bared down upon me as I shielded my eyes. All around, the camp was bustling as we prepared to continue our march west, through the mountain range the Krowikie had named Perun's Crown. The Narrow Pass in Astiwie lands was where my family had crossed from the world we'd known into the one I now called home. It was an arduous trek with so many people but possible, unlike the sections of the mountains farther south and the Mangled Woods in the north. Today, we started the climb.

Riders, both men and women, patrolled through the camp with their cavalry swords hung at their sides. As much as I hadn't missed the wars of my people, it was refreshing to be among my old clan's warrior women. The Krowikie were strong, but a girl with a bow or sword was dangerous to them. They'd never experienced wars on the steppes. Anyone who could hold a weapon was another rider in Zurgowie ranks.

I wound my way toward the outskirts of camp, where Wacław would surely be kneeling among the grasses by a tree, praying to his gods.

Outside the negotiations with the marzban and high priestess, our resident demon had become reclusive once we'd reached the clans. He hadn't returned to our group's tent last night. I couldn't blame him. Each day I had wept when I found myself alone, so instead of searching for solitude, I ran from it.

The thought of *his* gods still disturbed me. We hadn't told either of the clan leaders what we'd faced only days before reaching them. It was hard enough for me to grasp what I had been through. Obviously, Jaryło existed, as did at least Marzanna and Dziewanna. Did that make my clan's gods false, or were these simply our own in a different tongue?

I shook my head. Those questions were best answered by a priest or multiple mugs of oskoła. Unfortunately, I had neither. Any Zurgowie priestess who heard our story would scold me for associating with a demon, and our people didn't have alcohol except a fermented milk I despised. So, my mind toiled, sober and without guidance.

"Ara!"

I tore myself from my daze. Zakir, Bidaês's younger brother, trotted toward me on a bay Anshayman steppe horse, its short legs carrying its sturdy body as it stopped in front of me. With the slim, narrow-shouldered boy on its back, it seemed more like a bull than a horse. "Your brother doesn't understand who to start a fight with," I said.

The ends of Zakir's mouth curled for only a moment, but I had learned quickly that I would never get a real smile out of him. He was a timid alchemist who was fascinated with making my arrows more effective. Apparently, I was the only one willing to listen to his ideas, and based on the dark rings under his downturned eyes, he'd been hard at work.

"Bidaês has his ways," he said, glancing over his shoulder and lowering his voice. "Would you like to see what I discovered?"

I nodded. While Bidaês was a stubborn, annoying pony, his brother was a steady workhorse, gentle even at his most excited. The little smile returned to his face as he extended his hand and helped me mount the horse behind him. His tent was near the edge of camp, and I never minded riding instead of walking.

Unlike Zakir's demeanor, his workspace was scattered. Clay jars full of bubbling liquids covered the cloth mats he traveled with in lieu of tables. I kept my distance when we entered the tent. "Are any of these potions able to make my arrows pierce a demon?"

Curiosity flickered across his eyes, the gold of sand in the summer's heat. He shook his head and grabbed a capped jar with green liquid within. "The creatures your people call demons aren't my business. Why do you ask?"

Memories of the zmory crawling up the ridge toward Otylia and me flashed through my mind. I shuddered, forcing them away. "No reason. What did you wish to show me?"

Any hint of his suspicion disappeared as he shook the jar and opened it, releasing a putrid smell that stung my nostrils. He didn't seem to notice. "A new poison."

I coughed and stepped away from the vile odor. "And why would I need that?"

"You're a huntress, and this can bring down any animal with the slightest prick, I hope. Shouldn't ruin the meat either…" He cocked his head to the side. "I thought you'd be pleased."

"I am, but this is… surprising. Are you claiming I'm not a good enough shot to kill a deer without poison?"

"No! I… I…" He covered the jar again and turned away, babbling under his breath.

I swooped in to intercept the poison. "It'll be of great use. Thank you."

With a bow of his head, he allowed me to take it. "My pleasure, huntress."

A galloping horse approached from outside. I slipped the poison into my bag, offered Zakir a smile, and slid through the flap to see Xobas. He'd hastily thrown on his leather Simukie vest and thin, open-front jacket, but his stallion was golden in the sunlight. "*Commander* Xobas," I said. "What has you so active this early?"

"It's Wacław. A patrol found him lying by an oak and can't wake him."

"Alunam's wraiths…" I cursed. "All right, let's go find him."

I mounted the horse behind Xobas and only caught a glimpse of Zakir's disappointed face before we took off in a storm of dust.

Part 1
Isolation & Connection

1

Wacław

I could fly forever.

THE WINDS DANCED AT MY FINGERTIPS, willing followers more than obedient servants as I raced over the peaks of Perun's Crown. A laugh escaped my lungs and formed a thick fog that joined with the clouds around me. To fly was to be free of Jawia's pain for mere moments. It was bliss—but joy was as fickle as the gales.

I had slept by a tree each day since we'd found the clans. It was foolish, but whenever I laid my hands on one's bark and thought of the roots stretching deep below, Otylia didn't seem so far.

An unconvincing lie. Otylia was more distant than ever before, dragged to the depths of Nawia by Jaryło.

In recent days, I had defeated Marzanna's płanetnik called Eryk, negotiated a peace between our Krowikie tribe and the clans, and traveled through lands I never thought I would see. None of it mattered. The world was empty knowing Otylia was alone with Jaryło and Weles, who her mother had fled for years. *I'm coming for you, Otylka, whether Weles likes it or not.*

A cluster of cottages appeared through the clouds. Nestled among the hills covering southern Astiw was the village of Likiec—Eryk's home. The płanetnik had hung himself in hopes of saving his daughter, Yeva, years ago. In return for his loyalty, I had promised him I would help him free Yeva from her husband's abuse.

After losing Otylia, Kuba, and so many others on our journey, I didn't wish to fight, but I had given my word. Marzanna had not honored hers. I would not make the same mistake.

Dark clouds swirled north of the village. Lightning cracked and thunder rolled, feeding the power that surged through me as my fellow demon drew near. Revenge had a spirit of its own, but this was more than vengeance. There was love in Eryk's eyes.

"Wacław Lubiewicz," Eryk said as his wooden staff and scraggly, gray beard broke through the wall of clouds. "You have found my village, my home. For so long, it's been hidden from my memory, but you have brought me back to my Yeva."

As he drew near and knelt before me on the winds, I winced at the charred blood moon arcing from his temple to the base of his cheek—my mark. Jaryło had scolded me for letting the demon live, but what I had done was no mercy. That mark placed him under my influence. He had once served Marzanna, and now he served me. Did I deserve that service?

"Are you certain your daughter is still here?" I asked, motioning for him to rise.

He drew a heavy breath and gazed down upon the village. Anticipation filled his gray eyes, and I worried he would be disappointed after ten years. "You either leave Likiec by fire or the spear. If Yeva still lives, she will be here."

"Do you wish to confront the man alone?"

"I will have you at my side, if you choose to do so."

When I nodded, he clutched his staff and dove with the fury of the storm. I followed, and the air tore through my hair and loose tunic as we shot toward the edge of the village. My hand drifted to Kwiecień, the golden Moonblade of the fourth moon, at my back. I had yet to use Jaryło's sword in battle. I hoped tonight would not be the first.

Eryk landed in a wooded patch just south of a lonely cottage. It was no larger than Mom and my single room house in Dwie Rzeki, and smoke billowed from a window facing us. To the northeast lay a fallow field, where barley or wheat would've normally been planted if not for Marzanna's extended winter. It was deep in the night. Beyond the sound of the storm, it was eerily quiet, and a fog hovered as the dark clouds neared.

"I've waited too long for this moment," Eryk said as I slid through the shadows behind him. "It seems a dream."

"I don't dream," I replied. Though it was meant to be a joke, it didn't come off as one, and his gaze met me with narrowed eyes.

"If only I didn't." The storm swelled around us with each of his breaths. "Each day, when I shut my eyes, I see only Yeva's face. But because of you, now, I can have peace."

If only peace was so simple.

Part of me believed that finding Otylia would calm my soul, but I knew better. After all Marzanna had done, I could not rest until her looming threat was over. My chest tightened at the thought of what I might become in the process.

Eryk stepped into the light of the waxing moon. His gray cloak dissolved into the fog and remained barely visible as I followed mere strides behind.

Whispers circled us on the winds, strengthening as we approached the cottage. *"Kill him,"* they hissed. *"Make the fool suffer."*

As Eryk pulled open the door, they pounded my ears, my mind—not the gods of the winds but dark spirits, feeding on revenge.

"Mutilate him! Ensure he never sees the grasses of Nawia. Make him like us…"

Screams echoed in the confined space as gusts tore through the house, extinguishing the hearth and sweeping bowls and mugs off the table. A man clothed in nothing but a pair of roughspun trousers staggered back as he clutched a spear.

Behind him cowered a frail woman. She stared up at Eryk with an unknowing gaze, and I thanked the gods I was invisible in my soul-form.

"Out, demon!" the man shouted, jabbing the tip of his spear at Eryk.

It was no use. Eryk charged forward and wrapped the man in the winds. He pulled the air from the man's lungs, slowly suffocating him as Yeva pled for it to stop, but despite her cries, the spirits were louder, their wills stronger.

"Hang him! Let his breath linger only enough for him to live in agony."

The voices prodded at me. They wanted my rage, my hatred, but unleashing that power would only bring pain. So, I turned away from them, grabbing Eryk's arm as his hand closed around the man's throat. "If he becomes a demon like us, then she'll never rest."

"Death is too kind an ending."

"What good is revenge if you sacrifice Yeva to get it?"

Eryk looked at Yeva, curled up in the corner with an amulet of Mokosz clutched in her thin fingers and a prayer to the goddess on her lips. He winced before loosening his grip on the man. "Go far from this place. Take nothing and leave my daughter. You shall never harm her again."

The man stumbled back, gasping for air. His breaths were weak as the winds tore around him, but hatred filled his eyes. "You haunt me, old man?"

"Father?" Yeva asked. "Father!" She pushed past her husband and embraced Eryk, who clung to her like a father to a newborn child.

Eryk glared at the man over his daughter's shoulder. "Go, before I question my mercy!"

The man lunged for his spear, but before his fingers graced its shaft, lightning arced from Eryk's palm. He didn't have the chance to scream.

Around us, the spirits howled in dismay at the man's quick death. They broke from the winds and swarmed us in a tide of black smoke as Yeva screamed and tried to hide.

"You deny us the man," they hissed, *"so we will take the girl."*

A force threw me into the wall. It was impossible to see the spirits in the dark, and their talons ripped through my tunic as I froze, my breaths caught in my throat. *I can't fight them… Not now…*

Their strikes sent visions of Otylia's death rushing through my head. The blood. The fear in her eyes. It was too much… *I couldn't save her…*

"Run!" Eryk shouted to me, bursting through the door with Yeva.

I shook myself from the shock and followed. Disoriented, I caught hold of the winds as I reached the doorway. They were weak, more distant than before, but when the spirits dove ahead, thrashing at Yeva, I drew Kwiecień and took flight. The sword shone in the moonlight, all its power radiating from its sharp edge as I swung at the first visible spirit. Its shrieking tore at my ears, but the blade didn't waver. Gold sliced through the wisps of black.

The stench of death hung in that vapor, and dread rose within me once again as the four remaining spirits flooded the open air. Their bodies seemed to fade in and out of reality, their feathered, black wings snapping through the air as talons extended from their hands and feet. *What are they?*

Rain poured as Eryk spun his staff and called the winds to deflect the spirits' attacks. But they were quicker than Eryk's gusts, slipping through his defenses and grabbing hold of Yeva.

I hesitated before following. Each movement felt forced, as if I were swimming upstream. The rage lurking within hammered my head, but I ignored its call as I skipped above the spirits. That pain would destroy me. I wouldn't let it—not with Otylia and so many others relying on me.

With the spirits below, calling a lightning strike was tempting, but just keeping myself airborne was a struggle. I couldn't afford to drain my *żityje*—my life force—as I had twice before. Though I'd focused on that energy during our time with the clan, I still had little grasp of it beyond sensing roughly how much I had left while in my soul-form.

Two of the creatures carried Yeva into the sky as the final pair split and lunged at us. I blocked the first's strike with Kwiecień before countering. The blade felt light, nimble compared to the winds, and I let my instincts from years of Xobas's lessons guide me. When its talons swiped at my head, I followed its movement, ducking before sending Kwiecień's tip through its heart—if it had one.

My cheeks burned with the chilled gales. Below, Eryk's wind blast killed the other spirit, but the final two were little more than flickers of black in the dim light. If Yeva hadn't been thrashing, they would've slipped away. She did, though, and her kicks dislodged one of the creatures, distracting it long enough for Eryk to close in and send a bolt of lightning into its head.

The spirit dissolved as the remaining one climbed ever higher. Yeva screamed, but it gripped her wrists, not giving her a chance to fight free. Though Eryk's winds swore and cursed the spirit, it increased its pace.

Why am I so slow? I was a płanetnik, a demon of the winds, yet they gave no heed to my call.

Clouds soon enveloped Yeva's dress. I flew on without direction, and when lightning cracked, it revealed nothing but rain and a sea of gray.

"Follow, my boy!" Eryk's shout rang from below. Sweeping past me, sparks cracked from the end of his staff.

His energy pulled me through the clouds, battering me against the turbulent air within. I had no idea how Eryk knew where they'd gone, but he charged on without hesitation. Only the winds' senses guided me behind.

A disturbance split the clouds ahead and tore the storm from our control. I fought, but the winds defied me. Without their lift, I dropped like a stone.

What is this?

A scaled, wingless beast of deep gray hovered above. Yeva screamed from the serpent's coiled grasp as it roared, displaying jagged teeth and lightning cracking within its maw. When the *snap* hammered my ears, I dove to the side. Not far enough.

The bolt shot toward my chest as I raised Kwiecień into its path. Lightning met Moonstone in a blinding flash, sending me reeling.

My mind spun and the ground rushed ever closer. I called for the winds. For north's power. For south's heat. For northwest's tempests. None answered my plea until panic snapped through me as I reached the treetops. Cervenko's east and Dogoda's west winds collided to stop my fall. The impact sent a shock up my spine, but I rolled on the soft west wind as another bolt shot past. Static made my hair stand on end.

Why'd you wait so long? I asked the winds. *Why respond now?*

Answers would have to wait since, above, the serpent roared and Eryk wielded the tattered rope that had once entrapped his throat, throwing it over the beast's head. I took a relieved breath, but the serpent swung its tail and clattered the płanetnik in the throat. His storm faded as he tumbled.

I sent the west wind to cushion his fall. *Žityje* poured from me, far more than I should've needed for such a simple command, and with the serpent's control of the storm, I struggled to fly toward it. Fear rose within me. The serpent had turned to flee, Yeva still in its grasp, and it would be out of sight in seconds. I couldn't fail. Not again.

But no matter how hard I tried, the winds wouldn't answer. Tears stung my eyes watching Yeva disappear into the storm, her face flickering to Otylia's before vanishing completely. I pushed them away. Sorrow wouldn't save Yeva or Otylia. I had to be stronger, to overcome the weakness that had allowed Jaryło to take Otylia from me.

It wasn't enough.

A sea of black met me on the other side of the clouds. Still, I flew on for some time until I was far from Likiec and the storm, but there was no sight of Yeva or the serpent anywhere. I'd lost her.

My grip grew limp on Kwiecień as I stopped and stood on the air. It was quiet here, peaceful, but my souls were at war as I contemplated defeat. The demon's rage and the mortal's loss. Both felt like a hot iron driven into my skin, so I ignored them, drove them deep into me until nothing remained but a cavern in my chest. Empty like the sky.

Eryk reached me sometime later, bringing the rain clouds with him. I didn't know how long it had been, but Dadźbóg's sun peeked over the mountains in the east. *I don't want to go back.*

What did I want? To save Otylia, bring peace to Jawia, save my tribe and the clans, or just float through the sky, feeling nothing but the gentlest breeze against my skin? I didn't know.

A new surge of pain clutched me as Eryk stared into the distance, blinking away tears. Sorrow, raw and unyielding. Its weight tore me down less than a moon after losing Otylia, but Eryk had waited years to see his daughter again. Did the longing dominate his mind too?

"I'm sorry," my voice said, lost on the winds.

He took a heavy sigh as the rain fell upon us. "Wacław, this is not your doing. In taking your mark, I was able to see Yeva again, to see the woman she has become. Words cannot express how thankful I am." His voice cracked as he dropped to a knee before me, and I looked away so my heart wouldn't shatter with it. *Not now.* "My curse erased the location of my home from my mind, but you returned me here. Yeva is not gone forever. I will search for the chała that stole her from me, and I will ensure she has the life she deserved."

"Please, don't kneel," I said. "You took my mark in return for a promise—one I failed to uphold. You are free from my will. If I were to force you to endure this bond, then I would prove myself a *real* demon."

Standing, Eryk raised a hand to his marked cheek. It was odd to know I had done that to him, as if I had some right to claim him as mine, like Marzanna had done to me. "I will serve you once I find her," he said. "Whatever you ask, I will do what I can as long as it is within my power."

I looked to the mountains of Perun's Crown with the cold rain trickling down my face. It stung, but I invited the distraction from the resentment growing within me. At Marzanna for the destruction she'd wrought. At Father for abandoning me, abusing me. At Jaryło for taking Otylia from me. And at myself for failing to stop him and Yeva's abductors. My demonic soul fed upon that anger, demanding it fester. No, the void in my chest was better than that craving.

"You aren't my servant," I insisted, holding my Frostmarked hand into the rain and letting it slip through my fingers. "That mark would allow me to influence you if I wished, but I wouldn't be much different than Marzanna if I did. Go, find your daughter. When you return, it is your choice what you wish to do. Gods know Jawia has enough people forced to fight against their will already."

"If you were not so young," Eryk said with a nod, "I would have offered Yeva's hand to you in repayment for what you've done. To not only avenge my death but to help me fight the chały that threatened my daughter..."

My mind turned to Otylia again, and I closed my eyes for a moment as another wave of sorrow hit me. "Even if that were Yeva's will, I couldn't have accepted anyway. There's... another..." I shook my head. *Focus.* "You mentioned chały? The one Marzanna sent before was nothing like those."

"Demons are not all alike. Chały are shapeshifters and dark spirits. They are the foes of we płanetnikami. We are meant to build the clouds and lead the storms—when not abused by rogue gods—but they only destroy." With a stab of his staff into the clouds, he hummed in thought. "The morning comes."

"It does," I said with a sigh. The others would be expecting me. In recent days, Ara had expressed fears I was spending too much time in my soul-form. She believed it dampened my mind and mortal soul. Perhaps it did, but it was an escape I needed. Others had dreams. I had only the winds.

Eryk laid a hand on my shoulder. "I wish I could offer you more assistance in finding the girl, but Cervenko may know more. Seek him on his eastern wind. Then, pray we both find the ones we love."

I nodded, and he flew into the clouds.

At first, I moved to return to the clans, but I let the rain fall upon me a few minutes more. In the east, Dadźbóg's early light cast a golden halo over the mountains, splitting into a rainbow of a hundred colors as the clouds drifted away. To gain hope from such a thing was childish, but I let it cover my hurt and regret.

My hand closed around the bow of Dziewanna at my chest—Otylia's amulet—and I prayed to both mother and daughter, "May the coming day bless us with hope and the night gift us peace. Show me the way to you, my Otylka, and let me stray from that path under neither sun nor moon."

2

Otylia

I'm dead.

IT WAS MY FIRST—ADMITTEDLY STUPID—THOUGHT after Jaryło sliced my throat. Of course I was dead, but death wasn't what I'd expected.

Father claimed souls wandered for forty days before journeying to the Smorodina River that divided Jawia, the realm of the living, from Nawia, that of the dead. Instead, I knelt among the mosses in a dense swamp of willow, birch, and alder trees. Above me spread a tapestry of vines and lush, full branches that wound around each other, allowing only a few streaks of daylight through. Roots stretched from the ground to an enormous tree whose trunk somehow began high above.

A chorus of frogs echoed across the swamp as I felt the familiar moss. It was soft, as it often was after a storm. The smell of rain against the dirt and bark filled the air as a droplet fell on the tip of my nose. With an exasperated breath, I flicked it away.

Where am I?

The swamp felt familiar, but I had never seen it before. Dziewanna's… Mother's… power allowed me to sense a forest's spirit, and this one buzzed with life unlike any in Jawia.

A wind whispered among the trees and blew a few stray strands of black hair into my face. *Is Wašek alive?* I thought as I forced myself to stand. *Gods, I am a fool.* Here I was, dead, and I was worrying about my demonic—what? It was obvious our relationship had moved beyond mere friendship, but he was a demon and I a goddess. What did that make us?

I gripped my head in my hands and screamed in frustration. We'd been so close to the clans. But Jaryło had ruined everything.

I clasped my throat where Jaryło had sliced it. No scarring remained. He'd only killed me when something struck him. I assumed Wacław had found a last ounce of *žityje* to drive Marzanna's Thunderstone dagger into the god's back, but that concerned me more. His black veins had already returned before Jaryło's betrayal. If he'd used the winds again… "Gods help him."

"It is an odd thing, praying to yourself," a rough voice said from behind me.

I spun and reached for Dziewanna's power. The roots beneath me grew around my legs like an armor as the trees awaited my command.

A bearded gray man studied me, his head donned with cattle horns and his body with a cloak of bear fur. Slowly, he shuffled through the shallow swamp waters with the help of a willow staff that curled over itself at its peak. His steps didn't disturb their calm, and as he passed through a beam of light, his eyes shone green.

"You have your mother's spirit," the man said as he leaned against his staff and studied me.

Weles… I gritted my teeth, fighting back my fear at meeting the god of the underworld. "And I have none of yours. Where is Jaryło?"

He chuckled like an old man entertained by a child. "You possess her mind too, I see. Jaryło is here, as are you and I. Tell me, little one, do you know where that is?"

"Nawia, but I haven't crossed the Smorodina."

"Gods need not cross the stinking river nor wander like aimless human souls. Besides, Marzanna's minions control the river, and she is not known to be kind to those who kill her pets."

I scoffed. "As if the mistress of death shows favor to any but the cruel."

"Is the boy cruel?"

"Anything but."

Weles placed his hand on the trunk of a willow. His fingers followed the grooves in the bark. "Yet he is a demon, and demons are a corruption of the natural balance—the World Tree's bastards." He raised his gaze to the oak high above.

"Wait…" I stumbled back, gasping. "*This* is the base of the World Tree?"

"Indeed it is." He approached a cluster of roots directly beneath the tree. They twisted together but formed a gap large enough for a person to enter into. "This is the Heart of Nawia, where the World Tree's roots lead to the realms above. Demons threaten this bond between the realms. Whether the boy believes so or not, he is nothing but a tool of destruction. Why else would Marzanna be so fond of him?"

"Why the questions, Weles? You're a god. Surely you know more of Marzanna's schemes than I do."

A grin crossed his weathered face. He drove the staff into the ground, and the walls of vines creaked around us. "There has been much secrecy in recent moons, and all the whispers lead back to her. It is no surprise she wishes to take Jawia for herself. But why now? That is the question neither god, demon, nor man can answer. None except Marzanna herself."

When he raised his hand, roots from both above and below wove themselves into a throne before the Heart. He sat upon it, never taking his gaze from me. "I fear her allies stretch far further than any of us expected. For some odd reason, however, that płanetnik of yours has her attention more than any other."

"Why the concern now?" I asked, brow furrowed. "You didn't seem to care when he was dying—when I saved him. Why should I listen to you at all? You *killed* me."

"Is it too much that I ask to see my daughter?"

I clenched my fists and spat at his feet. "I'm not your daughter! A father doesn't tell his minion to slice his daughter's throat." I huffed, my hand returning to where the Moonblade of Kwiecień had drawn blood. "Mother fled from you because she saw who you are. Now she's trapped by Marzanna. I'll do whatever it takes to get her back, and I'll do it without you."

He leaned forward, clutching the cane between his palms. "What if I said the only way for you to rescue her is with my assistance?"

"Then I'd say I don't believe you." I lowered my head. Unwelcomed tears burned my eyes as I remembered Mother's embrace in the Lake of Reflection. She'd given up everything for me to be free from Weles. I wouldn't allow her sacrifice to be in vain.

Shadows hung over Weles's face as he settled on his throne. "Don't be a foolish child. You are little more than a godling, powerless against Marzanna until you Ascend."

"Ascend?"

"All the power you currently possess is channeled from your mother or grandmother, but as gods, our strength lies with the forces of the Three Realms we control and protect. I rule over Nawia and the lowlands of Jawia as well as sorcery, cattle, bears, and elements of nature. Your mother nurtures the wilds where no man may go, the game that men hunt, and the mares they ride. Soon, you will earn your place, but before then, I cannot allow you to leave. An un-Ascended goddess is vulnerable. Marzanna could slay you forever if she were to discover who you are."

Earn my place?

In the little time since Mother had told me she was Dziewanna, I hadn't comprehended that I could be the goddess of something. It had been complex and frustrating enough to grasp that my parents were gods. Knowing that I would have power over a domain was too much. All I wanted was to return to my friends and find Mother. I wasn't a goddess. Goddesses were beautiful, graceful, and respected, not outcast witches who no boy bothered to catch a second glimpse of. *No boy but a demon.*

"You say she could kill me," I said with one arm held across my body. "How? Aren't I immortal?"

A weight filled Weles's eyes. "Until you Ascend, you possess immortality like that a demon—an impossibly long life unless you are killed by curse or blade."

I winced, remembering Wacław's blackened fingers. *He actually saved me from Marzanna's Curse…*

"Jaryło wished to bring you here by less violent means," Weles continued, "as it required a large sacrifice of my *żityje* to recover your soul when you died. In the end, it matters little. You will Ascend when the time is right, and your place among the gods will be set."

"How am I to know my place when this has fallen upon me in mere days?" I asked. "You can't keep me here while Jawia is falling apart!"

Weles waved his hand dismissively. "The land of the living never lacks chaos. Marzanna is not the first to covet it for herself, nor will she be the last. Your mother is immortal and so shall you be. We will wait until you are ready. Until then," he said, turning away and staring up at the World Tree, "I will teach you the ways of the gods so long as you leave your old life behind and take your place by your brother's side and mine."

I felt sick as I crossed my arms and stepped back, leaving the roots' protection. "Just a few weeks ago I said the same thing about whoever ruled our tribe's lands, but there are things, people, worth fighting for. I'll find my own way."

As I turned away, the trees creaked around me.

I ran.

Water soaked my legs as I slid through the trees and their shadows, hoping to leave the god behind. My weapons were now enemies as branches and vines shot towards me. They scraped my arms and tore my dress, but I didn't stop. I couldn't.

Weles wished to trap me in Nawia for an eternity until I was powerful enough for him to use for his own will. I'd seen it in his eyes. He was no different than Marzanna, and it didn't matter he was my father. Ascended or not—I would not be tamed.

I burst into the light drenched in swamp water and sweat. An endless plain lay before me. Flowers of violet and red, blue and yellow, bloomed upon its hills and grasses swayed in its valleys. Cattle and horses grazed under the sun as people in pure white tunics wandered among them. I struggled to find my breath as its beauty caught me.

Then I heard the snakes.

They were everywhere at once. Branches shot from the trees and entrapped my arms as the serpents slithered up my legs, winding around them like relentless vines before digging their fangs into my skin.

I fought and I thrashed, but my body was weak. When I reached for the power that had saved me from Yuliya's ice, there was nothing. My mind drifted, and though I tried to scream, my voice was only a whisper in the void.

3

Wacław

Xobas is going to be angry.

MY SKIN WAS COLD AND MY MIND DULL by the time I returned to my physical body under an oak. Sosna, our fox companion sent by Dziewanna, was curled alongside me. She yapped at the sight of my open eyes.

At least she's always happy to see me.

As I rolled over, Dadźbóg's early light covered the grasses of the steppe, haloing Xobas and Ara. "Quite the welcome party," I said.

"Thank the gods. We were getting worried," Ara said with a laugh that sounded more like relief than anything.

Xobas huffed. "You were spotted by a sentry. The marzban and high priestess will ask questions."

I held my hands to my aching head. That night had been the longest I'd ever been in my soul-form, and as I looked from them to the camp in the valley below, dizziness overtook me. "It is the responsibility of leaders to question strangers. Our own people hate me, so why would the clans be any different?"

"You're avoiding something," Xobas said. "Where did you travel last night?"

With a sigh, I pushed myself off the ground and wrapped my

cloak over my shoulders, covering Kwiecień. "To Likiec, an Astiwie town west of the mountains. Eryk's daughter was there, and I had to fulfill my promise to help him free her. Unfortunately, a band of chały had another idea entirely."

"That would explain the gash on your arm," Ara said.

I instinctively covered the red stain bleeding through the shirt the Simukie had given me. It was lightweight, and unlike my tunics, it didn't stretch past my upper thigh. I felt exposed. But the clothes had been a gift—one I had already ruined. "It'll be hard to come up with an excuse for this."

She shrugged. "We've confronted worse. C'mon, I'll clean up the wound and then we can help Narcyz tear down the tent before he kills us."

The camp buzzed with riders patrolling and people preparing for the trek through the Narrow Pass. Though they tried to hide it, I caught their glances. Xobas and Ara may have left the clans, but at least they *looked* like they belonged, unlike Narcyz and me. Not that lacking the ability to speak the clans' shared tongue well had stopped Narcyz from pursuing every girl who so much as smiled at him.

He and Bidaês, the high-chinned eldest grandson of Marzban Katiôn of Simuk, were scuffling in the tent when Ara and I arrived. More than one bruise graced Narcyz's cheek, and Bidaês's nose was crooked and bloody. *At least we're good at making friends.*

I shot between them as Narcyz growled and swung, missing his target but striking my shoulder. Whatever he saw on my face forced him back. Fear replaced his anger, and he stammered before shooting Bidaês a glare. "Sorry…" he said without direction.

"Don't you have your own preparations for the journey?" Ara asked Bidaês as she tapped her foot.

Bidaês plowed through the tent flap, not bothering to reply. *Forcing him away was the wrong call.* I had quickly figured out during my negotiations with the clan leaders that Bidaês was interested in nothing but furthering his own ambitions. Regardless of my feelings, though, he was the brother of the Simukie heir—a future commander. We needed his loyalty.

As Ara sat me down and examined the slice from the spirit's talon on my arm, Narcyz muttered to himself and threw the few things he had left into his bag. Sosna circled him, demanding attention. He gave none.

The past week had taken a toll on Narcyz. I saw it in his sluggish movements, the way he'd avoided me at all costs, and his desperate chase of the clan women. He was lost without a purpose, like I had felt before all of this had begun. This fight against Marzanna wasn't his, but no matter how much he complained about the journey or me being a demon, I was glad to have him.

Ara applied an ointment she'd likely received from Zakir, the younger and more timid brother of Bidaês. Unlike his brother, the Simukie heir had been a consistent helper and educator with the culture of the clans. Ara couldn't keep her eyes off him.

When she finished, Ara paced over to her bag, tapping her fingers against her thighs. "Did Eryk offer any way for us to find Otylia?" she asked over her shoulder.

A pang struck my chest as I traced the wound. "No." Besides dying, none of us had figured out how to reach Nawia—especially doing so before Jaryło used the next Moonblade's power to recover upon the start of the Maj moon. As a demon, though, even death wasn't an option for me. Oblivion would be my end.

"We will find a way." Turning away, she pursed her lips and shook her head, her eyes red. "If anyone knows of one, it would be High Priest Dariusz. I figure he'll want his daughter back too." I raised my gaze to her as she sighed. "All right, maybe she's not *technically* his daughter, but still... Whether we need to make deals with grumpy priests or your gods, we will get her back."

"*Our* gods are the only real ones," Narcyz said as he threw his pack over his shoulder. "And they don't like doubters."

"They don't appreciate people calling their szeptuchy witches either," I replied.

Narcyz smirked. "You get a fancy sword and all of a sudden you have a spine. Maybe I'll stop talking if you let me hold it. I can't imagine the look on Father's face when he sees that blade. It's any smith's dream to see a god's sword."

I flicked my cloak to the side and slid Kwiecień from its leather sheath. For a moment, I studied the golden blade and the engravings on its flat before handing it to Narcyz. I assumed the symbols to be the old tongue, but it was impossible to know when only the gods and szeptuchy spoke it. "I still don't understand how a sword can control whether or not Jaryło can heal and return from Nawia. It seems far too simple."

Narcyz's eyes widened as he gripped the blade by its hilt, holding it as if it were a child. "Swaróg's hammer is powerful if it can make this. That dagger of yours and the Moonblades are impressive."

"As are all gods and spirits," Ara added. "There's so much we don't understand."

"Then we will wait until we reach Dwie Rzeki with the clans," I said. "Dariusz *must* know more."

A horn sounded from outside. *Time to go.* Narcyz returned Kwiecień to me before I tossed my scattered things in my bag and helped the others take down the tent. Less than half an hour later, we mounted our horses and began the march toward the Narrow Pass.

Clan riders surrounded us with all their belongings either in sacks on their horses' sides or pulled by wooden sleds. The Simukie considered their bond with their mounts inseparably sacred, but High Priestess Rasa Kolah had allowed us to borrow a set of Zurgowie stallions. They were quicker and smoother than my horse back home, Tanek. Still, I wished for a more familiar mount, as this one seemed disappointed by every instruction I gave it.

The grasses parted around us as the steppe slowly gave way to trees, still dark and naked without Dziewanna's power.

After our journey through the Mangled Woods, I watched each shadow in expectation of Marzanna's demons or cultists. Our victory over Eryk and Yuliya had only delayed her, and dread never left me, even beyond the reach of that cursed forest. Marzanna was watching. I knew it. The moment I put my guard down, she would strike, but we'd come too far to fail now.

The slope grew and cliffs narrowed the trail on each side as Dadźbóg climbed the sky. Each step towards the sun brought his fire closer, but an uncomfortable, dry warmth was better than a chill. My frostbitten fingers throbbed each day, reminding of me the sacrifices we'd made to stay alive—how close both Otylia and I had come to death because of Marzanna. In the end, she'd taken Kuba anyway, and Otylia was a realm away.

Ever since my *żityje* ritual with Otylia nearly a moon before, a tether had connected us in our most dire moments. At times, her pain was mine, as if we were joined by some force neither of us understood. Our bond had become faint since her descent to Nawia, but I could still feel her fear and anger. Those same emotions stirred within me, trying to lure me into their embrace. I refused. This emptiness was better than confronting that pain… I shut my eyes and took a breath. *We'll find answers in Dwie Rzeki.*

It was midday when Xobas found me among the crowd, his mount much more controlled than mine. "The marzban wishes to speak with you." He lowered his voice. "I believe now is the time to tell him the truth of your power. He is a level-headed man, a potential ally, and he may know more of the Frostmarked Horde than he has said."

"Can we trust his discretion? Even if he can help, I would prefer all of Jawia not know about my… condition."

"Katiôn neither trusts High Priestess Rasa nor does he break a vow. Your secret will be safe with him."

I nodded. "If he's earned your respect, then he deserves mine. Lead the way."

Marzban Katiôn had been the more reasonable of the clan leaders during our negotiations. When Rasa had refused to settle her zealous clan in the same territory as the Simukie, Katiôn chose the more vulnerable eastern lands of the southern hills. The man was principled and wanted what was best for his people. Unlike our own tribe's chiefs, though, he understood not everything could be accomplished with brute force.

Dust filled the air as we trotted through the parade of riders. Even with the incline, the horses were unbothered and mine seemed to enjoy the opportunity to stretch his legs, if only for a minute.

From atop a long-legged chestnut stallion, Katiôn's skin gleamed with sweat beneath the steppe sun. Despite being of middle age, he had fewer wrinkles than most men in their twenties. His thoughtful glances and the tan cape draped from his right shoulder, however, gave him a calm, regal presence.

He turned to us when he heard our approach, sending his pony tail whipping through the air behind him. "Ah, Wacław. I'm glad to see you are getting on better with your horse after last night's incident."

I raised a brow at Xobas, who flashed a grin before nodding to the marzban. "Yes…" I said, guessing at Xobas's explanation for my injury. "I rode in my village, but it's safe to say my skills are not as fresh as your own riders'."

With his face to the sun, Katiôn chuckled. "I imagine not. To ride is to live for our people. When one is separated from their horse, they are separated from their own spirit." He gripped his reins and sighed. "I wished to ask you about the lands that await us—as well as your people."

"Of course. The territory that will be yours is as alien to you as the steppes are to me."

The sun descended toward the horizon as he asked many questions about our lands' fertile areas, rivers, animals, and the people of Krowik, Astiw, and Solga. Xobas added clarity at first before quieting enough for me to forget he was there. Katiôn's curiosity seemed genuine as he tolerated my explanation of our gods, allowing me to tell even tales I had once thought were meant only for children. Ever since the Drowning of Marzanna, they had become all too real.

"Many of your stories speak of witchcraft and demons," Katiôn said at a point where the ground leveled to a rocky clearing. "Is this why your people believe the forest between us is so dark and irregular?"

I glanced at Xobas before returning my gaze to the marzban. "There is a lot I haven't told you. Can I trust that all I'm about to say will remain between us?" My chest tightened as I feared his response to the truth. Xobas trusted him, however, so I would too.

Katiôn studied the trees. This high up, pine had become dominant, and they clung to their needles despite the lingering cold. The deep lines above his brow deepened as he replied, "If we are to have a successful alliance, we must trust each other. Speak candidly."

"Very well."

I told him about our journey, Marzanna's call, and my demonic soul. I told him of Juri and Jaryło, zmory and wiły, and szeptuchy and Frostmarked. If he was to understand the threat we faced, he needed to know everything—everything except Otylia and the Lake of Reflection. That was not my story to share.

Katiôn did nothing but listen and nod, guiding his people forward as the climb began again until Dadźbóg's light touched the horizon. We'd reached an area where the path widened and the ground was level enough to camp for the night. He ordered the riders to spread the word before dismounting.

"Leave your horse with Xobas and walk with me," he said. "There seems to be much about the world beyond the mountains that I do not understand."

I did as he said, offering Xobas a parting nod before he disappeared into the crowd. Despite my old trainer's silence, his presence had calmed me both now and during the negotiations. Away from him, I realized how unprepared I was to be speaking with a clan's warlord.

Katiôn led me higher through the thin trees to a ridge along the northern edge of the pass. Here, the light had all but faded as the mountains blocked the sun, leaving nothing but a dark hue over the lands we had traversed in recent days. My pulse raced in anticipation of Katiôn's reply to my story, but a calm took me at the sight.

Before flying the first time, I had never been at such heights. Jawia's beauty was incomprehensible from here. Even in the darkness, the hills and cliffs of both gray and brown were nothing but magnificent. They seemed to proclaim Perun's power over the heights with each slope. Yet, though I tried to let myself enjoy the moment, sorrow washed it away quickly. I saw Eryk's longing gaze in each cloud, Otylia's wicked smirk in the earth, and Kuba's ridiculous theatrics in the trees.

"What lies east of the Anshayman Steppe?" I asked, forcing myself from the silence.

Katiôn held his arms behind his back, standing straighter than any man I'd met. The breeze guided his cape behind him and made the horse emblem upon it seem to gallop. "Mountains far smaller than these but enough to prevent many from passing—until the Horde. Beyond those, I have only heard rumors of a desert where sand serpents roam."

"Do you believe those rumors?"

He turned to me, and age seemed to weather his face as he sighed. "In time, I've learned when a story is true and when it is false. Even among those tales demented by generations or told by liars, there will always be a grain of the truth."

My hand traced the hilt of Marzanna's dagger at my side. "And do you believe me to be a liar?"

"If I thought you were a liar, we wouldn't be having this conversation, but only in the legends have I heard stories like those you told me." He studied me, his gaze heavy. "Though the Zurgowie have their sorceresses, my people do not differentiate those you call channelers from demons. All who alter the world are harbingers of chaos."

I swallowed. "Problems have followed me ever since I discovered my power..." *Ever since Otylia revealed it.* "I would understand if you believed me to be a risk to your people."

With a deep sigh, he shook his head. "From the moment the Horde arrived on the Anshayman Steppe, we have been in danger. Your arrival has given us hope and a new chance. But show caution. Rasa and her priestesses will either interpret your stories as deceit or will kill you for serving the dark god they call Alunam. We cannot afford a rift between our peoples at such a fragile time."

The high priestess's dedication to her gods would have been admirable if it didn't conflict with everything I had seen in the past moon. Ara and many other refugees had fled the Zurgowie because of Rasa's zealous wars. To know the truth could ruin all we'd worked for was not a reassuring thought. Luckily, I had spent my life treading lightly around Father's aggressiveness; though, I hadn't been all that successful.

"Tell me," Katiôn continued. "If this goddess, Marzanna, caused the droughts and blizzards that drove people to this Frostmarked Horde, what is stopping her from starving your people? The trees remain barren and the plants withered."

"She has captured Dziewanna," I said, "but as long as Marzanna doesn't hold Jaryło's Moonblades, she can't exert complete control without the help of demons. At least for now."

"And that is why she needs you."

I stared down at the scar of Marzanna's Frostmark on my palm. The phantom burn pulsed as if another of her demons were near. "It seems so."

His hand fell on my shoulder. "I do not envy you, Wacław, but know you shall not carry this burden alone. Though I do not believe this woman to be a goddess, she is a threat to my people. When the time comes for us to face our enemies, we will face them together. Trust me, and trust my grandsons. They will stand by you."

"Thank you, marzban." I gripped Dziewanna's bow. "I pray I will not need your support, but after recent days, I fear there are few gods that would answer my call."

With a grin, he nodded toward the camp. "This is why we bond with the horse. When we call, they come, and never in their lives will they betray us."

4

Otylia

I hate dying.

I WOKE TO A CHOKING FOG. My hands were bound with vines, and I lay on a soft bed unlike any I'd felt. Silence hung in the air.

Whatever venom had flowed through my veins lingered. Sluggish, I shifted to get a better view of the room around me, but there was only a weeping willow and its roots that jutted from the ground, forming the bed's frame. Etching covered them—symbols of the old tongue—only some that I recognized.

Father would know them.

But Dariusz wasn't my father. Though he'd raised me and taught me the ways of the gods, his blood was not mine. He'd been a cold and demanding guardian, but as I traced the etchings with my finger, I wished for his presence. It didn't matter if he would've scolded me. Harsh words and a push to improve seemed far better than being trapped in Nawia.

My heart suddenly pounded my chest. *I can't stay here.*

I swung my legs over the side of the bed. No matter what Weles had planned for me, I wanted none of it. I would find Mother and figure out my "place" without his deceit! My legs didn't get the message.

I wobbled the moment I tried to stand. Each foot acted of its own accord, digging into the damp dirt before giving way. With my hands bound, I fell face first into the muck.

"Gods…" I muttered as I peered through the mist. There was still nothing but the willow, its branches arcing over the bed like a falcon's talons, so I crawled into the abyss. Pain arced up my arms as I twisted my sore wrists in the vines and pulled myself through the dirt. No matter how hard I tried, my legs dragged behind me, useless.

Time passed slowly. I struggled for every inch, but the venom faded the further I went. Soon, I could raise my knees. Slow and weak, they still quickened my pace, and I reached a wall of twisting vines that stretched into the fog.

What is this place?

I grabbed the vines, using them to pull me along. The wall seemed to stretch forever, but as my arms strained, I thought only of Mother and the smile she'd worn in the Lake of Reflection. Pain meant nothing when she was trapped by Marzanna. Only I could save her, and that meant escaping Weles's grasp.

My fingers bled by the time a pair of doors appeared. They were crafted from a dark wood and stood as tall as two men, morphing into the vines at their outer rims. When I dragged myself to their base and pushed, they refused to give.

I yelled and slammed my fists into them. With each blow, I cursed Weles and Jaryło for what they'd done to me. It didn't matter how long it took. I would escape. Then I would make them pay for my death.

My knuckles bloodied quickly, each strike leaving a crimson spray that slowly dripped down the doors. I needed to get out of the room. I needed to get back to Jawia. Marzanna only grew stronger with every passing minute, but I was too weak to even open a door.

"No!" I growled through gritted teeth. "Weles won't win."

The mists swirled above me as I took the vines in my bloody hands and forced my legs to hold me. Handles of gold glinted just above my head, but anguish trapped my mind. Every limb was fire and pain, every second an eternity as I reached for the closest handle. My fingers graced its surface. With every bit of strength left, I pulled it open before dropping to the dirt.

Darkness swallowed my vision. The world felt distant, my limbs weak. *Keep going.*

I clenched my jaw so hard it hurt, but it distracted from the dread creeping into my heart as I staggered into the room beyond.

Here, it was fogless and dark. Only a few stray streaks of light shooting through the canopy above offered any glimpse of the space. The walls of vines were closer on each side. Roots peeked above the ground before dipping to the depths among the short grass.

A solitary beam illuminated another weeping willow at the room's center. A bed of violet basil flowers grew at its base, and unlike the ominous aura of the first, a power seemed to radiate from this one's branches. It called to me—a familiar burst of life I'd felt so many times when I channeled.

"Mom?"

Dziewanna's spirit danced among the catkins above me and ignited my drained soul with *żityje*. The air hummed as I scrambled to the willow and knelt among its roots. Bloodied and exhausted, I laid a hand on its trunk, whispering a prayer to her on the still winds. No response came but a warmth flowing from the tree. It was enough.

I rested against the willow for a long time—longer than I should've. The snake's venom had taken its toll, but I *would* prove Weles wrong. Ascended or not, I was strong enough to return to Jawia. I had to be. Mother had protected me from Weles for years, and now it was my turn to free her from Marzanna's grasp.

A twig snapped across the room.

I shot to my feet as a great bear stepped from the darkness. It advanced on its hind legs, thin beams of light revealing the beast's brown and oddly manicured fur. When it reached the edge of the willow's branches, it bared its jagged teeth and loosed a roar that tore through Dziewanna's hope and left me crumpled at the willow's base.

"Show no fear," Mother's voice whispered to me from my memories. *"You are stronger than the wildest beasts, my child."*

"What do you want from me?" I asked, meeting the bear's gaze.

"I want nothing but to help you, little one," it replied with a voice far kinder than I'd expected. "My name is Ivan, advisor to Master Weles. What brings you from your bed when you remain so weak?"

Pushing away the stabbing pain, I gripped the tree's bark and pulled myself to my feet. "Help me leave. I need to find Mother. Nothing else matters."

"Doesn't your own life?"

"Obviously not! Your master had me killed so I could suit his purposes."

"You see him as a monster, like she once did." He glanced toward the willow when he said *she*.

I narrowed my eyes. "Mother took me away because she still saw him as one. She wanted me to be free from his grasp, but I fell into it anyway."

Ivan broke the binds at my wrist and dropped his front legs. Even on all fours he was nearly as tall as my chin, and a foul odor of fish hung from his mouth, forcing me to stagger back as he sighed. "Oh, how Dziewanna did not wish to marry Weles. She was a wild creature, beautiful and bold unlike any woman either Weles or I had ever seen. The master became hopelessly fond of her. For years, she wasted away in these swamps, fleeing to Jawia whenever she had the chance. Her bond to him was not so easily broken, though, so she always returned from her escapades. When she did, Weles would await her with gifts of jewels, pelts, and servants of both animal and spirit. Yet even these did not please her."

"Mother was never interested in wealth or the prizes of a married woman," I said, smiling at that. "Nothing could tame Dziewanna."

"Yes, the freedom of the wilds would always be more than gold to her, but she treasured Prawia, the realm of Perun and the gods, more than all. You have heard the story of her rebellion, have you not?"

I nodded, leaning against the tree to support my wobbling legs. "Dziewanna believed Perun to be the wrong ruler of Prawia, so she fought to rule it and all of the Three Realms herself. But she failed. That's why she was forced here in the first place."

Ivan drew closer, and I slid down the willow's trunk as he sat next to me. "Dziewanna saw her father as corrupt," he said, "obsessed with his war against my master instead of helping the people of Jawia. She believed Weles to be no better, especially after he kidnapped Jaryło when he was merely a baby. Though Dziewanna's cause was just, she was only a newly Ascended and naïve goddess who let her ambitions get the best of her."

"What's wrong with wanting change?"

"Nothing. In fact, change has always been quite the thing most gods have been poor at. Your mother, though, failed to realize the strength of patience. Perun loved her dearly, and after years of watching his older children squabble, he had wished to gift Jawia to Dziewanna so that, together, they could end the fighting. Instead, she received no inheritance at all." The bear chuckled—an odd sight. "Your mother's passion was her greatest trait and her ultimate downfall."

My hands trembled as I dug my fingers into the dirt, seeking the power I'd felt before. It lingered but was dull, distant. *Did I ever really know her?* Was her ambition really so harmful, or was Ivan telling the story Weles wanted me to hear?

"Weles brought you here to convince me to wait, to trust him." I shook my head at myself. "I'm such an idiot."

He chuckled. "You remind me of her. I mean that fondly. Master Weles may be far from perfect, but he could make Jawia yours, Otylia, if you do not surrender to mortal desires."

"Don't lecture me!" My knees ached as I stood, but they held as I surveyed the room, looking for an escape. "Mother didn't surrender to Weles's temptations and neither will I."

Another set of enormous doors lurked opposite the first. *I could run, but Ivan would be faster.* Being eaten by a bear did not sound appealing—I needed a distraction.

"Yet Weles did tame the wild goddess," he said, noticing me eying the doors.

I hesitated. "Mother said she had a moment of weakness."

"Did she?" He seemed to grin as he glanced at the flowers among the tree's roots. "Weles brought her a type of basil that only grows in Prawia or the deepest, untouched wilds of Jawia. All the riches of the Three Realms could not convince her to stay, but that flower won her heart for far more than a moment."

"You're lying! Mother would never have stayed with him."

As I stepped away, Ivan rose with his head bowed. "Dziewanna spent many a year in Nawia. I do not know if she loved the master as he did her, but she always returned to him freely. Well, she did until you…" He sighed. "You have little reason to trust me, Lady Otylia, but I wish to protect you from both Master Weles and yourself. There is much you do not unders—"

My fist struck his nose. The great bear reeled back with a roar as I bolted away with everything I had left.

"Lady Otylia!" he huffed. "Please, I can *help* you!"

But I leaped for the handle and tore open the doors, sending light spewing over me as I ran blindly into the next room. When I glanced over my shoulder, the last things I saw before the doors slammed were Ivan's bared teeth and a sea of violet basils encircling Mother's willow.

I'll find you.

Light flooded everything beyond the door. I covered my face and pushed forward, but the endless rays pierced my eyes as they watered, begging me to shut them. I didn't. With Ivan only strides behind, I needed to put as much distance between that room and me as possible. No matter what peril Weles had waiting for me, it couldn't be worse than Ivan's claims about Mother.

That was before the hissing began.

It came from everywhere. I couldn't see the branches, but it sounded as if a swarm of snakes hovered above me as something larger cracked the foliage behind. *Not again.*

I charged into the light without direction. Sweat poured down my face, burning my already stinging eyes. I cursed Weles as I tripped on roots and stones. Scrapes covered my knees and blood from jagged cuts trickled down my arm, but each time I fell, I pushed on.

Soon, the chorus of noise drifted away as rock replaced dirt beneath my feet. I collapsed, desperate for each breath. *Why does it have to be snakes?*

I rubbed my irritated eyes. Wolves I could try to fight, but the serpents tailing me were a mass of venom ready to kill me slowly. At least wolves were generous enough to go for the jugular.

A shadow hovered over me when I moved my hands from my eyes, revealing the massive ravine less than twenty strides ahead. I would have to return to the forest. But as I struggled to stand, the shadow loomed closer. Catching my breath, I turned back to the woods.

A snake's giant head towered over me. Its tongue flicked at the air ahead of its golden scales, slinking and slithering through the rays. With the hissing of the others approaching from the forest, its green eyes narrowed to slits before it lunged.

I dove to the side as the snake's fangs ripped through the place I'd knelt moments before. Its body coiled upon itself as it prepared for another strike, but I didn't give it the chance. I scampered over the uneven stone ground, running along the tree line and dashing each direction to avoid the snake's strikes.

My thighs ached with each stride. Since I'd awoken under that weeping willow, it seemed I'd done nothing but struggle forward, but this had to be Weles's doing. Whether it was torture or a test didn't matter. I would survive.

The ravine curved across my path, forcing me closer to the woods. Hissing echoed around me. No matter how fast I ran, the giant serpent was never more than a dozen strides behind. I had no choice but to charge back into the trees.

What did Weles want from me? Was he trying to awaken my powers, teach me a lesson, or something else?

I didn't know, so I ran. Numb to both pain and the stinging light, I sprinted through the forest and leaped over downed trees and snakes alike. But I couldn't escape the largest among them.

The giant snake struck out behind me, missing my ankles by

inches as my feet caught on roots. *It's too fast!*

I scrambled into a massive pine. Needles and branches tore at my skin, but I pushed deeper, too far for the serpent's fangs to reach. Its excited hissing circled me as I clung to the trunk and forced myself to breathe. *Now what?* I couldn't stay within the tree forever, but leaving would mean my death.

Needles crunched beneath me. I reacted too late.

Pain shot through my leg as I stared down in horror at the two holes in my calf and the brown snake slithering away. My weakness returned with the venom, and I collapsed to the dirt.

"Mother, help me," I whimpered. I knew she wouldn't hear my cry. Even if she could, she was trapped, and instead of saving her, I'd stumbled into Weles's own prison of roots and snakes.

"You cannot run from the dangers you face," Weles's voice said from the mouth of the great snake beyond the pine. "Nor can you confront them directly."

I gritted my teeth. "How do you expect me to win if I can't fight?"

"Every great power has its weakness. To defeat a stronger enemy, you must patiently find that flaw and then exploit it."

Weakness? I steadied my breathing and focused on the serpent's dripping fangs through the needles. *What's a snake's weakness?* My eyes widened. *That's it!*

Mother's potion lessons had mostly been about treating diseases. Once, though, a hunter had fallen at our doorstep, dying from a snake bite. She'd used venom itself as part of the antidote. Afterward, she'd explained how she would extract the venom from snakes hibernating in winter. But where was I going to find snow? Even if I created the anti-venom, how would I defeat the beast that towered before me?

"You may be frightened as your body weakens," Weles hissed, "but a god's power lies in their soul's *żityje*, not their body. More importantly, it lies not in your mother or your grandmother, but in you. To survive and complete the first Trial of Ascension, you must surrender your bond to them."

I glared up at Weles. "Never!"

His head lowered, bringing the serpent's nose into the tree's branches. "Then you will perish once again. You have proven your will to leave without giving me a chance to prove myself, but I cannot allow you to do so until you find your power and Ascend. These lands need not be torture for you, my daughter. You are the princess of Nawia, not a prisoner. If you choose to end this ridiculous game, then I will show you the truth and teach you how to heal."

"This isn't a game!" I flung dirt into his eyes and scrambled free from the pine. "And I'm not your little princess!"

He reeled back, hissing, "Very well. If that is your will."

Slits returned to his eyes as the ground slithered with snakes once again. Weles's tongue flicked the air, and I rolled away just as he lunged.

Dirt and blood filled my mouth, but I fought back to my feet and sprinted deeper into the trees. The ravine blocked the furthest edge, so I ran parallel to it and the wall of vines. There had to be *something* between them that I could use.

That felt like more hope than anything. Hope was all I had, though, and when the trees thinned, I smirked at what lay beyond.

The forest crawled up a mountain's side before giving way to a blanket of white. *That's it.* I began the climb, ignoring the monster's presence and the throbbing pain from the bite. With both Dziewanna and Mokosz's power distant, I had no chance to fight the beast. The snow far ahead was my only chance.

The world spun around me as I reached the first steep ridge. The venom was spreading through my veins, and my head felt disconnected from my body. Each breath became a struggle, slowing me as Weles hissed from below.

I grabbed a notch and pulled myself onto the rock wall. One foot at a time, I slowly crawled my way up as blood and sweat coated every groove my fingers found. Pain flooded my mind, but with so many places sore or stinging, it all became a blur.

When I reached the top and collapsed against a tree, I couldn't remember half the climb, but I'd made it. The ridge was at least fifty feet high. I was safe.

I took a deep breath and glanced over the edge at Weles. He hadn't followed. Though his eyes narrowed up at me, he only slithered back and forth before disappearing into the trees.

He was gone—for now.

My stomach turned as I continued my ascent. Before long, I dropped to my knees, vomiting what little substance was left. Mother's words to the hunter rang in my ears as I wiped the sick from my chin, *"First comes weakness, then vomiting, and after that…"* She had bitten her cheek, unable to finish. It was hard to know whether to curse or thank her now. If it was bad enough to make her hesitate, then I never wanted to find out.

I caught my breath after what could've been a minute or five. Time sped and slowed at random, and the landscape warped with it as I staggered my way toward the snow. Besides the sting of the cold against my skin, I felt only dread. Then I heard the cracking of the trees.

"Run!" I muttered to myself. "Go!"

My feet dragged like a drunken chief as the serpent slithered through the pine forest's shadows.

The snow wasn't far now, but my progress was slow as bits of stone and dirt slid down the slope with each step. Exhaustion ruled my mind. My breaths were shallow. And when my legs surrendered, I clawed my way forward, desperate to survive.

It wasn't enough.

"The first Trial is the key to the rest," Weles said. "You must let your mother go and embrace who you are."

Darkness lurked at the edge of my vision as I turned to face him. His serpent form loomed over me, eyes hungry as his golden body encircled mine.

I told myself I could fight him, that I could still survive. But as I reached for my *żityje*, demanding that Mother's power answer my call, I sensed nothing but a void.

Then the serpent struck.

5

Wacław

What is Weles doing?

NIGHT HAD COME EARLY IN THE MOUNTAINS. The rocks above cast deep shadows across the terrain as we rested without a tent on the hard ground. I lay alone again beneath the trees, and each gust of wind made them creak and moan, enough to put me on edge.

Twinges of pain had shot through my connection to Otylia ever since I'd left Katiôn. It wasn't the first time, but this was different. I felt her desperation, her drive to escape, and most of all, the toil her body was enduring. After a week away from her, I couldn't handle it anymore. I needed to find her.

What sounded like an animal call echoing through the mountains pulled me from my thoughts.

Refugees and warriors alike had spoken of an aspid that called Perun's Crown home. A hulking monster with the wings and a beak of a bird but the scales and fire of a dragon, it preferred solitude, but when disturbed, it could destroy armies without hesitation. Something seemed to lurk on the winds beyond that call. I hoped it was friendlier than the tales.

Despite my worries, I finally drifted to sleep and awoke shivering in my soul-form. I pulled my cloak tight and slipped through camp, heading toward the southern cliffs. Without Dadźbóg's warmth, the winds brought a chill that made my hair stand on end. I embraced them. *They're your friends now.*

Eryk had told me to speak to Cervenko. How? I'd sensed the east wind's presence many times, yet contacting him seemed another task completely.

My power still felt *wrong* tonight, but the winds carried me over the Narrow Pass. My fingers throbbed as I landed along a rock face, digging into the thin handholds. I stared up the cliff and reveled in my isolation from all else living. With each step up, I reached for the winds. Their answers were weak, and instead of a fluid climb, I clambered to the summit with straining shoulders and fingers that bled from gripping stone.

But the pain was worth it.

The sky stretched forever, its darkness only broken by the twinkling stars representing each living soul. The Kwiecień moon hung among them—a godless crescent that taunted me every night with its sword humming at my back.

Dread returned. As long as I held Kwiecień, Jaryło would struggle to return during the moon, but the gods were a mystery. When would he come for revenge? Or was he already punishing Otylia in my place?

The sword glowed in the light of its moon as I set its point against the rocky ground and let its odd power join with mine. Though I couldn't wield Kwiecień's magic, the gales rushed around me, blowing the chilled air through my cloak and hair. With them, I traced every inch of the mountains and forests beyond. Mountain goats, wolves, and smaller creatures of all kinds traversed the land. There was no sign of demons or the aspid.

When I released the winds, they took my energy with them. I staggered, barely catching my footing as I shook away the fatigue.

I understood my *żityje* more with every night, but my power still caught me by surprise at times. Some nights I could summon storm clouds or even lightning. Recently, though, just searching with my power was exhausting.

"Cervenko," I whispered into the gales. "I seek your guidance."

The winds swirled around the summit, howling in my ears, but no reply came. I sighed and gripped Kwiecień's hilt. *Now what?* Cervenko was known to be as reckless as a wild stallion—a trait more helpful in battle than discussion. Did he not want to talk, or was I doing something wrong?

I looked east, over the hills and steppe beyond. *Maybe I must go to him…*

Kwiecień tight in my hand, I swept along the cliff's edge. The sword had begun to feel more like a companion than a tool in recent days. Though Otylia would've called me foolish for thinking so fondly of a sword, knowing that brought a grin to my face.

Clouds gathered far to the east, near where we'd first found the clans. The air buzzed as I flew to their center, shouting through the storm, "Cervenko, grandson of Strzybóg, I seek your guidance!"

Lightning snapped. A gray stallion burst through the clouds, sparks crackling through its body as it struck my chest at full stride.

I collapsed through the storm, clutching my sword as the figure made chase. The flashes of lightning illuminated its flowing mane and the swirls of mist encompassing its form. Its bright blue eyes pierced my soul as I spun out of its way and steadied myself on a bed of air.

"Demon!" the stallion shouted on the winds. "My brothers and I aided you against the other of your kind, but we are no friends of yours. You manipulate us to your will!"

Cervenko charged before I could respond. I tumbled to the side. As he rushed past, I grabbed hold of his neck in desperation.

"Release me!" he demanded.

My ribs ached from the strikes as he bucked. Tanek had done the same many times as a foal, though, and I countered the move, swinging myself onto his back with the winds and gripping his mane. "I don't wish to manipulate you! Marzanna is a threat to us both, and I need your help to stop her."

"Betrayer! Schemer! Begone!"

We dove.

My arms and thighs strained and my eyes stung as I clung to the beast. With each spin I struggled to breathe, holding on with weeks of frustration and anguish taking over. Otylia needed me. No stubborn wind god would stop me from finding her.

Cervenko hit the dirt at full stride, the muscles on his neck flexing as I gripped a fistful of his mane in one hand and Kwiecień in the other. The flat of its golden blade burned against his skin, and he reared as I pushed it harder into him. "Relent and I'll release you," I ordered.

"Demons speak nothing but lies."

"From what I've seen, gods are no different."

His laugh bellowed across the sky as he skidded to a halt atop a hill of short grass. Ahead, smoldering fires blanketed the ground, where a camp of hundreds of tents had once stood. My stomach turned at the sight and smoke burned my nostrils.

"What happened here?" I asked.

Cervenko huffed. "Don't ask stupid questions."

Riders appeared over the next hill, their black horses and bone weapons just as Otylia had described. *The Frostmarked Horde.* They had destroyed yet another clan, and Cervenko sought to warn me. "Where did they come from?"

He tossed his head. "Beyond the mountains east of the Anshayman Steppe. An immortal sorcerer leads them, the one they call Koschei the Deathless. His army grows ever stronger as they burn the clans one-by-one, and soon, even your lands will not be safe."

The Horde cheered as a rider on a white horse appeared over the hill. With a long spear of bone in one hand and a decapitated head in the other, power seemed to radiate from him. His skin hung wrinkled on his cheeks, and a chill crawled down my spine as his black gaze locked on me. His lip curled.

"Is he a god?" I asked.

"No," Cervenko said. "Koschei is not a god, but neither is he a normal man. Though many warriors have slain him, he has returned each time. His body is immortal."

I stared at the white rider, his stallion carrying him across the steppe faster than any horse I had ever seen. The earth shook with each stride. "If his body is immortal, where lies his soul?"

"You asked the right question this time, but I do not know the answer."

As the Horde drew nearer, Koschei's gaze never left me. It was hard to know how far we'd flown, but the Horde was no more than a week's travel behind the clans. If they caught us…

I gripped Kwiecień, its hilt warming my shaking hand. "If you don't know where it lies, then who does?"

"Only the goddess of winter herself."

"Then there is little hope to defeat him."

"What hope does a demon have anyway?" Cervenko huffed. "Leave me. I've said everything I know."

He charged into the air. I held on as he spun, trying to throw me off his back a final time, but Eryk's words rang in my mind. "Wait!" I said. "I was told you could tell me how to get to Nawia—how I can save Otylia!"

He snorted and shot north even faster than before. With his storm whipping around us, only my hold on his mane kept me on his back.

I stared down at the blur of grasses below. *If only Mom could see me now.* What would she have thought of her demonic son riding the east wind over the steppes? I didn't know whether she'd laugh or simply shake her head, but my chest ached regardless. *I'll come home. I promise.*

We soon raced over the warped branches of the Mangled Woods. It seemed far more than a week ago that we'd wandered through those trees in search of the płanetnik. They had been covered in Marzanna's frost then, but now, even in the dark, the warped and naked branches stretched across the forest. The snow was gone—yet death's grip lingered.

"Death is inescapable, demon-born," Cervenko said, finally stopping over the woods, out of breath. We'd flown a week's worth of travel in mere minutes. "But Nawia is not for your kind."

Can he read my mind, or am I just that obvious? Either answer was disconcerting as I shook my head. My own brow was coated with sweat from the ride, and I lacked the energy to fight the impatience burning away at my core. "There must be a way! I have to reach Nawia before Jaryło's return in Maj if there's any chance of saving her."

He laughed. "I have never seen a demon obsessed with love, nor do I know a way for one to go to Weles. No one travels freely between the realms except Dadźbóg and Weles himself. Even if there were a way, your demonic soul could not enter paradise."

With a groan, I slid off the horse's back and hovered on the winds, my glimmer of hope fading. Anger replaced it. "There *must* be a way."

"There are many secrets among the Three Realms," Cervenko replied. "It would not surprise me if a route existed, but such a thing is not of my knowledge. Even my northwestern brother, Kyustendil, remains trapped in Nawia. If you were to help him escape too, then you would have all our loyalties—except Chorna." He scoffed at the mention of his northern brother.

The storm swelled around us as if it fed on Cervenko's power and the pain pounding in my soul. Intoxicating, it tempted me to surrender to its call. "I promise," I said as I took a shuddered breath. It helped me build a wall between my mind and the storm in my heart, but part of me loathed the return of that numbness. "I don't know if I can get Otylia back, but gods know, I'm trying. If I succeed and Kyustendil is there, I will do all I can to rescue him too."

"Very well. Tell this to Dogoda in the west and she may know more." Cervenko leaped into the storm with a dismissive glance. "Know, however, that you chase fantasies. Even if you save the girl, Marzanna will use Koschei's Horde to slaughter her before your eyes. But you're a demon. The sight of death is natural for you."

Then he dissolved into the clouds, leaving me floating above the Mangled Woods.

I took one last look at the trees swaying in his gales. In the past moon, they had swallowed so much of my joy, my dreams. Nothing could change what had happened, but as I returned to the clan camp, I promised myself I wouldn't let those we'd lost die in vain. They deserved more—Kuba deserved more.

6

Wacław

Maj draws ever nearer, but we're no closer to answers. How long can we linger with the clans?

"ARE WE SURE DARIUSZ WILL KNOW?" ARA ASKED from atop her chestnut horse as she squinted into Dadźbóg's early rays. Curled on the back of her riding pad, Sosna watched me with eager eyes. "I mean, if even a god doesn't…"

"She's right," Narcyz said. "Hate to say it, Half-Chief, but relying on the high priest ain't much of a plan. Not that we should be worried about Otylia when an *immortal sorcerer* and his Horde are coming to kill us."

Ara rolled her eyes. "Otylia is our only chance to stop Marzanna's Frostmarked. Dziewanna said so."

"Because we should definitely listen to the goddess who got herself captured," Narcyz muttered.

I grimaced, gripping my horse's reins hard enough to turn my palm red. After my talk with Cervenko, I'd made a decision—one I knew they wouldn't like. "Marzanna is weakened, but who knows for how long? Between her threat and Jaryło's control of Maj, we have to hurry. The clans won't reach Dwie Rzeki by the end of the moon."

"I know what you're going to say," Ara interrupted. "And we're coming with you."

"Absolutely not," I said. "When we reach Kynnytsia and convince King Boz to allow the clans passage through his lands, I will ride ahead. The clans will need the two of you to represent our tribe and guide them to Dwie Rzeki." The thought of riding by myself scared me more than I was willing to admit, but being alone with my grief felt better than holding the lives of my friends in my hands. At least with the clans, they would be safe.

Narcyz scoffed. "Xobas can do it. They've made him a commander already, so why can't he show them the way?"

"Right," Ara said. "He can ensure the clans make it, but someone needs to make sure *you* make it, Wacław. After what we did to Yuliya, Eryk, and her cultists, Marzanna will be looking for revenge. Just because you can summon lightning in your soul-form doesn't mean you can fight off demons and warriors with only Kwiecień during the day."

I shook my head. "We're talking about the underworld, not just Marzanna. Even if you come with me, I can't risk you two being trapped in Nawia—dead."

Narcyz scoffed. "I can handle it."

"Weren't you the one who wanted to fight for the glory of the tribe against the Solgawi?" I asked. "If you were to travel with the clans, you could ride with them to reinforce our warriors across the Krowik. They would see you as a hero."

He shrugged. "Yeah, but anybody can talk about fighting guys with pointy sticks. When Genowefa hears I slayed the demons of the Mangled Woods *and* traveled to Nawia—"

"Do boys think of nothing else?" Ara asked with a roll of her eyes.

I chuckled, but a pang struck my heart. *Am I any different?* Otylia hadn't left my mind since Jaryło had killed her. All we'd had was one kiss, yet I yearned for the next one more than anything. Losing her and Kuba in such quick succession had torn away a part of me that refused to heal. I should've been preparing for whatever lay ahead. Instead, remembering there was a world beyond that ache in my soul was a struggle.

My cheeks burned when Ara sighed, pulling me from my thoughts. "Apparently so," she quipped.

"What's that you said?" Bidaês asked sarcastically, trotting up to our group on a bay horse whose mane was woven in an intricate pattern across its neck. "I thought I heard you say you think of nothing else but me."

"Then your ears deceive you," Ara sneered as Sosna growled at the visitor.

"Why so jaded on a beautiful day like this?" Bidaês turned his head to the sun. "Even your fox is in a foul mood."

He wasn't wrong about the weather. A cool breeze skimmed through the pines and granted us a rare relief. On the steppe, my skin had burned and the lack of trees offered no respite, but it had still been better than Marzanna's chill. I ran my thumb along my frostbitten fingers. *She's weakened for now, but it's only going to get worse.*

"I trust Sosna's opinion more than yours," Narcyz spat. "She's good at knowing people's intentions."

"Of course…" Bidaês chuckled.

Ara adjusted her bow and quiver on her back, furrowing her brow as she did. "I saw a god kidnap my best friend less than two weeks ago. Whether the sun shines or not is the least of my problems."

The Simuk's eyes widened. "A god? You're joking, right?"

"It wasn't one of mine." She nodded to Narcyz and me. "Jaryło is a Krowikie god."

"Huh. You place your faith in gods other than your own?"

Her lip curled. "It's not faith to believe something you've seen with your own eyes. And I don't worship him—I want to kill him and bring Otylia back. That's why I'm going with Wacław to find him."

Bidaês stroked his stubbled chin. "And how exactly do you plan to do that?"

"Jaryło is in Nawia—what we call the underworld," I said. Katiôn had told me to trust Bidaês. As much as that pained me, Xobas believed in the marzban, so I would too. "Otylia is the key to defeating the Frostmarked Horde. We need her."

I need her.

His horse huffed, and Bidaês patted the stallion's neck. "Searching for myths and fighting gods. There's more to you than you've told us, son of Jacek." He paused. "Your father sent you to bring him an army, but you would rather seek revenge against an immortal than join his war. Why? Surely one girl can't be the difference against the Horde?"

I swallowed. *You have no idea.* The emptiness in my chest threatened to pull me in as fear and regret reminded me of those we'd lost. Beneath it roared a stronger blaze, one I refused to recognize. "She's a powerful sorceress. Even if she wasn't, I couldn't stop Jaryło, and now he's taken her. It's up to me to get her back."

Silence hung among us. Only the clacking of hooves against stone broke the still air until Narcyz cleared his throat. "Yeah, it sucks… But it could be worse, right?"

Ara shot him a glare as sharp as her arrows. "Ever heard of empathy, or does nobody really matter to you?"

Narcyz winced just long enough to make me wonder who that was. Genowefa? His parents? He'd spoken about warriors that he looked up to, but were they it? A scowl quickly replaced the pain on his face, though, and he gripped his spear as he pushed his horse into a trot. "Some of us only need our tribe. Not that *you* would understand."

He plowed ahead, not waiting for a reply.

"Well, that went perfectly," Bidaês said, his usual sarcasm dulled.

I half-expected Ara to nock an arrow, but she just growled into her teeth. "What are you trying to accomplish, Bidaês? We've seen a lot of death over the last moon, and you poking open wounds isn't making life any easier."

"Oh." Bidaês cringed. It was refreshing to see him show regret for once—even if it was only because he was obviously fond of Ara. "I want to help," he finally managed to spit out. "Let me come with you."

Is this all because of her?

Ara's lips formed a thin line. She shook her head, but Bidaês had regained his posture, sitting tall on his mount. "The things you've seen are like the legends our elders tell," he said. "I may not be heir, but I can prove myself to the clan in other ways."

I opened my mouth to reply, but pain shot through my leg. Bidaês raised a brow as I caught my breath and exchanged a worried glance with Ara. "Everything all right, Wacław?" he asked.

Something's wrong. The flashes of pain had become all too familiar since Otylia's death, and every day they became more vivid. Either she was suffering or the connection between us was growing stronger. Both options scared me in very different ways.

"I'm fine," I mumbled unconvincingly. My leg still throbbed, but I avoided the topic. "You sounded skeptical of our plan a few minutes ago. Why the change?"

Bidaês's face grew heavy as he stared down at his horse. "What you said about Otylia… I know what it's like to lose someone you love. My parents were slaughtered when the Frostmarked Horde attacked. I'd give anything to see them again." He looked from me to Ara. "If I help you get Otylia back, then maybe I can do something worth remembering, something to stop the Horde so others don't have to suffer like I did."

My gut told me no, but I saw his pain. Bidaês had always acted like just another arrogant warrior. Now, though, I questioned whether he was so simple after all. Besides, if I couldn't go alone, having another skilled swordsman was reassuring at least.

"I need time to think about it," I said, sliding my fingers across Otylia's bow necklace. "Just know you were right: There is more to the story. If you come with us, your life won't be the same. We will have to break from the clans once we reach Astiwie lands. I don't know when we'll rejoin them."

"We're leaving my homeland, probably for forever," he replied. "I'd say my life is going to change no matter what I do." He sighed and glanced over his shoulder, where Zakir rode alone, pulling a cart of his alchemical solutions. "All I ask is that you allow my brother to come too. He's fascinated with discovery. He wouldn't forgive me if

I were to discover a way to the afterlife without him. Besides, to become marzban, he must complete a grand journey. What's better than this?"

Ara's eyes lit up as I winced. Bidaês could hold his own in a fight, but Zakir would be in danger—we'd lost too many friends already. "This isn't a fun adventure," I said. "If Zakir comes, I need to know he can defend himself. He's your clan's heir."

"He's made poison!" Ara blurted out, blushing as she did. "He might not be great with a sword, but maybe he could use his alchemy to help us?"

This isn't a good idea. I cursed myself as I looked to the sky. *Why did I have to inherit Mom's kindness?* "Otylia was our healer. Having someone who can make potions—for healing or poisoning—could be helpful, but let us talk this over. The last time we invited a stranger into our group, it didn't end well."

"Since when am I a stranger?" Bidaês asked with a cocky grin.

"Well, you definitely are strange," Ara said.

I sighed and looked to the lead riders, the journey ahead weighing heavy on my shoulders. "I doubt the marzban and high priestess will react well to us all leaving. With your parents gone, Katiôn won't want to lose you too."

Bidaês held his chin high. "Don't worry about my grandfather. I will talk to him."

"That's exactly what I'm worried about," Ara grumbled.

"This is the only way?"

Xobas paced around the rim of his rounded tent. Despite the fire flickering at its center, a cold breeze slipped through the flap and sent a shiver down my spine.

I squatted by the fire and warmed my hands. *Why does saying goodbye to him have to be so hard?* Xobas had always been more than just a combat trainer to me. He'd been a mentor and the closest thing I had to a real father. Leaving him brought the same sorrow as walking away from Mom, and though I had promised them both I would return to Dwie Rzeki, home seemed further than ever.

"If we want to find Otylia before Jaryło recovers, then yes," I said. "Honestly, I don't know if relying on Dariusz is the right option, but I can't think of a better one."

Arms crossed, Xobas continued pacing, as if on patrol. "I knew this day would come."

"What do you mean?"

He sighed and stopped with his hand on the hilt of his cavalry sword. In the firelight, his Simukie leather armor seemed to glow against his dark skin. He truly looked like a commander. "When you told me you were a demon, I knew that, someday, I would no longer be able to fulfill your father's last order to me."

Slowly, I rose, watching him from across the fire. "What order?"

He hung his head, and sorrow met me again. In the years I had known Xobas, I'd never seen him hesitate. Father's death had wounded him. To me, Jacek had been a brutal overseer, but he had gifted Xobas a second chance. Though Xobas had given Father his undying loyalty in response, he'd failed to protect his chief. I hurt for him.

"The high chief was often a cold man," Xobas said. "That didn't mean he didn't love you."

When I closed my eyes, I saw every time Father had struck me. Every time I had disappointed him. Every time I hadn't been the warrior he'd wanted me to be. And the moment he'd turned me away before I saw my first sunrise—the moment he'd rejected love for power. *If that's his love, I don't want it.* I bit my cheek so hard it bled before taking a deep breath. Pain lingered in those memories, anger. It frightened me, and I ran from it, circling the room until Xobas caught my arm.

"Your father gave me one responsibility before we left: keep you safe. But after Bustelintin, it became obvious there were things you would face that I could not protect you from. I knew I would fail him."

"No," I said, raising my gaze to his. "You've shown me more love, more care, than he ever has. Xobas, I wouldn't be alive if you hadn't been there every step of the way from Dwie Rzeki to the Mangled Woods. Father failed me, but you never have."

He stumbled for a reply. Before he found the words, I embraced him in a hug, and he just stood there for a moment, stunned as the fire's crackle filled the tent. When his arms wrapped around me, I felt centered for the first time since we'd left the woods. Whole. The walls surrounding my heart lowered for that moment, and sorrow clashed with the flickering joy within. It was torture, wishing for hope and finding only pain. So, I rebuilt those walls as I stepped back and averted my gaze.

"I've never had a son," Xobas said, "but I'm honored to call you mine." Clearing his throat, he assumed a commander's stance with his hands locked behind him. "When the time comes for you to leave for Dwie Rzeki, know you've done well for your tribe. Jacek would've been proud."

I dug my foot into the dirt. "I doubt he would've."

"Regardless, you are doing all you can. It weighs on you—that much is obvious—but you are on the right path." Xobas peered out of the tent, scanning the patrolling clan warriors. "Marzban Katiôn's grandchildren may be outsiders to us. To him, however, they're the next Simukie leaders. This journey will help them prove that according to our customs."

"So, you think I should take them and go?"

He nodded. "I will stay with the clans and ensure they arrive in Krowikie lands. Those boys will aid you. Powerful or not, we all need allies in times like these."

"Thank you, Xobas," I said with a bow of my head.

With a smile, he patted my shoulder. "May your gods protect you."

7

Otylia

Worst father ever.

EVERY MUSCLE IN MY BODY ACHED when I woke in the same wooden bed as the day before. Had it been the day before? I groaned and rubbed my throbbing head. Time passed oddly in Nawia, and it was hard to know if I'd been here days or weeks.

A familiar sadness greeted me as I sat up. *Oh Wašek, why do you mourn for me?* The tether between us had revealed the other's pain at times, but ever since my death, I'd felt it whenever he thought about me.

It was often.

I wondered if he felt the same twinge when I thought of him. Granted, I hadn't had much time to ponder anything but survival. After my two disastrous experiences with Weles's snakes, Nawia hadn't had exactly put me in a romantic mood.

Gods… Romantic mood? What had Wacław done to me?

One stupid kiss after almost four years of silence and now I'd fallen for him. A hesitant boy. A demon. The only person who didn't make me feel alone. The one who gave me hope that maybe there was something good in the world, that life was about more than the squabbles of kings and chiefs, gods and demons. I'd resented him for so long. But as I clutched my legs under that willow and remembered the few moments we'd slipped away together, I wanted nothing more than to lie next to him. No words. Just his arm around me—knowing I had a place where I could belong.

"I miss you, Wašek," I whispered as my fingers drifted to my collar, where Mother's necklace had once lain. He must've taken it before I'd descended here. I took that as a promise he'd come for me, but I didn't intend to sit and wait.

My hands weren't bound like last time. Still, my wrists were red from the vines, and even with my hands free, I was too weak to swing my legs out of the bed. But as I rolled over, I noticed a bowl of bright orange fruit sitting on a table that hadn't been there before.

What game are you playing, Weles?

The sight of food made my stomach rumble. I'd never seen a fruit like this. Taking one in my hand, I felt its tough exterior, thicker than that of an apple. I pulled back the skin and winced as a sharp sour scent struck my nose.

"They're quite good," a voice peeped from the darkness.

I dropped the fruit and instinctively reached for Dziewanna's power. When I found nothing, I pulled my legs to my chest instead. "Who are you?"

A thin girl clad in a dress woven from leaves stepped into a beam of light. Her long brown hair flowed freely over her shoulder and down to her waist. Beneath her bulbous eyes, she had high, pronounced cheekbones that seemed to swallow her narrow face. "My apologies, Lady Otylia," she said, curtsying as she stared at the ground. "I am called Sabina. Your father, Master Weles, has sent me to care for you."

"Please don't call me that."

"Oh." She stepped back with her arms clutched to her chest. "My apologies, La—I mean—"

"Call me Otylia. I don't know what he told you, but I'm no lady. Nor am I his daughter."

"Right… of course, Otylia." She said my name carefully, as if she were afraid I'd punish her for saying it wrong. Then, with a deep breath, she smiled and swept over to the fruit, picking up the one I'd dropped.

"What are those?" I asked. "I've never seen them in Jawia."

She wiped away the dirt from the fruit's skin and held it out to me. "Master Weles calls them oranges. He says they only grow in the most southern Anvoranie city-states. They're quite sweet when ripe. You peel back the skin, so that one should be okay to eat… Unless, of course, you'd prefer a new one?"

I took the orange and examined it in the light. *Not the most creative name*, I thought, but I was starving. Who cared what it was called?

I tore free what looked like a slice of it. Unlike the skin, this inside was soft. I squeezed, and juice shot out of it. *Odd.* When I took a bite, the juice burst in my mouth, bringing a tartness that made me wince at first. But surprisingly, it tasted good.

"That's the weirdest thing I've ever eaten," I said with a laugh. "You said the Anvoranie grow these?"

I knew little about the city-states south of Perun's Crown. It was difficult to cross the mountains, so only the rare trader had come to Dwie Rzeki with rumors. Apparently, the Anvoranie had once held an empire with more land than both the Krowikie and Solgawi combined. None of them would say why it fell.

Sabina nodded rapidly, probably happy that she hadn't angered me. "Yes, around the city of Rustah! I can tell you more about them if you'd like?"

"Maybe another time." I ate another slice of the orange, then another. "Do you know what Weles wants with me? Why he keeps me trapped here?"

"Oh." She blushed—a bright pink against her pale cheeks. "I don't… I thought he'd told you?"

"He did, but I want to know why *you* think he's keeping me here."

"It's only the master's opinion that matters, not mine."

I finished the orange quickly and lay back down. The venom had done its damage. Just sitting up was already making me light-headed. "I care about your opinion," I said. "Weles had little more than veiled threats and lessons I need to learn before I *Ascend*." My tongue felt wrong saying that word.

Sabina clasped her hands in front of her and walked through the dim light. "Master Weles can be like that, but I assure you, he means well."

I scoffed. "Is that why he had me killed?"

"Desperate men do silly things sometimes," she said, glancing up from the ground to me. "I was young when he lost Lady Dziewanna, but everyone says he's never been the same since the goddess left. I can only imagine now that you're here, he's afraid to lose you too."

Does he actually care, or is he trying to use me like Marzanna did to Wacław?

I'd thought once that it would be impossible to completely know the gods. Father had called them ancient, wonderful, and far beyond our understanding. With every piece I learned about them, I found I understood less and less. And now I was supposed to be one of them. *How do I become something I can't grasp?* Was that why Weles was so desperate to keep me here—to teach me? Or was I just another weapon in the wars among the gods?

"Lady Otylia?" Sabina asked with concern. "I will leave if you wish to be alone."

I pushed away my thoughts for now. "No, I'd like the company for once. I haven't spoken to someone who isn't a god or a bear since I got here."

She giggled and sat along the wooden bedframe. "I assume you met Ivan then?"

"Yeah..." I said as the memory of Mother's tree made me smile. "I punched him."

She gasped and clapped a hand to her mouth. "Oh yes, that would explain his grumpiness the past few days. If you give him the chance, he's actually quite nice."

Few days? Had I really been out that long? I hated Weles for confining me while Mother wasted away. "You've been the one caring for me while I recovered?" I asked.

"I have." Sabina hesitated for a second, twiddling her fingers before working up the courage to speak again. "If you don't mind me asking, who is Wašek?"

I blushed, then cursed myself for doing so.

"Oh." Another pitched giggle. "I see."

"It's not so simple. How do you know that name?"

"My apologies, but I overheard you calling to him in your sleep."

Wonderful. When had I become so reliant on him? "His name is Wacław—only I call him Wašek—and he's a demon. A living one."

Her eyes widened. "I've never heard of a living demon before."

I closed my eyes, fighting the throbbing pain in my head. "I thought them myths until I discovered his powers."

"Who is he to you?"

She's asking too many questions. I gritted my teeth. "Why do you care? You serve Weles. I've said too much already." I rolled over to face away from her. She was a stranger. Why had I trusted her so quickly, let her prod into my life? She would go to Weles when this was over and tell him everything I said—I knew it.

"I'll leave you then, Lady Otylia," Sabina said, her voice cracking. "When you're ready to be taken to Master Weles, I'll be outside the doors."

She stood, and the sound of her soft steps against the dirt faded. A door creaked open beyond the light, closer than it had been during my escape attempt. Before I could wonder why, tiredness washed over me, and I fell asleep.

8

Wacław

Whether it's in Dwie Rzeki or with the clans, everyone gives me that same look.

I PULLED UP MY CLOAK'S HOOD, but it provided little anonymity as I passed through our camp. With my light skin, I stuck out among the Zurgowie and Simukie. They eyed me wherever I went. I hadn't figured out yet if it was out of curiosity, fear, or resentment. All I knew was that my hair rose under their fierce gazes.

The flickering of campfires sent shadows across the ground as I crept toward a dense patch of fir trees alongside the trail. Though our tent had given the group privacy before, it wasn't built for such a narrow mountain pass, and everyone but the clan commanders had resorted to smaller tents or sleeping on unprotected bed rolls until we reached Astiwie lands. Anyone could overhear us in the close confines.

With a quick glance over my shoulder, I slid into the forest and found the downed trees where Ara and Narcyz had agreed to meet me. Ara sat on a log, whittling a stick while Narcyz paced. Sosna darted between them with her tail wagging and her tongue sticking out the side of her panting mouth.

"About time you showed up," Narcyz huffed.

I didn't bother to look at him as I joined Ara on the log and stretched my sore legs. Riding was easier than walking, but it hurt in entirely different places. "I needed to talk to Xobas about the plan."

"And?"

Ara rolled her eyes, but I allowed him that question. "He's hesitant to let us go, but he agrees that if this is our only chance to find a way to Nawia soon, then we have to take it. Gods know time is running out before the Horde arrives and Marzanna attacks again."

"Doubt that's the only reason you're in a rush," Narcyz said, grinning.

"No, it's not, but my motives matter less than getting her back." I winced with the phantom sting from my connection to Otylia lingering in my calf. "She's suffering—I can feel it. Ever since she…" Her death flashed through my mind again, catching my thoughts. *Can I really save her?* I tried to push on, but my doubts lingered. "The spurts of pain have been more frequent lately. Whatever Weles is doing to her, we have to stop it."

"How?"

"I don't know, but Dziewanna said I'm the only one who can save Otylia, and Otylia is the only one who can save her." Sosna ran over to me. I patted her head, remembering the goddess's words. "Dziewanna gave the last of her *życie* to keep me alive. She believed in me, and I don't plan on letting her down."

Ara took a sharp chunk out of the stick. "None of us do, but we don't need *him* to find her."

"Bidaês is arrogant and annoying, but he knows how to fight. There are so few people we can trust. He wants to help us, and I'm not one to turn away an ally when we're desperate. Plus, we don't have a healer without Otylia. Zakir won't come if we leave Bidaês behind."

"Why not?" Ara asked, her gaze fixed on me and her fist tight around her hunting knife.

Narcyz scoffed. "Worried he doesn't stare at you too?"

Ara shot to her feet and threw him to the ground before he could move. Blade in hand, she knelt over him and held its edge to his throat. "You're right, Wacław. Maybe we should bring him and leave Narcyz behind."

"The more energy we waste fighting each other," I said, "the happier Marzanna becomes. We don't have to be best friends, but we need each other if we're going to survive what's ahead. If bringing the brothers along keeps us alive, then that's all that matters to me."

Ara rose, sheathing her knife. "Fine. Let them come—for Otylia."

Narcyz grumbled. "What she said."

"Good." I took the straw płanetnik hat from my head and ran my fingers across its brim. Wearing it felt like an admission of what I'd become. *It doesn't matter. Demon or not, I'm bringing her home.* "They'll be here in a few minutes. Let's try to keep the scuffles to a minimum. I'm already dreading telling them the truth without having to break up another fight."

"Since when are you in charge?" Narcyz asked. He cracked his knuckles and sat on the other log. "Xobas was always the one giving the orders before."

I hesitated. Why was I taking lead? Being the center of attention made me nervous, but I felt responsible for both Otylia's fate and the clans'. Was it guilt for accepting the dagger in the first place or something else? Ever since the golden egg had awoken my power, I'd felt the craving for more, but this was different, a duty. That didn't mean I wanted it.

"I don't know," I admitted, "but everything seems to be forcing me to act. Believe me, I'd rather anyone else have to deal with this."

Suddenly, Sosna growled and shot to my side. I pulled Marzanna's blade, but a laugh greeted me.

"You invite us to a meeting and then ambush us. Nice start," Bidaês said, smirking as he stopped in the middle of the triangle our group had formed. "You really should get that fox of yours under control. She always looks ready to strike."

Narcyz huffed. "Good girl."

Zakir kept head down in thought, lingering near the moonlit trees. My eldest half-brother, Mikołaj, would've been offended at the boy's indifference, but in the short time I had known Zakir, I'd welcomed his relative quietness. He was probably figuring a new alchemical formula instead of bothering with our quarrels. Though I had no idea how his potions worked, Ara was convinced of his skill. That was enough for me to do the same.

"I'm honestly surprised you decided to come too, Zakir," I said, sheathing the dagger, "but I'm honored to have you with us."

Zakir thought for a moment before replying, hushed, "Bidaês tends to be rash in decisions like this. However, I see the potential for me to learn so much more about the world while completing my required journey as heir to the marzban. There has to be some *substance* behind witchcraft and the creatures you call demons."

It's called žityje. I doubted his technical mind would be satisfied with such a simple explanation, so I stayed quiet.

"I wouldn't call myself *rash*," Bidaês said. "I just know a good opportunity when I see one."

Sosna sniffed around him before running to Zakir and giving an excited yip, bringing a smile to the younger brother's face. "Opportunity and risk are not the same, Bidaês. Grandfather would have us know as much."

Bidaês waved a dismissive hand. "Whatever." He turned to me and crossed his arms. "What's the deal? Are we coming?"

My foot tapped against my will as I swapped glances with Ara. I'd just said we needed to trust them. Still, revealing the truth had my stomach tied into a knot. It had been hard enough to tell Xobas and the others, and I had known most of them for years. We'd only met the brothers a week before.

"Well?" Bidaês asked, insistent.

I pointed to a downed tree. "You both can come, but you should sit. There is a lot I need to tell you first."

He gave a skeptical look before sitting. Zakir didn't join him, instead wandering through the trees to stand near Ara.

Hesitation closed my throat as they watched me, expectant. What would they say? Would they turn the clans against me and ruin everything? Who was I to lead them west, where we'd surely find more danger? I had failed Otylia and Kuba, so why would I succeed with them?

"I…"

Bidaês slapped his thighs with an exaggerated sigh. "Spit it out!"

I looked to the trees, beginning at the hardest truth, "I'm a demon called a płanetnik."

"You're a *what*?" Bidaês exclaimed, his eyes wild and his fingers dug into the log's bark.

"Huh," Narcyz said. "Apparently he's deaf too."

Bidaês held his chin up, and my heart was heavy as I continued, "I didn't react much better when I found out a couple moons ago. Please, just let me explain."

"Tell me everything," Zakir said, scooting to the edge of the log. There was a rare dose of excitement in his voice before he resorted to whispering to himself, "Need to know more…"

"Fine." Bidaês held out a hand toward me. "Tell me why we should follow you, demon spawn."

The insult struck home, and I hesitated as doubts gripped me once again: about myself, about trusting the brothers, and about staying with the clans. Why couldn't I leave all this behind and go to Otylia? The clans needed me, but were they really worth it?

Ara's gaze met mine from across the clearing. Offering a smile, she nodded, and my worries faded slightly. These clans were hers and Xobas's. We needed them to defend Krowikie lands, but even more, they deserved to have a chance away from the Horde. I was the proof of our agreement, so I would stay for them. No matter how much it hurt to delay my search for Otylia.

I recounted everything that had happened since the morning of the Drowning of Marzanna. With Katiôn, I had hidden Otylia being a goddess, and I did the same with them. It wouldn't be necessary for the brothers to know until the time came for us to enter Nawia—if we actually found a way there. Besides, it was enough of a shock for them to learn I was a demon.

Zakir took in the stories with his usual silence, occasionally whispering something to himself and then returning his attention to me. Bidaês interjected randomly, and when I finished, he shot to his feet.

"I can't tell if you're pranking me or not!" He ran his hands through his curled hair, giving him the look of a lost hunter. "Not only do you claim you have powers, but you've fought a *god*? All right, then. Show me these storms of yours."

"My connection with the winds only works when I'm asleep," I said, trying to remain calm as frustration battered the walls within me. The demon's will or mine, I couldn't face it, and unleashing that darkness would only turn the brothers away.

Brow furrowed, he threw his arms out in either frustration or exasperation. "Of course you can't!" *Definitely frustration.*

"He's telling the truth," Ara said with her arms crossed and hip out. The pose reminded me of Otylia, but without the ability to channel, Ara was far less threatening.

I slid both Marzanna's dagger and Kwiecień from their sheathes. "You've seen these blades before, but I didn't tell you they're made of Thunderstone and Moonstone—capable of killing gods. Kwiecień was one of Jaryło's swords before I killed him. If you still don't believe me, I can show you the winds when I sleep tonight."

Zakir walked toward me, carefully placing each step as if he were worried he would trigger a trap. "Why can you only channel your power when you sleep? It shouldn't matter if your soul is in your body or not." With a huff, he turned away and muttered to himself, "Have to study this further. So many variables…"

Bidaês never took his eyes off me. Though he tried to speak, each attempt came out as little more than a nervous stutter.

"Congrats, Half-Chief." Narcyz chuckled. "You finally shut him up."

"Now's not the time, Narcyz," Ara said.

I sheathed the blades and closed the distance to Bidaês as Sosna curled defensively around my leg. "I understand that this is a lot to process at once. If you don't want to come with us, I would understand that too. What lies ahead is dangerous, but I have to go if both your clans and our tribe are to survive."

Bidaês shook his head and paced to a fir tree, tearing off a twig with a *crack*. "Does my grandfather know?"

"Yes, I've told him everything you now know."

"And he didn't care?" He scowled. "The Frostmarked with the Horde. Those bastards killed my parents!"

I stepped back, clutching my Frostmarked palm, still pulsing. "Bidaês, I'm sorry. I know there's nothing I can do to fix that, but I promise you, everything we're doing is to stop Marzanna and her Horde from taking more lives. This mark represents one of the worst mistakes I've ever made. Though I'll likely bear it the rest of my life, it doesn't define me."

He stormed forward, coming within inches of me as his eyes bore into mine. Bidaês was one of the few who matched my height, and I wavered under his glare. "I offered to come with you because you lost someone," he snarled. "You said Otylia could help me get revenge on the Horde, but how can I trust you when you're one of *them*? You won't even show me your power. How do I know you won't throw me to your Frostmarked friends the second we break from the clans?"

"No one said you have to come," Ara said.

"If he won't shut up, we'd be better off without him anyway," Narcyz grumbled.

Bidaês backed away, still studying me with narrowed eyes. "Tell me something: If you could choose to give up your power and be fully human, would you?"

I ran my finger across the tapered edge of my płanetnik hat. *Would I?* After more than a moon, Marzanna's mark still burned on my palm. I had been just a tool to her against Jaryło, but she'd unlocked my power, accidentally allowing me to defeat her cultists and her płanetnik. What would've happened if I'd never controlled the winds? Who was I without my night wanderings, without this power that had so quickly joined with me? Would I have mended my relationship with Otylia anyway?

My breaths were weak when I met Bidaês's stare. I knew the answer he wanted, but I couldn't give it. Without my connection to the winds, I would've still been nothing but a farm boy with little purpose, watching Otylia from a distance with a bleeding heart and no courage to meet her. No one would have ended Marzanna's winter. The clans would be destroyed, swallowed by the might of Koschei's Horde as they desperately tried to face the Astiwie in their way. No, I couldn't surrender my demonic soul. *What does that make me?*

"You're too much of a coward to give me an answer?" Bidaês snapped. "Or are you afraid of what your friends will think of you when they know the truth."

"Stop it, Bidaês!" Ara yelled.

I took a soft breath. "No, he's right." My heart ached as I paced toward them, remembering everyone I'd failed to save, even with my power. "Before, I would have given it up in an instant, but I can't just stop fighting. To surrender my demonic soul would be sacrificing Otylia to Weles and allowing Marzanna to slaughter us with her Horde. This part of me is dark—I feel its desire for power like a growing fire, desperate for fuel. But if I must lose myself to save those I love, then so be it."

I looked away. Admitting that was like leaping into the void in my chest and letting the pain and hurt within consume me. "If you choose not to come because of that," I continued, "then I can't blame you. Alone or not, I'm going to find Otylia. It's up to you whether you want to help save your clan. Think about it. Either way, I plan to split from the clans once we're past Kynnytsia."

Bidaês clenched his fists, but before he had the chance to speak, I rushed through the woods. Exhaustion, both physical and emotional, smothered all else as I watched the trees sway with the wind and felt it blow through my hair. I knew I'd likely said too much. It didn't matter. If they were to follow me to Nawia, they needed to know the truth.

9

Otylia

She's lying to me. Using me.

SABINA STOOD ACROSS MY BEDROOM with a new dress in hand. It was the brown of willow bark with flashes of green on its skirt. Similar to the ashen one I'd worn since we'd left Dwie Rzeki, it stopped just below the knee to avoid brush.

"Do you like it?" she asked, expectant.

I cocked my head to the side as I paced toward her, examining the patterns that seemed to twist like vines around the skirt's ruffles. The smile came before I could stop it. It *was* a beautiful dress. "I guess?"

Sabina squealed and spun it around. "If 'I guess' is aligned with a smile like that, I can't help but wonder how you smile when you see *him.*"

"Don't talk about him," I snapped, fighting the pit in my stomach.

"I'm sorry…" She hung her head and laid the dress on the bed. "I thought—"

"You thought we could be friends because you brought me oranges and a dress?" I stopped in front of her. Though she was at least a head taller than me, she was thinner than any human, and she backed down. "You want me to trust you, but you didn't tell me you were a forest nymph, or that Weles sent you to get information about Wacław."

Tears stramed down her cheeks. She stepped back—I closed the distance. "I don't talk in my sleep," I growled.

She whimpered again. "I'm sorry!"

So was I.

Why does it hurt to intimidate her? I knew she was working with Weles, but a pang struck my chest as she wept. Was I so desperate for a friend that I'd accepted the first person who bothered to even pretend that she cared? *Gods, I've been spending too much time with Wacław.*

I'd walked for nearly a moon with him on trails, fighting by his side after years apart. He'd saved my life. And I'd saved his. There had been a time when I'd wanted nothing to do with him. I'd felt only betrayal when I'd looked into his deep blue eyes—those stupid, caring eyes. That had all changed so quickly.

We're immortals. We have power, and the tribe hates us. We could've ignored Marzanna and created a life away from those idiots. Together. But we never had a choice, did we?

I turned from Sabina and ripped the dress off the bed. "I don't care that you lied. Everyone does to get their way. I just thought you were different."

No reply came.

It took everything I had not to look back at her. "Wait outside while I change. Then, you're going to take me to Weles."

"Yes, Lady Otylia. There is a pool in the other room if you wish to wash first."

I gripped the dress tight against me as her footsteps retreated. When the door swung shut, I released a sob of my own. It was short, but I needed to let myself feel the pain for a moment.

I died. Kuba sacrificed himself to save me, but I died anyway.

Everything had gone to plan until Jaryło had ruined it all. How long had he known? Had he just been waiting for us to defeat Marzanna's cultists for him? I screamed into the dress, holding it in my shaking hands as I promised myself I wouldn't be fooled again. Not by mortals. Not by demons. And not by gods.

I stared down at the dress, wetted by a few stray tears. Weles had sent it for a reason. He knew I'd resist staying here, and I assumed he expected me to ignore his gift. But this was a game—his game. I planned to win.

I dropped the dress on the bed before searching for the room Sabina had spoken of. Just outside the beams of light, the wall of vines split for a door that hadn't been there the last time I'd woke. It was narrower than the main doors, but its dark wood and golden handle was the same. Though it appeared heavy, it swung open with only a tug. I gasped at what lay beyond.

A pool of steaming water filled the room, washing warmth over me with the welcoming smell of spring flowers. On the land alongside it, roots stretched from the ground and formed a bar that held a towel and some type of robe that was soft to the touch. I ran my fingers through the plush fabric.

What is this place?

Doubt stopped me at the door. The room was inviting—too inviting to trust. After Weles's trick with the snakes and Sabina's questions, every muscle in my body was tense as I awaited another trap.

I glanced down at my ashen dress, dirtied from a moon of bathless travel. *I* could *use a wash…*

The dress peeled off me, taking a layer of sweat with it, but more remained. My normally pale skin was coated in dirt and dried blood from too many fights. Free from my clothes, I let down my guard, and instantly, every bruise and scrape reminded me of their presence. I felt horrible.

I left the dress in the grasses alongside the pool and stepped into the waters. They bit at my feet at first, tearing at the blisters and sores from weeks of walking.

With each step, I descended into the water until it covered me up to the shoulders. My muscles soaked in the heat as the grime fell away. I released my braid, tossing the bones and twine to the shore before diving beneath the surface.

A calm took over. I shut my eyes, holding my breath as my free hair drifted through the still waters around me. My mind emptied. My pain and soreness fled. And, against my instincts, I let myself relax.

It seemed like hours had passed when I surfaced. My hair clung to my face and chest, but I didn't care as I took in a deep breath of the steam. I'd forgotten the feeling of being clean. Though Dziewanna's wilds were my home, it was good to be free of their cling for even a moment.

I stayed in the pool for a while longer, trying and failing to not think about the inevitable confrontation with Weles that would follow.

Weles had me killed and brought to him for a purpose. I refused to accept that it was only so he could see me for the first time. Father had always called the snake god a trickster for a reason, but what was his plan? He needed me to Ascend and gain my powers as a goddess when *he* believed I was ready. Why?

Steam rose off me as I emerged from the pool and took the towel. But as I dried off, I noticed an object along the wall casting a reflection. *Glass?* Our craftsmen had only made cloudy, fragile creations from it that few people wanted. This unmarked plane was perfect.

I walked toward it, transfixed at the reflection of myself that I'd only seen in murky waters before. I believed I lacked the vanity of most of the girls in the tribe, but I couldn't look away from the girl in the glass. Those girls would've stared at themselves and wondered what boys thought of their hair, their skin, or the curve of their body. Instead, I studied every scar and imperfection.

The most obvious mark had been left by Yuliya's shard of ice. She'd missed, leaving only an arcing line from my cheekbone toward my lips, but part of me knew she would've killed me in that moment if she'd wanted to. Still, it had been a warning from both the szeptucha and her goddess. I had taken Wacław from her, and she would make me pay.

I traced the scar with a smirk. Something seemed right about it, and I remembered how strong I'd felt looking into the Lake of Reflection when it had glowed with power. Most girls would have panicked with such a mark on their face. I loved it.

Most of the other scars were new to me. With the boys around, I'd never had the chance to examine them, but I winced seeing them now. *How did I survive?*

A particular dark mark sliced across my side. It hadn't healed well, and the skin around it remained raised. A similar line ran from between my breasts to the base of my left ribs—narrowly missing my heart. And I could never forget the jagged claw marks upon my back, inflicted by the utopiec after the Drowning of Marzanna. The only serious wound that hadn't left a scar was Jaryło's. I assumed that was intentional.

What goddess wears scars like these? I asked myself, unable to step away.

Dziewanna had been stunning when she'd revealed herself to me. Wacław had described Marzanna as the same before Jaryło betrayed her. I was just a girl—barely a woman—but now I was to become a goddess. How?

I clenched my jaw and stepped away, grabbing the robe from the roots.

Mother's freedom had ended when Perun forced her to marry Weles. Marzanna had only grown wicked when Jaryło bedded another woman. Dziewanna had been captured because Strzybóg, god of the winds, had neglected to fight by her side.

Are all goddesses to be ruined by men?

I shook my head and covered myself with the robe, tying off its belt and taking one last glance at the glass. *I won't be.*

The sleeved dress Sabina had brought fit perfectly—suspiciously so. It felt good to wear something other than my travel dress after so long, though, so I tolerated it. Besides, I needed my focus for the real fight ahead.

Sabina silently led me through a maze of hallways. My bare feet brushed against the grass that covered the ground, and walls made of vines enclosed each hall, just like my room. Unlike when I'd fought to escape, there was no willow with Mother's basil flowers beneath it.

I watched Sabina's flowing gait closely. *What am I going to do about her?*

My anger had obviously wounded the forest nymph, but she'd proved that I couldn't trust her. That hurt. I was alone in Nawia, and having at least one person to talk to seemed better than complete isolation. Weles knew that—I wouldn't let him use it.

Eventually, Sabina stopped at a pair of giant doors, similar to those I'd face during my escape. I stared up at them and sighed. "What's with these doors?" I muttered.

Her expression was grim, and she struggled to look at me. "Master Weles increases his height to appear more powerful."

Curious. I would have to figure that out later. "He can do that?"

She shrugged. All the joy she'd had before was gone. I shouldn't have felt guilty for that, but I did each time her gaze met mine. "I'm sure the master can tell you more."

I pushed open the doors, revealing a wide dining room beyond. Vines and grasses still formed the walls and floors, but a variety of flowers wound their way around the room and gave it life. None were basil.

Above, a row of chandeliers made of roots and leaves hung over an elaborately carved table. Words from the old tongue lined its edge and created an intricately woven pattern.

Weles sat at the table's head, but even seated, his height was equal to mine. "Come, Otylia. I'm sure you are famished."

I hesitated for too long, and he raised his brow. *Don't let him win.*

I marched forward, studying the god. The room was brighter than the swamp where we'd met, but he looked *different* than last time, younger. His unwieldy beard and hair were a deep brown instead of gray. A long white tunic with red embroidered designs had replaced his bear furs, but the horns on his head remained.

He smiled when I sat across from him—as far away as possible. "Sabina told me you enjoyed the oranges from the Anvoranie, but they are certainly not a complete meal."

Though he awaited a reply, I didn't give one. My anger stirred. Through both Jaryło and his snakes, all he'd done was kill and torture me, yet I sat at his table. *What choice do I have?*

"I know you despise me for what I have done," he continued, folding his hands on the table. "Please understand, however, that I am only trying to protect you."

"I don't need *your* protection! You probably claimed to be protecting Mother too when you trapped her here."

"Trapped? Never did I trap Dziewanna here. In fact, I would say much of Nawia was her favorite place to be."

"Is that why she fled?" I gritted my teeth. "Ivan said she came willingly, but I've spoken to Mother. She was desperate to get me away from you."

With a sigh, he shook his head and raised a hand. A girl approached from behind him with a wooden plate. She wore the same leafy dress as Sabina, and by her bony face and extraordinary height, I assumed she was a forest nymph too. Another nymph dressed in blue approached, setting a plate in front of me as the first nymph did the same. Then, without a word, they left through a set of doors across the room.

I studied the array of food—beef, bread, and a batch of familiar wild strawberries. The strawberries were a pleasant surprise. Mother would send me out in summer to collect them for meals, and I had always loved their sweetness. *Does he know?*

"Please, eat," Weles said, grabbing his wooden fork. "I think you will enjoy the meat. It is from the finest beasts in all of the Three Realms."

As he stabbed his meat and took a bite, I slid my wooden knife up my sleeve. I felt exposed without my channeling, but even a knife was better than nothing. "The stories are true, then?" I asked. "You stole Perun's cows."

He chuckled. "*Stole* is one way to put it. I am the god of cattle, so is it wrong for me to protect the best of my beasts?"

"Do you steal everything you want to 'protect'?" I quipped, still not eating. My stomach rumbled at the sight of food, but I would show him I was strong.

"You are determined to despise me, little one," he said as the nymphs returned with glass jars full of a burgundy drink. They placed one before each of us along with a wooden goblet. Weles poured some of the liquid and drank it quickly. "Have you ever experienced the bliss that is wine? Alcohol in its greatest splendor."

"Szeptuchy are forbidden from drinking alcohol. The priests believe we could be swayed to misuse our powers under its influence."

A grin crossed his face as he took another sip. "You are no szeptucha—the first Trial demands you admit as much—and I have no desire to sway you."

"And *I* have no desire to trust you."

"Then it seems we are at an impasse."

We sat in silence for a while. He ate and drank while I stared down at my plate, starving but unable to convince myself to take a bite.

The man—the god—if front of me was supposed to be my father. He could never be that. But what did he want from me? There had to be something more than wine and strawberries.

After a few minutes, Weles dropped his fork and glared across the table at me, any touch of fatherly kindness fading. "What must I do to make you eat? You may be a goddess, but you've already died twice in two weeks. It would be damaging for your health and my *żityje* if you did so again."

Twice? I bit my cheek, trying to avoid snapping. It didn't work.

"Jaryło killing me wasn't enough?" I shouted, suddenly on my feet. "Why do you obsess over protecting me when I've lived my entire life without you? I don't need a protector. I *need* to get back to my friends and stop Marzanna from destroying Mother's wilds and our tribe. If Ascending means playing your stupid games with no answers, I don't want it! Either quit hiding behind lies or let me leave."

He rose, a condescending smirk crossing his face. I'd seen it enough from Father. I couldn't take it anymore—not after all Weles had done.

"There is much you must learn over many moons, my daughter," he began.

I didn't let him finish. "Fine, I'll be in my room, waiting for you to show me the way back to Jawia."

I tore out of the room. My skirts flew around me with each stride, and it felt freeing to leave him behind. He'd lied and tricked me enough. Now, it was time for him to play my game.

10

Wacław

Was it a mistake to trust him?

I RODE ALONE the day after I had revealed the truth to Bidaês. From the moment I'd woke, Narcyz had muttered endlessly about my choice to invite him on our journey, despite his initial agreement to let him come. His complaints usually mattered little to me—especially after a moon of hearing nothing but them—but this one had me unsettled.

Our third day in the Narrow Pass dragged on because of my isolation. It didn't help that the cliffs had closed in the further we went. As I gazed up at the ridges on either side, more than a hundred feet high, the route's name felt fitting. The trail remained wide enough for seven horses, but dread crept over me in the shadows of the rocks.

Bidaês rode ahead with his grandfather. *Odd.* He tended to avoid Katiôn, opting to ride among groups of girls or warriors guarding the sheep and goats in the back. He'd spent all day speaking with both Katiôn and High Priestess Rasa, though, and I was growing suspicious.

Now I'm just thinking like Otylia.

Otylia would've scolded me for revealing everything to the brothers. While Zakir had been curious, I feared Bidaês would expose me to the Zurgowie. Ara had told us all about Rasa's aggressiveness, and I'd left the peace negotiations with an understanding of how destructive the zealous priestess could be.

When Dadźbóg descended into Nawia, we made camp in the narrow space between the cliffs. Hunger panged my stomach, but I ignored it as I watched the souls' stars flicker in the cloudless sky.

The Kwiecień moon was nearly full now. With every passing day, I felt the sword's power swell—some form of its own *żityje* that I still couldn't grasp. Jaryło would be able to return at the next new moon, Maj, but we were free of his schemes until then.

I slid my finger along the flat edge of the golden blade, remembering Marzanna's threats.

It seemed an eternity ago that she'd demanded I kill Jaryło and steal his seven Moonstone swords. She'd threatened Father, then my entire family. I'd lost the first, but would she kill all of them? Mom? The pulse of my Frostmark made me shiver at that thought.

Now that I sat with a Moonblade in my hand, I felt like a fool. Both gods had used me. I had never asked to be in the middle of their battle for control of the seasons, but everything I did helped one of them defeat the other. I had set out to defeat Marzanna. Killing Jaryło, taking Kwiecień, and focusing on bringing Otylia back from Nawia all made that harder.

Did I have a choice? If I had let Jaryło live and keep his blade, would Marzanna and the Frostmarked be weaker? Had I eliminated the last spring god, clearing the way for her to control Jawia for herself? We'd defeated Eryk, Yuliya, and most of her cultists, but it would only delay her inevitable attack. Had it all been part of her plan? Koschei and the Horde were rushing toward us as we rested, and surely Marzanna's frost would return once again. The clans had fallen. Soon, the Astiwie and then the Krowikie would follow. What the Horde didn't destroy, the endless winter would.

Shaking, I held my head in my hands. *I risked everything to try and save Otylia. I still am.* Doubt clenched my chest, but as I stared down at my frostbitten fingers, I knew the truth.

No matter the risk. No matter the pain. I would do whatever it took to protect her. She was my first friend, my first love, and the only goddess that I adored.

"There you are!" Ara said, a twinge of annoyance in her voice as she jogged to me with Sosna at her heels. "Narcyz and I have been looking for you all day."

I looked from Kwiecień's glowing blade in my lap to the cliffs towering behind her. "I know it was a mistake."

She sighed and crossed her arms. "All of us agreed to it either way." Sosna zipped through her legs to me, and Ara chuckled. "Okay, maybe not *all* of us, but we need all the help we can get. Annoying or not, Bidaês is Katiôn's grandson and good with a sword."

"He might expose us to Rasa," I whispered, glancing around to make sure no one was nearby to overhear. "He could ruin everything… If I haven't already."

"All right, what's going on?" She sat cross-legged next to me. "Come on, you can trust me to keep it quiet."

I squeezed my eyes shut. It was stupid to pity myself so much, yet I couldn't fight the sorrow and anger that clashed in my heart. The latter scared me more than I was willing to admit. "Everyone is relying on us: Otylia, Dziewanna, the clans, our tribe…" I took a heavy breath. "Before, I was just the Half-Chief, being scoffed and laughed at. Now it feels like everything is on my shoulders, and I have no idea if I'm making things better."

Tears streamed down my cheeks. Though I cursed myself for crying again, I let them come as Sosna set her head in my lap, gazing at me with worry. "I killed a god to save Otylia," I continued. "A god! But she died anyway, and because of me, there's no one left to stop Marzanna from reaching her full power. Even now, I'm focused on bringing Otylia back. I should be helping the tribe and stopping the Horde. I should be completing the last order Father gave me. Instead, I *know* I have to find her. The world is falling apart around me, but every moment I have to think, I think about her."

Now Ara was crying too. She wiped the tears away and sniffled. "Otylia would hate us for pushing everything aside. She'd want us to keep fighting Marzanna and the Horde without her, but in truth, she's afraid of us loving her so much that we'd do it for her anyway."

I smiled at the thought of Otylia wrinkling her nose—like she always did when she was frustrated. "What kind of demon am I if I love a goddess?"

"One who doesn't let being a demon determine who he is." She smirked. "Bidaês is an idiot to push you away just because you bear a Frostmark, but I don't think you're wrong to trust him. If we can't trust in each other when everyone is against us, what else do we have?"

Her words calmed me, if only a little. We fell silent, and the winds drifted through the pass above us, whistling against the cliffs. Though I had appreciated a day alone, I enjoyed having her by me now. Ara was more straightforward than most. She couldn't channel or summon a storm, but she cared about people, especially Otylia. That was enough to let me feel human.

It was a long time before she spoke again, "I thought returning to my clan would be easy, that they'd see me as no different than them. I was wrong. My years living with the Krowikie and what I've seen of your gods have changed me. I don't quite understand it yet, but I'm not Zurgowie anymore."

She pulled her hunting knife and dragged its tip along the stone, carving a series of twisting lines downward from a single point. "The only place that made sense was with Otylia. I'll never be Krowikie. I can never be Zurgowie again. But around her, I'm just me."

"She's good at that," I said. "I guess when no one in the tribe accepts you, all you have left are the misfits."

"We really are…" She paused and cocked her head, analyzing her carving.

I chuckled looking down at it. "What is that supposed to be?"

Sliding the dagger back into its sheath on her thigh, she hopped to her feet. "Your gods all have symbols, right? Like the Frostmark

Marzanna put on your hand."

I nodded.

"So, I made one for Otylia—roots stretching from a cracked stump."

I stood beside her and smiled down at the emblem. "Why's it cracked?"

With a sharp nod, Ara grinned. "We all have our flaws."

"True, but she wears hers better than anyone, not that she has many."

She bumped into me and laughed. "Oh, I'm definitely telling her you said she has flaws."

My cheeks burned, but I smiled as I looked from Ara's carving to the bright moon. "Only if you also tell her I love all of them."

"Blah!" she gagged. "That will only make her even madder, you know? *Love* is a dangerous word for that girl."

"Probably." I shrugged. "But if she's calling me foolish, then at least something is right with the world."

It was three more days of riding until we reached the highest point of the Narrow Pass. Peaks surrounded us on every side, but without trees to block the view, we could see into Astiwie lands in the distance as we stopped to make camp.

How did we end up so far from home?

It had seemed both an eternity and a blink since we'd left Dwie Rzeki. So much had changed. At times it felt like I was living a stranger's life, just clinging onto the few familiarities I could find, but a voice in my mind told me this was better. My power was destructive and dangerous, yet it gave me a purpose, a chance to fix things. I hoped.

"Never thought I'd see Kynnytsia from the east," Narcyz said, dismounting alongside me. He'd struggled to get used to riding at first.

After weeks of fighting his stallion, though, he finally sat tall and confident on its back. He and I had despised each other once, but I found myself more grateful for his unwavering determination with each passing day. Whenever I hesitated to choose, he charged ahead.

"Honestly, I never expected to see it at all," I replied as I squinted and followed his gaze to the Astiwie capital, less than a day from the end of the pass. Like we Krowikie, the Astiwie preferred to settle among the trees, and only a few buildings were visible through their naked branches. *So similar to home.* I shook my head and sighed. *Yet still not the same.*

"It's one thing to travel through our own lands," I continued. "It's another to have passed through a forest our fathers called cursed, traversed the steppes with clans our ancestors never dared to meet, and now cross Perun's Crown into Kynnytsia… I'm just a farm boy who's spent far too much time awake—whatever the form. I never wanted any of this. Treaties and wars and epic battles between demons and gods are meant for heroes, not someone like me. Less than two moons ago, I was nobody, but now four tribes are relying on me to stop Marzanna and her Horde."

He scoffed as he took his reins again. "You're the kid of the high chief. We didn't like you, but that didn't make you nobody."

We began the preparations for supper with the rest of the clansmen when Dadźbóg hovered at the horizon. With each day we'd spent in the Narrow Pass, Katiôn and Rasa had grown more restless, and our rides had become longer because of it. The Horde was closing in. No one wanted to be caught in the mountains if they arrived.

When they arrived.

Marzanna's cultists had left horrors behind in Bustelintin. Warriors had been killed, women and children slaughtered. A chill came over me as I remembered Koschei's glare. It had been cold. Lifeless. Deathless. Something told me he was capable of more than those cultists ever were.

Focus on what you can do. Find Otylia. I'd been holding my breath unconsciously, and I let out a cough as I sighed deeply.

"Jeez, Half-Chief," Narcyz quipped. "If you can't even breathe, how in Weles are we going to make it to Nawia?"

My face was red when I finally recovered. "I might have to die to get there. Perhaps the practice is worth it."

"You actually think that?"

I felt the hilt of Marzanna's dagger, its cold breaking through my numbness. "I haven't known what to think ever since I met that leszy, but if we're going to save Otylia, we need to be prepared for anything. Marzanna, Weles, Jaryło, demons… we've got quite the list of powerful enemies." A disturbance came from across the camp as Zhaleh, the right hand of Rasa, approached with a band of the high priestess's guards. "And I have a sinking feeling that list will grow."

Narcyz clenched his fists as the guards flanked us. Both men and women, they had bows like many of the Zurgowie, but their primary weapons were lances as long as two men were tall. I just hoped never to find myself impaled at their sharp end.

"Wacław Lubiewicz," the young priestess began, curt, "High Priestess Rasa, chosen speaker of Otlezd and his Uzeša Teṇpa, will eat with you tonight. Will your companion excuse us?" She didn't lower her hood, and her deep brown eyes glared at me from beneath the shadows it cast. With the green lines streaking across her face like a fighter's war paint and a padded sleeve for her tamed eagle, she was *almost* more threatening than Rasa herself.

Zhaleh's words had been more a demand than a request, so Narcyz rolled his eyes and stomped away, muttering lewd alterations of Rasa's title to himself.

"He dares to mock Otlezd's representative among mortals," Zhaleh spat as she swept aside her green cloak and reached for a dagger. "I have killed for less."

Taking a sharp breath, I held out my arm to stop her from drawing the blade. "Believe me, there were times I wanted to kill him too, but Narcyz is someone you'd rather have on your side than against you."

She scoffed and turned away. "Follow."

As we wound our way through the crowd toward Rasa's tent, I

realized there were no Simukie in this section of the camp. The differences between the clans were slight at first glance. In recent days, though, I'd noticed the Zurgowie's sun amulets of their god Otlezd and the distinctive side-shaved haircut their adults wore. They also kept their horses together in a central location while the Simukie never strayed far from theirs.

"Isn't that the high priestess's tent?" I asked as we passed the circular tent, two more guards posted outside of it.

"You should have learned by now, westerner," Zhaleh replied. "We do not eat inside a structure. To do so is to be away from Otlezd's light, where Alunam's corruption can poison your food or drink."

Rasa wasn't far, though, sitting cross-legged on a blanket embroidered with symbols I'd seen worn by members of her clan. She rose at my arrival, and though the high priestess was thin, wrinkled, and short, I swallowed in fear. Ara had told me far too many stories of Rasa's aggressive wars in Otlezd's name. Anything I said could ignite her passion against the Krowikie.

"Welcome, Wacław," she began, her voice frail as she removed her hood, revealing her own green face paint. "Join me."

I nodded, and we sat across from each other on the blanket. During the negotiations over the Southern Hills, I had figured out Katiôn quickly and, through Xobas, had learned to trust him. I had no such confidence in the woman before me now. Nor did I know what she wanted.

Zhaleh took her place beside the high priestess as the pair silently waited for a man to set out a clay cup of milk and bowl of yogurt for each of us. Everything the clans consumed came from the sparse pickings of plants in the steppes and the animals they'd brought along the way: mainly goats and sheep. Even after weeks with them, I hadn't transitioned well from our tribe's grain-heavy diet.

Once the man left, Rasa sipped her milk. "Have you tasted *koumiss* before?"

"You mean milk?" I asked, unsure what she meant.

"It's fermented mare's milk," Zhaleh interrupted with a huff. "Do you pay attention to nothing in our clans?"

Rasa laid a hand on her apprentice's knee. "Calm. Otlezd asks that we show even the ignorant the way to him."

So that's *what this is about.*

"You have chosen quite the odd group to travel with," Rasa continued. "A boy unable to hold his tongue, a commander who abandoned his people, and a girl who has drifted with Otlezd's light."

I shrugged and took a sip of the *koumiss*. Sour, bitter, but I drank it anyway. After Zhaleh's outburst, angering them further didn't seem like a good idea. "Sometimes we don't choose our companions—fate has a knack of doing that for us, for good or ill. I would be dead without Narcyz and Ara. Narcyz, especially, may not be my best friend, but I owe him my life."

"That is an honorable thing, Wacław Lubiewicz, yet I have to wonder if you can have honor while worshipping gods who can foment wrath against their own people."

My thumb found Marzanna's mark, but I didn't allow the demon's anger to answer her taunting. "Do your gods not punish those who wrong them?"

"Through the Uzeša Teṇpa, Otlezd punishes those who act wrongly—those are not the same thing. From the stories I have heard, your gods cannot even agree which of them rules what elements of the world. They clash, leaving your people to suffer." She ate a spoonful of yogurt before meeting my gaze, the end of her mouth twitching upward. "Tell me, do they sound like gods worth worshipping?"

I remembered Dariusz's preaching to our village and repeated it with little thought, "Our gods protect us, nurture us, and provide for us. But they are imperfect, as we are. Perun is prideful and Weles envious, drawing them into battle. Marzanna is resentful and Jaryło disloyal, and their conflict creates the seasons. Though we fear them, much of it is an understanding that there are beings more powerful than us. Is a god worth worshipping if they are nothing like their people?"

She raised a brow. "Yet you worship this Marzanna and other, darker gods."

"No." I gritted my teeth, fighting the demon as my Frostmark stung. "I don't worship Marzanna, but a good friend said that it does not take faith to believe in things you've seen with your own eyes. The goddess of winter and death is real—I've met her. If our religions are meant to seek what is true, then it doesn't matter if the gods and spirits we believe in are righteous or good. All that matters is that they are real, and that's why we fear the worst of them."

Zhaleh scoffed, but Rasa clicked her tongue at the girl before turning to me. "If all you believe is what you have seen, then you are lost, child. Without faith, there is no hope, and without hope, we are nothing."

I shut my eyes and remembered the look Otylia gave me moments before her death. Beyond the shock and anger, I had seen her faith in me. She'd believed I could save her, but I couldn't. *What faith can I have when all my gods are quiet, beaten, or against me? Well, all but one.*

I gripped Otylia's necklace—all I had left of the girl I loved. "I disagree, high priestess. Faith may grant hope, but it's a blind hope. Warriors have faith in their chieftain, yet a chief does not know each of his thousands of warriors. He will send them to die in a war for greed or power. No. Faith is nothing without love because love is a bond—a bond that strengthens both weak and powerful."

Rasa considered that for a moment, her eyes more thoughtful than stern. "Perhaps I was wrong about you, child. Love is essential to belief." She nodded to Zhaleh, who extended her padded arm to the side. "Otlezd loves us and we him. It is through his power and the Uzeša Teṇpa, his servants who control our world, that we are connected to nature."

An eagle shrieked overhead. I jumped in shock as it dove, swooping to Zhaleh's arm and standing upon it with pride. Zhaleh smirked and stroked the beautiful brown feathers of the golden eagle the Zurgowie had used as one of their scouts throughout the trip. "You Krowikie and your Astiwie brothers cower behind nature, not joining *with* it," she said. "Pretending it protects you is not becoming part of it. You cannot deny what we are forever."

Rasa held her hand to a talisman of the sun at her chest, woven from steppe reeds. "As a newborn grows, it is ever-dependent on its mother. This is how the gods see us mortals. Mere children. Yet, many who worship miss the essential truth that you, Wacław, have mentioned. Just as the newborn needs its mother, the mother needs her child, and so the gods need us. It is the natural way of things—a love that is inherent to who we are."

She rolled up her sleeves and unwound the talisman from around her neck. As she cupped the small sun, muttering a prayer, I examined the large veins crisscrossing up her hands and arms, where her skin showed patches of scars I dared not question. *This woman is more than I thought.*

Once Rasa finished the prayer, she held the talisman out to me. "Take it, child. You do not yet know Otlezd's light, but I have prayed for this amulet to grant you his protection and guidance."

"Why are you offering me this?" I asked, taking it carefully. My Frostmark seared at the touch. "During our negotiations, you didn't seem to care much for me."

A smile crossed her face. It was soft, kind, almost like Mom's when she was proud of me. "I see potential in you. You may not be of our clan or worship our gods, but there is a goodness in your heart that is rare among men. When our clans were desperate, you freely offered help when many others would have taken up the sword. You seek the best for all, not only your tribe. It is a shame it is your brother who will be high chief and not yourself."

"Thank you, high priestess." I bowed my head. "I'm honored that, despite our differences, we may forge a new future for our people together, but I do not wish to lead."

As we returned to eating, she rolled down her sleeves once again and glanced up at me. "To lead is an opportunity many desire, yet the few worthy to do so rarely chase such power."

11

Otylia

I have to get out of here.

I PACED ALONG THE WALLS OF MY BEDROOM, desperately trying to see some way out of Nawia. My stomach groaned with each step. I ignored it. It didn't matter that I'd eaten nothing. Weles planned to use me, and though he wouldn't tell me how, I wasn't going to wait to find out.

When the door cracked open, I spun to face Sabina. My fingers gripped the knife I'd slid up my sleeve during dinner. *I can't trust anyone here.* "What do you want?" I growled.

Her eyes glistened in a stray beam of light. *Tears?* Slowly, she stepped toward me, and when she spoke, her voice was even quieter than before. "I'm sorry, Lady Otylia, for all I've done."

"No apology changes the fact you still work for Weles."

"You're right." She held her arm across her body and glanced over her shoulder. "There's… There's something I haven't told you."

She took another step forward, but I raised the knife. "That's close enough. Say what you came to say and leave."

A tear slipped down her bony cheek. "I'm trapped here, just like you."

I didn't lower the knife. With every second I waited to reply, Sabina seemed less confident, fading toward the door before turning away. *Does she think someone's listening?* Dziewanna's power could've told me if a spirit was lurking in the hall. But my connection to her was still useless here, so I crept to the door and listened for any sound beyond it. Silence.

"What do you mean, 'trapped'?" I asked, knife raised. Fear returned to her eyes as I advanced. "No one's listening, Sabina. You need to tell me everything. Now."

"Yes, Lady Otylia," she stammered as she fell back into the wall, her hands trembling before her. "I meant you no harm."

I stopped a stride from her. The knife's point touched the tip of her neck. It may have been only made of wood, but I'd felt its blade. Any pressure and I could draw enough blood to kill her. I was done with Nawia's lies. "Talk."

Between whimpers, she whispered, "I wasn't lying to you before. I *am* a forest nymph, like my mother, but my father was a human."

"Who?"

"An Astiwie warrior. I don't know his name."

I lowered the knife. "A half-nymph. Huh. Never heard of such a thing, but I'm not surprised a warrior would bed a forest nymph if given the chance."

She clutched her wrist against her chest, skirting around me. "Can we sit, Lady Otylia? I'm quite light-headed, and I fear I may faint."

Are all nymphs this frail? I nodded, joining her on the side of the bed, and she relaxed for the first time.

"I've lived in Nawia my entire life," she continued. "Weles says the warrior encountered my mother on a hunting expedition just outside the place your people call the Mangled Woods. Even beyond those woods themselves, forest nymphs live among the trees, and when he saw her, apparently he fell madly in love with her."

I scoffed. "Men are too simple."

"Have you not heard the effect we can have upon men?" A small smile flashed across her face, then vanished as quickly as it'd come.

"No. Father never told me much about nymphs, besides the four types: forest, mountain, water, and air. Then again, not sure any dad wants to tell his daughter about seductive spirits."

She grinned. "Especially considering yours fell in love with a goddess."

Love? Did they love each other? Father had raised me knowing I wasn't his, even after Mother died, but did that mean he loved her? I sighed. *I'm thinking far too much about love.*

"Well," Sabina said. "Mother, like many nymphs, convinced him to leave everything and join her. The Astiwie warrior vanished from Kynnytsia for weeks, but Mother pitied him. She released the spell. Instead of fleeing, though, he stayed another night with her… I was the result."

"Let me guess, then he ran from his responsibility and left her behind? Duty over love or whatever?" I waved my hand dismissively.

Her gaze drifted to the light. "Actually, no. The warrior asked her to marry him!" That subtle smile returned, lingering this time. "She agreed, but they knew their people wouldn't accept a nymph among them, so she called to Master Weles. He offered to make Mother appear as a human, losing her wings and sorcery, in return for Weles taking me as his servant."

"They agreed? What kind of mother does that?"

"I don't know." She wrapped her arms around her legs. "I've been raised by others like me—nymphs, mortal souls, and spirits traded to Master Weles for their parents' requests. All I wish for everyday is to see my mother even once."

I slid the knife back up my sleeve. Part of me regretted threatening her. After Weles's threats and her lies, it was hard to know if I could trust her, but this seemed different. There was a pain in her words, like that I felt whenever I thought about Mother.

"I understand," I said. "I'd give up anything to see Mother again, even after her hiding the truth."

"Then why do you have no desire to know your real father?" Sabina asked.

I bit my cheek so hard it hurt. *Why can't I admit he's my father?* I instinctively reached for my braid and the talismans within, but I'd left them along with my old dress. Never before had I worn my hair unbraided for so long. Free, it hung with a slight curl down to my chest, and my hand drifted through the strands as I thought. "I have a father who raised me. He may have been stern and sometimes didn't understand me, but he did love me—I think. It might be unfair to Weles, but I don't need another parent. I need the ones I had back."

When I looked up, Sabina's wide eyes were fixed on me. It felt odd talking to a nymph, yet she seemed more real than most people I'd met. Why did her support seem so unconditional, despite my treatment of her?

"Tell me about the world above," she said. "Jawia. I wish to know about all of it."

"It's grim. Between Marzanna capturing Mother and the Horde slaughtering the Anshayman clans, there might not be much left soon."

"Oh…" Her head drooped for a moment before she wiggled on the bed and scooted closer. "Anshayman? Is that the land to the east of the forests? And what about the trees and mountains—the ones they call Perun's Crown—and the Krowik river? Tell me about *all* of it!"

Gods, it's like she's a child awaiting a story from her grandmother.

I hesitated. Maybe I had been too harsh on her. I'd only been in Weles's home for at most a couple weeks and I was about to go insane. He'd trapped Sabina her entire life.

"All right," I said. "I'll tell you about all of it as long as, in exchange, you tell me everything you know about Nawia and Weles. Then, we're going to figure out a way for us to finally see both of our mothers."

Beaming, she embraced me in a tight hug. "Of course! Thank you, Lady Otylia. You have no idea how much this means to me."

I let myself smile, though I couldn't bring myself to return the embrace. Not yet. "Just don't betray me again."

"I won't!"

"Good." I took a deep breath and ran my hands through my ruffled skirt. "Where in the worlds do I start?"

The winding halls of Weles's home guided me closer to the swamp that encircled the Heart of Nawia. It was where I'd arrived and where Weles had made his first veiled threats. Nearly two weeks later, I was learning how to play his game—with Sabina's help.

Nothing had been the same since she'd revealed the truth about her birth. In turn, I'd explained everything I knew about Jawia to her. It was less than Wacław knew of the tribes beyond our borders, but Sabina had clung to every word. My mere existence in Jawia fascinated her.

Despite my initial reservations, it had felt nice to have someone who *wanted* to listen to me no matter what I had to say. Nobody had ever really bothered before. Well, except Wacław.

My hand reached for my missing necklace. *Where are you, Wašek?* I didn't know if the longing that fluttered in my chest was his or mine. Before, it had been obvious when his pain or emotion was affecting me, but now, they were less alien and more… natural?

I shook my head. *There's nothing natural about a goddess and a demon sharing žityje.* The whole thing scared me, yet when the tugs on our connection faded, I yearned to feel something from him. It was foolish. I knew it was. But that didn't make me want it any less. It didn't make me want *him* any less.

Gods. What is Sabina doing to me?

In the days since our first real conversation, Sabina had showed me everywhere she could in Nawia, but it wasn't much considering she wasn't allowed outside the swamps surrounding Weles's home. The paradise Father had always spoken of must've been beyond the cramped vines and trees here. I'd caught a glimpse of it when I'd first fled. I would need to reach it if we had any hope of finding a way out.

Until then, I had to gain Weles's trust. That meant passing the Trials… abandoning my szeptucha connection to Mother and Mokosz.

My jaw clenched at the thought of seeing Weles again, but he was the god of Nawia. If anyone knew the routes in and out of the underworld, it was him. Besides, I was curious what he could teach me about my power as a goddess—even if it was just to use it against him.

It was hard to admit how reliant I'd become on my goddesses' powers as a channeler. I felt empty with only the weak connection I held to them in Nawia. I touched the Bowmark and Mothermark on each side of my neck, tying me to them. Soon, they would be gone.

That was a problem for later, though. First, I had to confront Weles at another one of his meals. Despite him allowing Sabina to bring me my food directly after our fight, I knew he'd been awaiting my return. I doubted patience was one of his virtues.

I straightened my dress as I stopped before the dining room doors—normal height this time. The dress was another sent by Weles, apparently one Sabina had suggested. It was simple and light gray, like the one I usually wore, but instead of twine and bone amulets, its wide belt was made of leather and pulled the dress tight around my waist.

It was different, feminine. I'd hated that at first. When I'd noticed the belt had slits in it of various sizes, though, I'd changed my mind. Whether meant for weapons or potions, either would do.

A male water nymph, dressed in light blue robes, bowed to me and pushed open the doors. At least among Weles's servants, boys were less common. Was that because parents were more willing to sacrifice a daughter to appease Weles? I knew the answer to that.

Weles stood at the end of the long table. His height was that of the average man, yet he wore the same attire and appearance as last time. *Do the doors respond to his form?* The only other change was the length of his dark brown hair. It had been unruly before, but now, a woven mess of it stretched down to cover his shoulders.

He smiled. "I am glad to see you have decided to give me another chance."

Hardly. "I'm here to learn," I said, stern. "I've realized how little I really know about being a goddess—and about Mother—and I'm willing to listen if you're willing to teach."

"Not much of a compromiser, are you?" He chuckled. "I had expected you to be like her. My mistake was not realizing how much."

"Your mistake was killing me."

Another smile. "Fair enough. Sit, and let us actually enjoy a meal together. Once we are finished, then we can discuss your Trials."

"I was wondering about their purpose," I said as I sat.

"Surely you didn't expect your power to come instantaneously? An Ascension is a dangerous process, and there are many lessons you must learn. If you are not prepared…" He shifted and cleared his throat. "It matters not. You will pass the Trials in due time, I assure you."

Can a failed Ascension kill a god? I'd thought Father had known nearly everything about the gods. He'd known next to nothing—we all had.

Serving nymphs brought our food before retreating through the doors behind Weles. We ate in silence, only broken by Weles's occasional comments. He was trying. That was more than I could say for some fathers, but I cringed each time I looked at him. From the horns piercing his scalp to his constantly changing appearances, I couldn't grasp why he chose the form he did. I knew little about shape-shifting. Gods and many demons were capable of it, but did they have complete control over the end result?

"You are wondering about the body I have chosen," Weles said.

Can he read minds too? I didn't reply.

He grinned and pushed his plate to the side, folding his hands on the table in its place. "You may ask, Otylia. You *are* my daughter after all."

"I was questioning that, yes," I said through gritted teeth. Sabina had emphasized, as much as possible for her soft tongue, that I should avoid arguments, so I held back. "Do you choose your form, or is there another power behind it?"

"Finish eating and I will answer. Some things are best shown."

I raised a brow but complied. I was still starving, and the food was the best I'd had since Mother had died, maybe better. Not that I would admit that to him.

Once I had taken my last bite of the beef and grains, Weles rose, pushed in his chair, and grabbed his staff, looking at it with sorrow. "Follow."

The servants opened the back doors and bowed as we passed. I winced. The last thing I wanted was to be watched by the entire realm, let alone be their princess. I'd been the witch everyone avoided for years, but none of that seemed to matter anymore. My life—my old life—felt almost irrelevant. But I couldn't let go.

Weles led me through a series of identical halls of vines. Still, I memorized each turn and door we passed. The key to our escape could've been anywhere, and without knowing where to look, I studied everything I could. It wasn't hard with how slowly Weles walked.

He clung to the staff like it was life itself. *Ironic, for the god of the underworld.* Its curled top held a sapphire that I hadn't noticed before, and it glimmered in each ray of light that pierced the canopy above.

The staff kept him moving, though. For that I was grateful. His forward shuffle seemed that of an old man more than a god, only increasing my curiosity about the form he'd chosen. If gods were immortal, why would he want to live as a cripple?

Eventually, we came to a short hall that ended in a single door. It had a golden handle like the others, but its wood was simple. The vines kept their distance, leaving the door itself untouched except for a carving of Weles's Serpentmark—an inverted triangle beneath cattle horns. The horned snake. I hoped to never see another of his serpents ever again.

With a deep sigh, Weles held his staff before him and rested on it with both hands. "I assume you know a mark's power?"

I nodded. "Marzanna's dagger burned hers into Wacław's skin. It's supposed to grant a god influence over a person."

"Or a demon, yes. Truly, a mark can give a god power over anything, living or dead, granted the god is strong enough." He looked to me. "Symbols are powerful things—both marks and the old tongue. There is a reason we do not allow your tribes to use the written word."

He opened the door and stepped into the next room. I lagged behind, staring at his mark on the wood. *What power can a word have?* I'd spoken in the old tongue to strengthen my channeling. Was that it?

I wouldn't get answers standing there, so I followed.

The room beyond was small compared to the others I'd seen. Only one ray of light illuminated the space, shining on a bowl made of roots at the room's center. The twisting base beneath it wove through the ground and split the dirt at my feet. In the darkness, it was hard not to trip on the exposed roots, but Weles stepped over them with ease. His gaze was fixed upon the bowl and the dark liquid within.

"What is that?" I asked.

He didn't reply. Instead, he stared down at the roots and tapped them with his staff, muttering in the old tongue, "In death, there is life. In life, death. One cannot have one without the other."

I drew closer. Weles's presence felt cold, distant, as if he'd forgotten I was even there. He didn't look up when I reached his side and studied the contents of the bowl.

Blood.

"What do you know about *żityje*, child?" he asked.

A shiver gripped me as whispers swirled around the basin, too quiet to understand. I swallowed in fear. From the light to the pedestal, the pool reminded me of an altar—one to death itself.

"You wanted to learn, yet you ignore my questions?"

I tore my gaze from the altar. "It's the life force of all things," I said, my mind still elsewhere. "All living things have it, but most lack enough to use sorcery or any other power, even if they knew how. They regenerate their own *żityje*. But demons are dead, so they have to take it to survive."

He sighed and leaned against his staff. "Falsehoods, all of it—except the part about the demons."

"You'd let your priests spread lies to your own channelers?"

"Falsehoods and lies are not necessarily the same." He scratched his beard, which had invited insects from the swamp surrounding the palace. "*Žityje* is not a force but life itself. All actions, whether sorcery or simply walking, require it. In this, every creature both living and dead uses *žityje* and thus possesses the ability to harness it as well. Most beings have such little of it, though, that untrained channeling beyond the simplest spell would consume them. This is the problem both you and your demon boy have faced."

Pausing, he stared up at the hole in the roots above, where the light spewed through. "Do you know why we call our servants szeptuchy—whisperers?"

I shrugged. "We channel our god's strength, and often that involves chanting in the old tongue."

"And did I not tell you that words have power?" I didn't reply, and he shook his head. "Oh, child, how little you know of the threats you face."

Why does he always speak in riddles? I remembered the szeptuchy I'd known and demons I'd faced. We knew demons drew *žityje* from living things. That meant they were literally draining the life of their victims, but what did that have to do with channelers and the bowl of blood in front of us?

Then it clicked. *No…*

"We don't channel a god's power," I said, stepping away from the bowl. "We channel their *life*… We drain from their soul just like demons do to people, and we can do the same to plants and other things. We're the same?"

"In a way." He nodded to the blood. "Gods require *žityje* too. Though we create some of our own, it is not enough. What does that mean?"

My breaths quickened as I made the connections in my mind. "Sacrifices," I said before looking up at Weles, horrified. "Gods don't have unlimited *žityje*, so they demand sacrifices and offerings to them… to us. The blood is the life of the sacrifice—the life you consume."

"So is the way," Weles said. His voice was solemn, but his sorrow didn't stop me from backing away.

Anger devoured my mind. I lost all my thoughts but one. "You're no better than demons!" I clenched my fists and stormed across the room. "You kill for your immortality. No, you make *us* kill for your immortality! At least demons face us themselves instead of sitting behind their priests and szeptuchy, feeding us lies."

"Hmm." He leaned more heavily on his staff, speaking slowly, as if he were contemplating each word. "Are we no different than humans or wolves, plants or fungi? All things consume *życie* from another. All things must die and pass along their life to another. Is this not the world's cycle? Have you not drained elements of nature when you channel your mother?"

He shuffled toward me, his eyes growing stern. "We are immortal, my child, but it is not because of sacrifice. Sacrifice and worship alter our forms and morph us into the forces we represent. The gods we must be. Lesser gods with no worshippers are reliant on their own creation of *życie* and may fade, yet they do not die as if they were demons. For a god cannot die forever. They merely vanish for a time, until they collect enough *życie* to manifest again and fulfill their role."

"Why am I here then?" I spat. "Why have I not vanished? And where is Jaryło?"

"You and your brother perished from Jawia because of his Moonblades." Weles jabbed his staff into the ground. The curled top unwound, and when it stopped, a deep brown blade extended from where a sapphire had once been.

Thunderstone. I stepped away.

He chuckled at my surprise. "Yes, even I possess my enemy's weapon. Stolen, just as I stole his cattle and Jaryło. Both Thunderstone and Moonstone can kill a god—temporarily—and their power to absorb *życie* from their victim makes them effective at doing so. Moonstone, however, can store *życie*, unlike Thunderstone."

"This is why Jaryło lies rooms away," he continued, "recovering until he can draw the *życie* from the sword of the Maj moon. Wacław was quite cunning to steal Kwiecień from him and prevent his return. Your recovery was a different story."

Weles paused and returned his staff to its original form. Only the creaking of its wood broke the silence until he spoke again, "An Ascended god can grant *żityje* to a mortal or the un-Ascended through items of power such as the golden eggs. To do so without one comes with great risk—unless, of course, you are of shared blood. This made it easier for me to bring you back before you awoke, lost. Your brother, however, has Ascended and is not my son by blood. To recover him to full health would require far too much *żityje*."

Wacław and I don't share blood. Is the cost of our ritual only our connection or something more?

I glanced over my shoulder. Weles was backing me into the wall, so I spun away and kept the altar between him and me. "I'd thank you, but considering you killed me, it was the least you could've done."

"That is fair."

"Why the blood, then?" I asked. "Channelers receive a god's *żityje* without touch or an item of power."

"Szeptuchy *channel* their god's life. They never receive it." He approached the altar and dipped his fingers into the blood. "Unlike demons, we cannot steal *żityje*. It must be freely offered to us as a sacrifice—either that of animals or mortals themselves."

I winced and backed further, arms crossed. "I don't care what powers that gives me. I'm not sticking my hand in there."

"Oh, child. You must to embrace your power." He raised his fingers to his mouth, allowing the blood to trickle into it.

I can't do this.

I scrambled into the hall. My stomach turned, and I stopped for only a second to vomit. Then I sprinted without direction. It didn't matter anymore where I went. If this was what it took to learn from Weles and become a goddess, I didn't want it. I would find another way out of Nawia. Nothing was worth drinking the blood of sacrifices.

Even immortality.

12

Wacław

What was Rasa trying to tell me?

WE MADE CAMP BETWEEN TWO PEAKS THAT NIGHT. Here, the valley channeled the winds into a howling force, and they surrounded me as I sat on my bedroll and pondered the high priestess's words.

She had spoken of the gods' need for us and my worthiness to lead. My fingers tightened around the sun talisman she'd given me. The Zurgowie called the god Otlezd, yet I wondered if he was the same as Dadźbóg. The whole conversation had left me unsettled. I wasn't sure exactly why. I was certain, though, that things were happening beyond my knowledge, only slivers of which I could understand. If I had learned anything from Jaryło, it was that cryptic conversations came from those hiding elements of the truth.

I intended to find out what.

Well, I intended to once I convinced my body to sleep. Each night it seemed harder to rest than the one before. The demon's rage stirred within me, and despite my exhaustion, my thoughts kept me up.

Tensions were high between the two clans. In recent days, we'd woken to reports of wolf attacks against a few Zurgowie families in the outskirts of camps. I found it odd that wolves would strike at such a dense group, let alone *only* the Zurgowie. Tonight, I would keep an eye out.

Shifting alongside me, Sosna yawned. *Or at least* she'll *keep watch,* I thought with a chuckle.

The dull ache of my tired muscles was drowned out by a different, sharper pain. *Otylka?* My heart raced and breaths quickened as I dared to imagine what she was enduring. That was what scared me the most. I couldn't have cared less about sleeping or eating knowing she was alone in Nawia. It would've been *less* worrying if every moment hadn't felt like a serpent tightening around my chest through our connection, but her panic was obvious, especially tonight. So, I stayed awake, praying to her and any god who would listen. If any did.

What is it like to forget about your worries and just dream?

There were times I would've given anything to dream, yet the idea of giving up my night wandering—and my powers—wasn't appealing. Someday perhaps. Not until I brought Otylia home.

Eventually, I yawned and stretched one last time. *Maybe the gods will grant me sleep.* As I tightened my cloak around me and lay on the bedroll, though, my weariness faded, replaced by fear once again.

"I'm coming, Otylka," I whispered.

The winds tore above, whistling on the crags. Some moaned, others screamed, but among them, I swore I heard a reply, *"Wašek?"*

I spun from my cloak but only succeeded at tying myself up in the process. "Otylia?" I breathed as I fought free. Even catching a breath was difficult as hope clashed with fear within me. "Is that you?"

Though the winds howled, no answer came. I listened, my heartbeat hammering my ears as the gales whipped through my hair and cloak. *Please. Please be her. I need you, Otylka.*

Silence.

I dropped to my knees, the hope I'd gained a moment before washed away, leaving nothing but that familiar numbness. Even our tether seemed loose now, disconnected. There was no feeling of panic nor physical pain—just an empty void where I had felt her before. That was worse than anything.

I knelt there a long time. I didn't have a clue what I was doing, but it felt *right* to be still under the moon and stars, among the winds. They were silent companions. When I felt the most alone, they were always there. The stars as the souls of our ancestors and the moon as the godless power overseeing the night and watching the demons it had created.

According to Dariusz, I was one of the moon's victims, born on the night of a partial blood moon. A sliver of the moon had avoided the eclipse that night. The Lake of Reflection hadn't shown me if that had kept a part of me human, but I considered it a safe assumption. Still, there had surely been other children born during a blood moon. Dariusz and the other priests couldn't have sacrificed all of them, could they?

Sosna snarled as steps approached from behind me. "Wacław? Why are you still awake?"

Bidaês? I rose, patting Sosna as I faced the Simuk—the older brother, never to inherit his clan's rule. *Such an odd succession.* "I could ask the same of you."

He glanced around to make sure no one was listening. "I figured you'd sleep more often, because… you know."

"Unfortunately, being a demon doesn't grant me peace of mind." I eyed him and the cavalry sword at his side. The demon hissed within me, but I denied its will to leap into a fight. "Why stray so far from your part of camp?"

His hand fell upon the sword's hilt. Subtle, but convincing enough for me to confirm my suspicions. "I wanted to take a walk and clear my thoughts. You aren't the only one with a lot on their mind."

Maybe I judged him too quickly tonight… again. "Considering the state of my soul or mourning your parents?" I sighed. "I could understand either."

"Can demons not read minds too?"

I laughed. "Only those of our victims."

He hesitated. "Wait… seriously?"

"Of course not. I may have power over the winds and weather, but your mind is safe from me."

As if on command, the winds picked up again and sent a chill through my body, ending at my Frostmark. I shuddered and pulled my cloak tighter. *Simukie clothes could do with a bit more heft.*

Bidaês turned to leave but stopped at the last moment. "A rumor is going around that Rasa came to you today."

"She did."

He considered that. "And what did she say?"

"Still can't trust me?" I asked, a hand on the Thunderstone dagger's hilt. There was a bite to my voice I hadn't expected, but this time, it felt good. "Last time we spoke, you insulted me. Why would you expect me to tell you about all my conversations now?"

"Because I'm coming with you."

I released the blade and crossed my arms. "How do I know you actually want to help?"

He swallowed, wariness lingering in his voice. "Zakir… He's decided he needs to learn more about what you call the underworld. We don't exactly talk about an afterlife among our people, and Zakir has never been one to back down from a chance at discovery. If he's coming, so am I."

"Your brother's skill with potions could be helpful." I marched toward him, letting the demon's anger slip from its cage. "But if either of you are coming, I *need* to know that when my life is on the line, you'll be there to fight beside me. I've seen Marzanna's cultists and channelers slaughter villages and massacre warriors. I've watched her demons tear apart the sky and swarm my friends." I snarled as memories flashed in my mind, raw, untainted. "Her curse can kill anyone we love in the blink of an eye—just like she did to my father."

Stopping less than a stride from him, I narrowed my eyes and clenched my jaw. "Prove to me I can trust you."

He raised his chin at my affront into his space. "I can't. You're always going to doubt me after what I said before, and as long as you bear a Frostmark, I'm always going to doubt you. That doesn't matter."

"No, Bidaês. *Nothing* else matters. Marzanna has corrupted so many people, and we've been betrayed before. We're traveling into the literal underworld. I already have no idea what we'll be facing, but without knowing I can trust the people with me, the journey is hopeless." I stepped back, thumbing Marzanna's covered mark on my palm. Ablaze, as if I were near another Frostmarked, it only fed the demon. "Tell Zakir I'm sorry. If the choice is between bringing both of your or neither, then we'll be fine on our own."

I turned away, but he called after me, "Wait!"

Without looking back, I growled, "What?"

"I'll tell you why I asked about High Priestess Rasa." He drew closer and lowered his voice. When I met his gaze over my shoulder, there was a new intensity in his eyes—desperation. "I'll expose her plans, the entire Zurgowie plot, all of it."

"Why would the high priestess tell you anything? You're the grandson of the Simukie marzban."

"Exactly. I have the most to gain from my grandfather and brother's deaths."

My chest tightened. "What are you saying?"

He grabbed my shoulder, dropping his voice to a whisper that sent a shiver down my spine. "I'm saying Rasa is planning to ambush grandfather, Zakir, and the Simukie commanders once we get past Kynnytsia, and she thinks I'm going to help her."

"All right," Narcyz grumbled with a fist to his forehead. "Which one of you wants to tell me why in Oblivion I'm awake right now?"

Bidaês stood with Zakir, his arms crossed. "We need to prevent a slaughter…" he said, "as well as the death of Zakir and our grandfather."

He explained High Priestess Rasa's plan to strike the Simukie in

Astiwie lands and take all the southern hills for themselves. It was shocking to see how possible the attack was. By surrounding the camp at night, the Zurgowie could eliminate both the marzban and his heir in minutes. Chaos would result, and the remaining Simukie would either surrender or fall, fighting a battle they had no hopes of winning without time to mount their horses.

"And why do I care?" Narcyz said when Bidaês finished. "The clans caused the threat in the first place. Having less of them in our lands is better if we don't want to be conquered whenever they decide the south isn't enough."

"The Horde forced the clans to move west," Ara snapped. Bits of stone cracked beneath her boots as she paced in the shadow of the cliffs. Sosna seemed no less anxious, digging through the earth at her side. "Even you're not dumb enough to miss that."

He shrugged. "Still."

I stepped between them. "Our opinions on the clans aren't important right now. An attack like this could kill hundreds, if not thousands, of people. We have to try to stop it."

"How?" Narcyz marched toward Bidaês, and Zakir stepped cleanly out of his way. "Why ask us when your grandfather is the marzban?"

Bidaês shuffled his feet. "He won't believe me."

"There's a good reason for that," Zakir said.

"It doesn't matter whether he has a good reason or not. Someone needs to warn him before Rasa ruins everything!"

"Why won't you do it, Zakir?" I asked.

He fiddled with the ends of his sleeves. "I feel acting with such little information is hasty. Hearsay is not enough to start a war."

"You have a good point." I steadied my breaths and stared up at the stars. *Why can nothing be simple?* "Bidaês, you told me this only after I threatened to leave you behind. If it's the truth and you actually wanted my help, why not ask outright?"

"We'd fought," Bidaês said with a shrug. "But you said yourself that we need to trust each other, so I'm willing to let go of my worries about you being Frostmarked if you just trust me on this. You will have my sword, and I'll cover your back no matter what we face." Despite the confident words, he refused to meet my gaze.

Ara waved a dismissive hand. "You talk a lot without actually answering the question. We still don't have a reason to trust your word."

"Fine." He stepped forward and drew a long, curved dagger. I reached for Kwiecień as Sosna yapped, but he held up a hand. "Zakir, Grandfather, and I spar occasionally with these dulled daggers. They can break the skin, but it's impossible to do much actual damage with them."

"Get to the point," Narcyz ordered, his spear ready.

Bidaês acknowledged his comment but turned back to me. "The Zurgowie gave me venom to coat the blade with. A small cut is all that's needed for it to slowly work through his body—long enough for his death to seem unrelated to the injury."

Narcyz kept his spear raised. "That venom could come from anywhere."

"No," Bidaês said. "It couldn't. Ara, you're familiar with Zurgowie use of the Anshayman viper's venom, right? All their warriors learn to coat their arrows in it, but no other clan knows how to effectively kill enough of the snakes."

Ara shrugged. "I'm familiar with it, but I've never used it myself. It taints a hunter's kill."

He stepped toward her. "Could you identify its smell or taste?"

She winced.

"Please." Taking her hand, he slid the dagger's hilt into it. "I know I'm asking you to expose your clan, but Rasa's wars have already cost too many lives. Don't let my grandfather's be one of them. Don't let Zakir's be one of them."

I stepped to Ara's side. "You don't have to do this unless you want to."

"Don't speak for me," Ara muttered, stepping in front of me to take the dagger. "I don't *want* to betray my clan, but they're not mine anymore. Otylia, you, Narcyz, Xobas… you all are the clan that matters now." With a sharp breath, she raised the dagger to her nose before gasping and flinging it into the dirt.

"Well?" Narcyz asked.

Ara turned to the cliffs, staring up at them with an arm held across her chest. "It's the venom. I'd recognize that smell anywhere after…" Her voice trailed away.

I placed a hand on her shoulder. "It's all right. You don't need to say anything more."

Zakir eyed his brother but bowed his head. "I'm sorry. I shouldn't have doubted you."

"We've all had our share of doubt," I replied, my chest tight as I pondered what disaster this would bring, "but what matters is that we figure out a way to stop this. We will reach Kynnytsia by nightfall tomorrow, so we need to be quick. I will join Zakir and Bidaês to talk with the marzban and Xobas in the morning."

Ara strode across the circle. "I'll scout out Zurgowie supplies, and Narcyz can cause a distraction. My parents always said Rasa likes to trick her targets. Hopefully we can find something."

Bidaês nodded. "Okay then, we've got *something* at least."

"It's not enough," I said, rubbing my sore neck, "but it's a start. And for now, that's all we have."

13

Otylia

I heard him...

WACŁAW'S VOICE HADN'T BEEN MORE THAN A WHISPER, but as I lay, shaking, in my bed, I knew it had been him. *"I'm coming, Otylka."*

I'd called back over and over. No reply came. Our bond had strengthened to the point I'd felt his breaths in my own lungs, but now there was nothing. It was like someone had sliced the tether between us, leaving behind a void that gnawed at my aching heart.

Was he actually coming for me, or was this another of Weles's tricks?

I wanted to weep and curl up under my bedroom's willow. Part of me hoped I would drift away and wake to it all having been a nightmare. I'd feel the warmth of my little room in Dwie Rzeki after the Drowning of Marzanna and hear Dziewanna's voice. I'd see Wacław at Lubena's farm, and neither of us would be a goddess or demon. We'd forget our years apart and ignore our fathers' quarrels. Life would make sense.

But none of it had been a nightmare. I groaned, holding my fist to my forehead and cursing Wacław. He'd poisoned my mind with foolish dreams, yet those dreams were all that drove me forward.

Sabina and I will find a way out of here. We'll escape, and Wacław will help us fight off whoever Weles sends after us. I won't be a blood-drinking goddess or the princess of Nawia. I'll be Mother's channeler—the one who saves her from Marzanna—and I'll keep Wacław's human soul alive. That's enough to live for.

Someone pounded on my door. I gritted my teeth and flung myself from the bed. The gray dress with the wide belt had become my favorite, but now, it was disheveled and covered in tears. I didn't care. Based on Weles's appearance at lunch, neither would he.

I scowled and opened the door, yelping as a bear towered over me.

"My apologies, Lady Otylia," Ivan said before dropping to all fours. "I did not intend to frighten you."

"You're a *bear*," I snapped. "What did you expect?"

"That is a fair accusation. We aren't used to visitors here anymore, not after Lady Dziewanna left us. Perhaps I got too carried away."

I rolled my eyes. "Like when you threatened me under Mother's willow? Why are you here? I don't want to talk with another of Weles's servants."

"If you believe me to be Master Weles's servant, you are ill informed. It matters little, though. He sent me to escort you to the lands of Nawia outside of his palace."

"He's kicking me out? All he's been doing is forcing me to stay!"

The bear shook his head. Despite having seen him before, the sharp teeth and foul breath still made me back away further. "You misunderstand. I wish to show you the beauty of Nawia beyond this swamp before you are to finish the first two Trials. You may return when you please."

The Trials? What is Weles planning?

I knew I should've been excited about the possibilities both of passing the Trials and scouting out potential escape routes. But after seeing Weles drink the blood of sacrifices—both human and animal—I couldn't help but be skeptical of the man, the god, who was technically my father.

When I nodded, Ivan led me down a series of halls. It should've felt freeing to leave my chambers, but they'd become my sanctuary. Nothing else in the palace made sense. Instead of passing the dining hall and the side room where Weles had showed me the pool of blood, there were just more vines as the walls wound without an obvious pattern.

And I could *sense* them.

Though it was only for a moment, I'd felt the vines shift behind us. I glanced over my shoulder. *Nothing.*

Nawia was a new world to me that became stranger every day. I couldn't afford to become comfortable. If we had any chance of escape, I had to be on my toes.

Finally, we reached a place where sunlight snuck through the walls. Ivan raised a paw to one of the openings, and the vines pulled away, allowing the light to spill over me for the first time in weeks.

"I'd forgotten the sun's warmth," I said as I stepped through the opening and took a greedy breath.

The swamp finished around us. Rolling plains stretched for as far as I could comprehend, covered with grasses of green and gold. The sky above was a crisp blue that seemed to flow as if it were water. Only a few rare clouds broke its purity, and a slight breeze blew my hair into my face. For once, I didn't care.

A memory flashed through my mind.

Wacław stood with me on a hill over a plain just like this. The sky was dark as the płanetnik's storm approached from the east, but Wacław's eyes were radiant, hopeful despite Marzanna's threats. In that rare moment of vulnerability, when I was lost without Dziewanna's presence, having him by my side made things feel okay.

I miss you.

"It is quite unexpected to see you weeping at the sight of a mere plain," Ivan said. "When we met previously, you seemed much more… blunt."

I wiped the tears from my cheeks. They'd come without warning, and I hated that they had come at all. Weles—and his servants—needed to see me as strong, not a weeping child. "Where did you want to show me?" I asked, ignoring his comment.

"Ah, yes. Still blunt." He rose on his hind legs and strolled leisurely toward the next hill. I hadn't thought a bear possible of such graceful movements.

We walked in silence for a while. Ivan seemed to be enjoying the sun on his face, and I was more than happy not to talk to him. As we crested the hill, though, I gasped at the sheer size of the landscape before us. "I've never seen anything like this."

"I imagine not."

Beyond the plains, trees towered hundreds of feet into the sky—willow, birch, and alder among others. Golden cattle grazed on the grasses, and people, both clothed and not, danced around them as women sang songs to Weles and other gods. Far in the distance, a great sea stretched further than my eyes could see.

I looked up at Ivan. "Why does Weles hide in a house made of vines, deep in the swamp, when he has paradise beyond?"

"Hmm." Ivan dropped to all fours again and examined the dancers. "I imagine the responsibilities of a god weigh heavily on him. The master works tirelessly to protect as much of Nawia's grandeur as possible, yet this means he rarely experiences the rewards of his effort." He turned to me. "Except when he sees you, Lady Otylia."

"I'd hardly consider me a reward." I paused as the memory of the sacrificial blood stained my thoughts. "And what efforts? *Mother* raised me. She sacrificed herself to keep me safe from Weles, but here I am, trapped in the swamps he sequesters himself in."

"You underestimate the difficulties he endured to bring you here and how hard he has tried to make you feel at home. The master has struggled to find joy ever since Lady Dziewanna left, yet in the past few weeks, he has smiled more than I have seen in decades."

"Then I would've hated to see him before," I grumbled as I sat. It was soothing to dig my fingers into the dirt and feel the blades of grass brush against my hands. With Marzanna's winter halted for now, Jawia wouldn't freeze, but Mother was weak—Jaryło was dead. No life would fill the void Marzanna had made until they returned. *Ironically, Wacław killing him just helped Marzanna more.*

Ivan sat next to me, and I grinned at the eight-foot bear flopping onto his bottom. "Indeed, it was quite a depressing time for all of us. The master's war with Perun is ever-heavy on his mind, yet when he discovered you, he thought of nothing else."

I didn't reply for a long time. Knowing Weles had wanted me so badly was disconcerting, but it also felt nice to be wanted. If only he could have been anyone else.

"How did you end up in Nawia?" I asked. "Were you a bear before, or is that Weles's version of a sick joke?"

Ivan rocked back and forth. "That is a story of significant length, Lady Otylia. Are you certain you wish to listen as an old and long dead bear tells of his life on Jawia? I could hardly blame you if you were to say no."

I knew I should've pushed him to show me more of Nawia, but my curiosity was stronger. "You know a lot about me," I said. "It's only fair I get to hear your story."

"Very well," he began. "My tale is from far ago, before the united tribes of Krowik and Astiw. It was a time when we were warring and divided among many small kingdoms and tribes. In the cradle north of Perun's Crown, near the village you now call Klist, there was one particular kingdom whose name is long forgotten by your people—Królestwo z Dębu i Wierzby, the Kingdom from Oak and Willow. Our people were with the forests and they with us.

"There were many other forces within Perun's protected lands. Among the western hills, where the Solgawi now rule, lived a tyrant who gripped his people with demon-like claws. He reaped what he did not sow, and all who fled him were torn to shreds by his army."

"What was his name?" I asked.

Ivan shuddered. "Koschei we called him—the lord of death, taker of lives, and master of sorcery."

Koschei… The name felt familiar, yet I was sure I'd never heard it before. *Odd.* "Was he a god? A demon?"

"Neither, Lady Otylia," Ivan replied with a shake of his head. "Koschei was merely a man corrupted by his will to rule all the world. Like many kings before him, and many after, he sought whatever his heart desired, taking it no matter the cost for his people."

"You said this story would be about you." I pulled in my legs, holding them as I gazed over the sunlit landscape. "What does a warlord and an old kingdom have to do with it?"

"Ah, yes. I told you the tale would take some time to share. I do promise this is all relevant, but if you wish, we can continue another time?"

"No, you can keep going."

He took a deep breath of the warm air and settled again. "Where was I? Right. Koschei's corruption touched all of his kingdom, stretching from the great North Sea to the ranges of Perun's Crown in the south. For decades, his armies had swept east toward the Krowik River. Koschei had become quite old by then, and his attacks became more frequent and aggressive with each passing year. It mattered not to him how many men he lost slaughtering innocent villages. All he desired was complete victory.

"Now, Lady Otylia, I enter the story. For I was a boy at the time, no more than a year or two older than yourself. More importantly, I was the heir to the Oak and Willow crown and needed a wife to make queen when my time came to rule."

"So, you *were* a man once," I said.

With a nod, he smiled. "Indeed, I was. And the woman I married was the finest in all of Jawia: Princess Marya Morevna. Few men were as skilled a fighter as she, and fewer still would have dared to ask for her hand. I did, though, and she chose me to be her husband, uniting our lands. Those were the happiest days of my life. I spent each moment with her, whether in our village or in battle against Koschei's men.

"Soon, I became king, and each of my father's responsibilities passed on to me. Life became difficult. My burdens were heavy. I watched Marya's will fade as we received the reports of more villages falling to Koschei. My wife became distant and depressed until she came to me one day and professed her desire to slay the dark king herself. I pled with her not to, but she would not heed my warning.

She left without me."

I fingered Mokosz's amulet at my wrist. "Facing him alone… Marya sounds like a brave woman."

Ivan chuckled. "Most would say foolhardy, yet none could stand in Marya's way. Not even Koschei. She returned after many moons, dragging him by his withering gray hair before throwing him into our dungeon. Marya said no one was ever to see Koschei again, but my curiosity got the better of me."

"Why do men never listen?" I shook my head. "You didn't stop and think about *why* she told you not to confront a dangerous sorcerer?"

"That is a fine question, yet I was foolish. I could not resist facing the man who had slain so many of my people. This was my undoing." He held a paw to his cheek as sorrow filled his eyes. "Koschei was constrained by iron chains within the dungeon, and he begged for water when I entered. I considered myself a kind man and complied."

I smirked. "I doubt that went well…"

"Indeed." The old king sighed. "The moment the water touched his lips, life seemed to return to him. He threw me aside and swept out of the room, taking my precious Marya with him. He was so swift neither I nor any of our guards could lay a finger upon him. His armies were defeated and his lands free from his reign, but he had taken my wife—nothing else mattered. I left on the fastest horse I could find, searching for them all across our lands.

"I followed their tracks to the southern hills, where I found them riding east, toward the Narrow Pass. For days I chased them, but Koschei's mount was too swift. I tried stealing away Marya while he hunted, but, with little effort I presume, he caught and defeated me. Thrice this happened. And on the third occasion, he chopped me up and sealed me inside of a barrel." With a yawn, he stood and stretched. "Let us continue this story on the move. I fear my legs will grow stiff."

"How did you know? Weren't you dead?" I asked as I rose and

walked alongside him across the plain. By now, the dancers had strayed away, leaving only the cattle in the fields. *Where do they live?* I considered asking Ivan, but he seemed lost in his story.

The bear walked with his paws behind his back like an old man pondering life. "I had three sisters. Each was wedded to a wizard attached to a bird—the Falcon, Eagle, and Raven. When they discovered me in that barrel, floating down a river in the east, they put me back together."

I snickered. "Okay, now I know you're lying."

"How so, Lady Otylia?"

"Witches and wizards can only channel a demon's power!" I spun around in front of him, backing up as he continued forward. "And no demon could bring a dead man back to life."

"You misunderstand. In those days, there were wizards powerful enough to channel their own power as well as that of the artifacts they possessed. These three were among the most skilled alive, I believe. Beyond that, I understand little of sorcery. They saved me, and that is what matters in the end." He gave me a judgmental look, one I'd seen many times from Father. "May I continue?"

I held his gaze for a second, then fell into pace with him again. He had been a man in life, but I didn't want an angry bear as an enemy.

"I will accept no reply as a 'yes,' " he said. "Now, the wizards explained to me the power of the man they called Koschei the Deathless."

My stomach churned at his name. *Why have I heard of him?* It was unsettling to know of him but not know *why* I did.

"Koschei," Ivan continued, "possessed a magic steed faster than any horse in the known world. The only way to secure another like it was by finding the witch who created the Mangled Woods."

"Who?" I spun toward him in excitement. The source of the Mangled Woods had always been curious to me. The chance to ask someone who had met her was one I never thought I'd have. "Father told me about the witch, but even he didn't know much."

"No priest would. Baba Jaga was a private woman, secluded from all except those either brave enough to seek her out or simply lost among her trees."

Baba Jaga. I told myself to remember that name. *If this Koschei is so familiar, she may be important too.* "Do you know how or why she created the woods?" I asked.

"That is a story for another time, as it is a lengthy one of its own." We'd reached the forest, and the cattle scattered at the sight of Ivan. Far above, the tree tops swayed in the wind. "Baba Jaga lived within the Mangled Woods, beyond a river of fire. Her hidden house rested on chicken legs and skulls adorned her fence, but I did everything I could to reach her. It was a perilous journey. I nearly starved, as the creatures I discovered cried for mercy when I was to kill them for food. When I finally found her, the old crone told me I was to care for her mares for three days. If any were to escape, I would find my skull on a spike."

We wound through the trees, deeper into the wood. Other creatures scurried across the ground, just as alarmed as the cattle to see a giant bear.

"I failed every day," Ivan continued, "yet the animals I had spared along the way herded the mares back each night while I slept. On the final night, they warned me that Baba Jaga would kill me anyway, so I stole a mare and left the woods faster than I had ever ridden before."

I raised my brow. "The powerful witch of the woods let you just take one of her horses?"

"Of course not. The witch made chase, riding on a mortar and pestle, but the mare was too fast, even for her." He held his chin high, grinning. "I searched until I found Koschei. Then I waited until he left Marya at camp. This was how I had retrieved her before, but this time, Koschei could not catch us when I swept her into my arms. Though the sorcerer drew his blade, I swung my club and cracked his skull, ending his threat."

"That can't be it," I said, running my fingers along a willow's bark. Its touch reminded me of Mother, but I turned to Ivan. "A sorcerer called 'the Deathless' couldn't be killed so easily."

He nodded as we approached a river. Across it, a bridge made of winding roots stretched over the rocks. Symbols in the old tongue marked it: *The bridge home.* Hope for an escape burned in my chest.

"We believed the same," Ivan said, "so we burned him and scattered his ashes throughout Jawia. Koschei has never been heard from since."

For now. I couldn't shake the feeling that something wasn't right, but it didn't help that we were in the underworld. Everything was unfamiliar here, both stories and not.

"But that doesn't explain how you became a bear," I said.

He hummed to himself. "Indeed, it does not. That story carries on from this one, but we do not have time for it today, for we must cross the bridge."

"What do the symbols mean?" I asked. "*The bridge home.* To Jawia?"

"No, Lady Otylia. This bridge leads many of the newly dead to the villages beyond—where they will live forever."

14

Wacław

What would Mother think of me now, negotiating with distant clans and seeking Nawia?

NERVES GRIPPED ME ALL NIGHT as I sat in my soul-form atop the pass's northern cliff. I thought of home. Of Mom. Of Nevenka, my little half-sister. Of my horse Tanek. Of the laughs I had once had with Kuba. Of the adventures Otylia and I had as children.

Looking back, it all seemed so simple—watching the wheat, following Xobas's instructions, and worrying whether I'd done the right thing years before with Otylia. At least then I had been able to walk through the village and see her from a distance. It had been a foolish hope, but that little witch in the woods had never left my heart. Though I hadn't understood it then, I knew now that I had always loved her.

Why did I ever give in to Father's threats?

We'd spent years apart because of my decision, and during the *žityje* ritual, her pain had become mine. Years of feeling forgotten, alone. *I should've been there for her.*

I sat there on that cliff, staring at the camp and regretting everything, but I knew I never had a real choice. I'd been twelve, far too young to understand life or love. That didn't make it hurt any less, and I clenched my fists, remembering all Father had taken from me. Whether mine or the demon's anger, I didn't care. Maybe his death had been a good thing.

No, I told myself. My demonic soul influenced my emotions, my thoughts, more with each day. I wouldn't let it take me.

It seemed an eternity before Dadźbóg rose in the east, peeking over the mountains of Perun's Crown. My mind was in a fog, but we would need to speak to Xobas and Katiôn as early as possible. Neither would take Rasa's betrayal well. Unlike the high priestess, Katiôn had been compromising and supportive of the clans' cooperation, and its end would crush him.

But both he and Zakir would live.

Arms extended, I leaped from the ledge and free-fell toward the earth. The air rushed past me, whipping through my hair and cloak as I flew straight as an arrow. Then, just as I was about to reach the rocky ground, I called the winds and burst over the camp with a rush of speed. The thrill helped me forget the trials ahead, but those worries returned as I landed a few strides from where my body slept.

The winds freed more than my body each night. Wandering invisibly in my soul-form had been part of my life as long as I could remember, and the quiet beneath the moon offered a rare respite from the business of the day. I spent nearly as much time alone at night as most people spent awake, granting me hours to ponder. On days like this, though, that wasn't a gift.

Narcyz scowled at the sun nearby as I returned to my body. He watched the process, and when I woke, he shook his head. "I'll never get how that works."

I chuckled, tightening my cloak around me as I pushed myself off my bed roll. Despite being warmer than last night, the morning was chilly. I missed the embrace of my heavier tunic. "Honestly, I doubt I will ever understand it either, and I've done it for years. Some things, I think, should stay mysteries."

He huffed and slid his weapons onto his back. His wooden shield was chipped but in better shape than mine had been in, even before my battle with Eryk over the Mangled Woods.

After weeks without it, I regretted losing the one thing Kuba and I had used to mark our friendship—our matching shields. I'd wanted another at first, but the Simukie shields were far too small and light. The Zurgowie carried none, opting instead for bows or two-handed spears and staffs. It was an odd tactic considering their near-complete lack of armor. To them, though, speed countered an enemy's brute force, and I couldn't argue with the success the Zurgowie had claimed in battles of the past.

I hesitated with a hand on my pack. Even if I had found a new shield, it wouldn't feel right. Kuba and I had painted those shields when we'd barely been old enough to hold them. Part of him had always been joined with it, protecting me. Gone, neither he nor it could be so easily replaced. *May Nawia grant you peace, brother.*

We finished packing our things and hauled them to our horses. Like the Simukie, we tied them near our tent. I was grateful to avoid the Zurgowie guards around their clan's gathered mounts. Rasa's potential betrayal didn't mean they all wished to fight, but I tensed beneath her warriors' gazes.

The clans rose swiftly. Within an hour of daybreak, we were on the move again, and I found the Simukie brothers near the front of the crowd. Zakir was deep in thought as normal, mumbling to himself as Bidaês fixed his curled hair that had become more of a mangled mess.

"Ah, so our demonic friend arrives," Bidaês whispered with a smirk.

How is he smiling? Our next actions could pit the clans against each other, but he seemed as excited as a boy before a festival. "It would be better not to speak about my condition in such a public area," I said. "There are ears everywhere, whether you whisper or not."

Zakir looked up, though his fingers still worked on the air as if it were a puzzle. "The art of silence is alien to him."

Bidaês shot his brother a glare before pushing his horse into a trot. "C'mon. We need to talk with grandfather and Commander Xobas."

Following close behind, I guided my stallion through the crowd.

I could feel the young bay's excitement at doing anything more than just walking, and he surged with each stride. It hammered my sore thighs, but I let myself enjoy the cool morning breeze as we wound through the clans, up to Katiôn's position.

The marzban rode alongside Xobas with his back straight and chin held high. His horse's motions were fluid as he guided it to the side and away from the crowd. I admired how well Simukie riders knew their mounts. It wasn't surprising considering their religion's sacred connection between rider and horse, but that only added to their elegance—at least when they weren't at war.

"What is it you want to speak of?" Katiôn asked. Bags had formed beneath his eyes. "If all three of you have come to me so early, then I do not expect it to be positive news."

Xobas nodded. "But if Wacław is part of the group who brings it, then it must be important."

"It is High Priestess Rasa, grandfather." Bidaês began. "She is plotting to assassinate you, Zakir, and our officers."

Katiôn's expression soured. "You should be more careful to throw such accusations around."

"Let us hear them out," Xobas said. "I believe these boys have already discussed this at length, possibly with two others I know well."

"We have," I said, trying to swallow my doubts. "Though we were skeptical of Bidaês's claim, he showed us his sparring dagger. Rasa covered its edge with Zurgowie venom that would kill both Marzban Katiôn and Zakir slowly once we passed through Kynnytsia."

"Then," Bidaês added, "she would take advantage of your death to kill the commanders loyal to you."

Xobas tightened his grip on his reins, his brow wrinkled and his teeth bared. "What have you gotten yourself into? Did you offer to help her?"

Bidaês nodded.

"Ara confirmed the venom is from the Zurgowie," Zakir said. He reached for his belt and pulled a small clay vial. "I've been working on a remedy. It's not much, but it might be enough to counter its effects."

Katiôn accepted the vial. "Now that we know of the plot, one would hope I won't need this, but thank you, Zakir. Your clever mind is ever an aid." He turned to Bidaês. "How did you convince her you truly were willing to kill me? You aren't my heir, yet you are strong-minded—not exactly who a zealot like her wants in an opposing clan."

"Strong-minded is putting it lightly," Xobas muttered. "It was a mistake to involve yourself in this plot."

"Rasa is blind," Bidaês said. "She believes me to be a child who could be manipulated as marzban. It wasn't hard to play the part she expected of me. I know I should've said something sooner, but it took some time to ensure she didn't doubt me."

Xobas sighed deeply. "This leaves us with little time if she wishes to strike so soon, but why has she waited until now?"

"Perhaps she feared Wacław would suspect her," Katiôn said. "Considering her clan's rough past with the Astiwie, it is unlikely the Zurgowie would have been allowed through their lands without his word of our agreement. To save this treaty, though, I will speak with the high priestess."

"I agree, marzban." Xobas glanced over his shoulder to the back of the convoy, where Rasa rode with her personal guard. "The Zurgowie are skilled horsemen. It would be best to avoid a battle with so few of us left."

Zakir drank a few sips of his water. "I will attempt to make more of the antidote. My supplies are few, but some is better than none."

Katiôn patted him on the shoulder. "Good. You bring honor to our bloodline with your efforts."

"When will you confront her?" Bidaês asked, puffing up his chest. "I should be there."

"No, you should not. It is your recklessness that has put us in a horrific position mere days before we were to reach the Tribe of Krowik."

Bidaês tried to defend himself, but the marzban waved away his appeals. "High Priestess Rasa has wished me dead for a decade, but

I suspect it is only because of your intervention that she considered acting. Now, whether you succeeded in killing me or not, she plans to strike the clan our family has ruled for a century. If this descends into slaughter, then it will be *your* legacy, boy."

Katiôn took a sharp breath before continuing, "I will address this with the high priestess when we have arrived in Kynnytsia. Something tells me having the Astiwie army present may be our best hope of avoiding a war. Until then, leave us. I must speak with Commander Xobas and young Wacław."

What does he want with me? For once, the problem didn't seem to be mine, yet I still found myself in the middle of a war so much bigger than me. *Just my luck.*

Zakir bowed his head. "Thank you, grandfather. Let me know if I can be of any help."

As his brother cantered away, Bidaês gritted his teeth. "You'll thank me when we reach the southern hills."

"That may be," Katiôn said, "but you have much to learn about diplomacy."

With that, Xobas raised an arm, signaling to Bidaês that it was his time to go. The elder brother turned to leave but held his gaze on me for a moment too long to be comfortable. I couldn't shake a feeling there was more to this. Feelings didn't matter in war, though—at least not according to Father.

Katiôn pursed his lips when Bidaês was out of earshot. "That boy will be my death, either by foolishness or the blade."

"All men were boys once," Xobas said. "His grit is admirable—despite his rash actions. I know some who would do well to move more quickly." He winked at me.

I knew he was just trying to make me smile, but I couldn't muster one. With an impending war between the clans, any hope of riding ahead once we reached Kynnytsia was fading fast. I *needed* to find Otylia before the end of Kwiecień.

"Wacław," Katiôn began, pulling me from my thoughts, "Xobas tells me you wish to leave our clans once we receive permission from

King Boz to cross his lands."

My shoulders slumped. "That had been my goal before Bidaês told me about High Chieftess Rasa's plan."

"I have never known you to speak anything but the truth. Tell me, how dire is this Otylia's situation?"

I looked to Xobas, but he nodded for me to continue. With a deep breath, I checked again to ensure no one was listening and moved my horse closer to Katiôn's. "She's in Nawia, stolen by a god who betrayed us. If we are going to save Dziewanna and bringing life back, we need her."

"This is… unexpected." He scratched the shaved side of his head. "I knew you had left out something before, but this is unlike anything I have known. How do you intend to retrieve this girl from this place you call the underworld?"

"Honestly, I don't know. Our hope was that Dariusz—Otylia's father and our high priest—would know a way."

"Our? Do you mean your companions, Narcyz and Ara?"

We reach the end of the cliffs, and the trail entered a scattering of trees as it descended toward Astiwie lands below. "Yes, though for such a long journey, I would like to bring Zakir as well. Otylia was the only healer we had, and without her, we could find ourselves in trouble far too quickly."

"What of Bidaês?"

I winced. The sound of hooves against stones and dirt surrounded us, dulling my thoughts. Bidaês had shown that he trusted me enough to bring the truth to Katiôn. Why did I still hesitate in giving him the same belief? "He is determined to come if Zakir does, but I'm not sure it's for the best."

"Bring him." Katiôn reached up and touched an oak branch hanging over the trail. "If this journey, and this girl, truly is the only way for life to return to the world, then you will need all the help you can. I imagine an army would cause more attention than you would like. However, Bidaês may make as much noise as a few hundred men."

"You're willing to risk the future of your people for me?" I looked from him to Xobas. Both of them had earned my respect, each in their own time, and it hurt knowing I would be leaving them behind.

He slowed his horse and patted its neck. "As a mount will do everything for its rider, I will do all I can for my clan. I have seen the Horde your gods have spoken of. I would be blind if I were not to see the death of the wilds around me. Neither you nor I completely understand what lies ahead, but you may have the power to stop it. I would be a fool not to help your cause."

I gripped Dziewanna and Mokosz's necklaces at my collar. *Maybe they are watching over me.* "I'm honored by your support and belief. If only I could find the same in myself."

"All great men have doubt," Katiôn said. "Only the terrible ones do not. As for Bidaês, you are doing me a favor by forcing him to step up and do real work. Besides, I already stole one from your group."

"No one was stolen," Xobas said, rounding Katiôn and stopping in the shade. "Shame sent me from the clan, and honor has given me a second chance."

Shame? I studied the scar on his arm. It had been a long time since I had asked about it, and the one time I did hadn't ended well. What did he have to be ashamed of?

"It is our tradition to forgive one great regret," Katiôn said to Xobas before turning to me one last time. "No matter what occurs between Rasa's clan and mine, I will ensure you begin your journey with a full stock of supplies and our freshest horses. There are some things more significant than the quarrels of man."

I stuttered, trying to find a reply, "But, my marzban, your horses have a spiritual connection with you. It would violate your beliefs for me to take them. I can't do that."

"You do not have a choice, Wacław Lubiewicz. You will take the mounts, and they will be a sign to your gods and demons alike that the Clan of Simuk stands against the darkness. Treat them well. They are yours as long as they live—to a Simuk strider, the bond between them and their rider is one of bone and blood."

With that, he nodded before urging his horse into a gallop along-side the trail, the sun shining on his head as he went.

"You chose a good man to serve," I said, smiling at Xobas.

He looked at me with pride. "I consider myself fortunate to be in the presence of the men who may save us all. After all I've done, it is more than I deserve."

15

Otylia

Forever.

IVAN'S DESCRIPTION OF DEAD SOULS LIVING BEYOND THE RIVER COMMANDED MY THOUGHTS. I was an immortal goddess. I would live forever. But what did *forever* mean?

Nightfall came by the time we reached the first cottages. No, these houses were far too large to be cottages. They were built from roots jutting from the ground or wood from the amazingly thick trees surrounding the village. Most of the homes were multi-level, and I felt the urge to rush inside and discover how they could support a second floor. Along their walls, they had slits half-a-stride wide. Patterned fabrics covered some, but others were open, revealing rooms with brightly colored furniture.

Ivan smirked, baring his teeth a little too much. "You are wondering about how the homes are built, are you not?"

"Weles is capable of quite a lot," I said, my voice slipping.

"He is a god, Lady Otylia. He is capable of far more than putting together sticks and stones."

Like drinking the blood of his priests' sacrifices? I forced away the thought. Obsessing over my disgust wouldn't get me back to Jawia, back to Wacław.

Then I stopped. Despite the dyed fabrics and elaborate homes, something was wrong. "Where is everyone?"

With a wave, he continued walking, tucking his paws behind his back. "Where do you think we are headed? Even goddesses must attend feasts—especially when they are to celebrate your first two Trials."

"A feast? My last one didn't end well..."

Ivan reached a paw out to me. "This celebration will be far better than the Drowning of Marzanna. Trust me."

"Let's go then." I slid past him, ignoring the offer. Typically, I would have avoided a gathering of so many people, but after weeks in isolation, I was willing to settle for the dead.

It wasn't long before the curling smoke became visible among the trees. A bonfire glowed a hundred strides away, higher than the tallest of men. Around it, dancers similar to those we'd seen earlier followed the beat of heavy drums and another instrument that flowed like a river. *At least they're clothed this time...*

Ivan dropped to all fours and smiled. "Come along!"

I chuckled and moved to follow, but something held me back—fear. It had been a long time since I'd mingled with such a large group. I hadn't enjoyed it before, yet the allure of talking with someone who was just a regular human was tempting. Still, the people of Dwie Rzeki had never accepted me. Why would these be any different?

A tall figure broke from the musicians. He wound through the trees, heading in my direction, and I instinctively shuffled into the shadows. In the firelight, the boy's hair was like ash and his skin unnaturally pale. A long tunic of blue, trimmed in white, draped down his body.

He drew closer, spinning a wooden flute between his fingers as he walked. His eyes wandered everywhere else, but he was coming for me. The question was why.

Stopping beneath the next tree, he played the flute. Each note brought a swift breeze through the trees as he played. I'd never heard a song like it, and while I listened, creatures scuttled through the forest, racing past me to gather at his feet. He continued to ignore me as a crowd of the animals—squirrels, mice, and birds alike—grew around him. Soon, the ground between us was covered in them.

Is he going to just stand there? I dug my heel into the dirt. I had no desire to speak to the random boy, but he had approached me, and his false ignorance of my presence was irritating at best.

Eventually, I gave up waiting. "What are you doing?" I said, harsher than I'd wanted to.

He turned to me, but the song continued. Then, he bounded into the air, floating over the crowd of animals and landing a stride from me. I made it two.

With one last note that he held far longer than necessary, he stopped playing. The animals scattered behind him, but if he noticed, he didn't care as he offered me a grin. "I could ask the same of you, Lady Otylia."

I furrowed my brow. "Who are you? And how do you know me?"

"Many know me as the fifth grandchild of Strzybóg and master of the northwest wind, but that is quite the mouthful. You may call me Kyustendil."

Grandchild of Strzybóg.

Father's legends said the god of wind had eight grandchildren who each ruled a directional wind. Wacław had claimed Cervenko, god of the east wind, helped him save me in the Lake of Reflection, but I'd never *seen* him. It was odd to meet a wind as a person. Then again, everything I'd seen for weeks had been.

"It's an honor, Kyustendil," I said, crossing my arms, "but what are you doing in Nawia?"

"Ah, little one, Ivan must have told you more than *that* by now?" When I didn't reply, he spun on his toes with a chuckle. "I may be only half-god, but my services are needed beyond just Jawia. I'm actually here right now to perform *essential* duties for Weles. However, if he hasn't told you of them, then those duties best remain secret."

I crossed my arms. "Everyone else has called him 'master.' Why don't you?"

"The winds have no master. We may assist gods and men, but we are ruled by none."

"And Master Kyustendil will assist us," Ivan said as he lumbered from the shadows, spurring another wink from the wind god. "In time."

"You still haven't told me how you know my name," I said.

Kyustendil snapped his finger and fluttered his arms. "I am the wind," he said, hovering a foot off the ground. "It would be wrong for me not to know what has been spoken, especially when it is the name of Weles's daughter."

"I thought that was supposed to be a secret…"

"There are few secrets that can be kept from the wind." He waved his flute through the air. "Besides, Weles has a special reason for this festival, and everyone here knows who you are."

Why can't he say anything directly? "If you know everything that's been said, then you have heard Marzanna's plans?"

"It is an unfortunate thing to hear so much yet understand so little," he said, dancing around a willow. When he neared me again, I shivered as a chill blew through my hair. "Marzanna protects her underlings, weak as she may be—for now."

"What do you know?" I stepped toward him, insistent. "We weakened her, but she'll return stronger. When?"

"Oho." He giggled and twirled once again. As he spun, I pondered what he'd do if I snapped that stupid flute. "You truly are like the wild goddess. I'd wondered how much you learned from her."

I sighed and pushed away my annoyance at everyone comparing me to Mother. "You didn't answer the question, *again.*"

"I believe you will find Lord Kyustendil quite fond of that," Ivan said.

"Already have," I muttered as a cheer erupted from the crowd.

Ivan followed my gaze to the dancers around the fire. "Ah yes, the ritual for the second Trial has begun. We shall join them in time, but you must first pass the Trial of Isolation."

I wrinkled my nose. *Isolation?* There were still answers I needed to force out of Kyustendil, but Ivan didn't seem to be asking.

"Go along, Lady Otylia," Kyustendil said with a bow. "There are other matters I must attend to, but I have a feeling we will speak again soon."

He leaped into the air and shot toward the treetops far above. A melody flowed behind him. *What a strange man.*

"We will indeed speak with the lord of the northwest wind again," Ivan said. "First, however, I must introduce you to Vlatka."

He led me from the crowd and into the darkness of the woods. The music faded. A chill crept over me with each step. Soon, even the moonlight failed to split the canopy.

My eyes adjusted to the darkness, but they caught little more than shadows drifting with the night breeze. Creatures rushed across the ground near my side. Strange, alien things. I studied them for a few moments before looking back to Ivan. "What are—"

The bear was gone.

I spun, reaching for Dziewanna's power. A realm away, it was nothing more than a faint whisper, and I cursed Ivan for leaving me here.

He'd called this the Trial of Isolation. Based on Weles's threats before, I would have to surrender my connection to Dziewanna and Mokosz. I felt their marks on either side of my neck as a creature made a clicking noise nearby. *Is that the entire Trial?*

The frame of a woman appeared ahead. Short with a stout frame and round cheeks, she seemed far less ominous than the shadows creeping around me. But this was Nawia. Everything was strange.

"Who are you?" I called out.

The woman smiled more joyously than I'd expected as she approached. She was no taller than my collar, and her eyes shone as she stared up at me. "I've waited a long time for this," she said before her smile faded. "Unfortunately, I'd hoped to wait longer…"

"I can relate."

She snickered and ran her hands along the sleeves of her simple brown dress. "There is so much you don't know, Otylia, but I won't trick you. Not like Weles or that idiot he calls his son. You can call me Vlatka—your mother's favorite witch."

"Witch?" I cocked my head. "But witches—"

"Channel demons?" Vlatka asked, folding her arms. "Meaningless lies created by those with a spear up their rear. It doesn't matter what I am, though. Just what you are, and what you must do."

"The first Trial. Isolation."

With a heavy sigh, she took my hand. "Weles didn't think you'd complete it with him there, but he knew Dziewanna trusted me."

I pulled myself free from her grip. "You don't call her 'lady' or him 'master' like the others."

"A witch calls no one her master." Her gaze lowered. "Nor do you use such formalities with a friend. Come, and let's get this over with."

She led me through the trees to an altar with a solitary blade upon it. "Isolation is not a positive Trial," she continued. "Channeling is needed to begin, but I cannot complete it for you."

Dziewanna's remote power lingered in my soul as I approached the altar. Mokosz was absent. I yearned to feel the flow of time in the Great Mother's rituals once more, but time, ironically, had run out. To escape and free Mother, I had to Ascend. That meant breaking my bond with both goddesses.

I clenched my fists at that thought.

Noticing my hesitation, Vlatka laid a hand on my back. I tensed. "Weles wants you to Ascend slowly," she said. "He can't control you once you've Ascended, at least not without Jaryło's help. There are those of us who would rather the pace be swift now that you're here…"

"You're defying him," I replied, brow furrowed. "Why? Is Ivan one of you? Sabina?"

The ends of her mouth curled. "Like I said, he isn't my master. But the less you know of us the better until the time is right. Weles's ears could be anywhere. For now, rid yourself of your marks to complete the first Trial. The second, Connection, awaits you after."

My heart hammered my chest. Four years before, I'd sworn to obey Dziewanna and Mokosz for my entire life, to serve them until death. An unbreakable vow—for a mortal.

But Mother didn't need a szeptucha. The tribe never had.

My hairs rose as I stepped onto the stone circle surrounding the altar. What I must do weighed heavy upon my shoulders. The fear of a younger me, clinging to her goddesses to fill the void Mother's death and Wacław's absence had caused. I *knew* I needed to grow up, become my own woman and goddess. That child within me, though, cowered at the thought of being abandoned again.

I closed my hand around the dagger's hilt, the world fading at its touch. My breaths caught, but when I looked back to Vlatka, she was gone.

Isolation.

Upon my return to Weles, I would press him more on the Trials and their meanings. Curiosity of them clashed with my childish fears as I stood there for too long, staring down at the cold iron blade. Mother would've urged me on. Father would've chided me for breaking my vow.

Did it matter? Dziewanna was trapped in Marzanna's grasp, and Dariusz was a realm away. I had leaped the flames at the Drowning of Marzanna. I was a woman, not a child whose parents decided her fate. The decision to complete the Trials was mine to face alone. I couldn't fail.

Gripping the dagger with both hands, I pressed its edge to Mokosz's Mothermark on my neck. My breaths quickened. I wished to close my eyes and let my hands guide themselves. But I held the blade still, not trembling like that weak girl who'd wept in the woods four years ago without her mother or best friend. No. Alone or not, I would be strong. For Mother. For Wašek. For myself.

I bit my cheek and sliced away the Mothermark.

Blood poured down my neck as a fire met my veins. My mind drifted, my hand wavering against the blade. The emptiness that followed was worse than any physical pain—not sensing Mokosz or her bond with earth and time itself—but I couldn't stop. Weles expected me to falter, to allow him to use me for his will. He would see no such frailty in me. Only a proud, independent goddess would greet him as I passed the Trials. Even if that strength was a lie.

Tears burned my eyes as I raised the bloodied dagger to Dziwanna's Bowmark. I would carry on. I would defy Weles. And no one would see my tears.

The blade tore flesh.

I dropped to my knees. The dagger slipped to the stone ground with a *clang* that echoed through the woods for what felt an eternity. No matter how hard I fought, the tears came regardless as I cradled myself against the altar. Alone.

"Mom?" I whispered to no reply.

I'd thought her power to be distant before, but it had been a roaring fire compared to the hollowness within my soul now. After four years of serving the goddesses, I'd grown accustomed to the noise of the wilds around me as time flowed past. Without them, only my thoughts remained. They were more frightening than anything.

Stand, I told myself. *Vlatka will see.*

With a tumult of emotions trying to drown me, I grabbed the dagger and pushed myself to my feet. The moonlight returned as I did. Dull, as if the world had lost its color. Only the blood staining my dress and dripping from the dagger's tip broke the sea of gray.

"You did it," Vlatka's cheerful voice said. "Dziewanna would be proud."

A scoff escaped my lips. I couldn't look up from the crimson pooling at my feet. There should've been so much pain from the slices along my neck, but it was smothered by something stronger, heavier.

Her approaching steps against the stone hammered my mind. "You doubt your mother would want you to pass the Trials?" she asked.

"Why did Mother trust you?" I snapped, glaring back at her. "I completed the Trial for her, but even you are hiding things from me."

"Dziewanna feared this day would come, despite all she'd done to free you from this place." She stepped closer and lowered her voice. "Do you trust the nymph? Sabina?"

I nodded.

"Good, then we will send you messages through her." With a

glance into the woods, she snatched my hand, sliding something into it. "The palace's vines obey their master, but we will tell you the truth when it is time to prepare."

"For my escape?" I asked, furrowing my brow.

Vlatka turned away with a shush. "Weles awaits you. Best not to whisper things that could ruin everything. Ivan will come for you in a few minutes. Until then, take the time to look at yourself in the mirror."

Mirror?

Before I could question her further, she slipped into the shadows. I gritted my teeth. For once, it seemed like others were on my side in Nawia. But Sabina knew little, and Vlatka, Ivan, and Kyustendil were afraid of Weles hearing. *So close to the truth, yet so far.*

I turned back to the altar, where a tall plane of glass—similar to that in my bathing room—reflected me in the moonlight. A horrific sight.

Streaks of red ran from my cut neck down the gray dress, clashing with its brown and green embroidery. Between the wounds, dagger, blood, and my unruly hair, I appeared as a demon from Father's legends. Something about that made me smirk.

I uncurled my free hand to reveal a thin sheet of white that Vlatka had given me. It had become crinkled within my fist, but the black markings of the old tongue remained visible upon it.

What is this?

The words seemed gibberish to me. Even the priests and szeptuchy who could read *some* of the old tongue knew only a fraction of it. Of that, little was written except carvings or paintings. Weles had claimed words held power. Was this odd sheet related to that?

I cursed and spun, stuffing the dagger into a slit in the belt. It was my first weapon in Nawia. Though I doubted Weles would let me keep it, it was reassuring to have the blade. If only the note were so simple.

Then it hit me. *The mirror…*

Vlatka's statement about it had been odd, but as I stared down at the note, it made sense. The words weren't unfamiliar. They were *backward.* Holding up the sheet to the glass, I examined the phrases upon it. Some of the words were new, but context provided enough clarity. When the whole thing finally formed in my mind, I gasped, slipping the sheet away as Ivan's voice came from behind me.

"Lady Otylia," the bear said, his voice airy and sweet, "the second Trial is prepared."

I barely heard him. Instead, I clutched the crumpled note to my breast as my breaths grew heavy. The mirror loomed over me now, like the truth it had revealed moments before. One that changed everything.

Mother never abandoned me…

16

Otylia

You are not alone, Lady Otylia. We are those loyal to Lady Dziewanna. Many of us were stolen from Jawia by Weles before we could ever live. In this, you are like us: bound, trapped. Yet, your mother foresaw your capture and ensured we would be ready. You deserve to be free—as do we all—and, together, we will make it so.

EVERY WORD OF THE NOTE HAD MY HEART RACING as Ivan led me toward the bonfire and the dancers around it. Against the cold void of my goddesses' absences, its heat washed over me like a powerful river. I'd lost so much in the Trial of Isolation. The next moment, Vlatka's note had revealed Mother's plan. Hope had come with it.

You always knew the answer, I silently prayed to Mother. Her bow no longer marked my skin, but I hoped she heard me in Marzanna's grasp. *I'll escape, and then I'll find you.*

Those near the fire were conducting a ritual dance I hadn't seen before. The men wore wooden masks with antlers while the women adorned bear and wolf pelts on their heads, chasing the men around the flames. The dancing women's chants surrounded us as they praised Weles and Dziewanna, calling for nature to be healed by their presence. I sensed a primal energy growing among them.

The second Trial—Connection.

I knew nothing of the other Trials besides the hints Weles's servants had offered. Isolation still had the world seeming a dull gray, but if the name of the first Trial's sister was any hint, it would be kinder. I prayed it was.

We stopped before the dancers. The ferocity of the women in the chase almost seemed *real.* They growled and darted after the men, who glanced back before scampering away. What was beneath their masks? Fear? Or a smile?

Before I could ask Ivan, someone threw a pelt over my head.

I stumbled in shock. A woman grabbed my arm and suddenly I was circling the fire with their pack. No matter how hard I fought, she held on, and my mind spun as their song swallowed my thoughts.

"Weles, lord of the earth and all beneath it, give us your strength."

"Dziewanna, queen of the wilds and beasts, flow through us like our blood."

"Otylia, lady of what will come, join us."

As we ran, the women morphed around me, transforming into the animals they wore. My consciousness changed with them, and excitement filled me at the sight of the men ahead, no more than deer and elk. They fled, yet they were helpless.

My strides were long and powerful. Each of my muscles primed for the kill. A growl tore through my throat as I leaped forward, ahead of the wolves and bears at my side. Even they were slow compared to me.

A deer stumbled. The fire reflected the fear in his eyes as blood pumped through my veins.

Kill.

It was my only desire. No, my only *need.* I was a swift fox, my fur black streaked with white, giving it an illusion of silver. I'd been hungry for days in the wilds, and it was time to feast.

I struck as the deer staggered on weak legs. Though it swung its antlers toward me, desperate to survive, I dodged them easily. My claws met flesh and my teeth tore into muscle. The thrill surged through my mind and body, unlike anything I'd felt before. This kill, this victory, was mine alone, and nothing could take it from me.

The world snapped.

My legs failed as reality swept the thrill away. I collapsed alongside the fire, panting and shaking as I tried to grasp what had just happened. Though the heat seared my skin and tears burned my eyes, I refused to move. A strange substance coated my tongue. My body felt alien, *wrong.*

What happened to me?

Laughter echoed from above. I forced myself to look at the man in the dirt beside me. He was incredibly thin with deep lines above his brow. Crimson seeped from a slice across his jugular, staining his graying beard and white tunic. His eyes were empty.

That taste…

I screamed as hands grasped me. I fought them. My fist struck a nose, my elbow a chin, but they were strong, and there were far too many. They pulled me to my feet, laughing and cheering as if I'd won a festival game. But this was no game. I'd seen the man's blood, tasted it on my lips.

I killed him.

My strength failed. I would've collapsed if there hadn't been so many arms holding me up. Voices surrounded me, but they were distant whispers. Everywhere I looked, smiles met me as the ritualists ignored the man dead just strides away. I wished it had been me instead.

"Lady Otylia has passed the Trial of Connection!" someone shouted from across the fire.

More cheers responded as the crowd carried me toward the voice. I couldn't resist. It took all the strength I had not to pass out, and when they set me down on the cool earth, I collapsed into a ball.

"There is no reason to weep, child," the voice said, standing over me now. "By becoming one with the silver fox, you have taken the next step on your journey toward Ascension."

The silver fox? I struggled for each breath as I brushed away the hair covering my face. Before me stood a man wearing a bear pelt over a mask of bone. Sharp horns jutted from the mask's top and red coated its mouth. "I don't understand," I managed to sputter.

The man knelt before me and removed his mask.

"Weles?" I spat, rage replacing my shock. "Why? What is this?"

The god smiled with pride. He had taken his older appearance again, and his gray hair and beard flowed over his deep red robes. "This festival has been conducted for every god in one form or another—the second Trial. We must join with a creature whose form we can take at our choosing. The silver fox has chosen you, as the bear chose me and the wild mare your mother. Gods can take many forms, but it is this creature that is your greatest connection."

"I killed him!" I pushed back from Weles, scrambling away until it felt like the flames would burn my back. As I did, the silver fox pelt slid from my head and dropped to the dirt between us. "You made me kill him!"

Weles shuffled forward, his steps weak without his staff. "Do you know why souls wait in Nawia?"

I scowled but shook my head. Father had spoken of Nawia as an eternal paradise, not a place where a soul could die again.

"Nawia is simply a resting place," Weles continued as he reached down to collect the fox pelt. "All non-demonic souls are immortal—god or not—and they rest here for a time, restoring their *żityje* before they are reborn in Jawia. When they are ready, first, they must choose to leave this body behind and forget their last life." He stopped be fore me. "Do you understand now?"

His words made sense, but the taste of blood lingered on my tongue. Every time I pictured his corpse, I started shaking again. "He volunteered to die?"

"To be reborn, child." With a heavy sigh, he held a hand out toward me. "Come, and let us watch."

Why must the underworld be nothing but mystery? I steadied my breathing as he helped me stand. My legs wavered and my heart ached for Dziewanna's presence. I gripped his arm while the women gathered around us, taking the pelt of the silver fox and placing it on my head again. I cringed at its touch. How was I supposed to bond with something that had already horrified me?

I hated the ritualists' joy. Maybe after years in Nawia, a death leading to rebirth was exciting, but the lies around the ritual disgusted me. Ivan claimed to be a friend yet had led me here to kill. He'd said this would be better than the Drowning of Marzanna. All I felt was fear and disdain.

Weles approached the flames with me at his side. Sweat already coated my skin from the shock, but now the heat was enough to make me dizzy.

"This ritual is a special one," he began. "While many men may choose to return to the lands of Jawia and leave behind all they knew, few receive the chance to do so with their memories and in the form of their choosing." He smiled widely at me. "This is the gift Lady Otylia has given to Illya by allowing us to put his body to rest."

With a nod to a group of men, he stepped back. The men carried Illya's body to the fire and placed it within, but I did not wince at the smell of burning flesh. Not after I'd watched Mother's body turn to ash as I wept, heaped the corpses of twenty of our warriors into the fire at Bustelintin, and lost my bond to my goddesses. No, I wouldn't weep. Death, and releasing souls with fire, had become too familiar to me.

Yet still I trembled.

Weles spoke as if I had given this man a gift. But as I watched the heat sear his skin and muscle, I regretted it. If these terrible Trials were the first steps to my Ascension, what would come next? How could it be worse than murder and surrendering all I'd known?

"Reach into the flames," Weles whispered, placing a hand on my shoulder. "Then call forth his soul in the tongue of the gods."

My eyes widened. "You want me to stick my hand in the fire?"

"It is part of the Trial. Show them you are a goddess—not afraid of fire or death."

I failed half of that… I took a sharp breath and lumbered forward, forcing my legs to hold me. The heat scorched my skin, but still I pushed on. I told myself the pain was nothing compared to the torture I'd faced trying to escape Weles the first time. This was my only hope of finding a way out—my only chance to save Mother and see Wacław again. Pain would not stop me.

I reached the edge of the fire itself. The blaze rushed over me, and I bit my cheek to stop myself from screaming.

Keep going.

I stepped into the fire, reaching into its heart as agony clutched every inch of me. My eyes burned. My skin charred. My fingers quivered.

Every word sounded faint as I spoke the words in the old tongue, "Rise, Illya, and claim your new life."

Žityje flooded from my veins. I gasped with what little energy I had left swirling into the flames. A white wisp floated above as I dropped to my knees.

Before me, the mist became a figure. I coughed and clutched my body, wheezing with every breath. *I'm going to die. Is that the point?*

With a swift bow, Illya flew upward until a nightjar swooped from the trees. They joined in an instant. Then, the bird sang its rapid call as it dove and landed on my shoulder.

The pain faded. Air rushed into my lungs, and I found my breath as the nightjar pecked at my ear. *Thank the gods, it's over.* I rose, stumbling more than striding like a goddess from the flames. The crowd backed away. Awe covered their faces, and they whispered among themselves as I stood in the center of their circle—alive.

Weles held his chin high and stepped to me. "Otylia, first daughter of Weles, chosen of Dziewanna, you have passed the second Trial of Ascension. From this day forward you shall bear the name 'Otylia Welesiakówna, the Silver Fox of Nawia.' " He waved the bird on. "Go forth, Illya, and live spreading word of the goddess who gave you a second chance."

Part 2
Life & Death

17

Wacław

What could Xobas have done to carry such shame?

XOBAS RODE AHEAD WITH KATIÔN as I rejoined Ara and Narcyz amid the rest of the crowd. We weren't far from the outskirts of Kynnytsia, yet we'd seen no evidence of Astiwie warriors guarding the path. Considering they had heard the clans' warnings of the Horde's advance, I found that odd. Not that Father had ever thought me much of a strategist.

"What if we missed something?" Ara asked. She'd gripped her bow for the last four hours, probably expecting the Astiwie to be combative if they showed.

"If Marzanna's cultists razed Bustelintin," I said, "then who knows what else they could have done? She *is* the goddess of death."

Memories of the raid still haunted me. Whenever I wasn't picturing Otylia and Kuba's deaths, I saw my first kills over and over. Who had I become in the moon since? We'd lost nearly twenty people that day, and the cultists had slaughtered so many more before we'd arrived. It was hard to remember sometimes that Marzanna, not Jaryło, was the real threat we faced. Jaryło had taken Otylia from me, but Marzanna wished to take everything.

Narcyz smirked. "We've got two armies now. Doubt her cultists would stand any chance against the clans."

"Especially if they couldn't even best you," Ara quipped.

Narcyz's jaw hung open, but before he could jab back, a clamor came from ahead. Shouting and the clanking of shields against swords split through the trees. I willed myself to rush toward the noise. Instead, I froze, just like when the chały had swarmed me. A force gripped my chest, making each breath a battle as I remembered watching Marzanna's cultists slaughter other boys at Bustelintin. Was it happening again?

"Wacław!" Ara yelled as she drew her bow. "C'mon, we need you if the Astiwie are going to believe the agreement with the Krowikie."

I shut my eyes for a moment, enduring the torment of sorrow and fear. *Only you can stop this.*

"Wacław!"

When I looked to Ara again, I clenched my jaw and slowly nodded. I would mourn when the clans were safe, when Otylia was safe. But those memories… They were suffocating. How could I speak to King Boz of the Astiwie when I was the reason our own high chief, his brother-in-law, was dead? How could I pretend nothing had happened?

My head was still in a daze, but I finally managed to push my horse into a canter, following Ara as she weaved through the gathered crowds and knocked more than one inattentive observer to the ground.

Amid the chaos at the front, Xobas's head stuck above the rest on his mount as he forced the people back. A gap formed between the clan members and their leaders, who stared down at a line of two-dozen warriors clad in Astiwie blue tunics. Between them lay six bleeding corpses: three dressed in Zurgowie green, two in Simukie tan, and an Astiw with an arrow through his skull.

My heart sunk as I stopped beside Xobas and took a shaky breath. "Gods, what happened?"

He furrowed his brow. "There was a clash. We explained why we're here, but they won't allow us to pass without proof of an agreement with the Krowikie. Some idiots rushed them anyway." He waved his arm toward the dead. "This was the result."

"Not a good start." *I could've prevented this.* If I hadn't waited… "I have to explain who I am. They'll listen to Jacek's son."

"Wait." He nodded ahead.

A young man with almond hair and a blue tunic embroidered with gold approached Katiôn. He bowed his head to the dead for a moment before glancing up at the mounted clansmen. The wrinkle in his brow exposed his worry as his blue cloak flapped behind him, woven with the kalina emblem of the Astiwie. White petals and red berries. The flower represented purity and bloodlines—what Father had claimed the Astiwie valued above all else.

I recognize him.

Katiôn dismounted and handed off his blade to his guard before giving the Astiw the traditional Simukie greeting—two fingers touching the nose, then extended toward the other person. "There should be no bloodshed between us. Let us all lower our weapons." He nodded to Xobas, who ordered the Simukie archers to lower their bows.

Rasa remained on her horse, scowling. At her side, Zhaleh extended her arm with her golden eagle perched upon it. Her other arm was held high with an open hand, the signal for their own archers to be ready.

Nodding to both the high priestess and marzban, the Astiw raised his voice so that the crowd could hear, "I am Commander Andrij Myroslavovych Yakymchuk, and I am here under the orders of King Boz Vladyslavovych Kramarenko of the Tribe of Astiw."

Andrij… The messenger! He was the Astiwie messenger at the Drowning of Marzanna.

Andrij held his hands behind his back and scanned the crowd. "The king has commanded that our lands be closed to all travelers from the east. I'm sorry, but too many have died already. You must go back where you came from. You are not welcome here."

I studied Andrij. He was young for such a position, and his demeanor wasn't that of a confident leader. Xobas ordered with authority. Andrij seemed to be trying to convince himself of his orders. *How did he rise from messenger to commander so quickly?*

When Andrij finished, he raised a hand, and the sound of stomping boots echoed around us. Xobas cursed as I spotted them among the trees. "More archers," I whispered, my voice catching in my throat. "A hundred of them at least. From the look of it, they've got us surrounded."

"Hmm," he grumbled, spinning with his horse to watch every side of the Astiwie advance. "Your father will have returned this Andrij with instructions to allow the clans through. Either Boz has ignored High Chief Jacek, or he has received word of his death."

"Or Boz has had enough of easterners coming through his lands." I swallowed. "From what Father told me, he isn't exactly the most accepting man."

The unarmed crowd stirred as they realized what was happening. Women clutched their children as warriors from both clans formed a defensive circle around them.

Rasa watched her clan's fear with a stern gaze. "You fools!" she hissed at the Astiwie. "May Otlezd strike you down so that you drown in Alunam's eternal sands."

Katiôn held up his hands, attempting to appear non-threatening as he stepped toward the Astiwie warriors. "We mean you and your people no harm," he said. "Wacław, second son of High Chief Jacek of the Tribe of Krowik, is with us. He can speak for the legitimacy of our agreement."

Xobas nodded, and Commander Andrij watched me as I took a deep breath and guided my horse into the opening. I felt the eyes of thousands upon me. With women weeping and men shouting to the Astiwie archers, my shoulders were heavy with the weight of both the clans and Astiw's fates. *This can't come to war.*

"The marzban speaks the truth," I declared as firmly as I could. "You saw me in Dwie Rzeki, commander. I am Jacek's second-born, and I represented my father's wishes in negotiations with the clans. They shall have the southern hills for their assistance in our war against the Kingdom of Solga. If King Boz refuses to allow passage for these people, he will find three armies united against him."

Andrij gripped his spear, but his voice quivered. "You speak the truth—I know this—but this isn't my choice to make. The king does not respond well to threats."

I rode to Katiôn's side, forming a line between him, Rasa, and me. My words weren't enough. They had to understand the true force they faced, even if there would likely be no third army. The Krowikie warriors were occupied in the west, and I doubted Mikołaj would send them here if the Astiwie refused. If there was any hope for victory against the Solga, my half-brother needed the clans' help, but he wouldn't sacrifice his own men to ensure they arrived. He wasn't that brave.

But the Astiwie didn't know that.

"I speak no threats, commander," I said, dismounting. "I believe a threat would be surrounding thousands of unarmed refugees, but I know neither of us wants more unnecessary bloodshed. Tell them to place their arrows back in their quivers."

He nodded to me but remained silent.

Rasa spat as Katiôn and I exchanged glances. There was respect in the marzban's gaze as he mouthed, "Go alone."

My breaths caught, but I knew he was right. There was no way we'd make it through unless I talked with Boz. If only I had any idea how to convince him…

I gripped Mokosz's amulet at my chest, asking the Great Mother for protection. Each moment wasted was another Otylia languished in Nawia, but this was my duty. I had brought the clans this far. It was my responsibility to help the clans reach Krowikie lands, even if we lost precious days doing so. *I'm sorry Otylka.*

I stopped before Andrij and nodded toward Kynnytsia in the distance. "If you will not let us pass, then take me to King Boz. There must be an agreement we can reach."

"The boy does not have the power to speak for my clan," Rasa interrupted. She rode forward and pressed her fingers to an amulet of a winged woman at her chest. "By Teṇpa Āymaya, these lands have been gifted to us, and as High Priestess of the Zurgowie, I will see my people to them or perish trying."

She's going to start a war. Katiôn eyed her as she stopped before the Astiwie warriors, but she had spoken. It was up to Andrij now.

The commander flipped back his cloak and walked warily to Rasa, still keeping his distance. "I have heard stories of the horrors you inflict upon your enemies, high priestess," he began, "and I, for one, do not wish to be counted among them." He shook his head to himself as he looked from the ground to the crowd. "Marzban Katiôn, High Priestess Rasa, and Wacław, son of Jacek, may see King Boz. The rest of your people must remain here until he decides what to do with you all."

Katiôn bowed. "May the spirit of the horse bless you, Commander Andrij, for you have saved many lives this day."

Andrij sighed and pushed the rogue hairs from his face. "I wouldn't thank me yet, Marzban. You have yet to meet the king."

Homesickness struck me the moment the trail down gave way to the farms and cottages of Kynnytsia. It was all too familiar. Though their homes had only two walls—one in the front and back with their thatched roofs running all the way to the ground on the sides—the similarities were enough to make me dream of Dwie Rzeki.

In each field we passed, I saw Mom tilling the soil in preparation for the planting. In each doorway, I saw her smiling as I returned from exploring the woods. And in each bed of trees between farms, I saw little Wašek and Otylka, running and laughing as if there were no cares in the world.

Gods, I miss it.

We would reach Dwie Rzeki soon. I would see Mom and Nevenka once again, and then, I would save Otylia. If I was being honest, though, I had made no progress on how to reach Nawia. Even Cervenko hadn't known, and we'd found no other answers—not that there had been much to find in the Narrow Pass. Relying on Dariusz was a foolish hope, but it was all I had.

Rasa rode her bay horse directly behind Commander Andrij as

Katiôn and I fell in behind, neither of us willing to get in the high priestess's way. By interfering with my offer to go alone, she'd jeopardized everything. Yet, the gamble had succeeded.

That changed nothing about her plot.

Bidaês had said the Zurgowie would strike only once we left the Astiwie capital, but I was determined to keep on my toes. Dealing with the Astiwie hating the clans was enough. If things devolved into chaos now, all three of our tribe's allies would be killing each other while the Horde drew closer. I couldn't let that happen.

Before we could address a hundred years of clan rivalry, though, we first needed to face the king of the Astiwie. The man was the brother of High Chieftess Natasza, Father's widow. He wasn't my uncle, but a part of me clung to the slim chance he didn't know that. It was all the hope I had as dread entrapped my chest.

The trail ended with the trees. Here, more buildings encircled a large circular house. From the rancid smell, a tanner was to the west. *Odd to build it upwind.*

I held my breath as we continued on. Smoke rose from a stone furnace to our right, where a man guided a sword into the flames. I watched as he yanked the blade and swiftly grabbed a hammer, cracking its head onto the red-hot metal. The clanging rang through the village. *Narcyz would have loved to see that slice of home.* Only I seemed to notice the ironsmith, however, and the others were nearly at the hilltop by the time I trotted after them.

A pair of wooden doors marked the home's entry. As we dismounted, Andrij nodded to the two spearmen guarding the doors and pushed, revealing a narrow hall lined with bear pelts upon the floor.

I trailed Katiôn and Rasa. Boz would need my word to confirm the clan warlords' stories, but alongside them, I felt insignificant. They had been chosen to lead their people. I was just a discarded son with a power no one knew of. I didn't even *want* to lead.

We reached a circular room, where more bear pelts covered the dirt floor. An elaborate throne made of bone sat in the room's center, scattered carvings etched across its back and armrests. Along the back wall hung a massive gray and purple weave with a pattern similar to what I imagined dragon scales to be. It spanned ceiling to floor and stretched across the entire rear of the room, at least twenty strides long. I couldn't help but stare at the intricacy of its design. *It almost seems real.*

Footsteps brought me back from my thoughts. A clean-shaven man who appeared barely before his fortieth year entered from a hall to our left. He wore a fur-lined blue cloak embroidered in gold—bearing the Astiwie kalina symbol—and a crown of scales the same color as the tapestry.

My eyes widened. *Those are actual scales… The aspid. The tales of the demonic beast in the mountains were real. And they slayed it.*

As Boz paraded along with a girl, no older than my little half-sister Nevenka, I wondered what den we had walked into. *Bears. Dragons. What else is this man capable of killing?* Based on Andrij's warnings, I didn't want to know.

The king sat on the throne as the girl scampered down the third and final hall. For a minute, he studied each of us, and when he turned to me, I forced myself not to break my gaze from his thin, sharp face. It seemed like hours that he watched me, silent.

Then he smiled.

"In my years," the king said with a proud and powerful voice, "I have seen many things, but I never expected to meet the bastard child of Jacek."

Bastard. That word struck me like one of Father's blows. I tried to reply, but the words wouldn't come. The boys in Dwie Rzeki had mocked me for years, yet they'd never dared to call me that—never dared to label Mom as a mere mistress. Boz had spoken only one sentence. My throat burned already with the demon's rage. *Don't give him a reason to fight.*

"So you *do* know your place," he continued, cackling at my silence. "That's wonderful, because I feared you might try to walk into my home and pretend you mattered. Well, fear is the wrong word. Wouldn't you say, Andrij?"

Andrij clenched his jaw just long enough to be noticeable. When he replied, his voice was far more timid than before, "We fear no one, my king."

"Indeed we do not!" Boz exclaimed, smacking his fist against the throne's bone armrest and standing. A crazed look crossed his eyes as he paced in the space between us. "We are the Tribe of Astiw, rulers of the forgotten lands between west and east. We hold the Narrow Pass, skewering dragons and raiders alike while Jacek feasts on the Krowik River and grows fat."

He spun toward Andrij, his cloak sweeping behind his advance. "And despite all this, my own commander defies my instructions *again* and brings these easterners here along with a bastard! I told you to turn them away or kill them, not allow them to ride into our village as if it were their own."

Andrij shuffled back, falling into the wood wall. "I apologize, my king. They—"

Boz lunged. A knife flashed in his hand as he grabbed Andrij by the throat and held the blade's point to his heart.

He's insane! I reached for the Thunderstone dagger with one hand and instinctively tried to wield the winds with the other. In my physical body, though, they didn't answer.

Ahead, Rasa prayed under her breath while Katiôn stepped forward. "King Boz," he pled, "I ask that you not punish your commander for avoiding bloodshed."

I slipped around him as Boz glared at Andrij through heavy breaths. The dagger's cool metal hummed against my forearm, hidden beneath my sleeve. Though there were guards in the room, if it came to it, I needed to be ready to fight—not that I planned to.

"We forced him to bring us," I said, my breaths shallow and my voice raspy. *If this is a trap, Andrij is our only way out of this. He needs to live.* "But the commander left our people surrounded by your warriors, at your mercy. I am here to prove Krowik's alliance with the clans. It matters not who my mother is, only that my father sent me to help bring peace."

"Jacek's word means nothing!" Boz snapped. He studied my approach and flicked his tongue across his lips. "Don't think I can't see that dagger, boy. You stalk me like Weles, sending his beasts to scour my lands."

Weles?

Slowly, I raised the dagger and returned it to its sheath. "I have no desire to hurt you, only to talk without blades to each other's hearts."

He laughed. "The bastard thinks he knows how I should order my men." His hand tightened around Andrij's throat before he lifted the commander and threw him into the wall. Andrij's skull crashed against the wood, and blood seeped from his temple as he slipped to the dirt.

"This is madness…" Katiôn muttered, shuddering as I tore a strip of fabric from my sleeve to cover Andrij's wound.

"Madness?" Boz strutted to his throne and sat with his legs crossed. "No, marzban. Madness would be willingly walking into your enemy's lands with your cock hanging out."

Katiôn sighed. "Our people have never had quarrels with your own!"

"Perhaps *yours* did not, but what about the high priestess?" Boz leaned forward, spinning the knife between his fingers. "What does Rasa have to say for her slaughters of my people?"

As Katiôn glared back at Rasa, Andrij's hand closed around my arm. "He's going to kill you," he whispered, gasping for each breath. "Run. Leave me and save your people."

"I can't. The clans are surrounded."

He squeezed harder. "Tell them Boz finally finished me. They'll back down."

I shook my head. "Enough have died. We have a potion-maker who might be able to help you."

"Yes, Katiôn," Boz said, oblivious to our conversation, "the Zurgowie have been raiding our villages for years. And here their leader is, in my hall."

The king smirked across the room. He surely expected Katiôn to be surprised by Rasa's actions, but Boz didn't realize the marzban knew of her lies.

Katiôn sighed but stood tall with his arms held behind him. "It is not unexpected that High Priestess Rasa would act in such a way. She has clashed with my own clan for years, yet I had been led to believe she had changed her ways." He glanced over his shoulder at Rasa. "Bidaês told me of your assassination plans, High Priestess."

"My what?" Rasa sneered. "I have no such plot, nor would I gain anything from instructing raids on Astiwie villages. This man is of Alunam. He is a devil!"

"I do not know what sways the king's mind," Katiôn said, "but I am far too familiar with what you are capable of. That is enough."

A shadow seemed to hang over Boz's face as he rubbed his thumb across his fingers. *We need to get out of here! But how?*

Boz whistled, and six guards armed with swords swarmed Rasa. She scrambled away. The guards were faster. As she kicked and called to her gods, Boz rose and approached Katiôn, never blinking. "Give me the high priestess and you may pass. Resist, and I shall slaughter every man, woman, and child in your clan just as I did the ferocious aspid."

He spun, pointing his blade at me. "And *you*, bastard. Tell Jacek I hope he's enjoyed my sister. I have been quite fond of her absence."

Tell him in Nawia, lunatic. The demon in me snarled, and fear of what either it or Boz would do pushed me into action. "What of the Zurgowie innocents?" I asked, as I helped Andrij up. "They aren't the ones who raided your lands."

"No… No they aren't." He paused with the knife's tip to his lip. With another sweep of his cape, he marched to Rasa, his voice mocking. "The bastard makes a fine point, does he not, *High Priestess*? Maybe, I should just kill the men—and the boys who could grow to avenge their fathers. Yes… yes…"

Katiôn stammered, "That would not—"

"I will carry out your orders," Andrij interrupted, standing under his own power now. I tensed at his side, but as Boz grinned and looked back at Rasa, the commander whispered to me, "The warriors in the hills are mine. Trust me, and maybe we'll both make it out of this alive and much better off."

Taking a heavy breath, I nodded. *Why do I trust him?* Andrij had appeared meek in front of the clans, but I saw how he despised Boz. Based on the fragile balance of power among the triad before us, we could use that.

Katiôn eyed Andrij before trying to speak again. This time, I stopped him. "I believe this is for the best, Marzban." His eyes widened, but I shuffled toward him with Andrij, not breaking his gaze. "Our people will be safe and Rasa's scheme foiled. Together, *all* of us can continue on without worry once she is gone."

Please understand.

He hesitated, and in the gap, Rasa cursed my name, "I was wrong about you, child! You are nothing but a coward!"

I thought of the praise she'd given me, of the amulet to her god that she'd offered as a sign of trust, but none of that mattered. Peace between the clans was our only hope of reaching Krowikie lands and facing the Solgawi. She'd threatened that. She'd threatened Katiôn. Now, she would suffer for her sins. We all would.

"Very well," Katiôn mumbled, averting his gaze as Boz smirked and waved the guards away.

With a bow, they dragged the screaming high priestess out the door. Doubt beset me watching her go, but there was nothing I could do—even if I wanted to save her. Crazed as he may have been, Boz had made it clear the choice was the Simukie clan or Rasa.

Boz slid his knife into a hidden sheath beneath his cloak. "Commander Andrij, take these two back to their people. If they run, kill them. If they warn the Zurgowie, kill them. And if any of the Simukie try to stop your men, kill the Zurgowie women too."

Andrij bowed. "Yes, my king."

He led me to Katiôn, whose eye twitched as he watched Boz return to his throne. I would've done the same, but after what I'd seen in the Mangled Woods, Boz was just another demon—whether he had the soul of one or not. Luckily, demons were my specialty.

"We will get through this," I told Katiôn as I took his arm, my demonic rage pushing me on. "I promise you."

Following slowly behind, his breaths were fleeting. "There is evil at work here far worse than anything the high priestess was capable of."

We emerged into the daylight, and though Andrij limped, he walked with a purpose. He turned when we were out of earshot of the guards, his voice sharp. "You have not seen the least of it, Marzban. King Boz is a tyrant who has cursed our lands for too long, but with your help, we can end his reign."

18

Wacław

I have a terrible feeling about this.

UPON OUR RETURN TO THE CLANS, Katiôn and Andrij gathered the commanders among the trees, away from any curious ears. Bidaês and Zakir were present as well. The elder brother paced as we recounted our experience with Boz.

It seemed a dream—more a nightmare. Things had changed so quickly. Now, we had no choice left but to defeat the Astiwie king to reach Krowikic lands. Without the demon's passion driving me on, I felt lost, deflated. *Have I failed them too?*

As promised, Andrij had ordered his men not to threaten or harm any members of the clans. They kept their positions for now, though, in case any warriors loyal to Boz came to investigate. It wasn't perfect, but we at least didn't need to worry about archers from either side accidentally shooting at each other.

Xobas studied Andrij when we finished telling the story. "You intend to dethrone King Boz," he said, his tone flat.

"Yes." Andrij crossed his arms, appearing more confident than before, despite the gauze wrapped around his head. "While I have no intentions of ruling myself, Boz has been choking our tribe for too long now, and he's failed to uphold his promises to me. This is the perfect time to strike, as your armies combined with my warriors would be enough to defeat the garrison here. And that's before you consider the men who will defect when they hear."

"No one must hear," Xobas insisted. "If word reaches Boz of an insurrection, he will flee. We cannot allow this to become an extended conflict."

Katiôn held up his arms. "That is if we wish to attack the king at all."

"We have little choice," Zhaleh said, that eagle perched upon her arm. Like Rasa, she wore green robes with a golden sun woven onto the chest, and she'd shown no hesitation in taking the high priestess's place. "This king will attack *us* if we attempt to pass, and allowing Commander Andrij to slaughter our people is unacceptable. The best option is to take Kynnytsia, free the high priestess, and leave the Astiwie to squabble for the throne."

A sudden panic struck my chest, and I staggered into a tree, gasping for air. *What's wrong Otylia?* Her heart was racing. Then, I tasted blood.

"I see no reason not to strike as early as possible," Bidaês said. "Tonight even." He glanced at me. "Wacław, you look as if you've seen a ghost."

I definitely felt one. The panic lingered, but I took a deep breath and straightened my posture. Unfortunately, that didn't stop the throbbing of my Frostmark—which had flared up again. "It's nothing… I agree with you both. Though I'm not one to march to war, I don't think we have much of a choice unless we want to turn back and face the Horde. A quick strike will also prevent the deaths of our innocents and theirs."

Katiôn's lips drew in a thin line. "It seems we are trapped between an army and a tyrant. Very well, I shall support the attack."

The others continued to discuss plans as I sat at the base of an aspen and tried to steady my thoughts. My own worries joined with Otylia's. Within them, that unmistakable taste of blood spurred on my demonic soul…

I drew the Thunderstone dagger, running my finger along its

sharp edge. *I'll kill Weles if I have to. Anything to get her back.* My impatience grew with each day, but the only way west was through Astiwie lands. We would deal with Boz, address Rasa's schemes, and then I could finally ride for Dwie Rzeki. *If only it were so simple.*

"We have a plan of attack, then," Xobas said. "We strike at night and encircle them with our riders. They should surrender swiftly."

"Boz will become suspicious if we just wait here," I replied.

Katiôn held out his hands. "Any suggestions are helpful."

I furrowed my brow and3 65432studied the slope down to Kynnytsia. "The Zurgowie warriors should pull back to the mountains during the daylight. That'll allow Andrij time to convince Boz his orders were followed. Hopefully Boz will let down his guard, and once darkness falls, their cavalry can descend under cover of the trees and meet us here with Andrij's men."

Zhaleh shrugged. "I have no problem with this, but Boz only believes our men to be a threat. We'll leave our female riders here. We are allied for now. That does not mean I trust Simukie men with our unarmed people."

"I do not see why you distrust us when you have been the aggressors," Katiôn said. "My concern is not important, now, though. King Boz only asked for your men to be killed, so it should not be a problem if your women stay."

Xobas nodded. "Then it's settled. Prepare your warriors."

As the group dispersed, I stayed beneath the tree, allowing Otylia's emotions to wash over my own. I felt her hatred of Weles, her desperation to escape, and her loneliness. My heart ached knowing her suffering. But it was all I had of her, so if she hurt, I would too. At least then she wouldn't be completely alone.

Footsteps approached from behind. "You all right?" Ara asked as she and Narcyz crouched alongside me.

"That bad, huh?" I asked, faking a laugh.

"You never look good," Narcyz quipped, "but right now you look like someone killed that horse of yours."

Oh Tanek. I missed him. "A zmora tried. That didn't end well for it." Resentment against Marzanna, Father, and Mikołaj had ignited my connection to the winds as a płanetnik that night. That anger lurking in my demonic soul was powerful. A key to something I could never wield alone. Even now, its hunger bore into me, but I denied it, clinging instead to my sorrow and Otylia's pain.

Ara sat next to me and punched my arm. "So, tell me what's actually bothering you."

"Ow." I rubbed my arm. "Hitting me isn't the best way to get information, you know."

"I thought that was how you boys interact?" She smirked before adjusting her archery bracer. "Seriously, is it Otylia, or does it have to do with the rumors that we're about to attack King Boz?"

My head pounded. I held it in my hands, closing my eyes. "It's both, but Otylia's panicked and scared. I feel all of it. Weles has her doing something, and she hates him for it." I sighed. "Whatever it is, I don't think it's good. I taste blood, and she's never been this afraid before… not since our connection."

Ara pulled her hunting knife from its sheath on her thigh. For a second, she stared at her reflection in the blade before driving it into the ground. "Alunam!" she spat. "Weles must be the devil."

"We'll get her back," Narcyz said as he rose. "I was wrong about the gods being distant, and I was wrong about her. But one thing I know is that we're doing what's best. Helping these clans and fighting Marzanna—it feels right."

"You hated my people at one time," Ara said, smirking.

He huffed. "Yeah, and I hated both of you too. Either I got stupid or soft, you pick."

Ara chuckled and turned to me again. "Otylia's tough. If she's that worried, then we need to hurry, but obviously we're stuck right now." She grabbed her knife again. "There's no other clues in your connection? No obvious way for us to get to Nawia that doesn't involve riding through another warzone?"

I shook my head.

"Your gods suck."

"At least ours exist," Narcyz quipped, still pacing. "If your gods are anything like Rasa, then we're all better off if they don't."

Ara pulled in her legs. "Mother said things weren't bad before Rasa, but all I knew with the clan was war. It was exciting to be on the move all the time, exploring the steppe. The fear of an army swooping down upon us was the opposite."

"Well," I said, "Rasa is imprisoned by Boz right now, if that makes you feel any better."

A smile crossed her face. "It does. Though, I doubt he'll get the chance to kill her before we kill him."

"She was really that bad?" Narcyz asked.

Ara nodded. "Anyone who didn't follow our faith is the enemy to her, but she wouldn't allow anyone to go to other clans and convince them our gods were real. People starved. She claims to have honor for allowing women to join her armies, but that's just because so many of our men were dead. The boys told stories of her orders to kill children and unarmed women for no reason."

"Oh…"

"Get it now?"

I leaned my head back against the tree. "And now we're bringing her into our lands. Maybe I was wrong."

"Chief Mieczysław would've walked our army into a slaughter," Narcyz replied. "I used to agree with him, but if Otylia and the other diviners were right about the Solgawi numbers, we're doomed without the clans' cavalry."

"We might be doomed anyway if we're unprepared for the Horde."

He scoffed. "When did you become such a downer?"

"When a witch killed my best friend and a god stole the girl I love," I snapped. "Optimism is a luxury when everyone you know is dying around you."

He winced. "I didn't mean it like that."

"I know." I clenched and unclenched my fists, trying to release the tension in my core. The demon's anger molded with my passions, and it was becoming harder to tell them apart. "It's just that I can't help feeling trapped. I want to find her more than anything, but I can't leave the clans until we're in Krowikie lands."

Ara stood and slid her knife into its sheath. "Then we'll beat Boz fast. Is it true that we're striking tonight?"

"It is."

She smiled. Though I knew it was only to cheer me up, it helped. "Then soon, we'll ride free," she said. "We *will* rescue her, but first, let's rescue the clans."

The moon hung full in the sky. I knelt in my soul-form with Ara, Narcyz, and Zakir among the trees, waiting for the Zurgowie to arrive for our attack on Kynnytsia. My body lay within a cluster of rocks a few hundred strides up the slope—far enough from the impending battle to hopefully be safe.

I chose to remain invisible to all but Xobas, Katiôn, and my three companions. On the off chance anyone asked for me, one of them could vouch for my location, or, in the worst case, I could appear and hope the moonlight wasn't enough to make me appear *that* different. It was a risk, but I had seen the aspid Boz claimed to have killed. He may have been hiding sorcery of some kind from us. If he was, I needed to be ready.

Around us, Xobas rode about, relaying orders to his men. Andrij had done the same on foot before disappearing up the slope. His archers and spearmen would sneak through the trees to Kynnytsia's western gate while the cavalry charged the eastern one like madmen.

Though his information was imprecise, Andrij estimated Boz wouldn't be able to muster more than three hundred warriors for the fight in time. Between Andrij's hundred-or-so and the clans' riders, we had at least four times that number, which meant our quick strike should ensure neither side would suffer too many losses. The plan counted on Boz surrendering when he realized all hope was lost. I found that unlikely.

"What's taking them so long?" Narcyz muttered, rubbing his hands together to keep warm.

"I don't know," I said. "Zhaleh rode to them half-an-hour ago.

She should've been back by now." I called the winds, but they found nothing. The Zurgowie must've gone further up the trail than we'd expected.

Ara peered toward our camp. Even in the moonlight, there was little to see but trees and cliffs. "Speaking of people gone missing, where is Bidaês?"

"I haven't seen him since our meeting earlier," I said. "Zakir, any idea?"

He shrugged.

Well said. "Maybe he's with Katiôn."

"Or maybe he wimped out on us." Narcyz snickered.

The ground shook as the sound of a stampede approached from above. Ara and I exchanged looks as I shot to my feet and slid Kwiecień free. "They're coming too fast!" I said. "Stay here, I'll figure out what's going on."

Ara shouted an objection, but I was already in the air, lifted by the western wind.

I swooped over the trees, enjoying the chilled breeze sliding through my hair and cloak for a moment before turning my attention below. It was difficult to see in the dark, but then I spotted the Zurgowie cavalry galloping through the trees with no order. Screams pierced the air.

"Ambush!" someone cried.

Smoke rose from our flanks as the Zurgowie cavalry rushed past. My chest tightened as I dropped back to my friends. One of the blazes was near where I'd hidden my body, but the sounds of battle echoed around me. *Survive first.*

Searching for each breath, I could only watch our plan unravel. Arrows flew from below and struck the trees around us. Torches illuminated the attackers in Astiwie blue as they charged, far outnumbering our group.

"Take cover!" Ara grabbed my arm and yanked me behind a tree just before an arrow flew through where I'd been standing. She scowled and nocked an arrow of her own. "What were you doing?"

"I've seen that look," Narcyz replied when I didn't, taking cover behind his shield. "Wacław's got battle sickness. Gets your nerves."

I pulled Kwiecień, trying to shake that paralyzing fear. "I'll be okay." But Narcyz was right. It consumed every part of me ahead of battle, right when I needed my focus the most. Though the demon within me yearned to burst forth, I couldn't let it free. Hesitation was far better than whatever wrath it would bring.

Ara aimed her bow down the hill and loosed an arrow as Zakir hid beside us, clutching some type of clay jar. "Wonderful," she muttered before sending another arrow into the head of a figure fifty strides away. "Somehow, the Astiwie knew we were coming. They've got us surrounded."

"I bet that stupid commander did this," Narcyz snapped before rushing forward as three Astiwie spearmen arrived.

I followed, but with my invisibility, they focused entirely on Narcyz, making the kills far too easy. Instinct guided Kwiecień through the first's throat and the Thunderstone dagger into the second's gut. The demon hummed in pleasure as Narcyz readied his spear to finish the third. Instead, Ara sent an arrow through his heart.

Narcyz shot her a glare. "Hey, that was my kill!"

She shook her head and ignored his outburst. "Andrij was with some of his archers a bit further south. They were trying to flank them like they were supposed to."

"Then who exposed the attack?" I asked.

No answer.

Smoke filled the air as the growing blaze revealed a dozen more Astiwie warriors rushing toward us. Ara loosed another arrow, missing by a finger-length. I threw out my arms and blasted them with the winds. The gust probably wouldn't kill them, but we needed to slow them down. If they had more than three hundred warriors, every second counted to let our commanders organize a defense.

As Ara shot again, I remembered my body. "I need a favor," I said.

"What? Talk fast."

Three more warriors closed in, and I spun, flinging them into the air before sending a gale to slam them back down. "The flames are getting close to my body, but I can't move it without leaving my soul-form."

Two arrows whizzed past us as she groaned. "We're kinda stuck here!"

"I'll do it," Zakir said, standing. "Tell me where it is and I'll move it away from the fire."

I studied him. Zakir had always seemed trustworthy, unlike his brother, yet I hesitated to allow him so near to me in my most vulnerable state. But my doubts were irrelevant. There were no other options.

Once I explained the spot to him, he nodded, turned, and lobbed his clay jar at a squad of archers down the hill. It exploded in a flash of sparks. Cries and shouts rang out from the archers. When I peered through the darkness, none remained.

"I need whatever that was," I said.

He grinned and bounded toward the flames without another word. *I owe him.*

"We need to fall back," Ara said. "I'll get Narcyz and join Andrij. Figure out where Xobas is and what in Alunam is happening." With one last arrow into an approaching warrior, she spun into the darkness.

Alone, I took a shuddered breath, fighting the demon's thrill as I shot into the air and over the battle that now covered the entire side of the mountain. Smoke blanketed everything and flames danced at the treetops. *I can't enjoy this.* The demon did, though, and it fed the winds as I watched the Astiwie warriors clamber up the shallow parts of the climb. Ahead, clansmen held choke-points where cliffs and rocks prevented any possible flanking attacks. Andrij's men defended one such postion just uphill from Ara. They'd likely been pushed back and found the first spot to hold.

Where are you, Xobas?

The winds swept me up again, toward the northern edge of the battle. But the haze blocked my vision, so I ducked lower until I was forced to dodge the trees.

My breaths caught at the sight of the Astiwie warriors here. They swarmed ahead in far greater numbers than Andrij had thought. Three hundred alone overwhelmed the clan's cavalry in the area, trapping their horses and preventing any chance of an effective charge. Around the fringes, clan riders picked off small groups of warriors, but they were too few to make a difference. Xobas was nowhere to be seen.

The winds grew unresponsive as I drifted up the mountain. It took all my strength just to fight the panic brewing within me, and soon, the gales dropped me to the ground ahead of a group of Astiwie warriors that were charging the clan camp. *Why do you abandon me now?*

Smoke smothered the warriors as they ran blindly through the trees. Even with fear dulling my mind, Xobas's training guided my invisible motions. Kwiecień slayed five in seconds. Those that remained halted their advance as they cowered behind trees and peeked out in hopes of seeing their attacker. But when I struck again, they saw nothing.

I caught my breath and stared down at the field of corpses. My stomach turned. Death was disgusting enough, but I'd slaughtered them in an unfair fight. And worse: I'd *enjoyed* it.

The Zurgowie cavalry raced toward me, their dark green cloaks flapping behind them, but it was over. Confused, they looked for who'd killed the warriors. I felt no pride, despite having protected the camp.

With the winds still weak, I slowly ascended. I flew higher this time, hoping to get a better view of the battle, but the flames had engulfed everything—a thick haze blanketing warriors and cavalry alike. Just the thought of diving into battle again made me hesitate. Though I had a decent amount of *żityje*, it was as if the winds dampened with the dread within me. The demon's excitement to kill lurked beneath it.

A roar ripped through the forest. Deep and gruesome, it stopped my heart as a stabbing pain struck my Frostmark. *What are you doing now, Marzanna?*

Screams followed before another roar echoed from the southern slope—right where my friends were defending with Andrij. Desperation drove me on as I threw my worries aside and chased the noise.

If the beast had caused that much panic already, I had to stop it before it reached the camp. So I flew faster, streaking toward the ridge.

I was too late. The corpses of Andrij's men hung from the rocks and blood covered the ground. Ara, Narcyz, and Zakir were gone.

A crash came from further up the hill. I charged after it, Frostmark burning as I dove around trees.

Ahead, Andrij's tattered blue and gold-trimmed cloak swept behind him as his remaining spearmen formed a shield-wall against a swarm of warriors. Narcyz stood among them as Ara and Zakir launched arrows and spark-bombs from higher up. Andrij shouted for his men to hold, but they were too few. Their lines crumbled just as I arrived.

It was a slaughter.

Andrij's warriors fled, exposing their backs as the Astiwie axmen descended on them. Half were dead by the time I plunged into the mob. I yelled in rage as I drove my sword through each of the attackers, diving around their attacks and slicing a path through to Narcyz, who smirked as he saw me. "About time!"

"I was busy," I snapped as I deflected an ax with the flat of my blade.

Andrij watched in awe. Blind to my presence but aware of his enemy's collapse, he ran forward, shouting for his retreating men to follow. The dozen remaining stopped and watched their commander charge the Astiwie alone. Then they yelled together and swept into the fray.

Sweat dripped from my brow as I rammed Kwiecień through yet another warrior's chest. Blood sprayed over me, but my tunic was already stained, my face splatted with red. A reeking smell covered the battlefield. Screams surrounded us as flames pelted the sky, burning those who drew near. When the final Astiwie warrior fell, I staggered back in horror.

This is war. I hated all of it. But the demon reveled in each death.

I exchanged glances with Narcyz. Our group included, eleven remained, and Andrij quivered as he stood over the carnage. "Wha… What just happened? They fell as if the wind sliced them open!"

Another roar shook the air up the mountain. *The camp!* Ara nodded for me to leave, and I returned the gesture before darting east on the winds.

The screams guided me toward the beast, but when I landed in a patch of ashen trees, there was nothing but a stray Astiwie axman. I growled and flung him into a tree with a blast. With all my fury, I swung Kwiecień across his throat.

As his body dropped, I released an exasperated breath. *What am I becoming?* The kills came too easily in my soul-form, and the demon's desire only grew.

"Wašek!"

I spun. The cry had come from the burned trees nearby, and though shouts and clashes surrounded me, I stared into the smoke and whispered, "Otylka?"

She drifted among the falling flakes of white in a dress of glimmering silver. Ash covered her hair, woven through a simple matching crown, and her green eyes glowed with power as she reached out to me. My anger, my fear, my sorrow all slipped away as I saw nothing but her—my Otylka, my love, my goddess.

She smiled with tears streaming down her cheeks. "I'm here, Wašek."

19

Otylia

The silver fox. What have I become? What am I becoming?

SLEEP DIDN'T ANSWER MY CALL THAT NIGHT. I dared not shut my eyes out of fear of the power that had possessed me. The ritual was over, yet I sensed a change within my soul. That alone was enough, but after washing my mouth too many times to count, the taste of iron lingered. Blood always left a stain—this would be no different.

Absent of sleep's embrace, I wandered into the depths of the warm pool in my chambers.

My body floated with neither dress nor pelt. Each brush of the water against my skin anchored me to reality as my mind drifted. The moonlight slipped through the vines and branches above, barely illuminating the room and making the pool seem an eerie black. The darkness was mine. Alone in its embrace, I was safe.

Who am I? What am I?

Questions I couldn't answer for the first time in my life. Mere moons before I had been Otylia Dariuszyczówna, daughter of Dariusz, chosen of Dziewanna, and diviner of Mokosz. The village had named me the wild witch, and I'd fallen into the role. Without Mother, I'd needed no one but my goddesses. They had been my life—my purpose.

But Mother had never left. From a distance, she'd watched over me, mentoring me through adolescence and heartbreak. I had lost her and Wacław so quickly, yet that isolation had been nothing but lies.

This time was different. Mother was trapped by Marzanna, and I'd lost my bond with her and Mokosz. Wacław was a world away, probably pursued by both Marzanna and the Frostmarked Horde. And Ara, gods bless her, was stuck with the boys after losing me. It had taken far too long, but now, I realized how much I needed them.

I wept.

Rage, sorrow, and regret swelled within me. Weles had forced me to kill an innocent man. It didn't matter that he'd volunteered. It didn't matter he would be reborn on Jawia to 'preach my name.' The god who was supposed to be my father had manipulated me. He was deceitful, and with every turn, he used me for his own plans. I had taken the first steps toward Ascension, but I felt no more like a goddess. Though the silver fox felt *right* as my bonded creature, each time I looked at the pelt I wanted to vomit.

I took a deep breath and dove. My hair flowed behind me as I reached for the pond's bed. When I'd stood, the water had been no higher than my nose, but now it seemed to go on forever as whispers called me further into the water's embrace.

The depths swallowed me whole with the voices luring me on. Time passed slowly as my lungs ached. I spun and hugged myself—an alien in my own form. Any semblance of security had been stolen by Weles's invasion, and I knew no way forward. My mind told me to finish the Trials and exact revenge, but my heart wanted to stop. Escape was little more than a distant hope.

My air ran out.

The voices devoured me as I spasmed and writhed. Despite the pain, I refused to surrender my descent, and I fought with each stroke until my consciousness slipped. Darkness drowned my sorrow. Darkness drowned my rage. Darkness drowned my world. Then my fingers struck earth.

Light shattered the void. Air rushed with the water into my desperate lungs, and my eyes seared as a woman appeared before me, standing on the pond's bed.

A kokoshnik embroidered in flowers and the purest gold crowned her head while a dress that seemed woven from the earth itself flowed down her body. Her smile was soft and her eyes kind. And when she reached out to steady me, hope returned to my heart.

"Great Mother!" I exclaimed, my voice piercing the water as if it were air. I dropped to my knees, clutching Mokosz's hands—naked and unworthy. "I've missed your voice, your guidance."

She knelt with me, cupping my scarred cheek in her hand. "Though Weles has prevented me from seeing Nawia for many years, your mother sought me here too, at the furthest edge of his power. The earth is mine, as are you, my child—bonded or not."

I hung my head and squeezed my eyes shut. "*Babcia*, grandmother, I've failed. Mother is gone. Jawia will wither without her, but I am trapped here, unable to help her."

"Look at me, *mała dziką*."

Little wildling. It was what mother had called me, and hearing it from her brought a calm to my heart. I raised my gaze to her. "My goddess, what am I supposed to do? How can I live here while those I love suffer without me?"

She chuckled as she pulled me close, cradling my head against her breast. "You were always such a questioning child, but Lady Destiny does not answer to such appeals, even those of goddesses."

"I never believed in destiny."

"Such a fascinating conclusion for a diviner to reach," she said, her hands working on my hair. "Yet, I should have expected nothing less from you. Rebellion runs in your veins, Otylia, as it does through your mother's, and that can make it difficult to accept the truth."

"What do you mean?"

"There are forces far beyond the comprehension of even the most powerful gods. Perun, Weles, and Swaróg combined cannot defy Destiny's will—not for want of trying. And you, my *wnuczka*, are destined for more than you can possibly understand."

She finished tying my hair into a braid that wrapped around my head. Her smile met me when I looked up, but I struggled to return it as sorrow held my heart. "Can you show me the way? If fate controls my path, then I have no choice anyway."

"The silver fox suits you." Folding her hands, she rose and paced along the muddy ground. "You are rogue, unique, and determined, but there is another reason Marzanna cannot defeat you." She stopped before me and offered a hand to help me up. I took it as she smiled with pride. "Cunning and free as the creature may be, the fox takes a single mate in life. One is bound to the other for eternity, and together, they are strong."

I studied her expression, young yet motherly. *Is she saying…* "Wacław?"

She nodded. "Yes, child. You may doubt the boy's love for you, but the two of you are bound by more than mere attraction. When you saved him from draining his human soul, you gifted him more than just *życie*. You gave him a portion of your immortal soul for a portion of his mortal one, joining you on a level deeper than anyone can know." Her hands gripped mine. "You are an essential piece of Wacław and he an essential piece of you. As long as you are apart, your souls will be incomplete, but together, you form a powerful whole unseen in the history of the Three Realms."

"But we were connected before the ritual," I said, shaking my head. "I don't understand…"

Mokosz pushed up my chin. "Destiny has her ways. Follow your heart and you will find your way back to him. I know you wish for me to give you the answer, but you have no need of my visions any longer, Otylia. You are a goddess who will soon Ascend and take a great power upon yourself."

"What if I don't want the power?" I yelled without meaning to. "I just want Mother and you and Wacław!"

"Oh, child. If only I could give you all you deserved. I cannot, but I shall gift you one last vision before I return you to your body."

My body?

A current swept the water away, tearing at my skin until I stood in a burning forest. Above, the great mountains of Perun's Crown cast shadows over the blaze.

A flowing dress and cloak of silver hung from my shoulders as I gasped at the fires ravaging the dry, lifeless trees. Flashes of blue, green, and brown tunics raced around me. Men shouted and clashed as smoke smothered the night sky, leaving a dull gray hue hanging over the earth. *What is this?*

Then came the screams.

A monster burst through the blaze with blood dripping from its jagged, crimson-stained teeth. I scrambled back in horror as the beast, covered in wolf-like fur yet standing with the figure of a man, lunged with inhuman speed and shredded another victim with its claws.

Demon…

As the demon devoured the flesh of its kill, I instinctively searched for Marzanna's Frostmark in its power, but my connection to Dziewanna was gone. What was this beast? None of Father's lessons had spoken of this.

Brown-clad warriors swarmed the demon. With shields raised and spears ready, they closed in slowly. Each of their breaths were heavy, and their bodies quivered as it roared. Then they charged.

Ten spears raced toward the demon's body—none struck. It vaulted over the warriors, landing behind their circle and ravaging their unshielded ranks. In seconds, seven men fell and those remaining tried to flee.

They never had the chance.

The demon killed them one-by-one as fighting rang out further downhill. I turned toward the sound, but smoke obscured sight beyond a few strides. All I could see were warriors in blue—who I assumed to be Astiwie based on the tongue they cried—falling back before running into dark-skinned warriors with green-painted faces. *They're fighting the clans?*

I shook my head. The Astiwie were supposed to allow the clans to pass. Unless Wacław had failed…

Then a force snapped tight in my chest. It split my mind and dragged me forward like the tether that had joined me to Wacław before. But this couldn't be the same. *Could it?*

I tripped into a sloppy sprint without another thought. Dashing through trees and smoke, dodging fires and warriors alike, I scrambled toward him with anticipation swelling in my chest. *I just need to see him, to know he's okay.*

The pull strengthened with every step, and though my lungs gasped and my heart pounded, I ran on. I felt his anger, passion, agony, and sorrow swirling within me. And when a golden blade sliced through the smoke, cutting down an Astiwie warrior just strides away, I cried out for him.

"Wašek!"

Battle surrounded him as he looked up from his kill with a start. His blond hair had become unruly, his brown clan shirt spattered with blood, and his eyes held a conviction I'd never seen before. He was different. But he was my Wašek—the boy whose soul was joined with mine.

"Otylka?" he whispered through the torrent of screams and clanging of metal, gripping my Bowmark necklace at his collar.

I reached out for him. "I'm here, Wašek."

His breaths were shallow as he clambered toward me, dropping Kwiecień and pulling me into his embrace. My heart felt full, yet I shook, holding him tight to me. I knew this moment was Mokosz's gift. It would not last.

"I'm sorry, Otylka," he wept into my shoulder. "I let him take you. I let Jaryło kill you."

"You avenged me," I whispered, running my hands through his hair and trying to remember every bit of him. The little smile he wore when I was near. The way he blushed when I challenged him. And his soft embrace when he held me in his arms. "Jaryło can't return until Maj, but even with him gone, there's no escape from Nawia. Not until I Ascend."

He pulled back, softly holding my cheek in his hand and gazing at me with eyes of blue against a sea of flames. "I'll bring you back, Otylka. We're going to Dariusz to find a way. It doesn't matter whether I have to slay Jaryło, Weles, or anyone else. They won't stop me from bringing you back."

Tears rushed down my cheeks as I clutched his shirt. I wanted more than anything to tell him everything—there was no time. So, as I felt Mokosz's tug on my soul, I kissed him with every bit of desire I had after weeks away from him. It was only a quick second of his lips pressed to mine, but my soul swelled with his, and time slowed as I treasured the moment of bliss.

"I miss you," I whispered.

He smiled with sorrow in his eyes. "I lo—"

The demon struck. Blood streaked through the air as the wolf-man tore Wacław from my grasp and threw him to the ashen ground. Wacław struggled against the demon and reached for Kwiecień, but it was too far.

I raced for the blade, fighting as Mokosz's power summoned me back to Nawia. When my hand closed around its hilt, the world slipped away, and with my last breath, I drove the sword into the beast.

20

Wacław

She's gone…

THE WORLD HAD MELTED AWAY as I'd held Otylia for the first time in what felt like years. She'd been as beautiful as the stars in the night sky, dressed in silver against her black hair. When our lips had met, my soul felt complete, the ache within it fading.

But that moment was over. Now, only pain remained.

A beast—half-man, half-wolf—towered above, holding me against the earth as it clawed through my tunic and struck skin beneath. I was defenseless. The winds were distant and my mind fogged as I struggled for breath. I'd dropped Kwiecień when Otylia had appeared, and I cursed my foolishness as the wolf-man roared and slashed at my neck.

The strike never fell. A shrill cry tore from the beast's jaws. It reeled back as blood splattered over me, allowing me to leap to my feet and gasp at Kwiecień impaled in the wolf-man's side.

She saved me again. No one had been near—no one but Otylia.

I swiped the blood from my face. It was red, not the usual black of demons, but there was no time to figure out why. With a roar that threw me back into a burning tree, the beast tore the blade from itself and fixed its dark eyes on me.

Great, now it has a god's sword.

Bits of bark scraped my back as the demon charged again. But I took to the air, bounding over the trees and landing where it had stood a moment before.

It spun to meet me. Blood poured from the wound on its side, but the beast didn't notice. It clawed at the ground as Kwiecień glowed in its free hand.

Let's see how you enjoy lightning.

I twisted the gales around the demon, distracting it as I surged above. It tore through the whirlwind and dove, but I was faster. Kwiecień's edge cut through the air beneath my feet, and an enraged howl echoed through the forest as I flew above the trees.

I shut my eyes and closed off the noise of the battle. *Focus.* The płanetnik's fury within me demanded to be released. It took everything to hold it back, and worrying about the rest of the battle wouldn't help me stop the wolf-man. For now, defeating the beast was all that mattered.

The winds circled the mountain's edge, but I went further, to the hills and valleys of the west. I soared higher than ever, calling each cloud I passed and pulling it into my wake until a great mass of them had assembled. I stopped and sensed each of their potential for rain and thunder. It wasn't enough, but there were no storms across all of the lands within Perun's Crown.

I'll regret this. With a shout, I tapped into the demon's strength and plunged my *żityje* into the clouds.

They swelled around me. Lightning cracked within them as the winds whipped through my hair and torn cloak. I held out my arms, grasping the tempest's power and letting it flow through me. My veins glowed with the lightning. My demonic soul had desired control of a storm more than I'd known, and with one finally in its grasp, it burned for more.

I dove east with a speed I'd never known. Dogoda's west wind was graceful, life-giving, but now it fueled my anger.

Within minutes, I reached Kynnytsia again. East of the village, the fires scorched earth and nature wherever I looked, but the clans' innocents had gathered further up the Narrow Pass. Though many had perished, it was a miracle even more had avoided the slaughter. Still, the Astiwie clashed with the clans below. The battle was far from won.

The storm unleashed a torrent of rain at my command, dousing the flames as I dropped to the ash circle where I'd left the wolf-man.

Kwiecień's golden blade was coated in crimson in its hand. Corpses circled the beast—brave clansmen who had dared face it alone.

I clenched my fists, drained of nearly all my *žityje* but enraged at the destruction both the Astiwie and demon had caused. The cries of dying warriors surrounded me. All of them should've survived to fight the Horde, but instead, our numbers dwindled as Marzanna watched us kill our own.

"This is *your* work, Wacław," the demon growled, stalking closer. "We could have joined with the Astiwie and slaughtered Rasa's minions! The Zurgowie have caused nothing but death and destruction, but you gave them mercy."

I know that voice. As I reached into the heart of the storm, I drew the Thunderstone dagger, my Frostmark pulsing. "Bidaês?"

"Yes, you idiot!"

He lunged, but I side-stepped, slicing the dagger across his extended forearm. A yelp slipped from him as blood seeped from his wounds. We circled each other, but Bidaês's breaths were weak, his gaze jagged. Veins of black covered where fur didn't.

"You're dying," I said, my demonic soul's anger joining with my own. *Control it.* "If you're anything like me, you can't keep using your power like this. Tell me everything and I'll let you live."

Baring his teeth, he laughed before ripping into a corpse next to him and devouring its heart in seconds. I staggered back. His dark veins disappeared and his wounds no longer bled. "We are creatures of death, Wacław, but you are unwilling to embrace that."

"I'm no cannibal," I snarled.

"And that makes you weak, just like humans."

I gripped the dagger and stepped forward, ready to strike. The demon in me wanted to kill him, but I saw the mortal in his eyes. He was fighting the same battle as me. "Bidaês, you are human!"

He held up his free claw and stared at it. "Do I *look* human to you? I am a wilkołak—a morph of wolf and man stronger than the greatest warriors and faster than them too. You and I are not meant to wait and listen to others. We were meant to rule alongside the gods."

"Your demonic soul is tearing you apart." I edged closer still. "Marzanna's using you, making you a slave of your ambition."

"I am no slave." He turned to me and swung Kwiecień through the air. "I am the *rightful* marzban of Clan Simuk, and I will lead my people against our enemies—slaying whoever stands in my way."

Sparks arced between my fingers as thunder rolled amid the sounds of battle. *I can't hold this for long.* "You did all of this so that you could be marzban? Your brother is the heir! You could serve by his side."

His jaws snapped, and he circled me, growling. "My grandfather is weak, unable to see when his enemies are ready to pounce, and Zakir is no warlord. You know what it feels like to watch your inferior brother be chosen to rule! Rasa would have attacked us eventually. When she did, they would lead us to our final defeat. Marzanna gave me a way to change that by allying with Boz and using his rage."

"Listen to yourself!" My boots crunched against ash as the rain continued to fall, suffocating the battlefield. Cries still came, but they were fewer. I hoped that was a good sign. "Boz's men are killing Simukie—your people. The Horde is worse! They killed your family."

He charged, slicing Kwiecień but finding only air as I dodged.

"Many of our warriors will die, but *I* will lead our clan into the future, Marzanna's future!" he growled. "My parents died because they wished to expose my condition to grandfather. I couldn't let them kill me—our greatest weapon in our survival. And survival is all that matters. Resisting the inevitable coming of the Horde is futile."

"Then you are my enemy," I said, tightening my grip on both lightning and dagger. Every ounce of me hated what I had to do.

Lightning snapped through the sky as Bidaês rushed toward me.

I rolled to the side and launched a bolt from my hand, striking his chest. Though smoke rose from his singed hair, he didn't slow. Kwiecień sliced toward me over and over. I scrambled away and shot bolts at him with every miss, and soon, splotches of charred skin patterned his body.

Why isn't it working?

When Bidaês charged again, I flung myself over his long reach. He leaped after me, and as I jumped, I dropped the dagger, leaving it just strides behind him. I waited for his attack, then dodged and lifted the dagger on the winds.

It missed.

My *życie* snapped as Bidaês stepped to the side, allowing the dagger to shoot past him and impale itself in a nearby oak. He grinned. "Smart trick, but not enough."

I heaved with each breath. The storm's power was draining what remained of my strength with each second. As the clouds blocked out the moonlight, all I saw of Bidaês was his wolf eyes, glowing in the night. Fear grabbed hold, and the winds retreated with it as he struck again.

Only ducking behind a tree saved me. Kwiecień cracked its trunk before Bidaês swung its golden blade again. I was quick too, but my head spun from fear and smoke inhalation. The winds wouldn't help either, and his attacks were getting closer as my energy waned.

I need to get that sword away from him. He was dangerous without it, but its long reach was deadly. Neither bolts nor wind were strong enough to hurt him. I needed to get to get closer, but how?

"There was one thing I didn't tell you about Marzanna's promise," he said, drawing closer. Confidence swelled in his gaze.

Keep him talking. Let him think you're drained. With a cough that was only half fake, I dropped to my back and scrambled away. "What?"

He chuckled. "Oh come on, Wacław. You're smart enough to know."

Just a little closer. I backed between a tight cluster of trees, clutching my stomach and reaching for the little *życie* I had left as the demon lurked within me. "You have to kill me," I spat.

The storm blew his thick hair as he stomped into the cluster. "Yes. And when I do, my clan will be blessed with abundant land. While your people crumble, we will rise." He raised Kwiecień and prepared to strike.

I was faster.

As the blade rushed toward my neck, I used its momentum, sliding away and commanding the winds to push it faster than Bidaês could control. The move took little *żityje*, and the sword embedded itself into a tree.

He growled as I ran. In his rage, he tore Kwiecień from the bark, but again, I pulled on it with the winds. The hilt slipped from his hands. Instead of flying to me, though, it soared into the mists. I cursed watching it go.

Now what?

Bidaês puffed up his chest and howled in rage as I ducked behind a tree, catching my breath. Marzanna didn't know I held the Moonblade. If she had, Bidaês would have run with it the moment it had touched him. I smiled knowing that, but my little victory faded as the winds alerted me to his charge.

The tree snapped. Shards sliced across my arms and face as I rolled away just in time to avoid his strike. *Thank the winds.*

I took off into the darkness. Only the winds warned me of trees or rocks as I ran with Bidaês panting behind me, cutting through the patter of the rain. With his wolf-like speed, he would catch me in seconds. Panic came sooner.

My chest seized. I dropped, the visions of death taking my mind again. *Not now!* Thunder cracked above. Each flash lit the forest, exposing the fire's destruction and the warriors clashing in the distance, yet even with the light, I dared not look back at my pursuer. I wished I could stop the battle. I wished I could save the innocents. I wished I could end Bidaês's chase. But I could barely keep myself alive with my depleted *żityje*. Anything that killed him would take me too. *Unless…*

When the lightning faded, I jumped into the dark branches of a tree. Bidaês lunged blindly, missing by inches as I landed above. He sniffed the air a few strides away, but the stench of smoke and death coated everything. I wanted to gag—the demon was stronger.

My heart pounded as I waited in the shadows, my desire for revenge pulsing with it. This destruction had been Bidaês's doing. He'd led his own people into an ambush. The storm fed on my rage, lightning snapping along my hands and veins as the płanetnik took over. My last safe amount of *żityje. This better work.*

I whistled.

Bidaês charged beneath the tree. I leaped upon his back, wrapping an arm around his neck and driving my other hand into his face. Pleasure filled me as he screamed with the lightning searing against his skin. He *deserved* to feel the pain he'd wrought, and though he clawed at me, I pushed harder. My fingers dug into his eye. Then, channeling every bit of energy I had left, I shot a bolt into his head.

Fatigue took over. His claws tore me from his back. I collapsed into the ash, heaving and covered in blood. My mind faltered as I stared through the lingering haze of gray. The storm faded with my power, and the last few drops of rain fell upon my face as Bidaês dropped next to me.

Is that it? He'd surprised me twice already, and part of me expected him to rise and finally kill me. But he only groaned before falling still, his face burned and blackened, his eye socket bleeding and swollen. The thrill faded. After all the pain he'd caused, there'd been no other choice. His struggle against his soul had been the same as my own. Was I truly any different when I'd given into the demon's call for revenge?

My back ached and my chest seared as I fought to stand. My *żityje* was gone, but I was alive.

Despite the battle raging in the darkness, a glimmer of hope burned in my heart. We'd lost so many people, too many, yet, from the sound of the clans' shouts, the Astiwie were being driven back. Marzanna's plot had failed. We'd survived to fight another day. In the end, I was grateful for even that.

I stumbled through the woods in search of Kwiecień. Dropping the golden blade had nearly killed me, and ironically, so had Otylia's use of it to save me. Though memories of her filled my mind, I forced them away—for now. Every part of me hurt, and the last thing I needed was to be reminded of her death.

Zurgowie warriors ran past, carrying their injured: one with an arrow in her leg and another slashed from collar to stomach. Blood coated their faces and clothes, red clashing with green. *Gods save them.*

It was a long time before I found the sword buried under layers of ash. The forest was filled with fallen warriors and their weapons. Only the flash of a well-timed lightning strike lit the blade's edge enough for me to see.

As I lifted Kwiecień, my arms were heavy. Bidaês had stolen it from me, but the Moonblade was still mine. Marzanna would soon figure out I held it, and she would surely come for it when she did. That was a problem for later. For now, I would take surviving and holding the sword as a win.

With Kwiecień safely in its sheath, I returned to the place I'd fought Bidaês. Darkness shrouded the woods, but the pool of crimson was obvious from a distance away. My heart stopped, however, as I drew closer.

Bidaês was gone.

How did he survive?

He'd been motionless just minutes before, his breaths faint, fleeting. Kwiecień would've finished the job, but I'd thought him already dead. Apparently, I was wrong. What worried me the most was that there was no trail of blood from the spot. Nor were there footprints in the ash. It was as if he'd simply dissipated or been carried away—by who?

I shook my head. He was gone, and there was nothing I could do about it, so I returned to where I'd seen Otylia. Marzanna's dagger was embedded in one of the trees nearby. As much as I wanted to forget the dagger and the omens it had brought me, its Thunderstone blade was invaluable.

My Frostmark burned as I neared the place. *Thanks for the help.* Soon, the dagger came into sight, its sleek black hilt splitting the night—as sharp as the blade's tip.

I let myself smile. *He might be alive, but I still have the blades.* Marzanna wouldn't rule the Kwiecień moon without the Moonstone, and though I still hadn't figured out the blade's power, it was better in my hands than hers. Five moons were enough, if not too many, for her already.

My hand found the dagger, embedded up to its hilt in an oak's trunk, but I didn't have the strength to pull. Maybe the demon did. After enduring its torrent of rage to defeat Bidaês, though, I had no desire to let it rule me again. It still lingered, trapped once again in that cage in my soul. No, I couldn't let it take over, no matter how tempting that power was.

A sharp pain shot through my ribs as I coughed on the lingering smoke and fell to the base of the tree, exhausted. It had been hours since the battle had begun. Dehydration numbed both my mouth and mind as my soul ached without *żityje*.

What use am I now? While warriors fought and died less than a hundred strides away, I was alone in the darkness. My friends had trusted me. They needed me to help them against the Astiwie, but I'd used everything in my desire to kill Bidaês. Zakir had moved my body, yet I hadn't seen him since. He'd put his life at risk for me—someone he had known for merely two weeks. Xobas had led the Simukie into battle, disappearing into the mists and never returning. I could only hope he was safe, along with Ara and Narcyz. *Otylia, Dziewanna, Perun, anyone protect them.*

Slowly, my vision faded. I fought to stay awake, to listen to the clanging of iron in wait of our victory—or defeat. But the fatigue was too much. I drifted, and when I closed my eyes, all that lingered was the haze of death and the taste of falling ash.

21

Otylia

I saw him.

I BURST TO THE POOL'S SURFACE, gasping and panicked. Reality's grip was cold, and I shuddered remembering Wacław crushed beneath the wolf-man.

One moment I'd been whole in his arms, the next, ripped away from him without a chance to say half of what I'd wanted to—what I'd needed to. It was like breath had been sucked out of my lungs, leaving me empty. Mokosz's vision filled had me with hope and fear, and as I stood in the pond, I wept knowing I wouldn't see Wacław again for a long time.

"Please be alive," I whispered. "I need you."

The horror of battle hung over me: the cries, blood, and flames that engulfed Dziewanna's wilds with a dark fury. It had reeked of death.

He's alive, I told myself. *He has to be.*

Wacław had faced more dangerous demons before. Well, I thought he had. The wolf-man was unlike any we'd seen, and based on its destruction of multiple squads of warriors, it was a powerful force. But Wacław had the storms. He would defeat it.

I forced my thoughts to end there. Wacław was fighting his way across Jawia to find Father and the way to Nawia, and I needed to be ready when he arrived. That meant completing the remaining Trials of Ascension—whatever those were.

Weles was convinced I would never be able to face Marzanna without Ascending. I didn't trust him, but I'd seen his fear. On that, he'd told no lie.

To accomplish anything, first I had to pry myself away from the pool's embrace. Mokosz was gone, yet her presence lingered in the waters. I didn't care that it may have been blind hope more than reality. It had been too long since I'd felt a mother's touch—my grandmother's would do.

I climbed to shore and reached for a towel. However, before I grabbed hold of it, the mirror called me back.

The pull happened whenever I bathed in the pond. No matter how hard I tried to avoid it, I found myself studying my face and every mark on my skin. This time, I barely recognized the woman looking back at me. The features were mine, as were the compact yet strong muscles I'd developed from years of running through the woods, but there was something different, something *wrong.* It was as if the body was mine yet the soul within no longer fit.

I ran my hand down my face and sighed. *Gods, I really am losing it. How long has it been since I slept?*

The silver fox pelt rested alongside the towel, taunting me. The ritual had only been a few hours before, but it seemed as if weeks had passed since I'd killed my first innocent. Sleep would remain a stranger tonight. I could tell that already. But I knew I had to come to terms with what I'd done—and what I had to do—if I was to pass the rest of Weles's Trials.

A salty taste coated my tongue. I winced and held my hand to it, cursing myself as I examined my reddened fingers in the moonlight. I'd bitten my cheek so hard it bled.

Get used to the taste.

My hand trembled as I stared at the blood, watching it roll down my finger and drip to the dirt. Weles had told me gods were weak without sacrificial blood. Whether it be human or animal, the offering's *żityje* gave them life… gave *us* life.

It was so simple. Father and szeptuchy offered sacrifices of crops, food, animals, and even enemy warriors so many times. We'd given willingly because the gods were essential to the world's existence, its natural cycle. Yet, as I dipped my fingers in the water and washed them clean, I despised myself for being a goddess. I wasn't needed. I wasn't a protector of the wilds or the crops, the lowlands or the mountains, the sun or the stars. I was a girl without a place—a goddess with no function.

I was nothing.

You don't believe that. I reached for my underdress, hanging from the vines, and slid it over my head. It didn't matter what I believed. Goddess or szeptucha, I had to save Mother, and the only way to do that was to Ascend.

With a sharp breath, I grabbed the fox pelt and felt its fur, remembering Sosna, the little red fox Dziewanna had sent to protect me. She'd fought by my side for weeks, and I hoped she was doing the same for Wacław. If the Astiwie were at war with the clans, gods knew he needed all the help he could get.

Still holding the pelt, I sauntered into my room and shivered at the chill away from the pool. *I'm getting soft.*

Years of harsh winters had made me resilient to the cold, but the breeze slipping through the slits in the roots above was enough to slow me now. I'd spent weeks in Nawia, trapped in the comfort of Weles's home. After the last day, though, I wasn't sure I wanted to leave it again—not if it meant transforming into an animal in search of a kill.

I slid into bed and curled myself within the fur blanket's embrace. My arms clutched the fox pelt, unwilling to release it for a reason I couldn't explain, as I shut my eyes and tried to think of anything but death and blood. But I saw only Wacław, crowned by a halo of flames as he looked at me with desperation in his eyes.

What were you about to say, Wašek?

His lips had whispered, "I lo—" before he'd been cut off by the beast's attack. Had he been ready to admit he loved me? My heart fluttered at the thought. Of course he would try to say something so important in the midst of battle, oblivious to the looming threats around him.

He loves me. Part of me had always known it, but the fact he'd said it, or tried to, made me smile and hold the pelt tighter.

To everyone else, I was just a channeler or a goddess—a power to be used. Wacław didn't care. He'd taken his Father's beatings to see me once more as a child, even after I'd harnessed sorcery I still didn't understand. He'd killed a god to avenge me, even though it risked our fight against Marzanna. And when flames and war had surrounded him, he'd run to me.

He loved me. Could I say the same to him?

Love would make us vulnerable. Wacław would've done anything to save me, and that was dangerous. The battles among gods and men were won by those without weakness, without flaws to be exploited. But Marzanna could threaten one of us to cripple the other. We would claw our way to each other, sacrificing all else to be joined again, but when would the sacrifice become too much?

I ripped off the blanket and forced myself out of bed. *Enough.* Speculations about my relationship with Wacław weren't going to fix anything. I clenched my jaw, threw the fox pelt over my head, and plowed out of the room.

The halls of vines wound every which way. I allowed myself to get lost in the maze.

My bare feet slid across the grasses, collecting a soft dew that hung on their tips. I focused on the feeling of each blade. I needed to focus, to forget about my feelings and fears. All that mattered was the Trials and understanding my power. Nothing else.

I didn't know how long I wandered for, but I eventually stopped before a narrow passage. My breaths caught as I stared down it to the single door bearing Weles's Serpentmark. *Why did I come here?*

As I turned to leave, something kept me there. I knew I should've run back to my bed and forced myself to sleep, but the room lured me closer. I relented to the call, pushing the door open and entering the small chamber. Where the sunlight had illuminated the bowl of blood before, now the moonlight offered only a slight glimpse of the root altar. All else was black.

The darkness was no obstacle. My steps cleared the exposed roots lining the floor with ease as I made my way to the bowl and stared down at the blood within. It appeared a murky gray now, but I remembered Weles drinking from it not long before. I stepped back. "No. I'm not like him."

A laugh cracked through the room. I spun, instinctively reaching for Dziewanna's power but finding nothing.

Near the door, a figure shifted, their boots cracking against the dirt as they slid a sword from their sheath. "I had hoped you would come here."

Jaryło's arrogant smirk met me as he stepped from the shadows with Maj's green Moonblade in hand. As always, his teeth were unnaturally white and his hair was bleached as gold as the sun, but a gloom hung over him. Whether it was the dullness in his eye or the lumbering of his gait, he was different. A grin crossed my face knowing Wacław had caused that pain.

"Come to kill me again?" I spat, holding my ground.

He huffed and cocked his head to the side. "Oh, my dear sister. Father has explained everything to you, yet you still blame me for bringing you home?"

I swung. Jaryło dodged too late, and my knuckles connected with his jaw, sending him staggering into the wall. "You stole me from my home!" He winced as my forearm pinned his neck. Despite his lack of resistance, I took pleasure in my moment of dominance. "I will *never* be your sister, you murderer."

"Murderer?" He laughed as blood dripped from his lip to his chin. "You are alive, Otylia, perhaps more than ever. It may take time for you to accept what I have done for you, but in your soul, you know I meant you no harm. If Wacław had not struck me with Marzanna's dagger, then you would have crossed from Jawia with no pain."

I drove my arm harder into his throat. "I didn't want to leave! Marzanna has my mother, and because of you, I'm stuck here instead of fighting to save her."

"Because of me, you live!" Flicking his gaze to Maj, he scoffed. "Marzanna would have killed you if you had faced her without Ascending, and then, we really would have been hopeless."

"What are you saying?"

He huffed. "Allow me to breathe, and then we can talk, deity to deity."

I glared up at him but stepped back. "You caused Marzanna's rage. Then, you lied to all of us and killed me, and now you want to *talk*?" I shook my head. "I knew from the moment I met you that something was wrong. Why didn't I trust my instincts?"

"Perhaps for the same reason you chose to wear that pelt after hating Weles for gifting it to you," he said, smiling as I self-consciously gripped the fur on my head. "You may not understand who you are yet, but your soul always has, Otylia. You are a goddess. No amount of fleeing from or struggling against that fact will change the very essence of who you are. If you are to Ascend, you must accept that."

"Stop making this about me!" I spun away. "All anyone wants to talk about is who *I* am or who I'm meant to become, but nobody cares what *I* want. My destiny or Ascension or whatever doesn't excuse you killing me and betraying my friends. You are the one who turned Marzanna into the goddess of death. You are the one who failed to protect Dziewanna on the equinox. You took me from Wacław, leaving him to face the Frostmarked alone. Why would I care what you have to say when everything you've done is push Jawia to the brink of destruction?"

He sighed and sheathed his blade as he paced to the altar. "Oh, little one, if only you knew the full extent of my errors. I have lived for hundreds of years, but immortality does not grant you immunity to the whims of the heart and mind. You will find in time that I have done all that I can to fix what I have broken. Without your help, I will fail."

"Maybe I want you to."

"You act determined and strong," he said, dipping his fingers into the blood, "but you are not fooling us. With Dziewanna gone, you are nothing but a desperate girl stolen from her childhood love." His gaze rose to me, and I shuddered at the ferocity in his eyes. "We can change that. Let us take you through your Ascension, slowly and in the correct time. Then we will make you a goddess to worship—and fear—by my side."

Is that all I am? I crossed my arms. "You're just like Weles. Stop speaking in riddles or I won't help you."

He chuckled and dripped the blood into his mouth, making me squirm. "Very well. Ask me a question and I will answer directly."

"Why do you need me? Weles is one of the most powerful gods. Surely the two of you combined could defeat Marzanna without my help."

With a wag of his finger, he grinned. "There is much more to the gods than any priest could possibly comprehend. Father may grant me safety while I recover in Nawia, but he is constantly under siege by Perun. A quarrel with Marzanna would only allow Perun to gain an advantage."

I scoffed and returned to the patch of light. "*Quarrel* is one way to describe Marzanna's Frostmarked threatening all of Jawia. Why is Weles so desperate to keep me then? Does he just want me to be another pawn for him to use against Perun?"

"Though Weles does not choose to interfere directly, he believes I should regain my control of the twelve moons of Jawia." He raised his arm over his mouth as he coughed, exposing blackened veins upon it, before leaning against the pillar of roots again. "In order to do so, though, I must take Marzanna's five Moonstones."

"Like your swords."

He nodded. "Precisely. Well, except for my poor beloved Kwiecień. No artifact as powerful as it should ever be in the hands of a corrupted demon, but we will fix that, won't we?" His eyes fell upon me again.

I thought of Wacław releasing the blade as he rushed toward me.

No one had told me everything about the Moonstones' powers, but knowing Wacław cared enough for me to drop Kwiecień was frightening. If the sword had ended up in Marzanna's hands…

"Your silence concerns me, Otylia," Jaryło said, tearing me from my thoughts. "Surely, you do not believe that boy should possess Kwiecień any longer? It matters not his intentions. He is a demon, and with the sword, his corruption could do irreparable damage to Jawia."

"If anyone is corrupting Jawia, it's not Wacław." I bit my cheek and narrowed my eyes. "You still haven't told me why you need my help or why you should hold all twelve moons. From what I can see, you've failed to protect the ones you have, and you don't seem to care about saving Dziewanna."

He took a raspy breath. With every minute that passed, his voice grew weaker, and his eyes exposed his fatigue. "I am cursed."

I stuttered for a moment, caught off guard but that blunt truth.

"Are you pleased now?" he said, throwing out his arms. "You wanted the truth?"

"What curse?" I asked once I regained my composure. "I know of none that could harm a god."

Another cough ripped through the room. "It is the same wretched thing that transformed Marzanna into the horror she is today. My infidelity and her murder violated nature. But we are gods. We are supposed to create and protect the natural order, not destroy it as if we were demons."

He quivered and looked up at me as he placed all his weight on the basin. "I do not know how to end the curse, but as long as we both live, I spend five moons in agony as crops wither. Dziewanna joins me every spring because I *cannot* kill Marzanna. The closer I come to her, the more my power is drained as punishment for my mistake. Only the Moonblades keep me alive long enough for the tribes to conduct the Drowning of Marzanna rituals and for Dziewanna to slay her."

"She's your only hope, yet you let her go?"

He scowled. "I did not abandon her! On the equinox, Marzanna came with an army unlike any assembled before. Demons, spirits, and dark creatures of the earth swarmed us. Even they should not have stopped us, but there was another *thing*. It was formless and dark at first, swallowing the earth. When Dziewanna attacked it, though, the darkness morphed into a great żmij—a black dragon larger than any I have ever seen. Dziewanna fell, and by the time I rushed to her, it was too late. Marzanna's servants had taken her."

"Mother told us she was trapped," I said, pacing around him, "but why would Marzanna keep her alive? And what becomes of Jawia now that you are in Nawia and she is captured? You said before that the płanetnik was helping her continue winter, but why does she still need demons if you're dead?"

"So many questions." He shook his head. "The curse Marzanna suffers, like mine, means she has little power when she does not possess the current Moonstone. It gets worse when we are both alive, but even with me here, she cannot bring winter back completely without the stones. Perhaps capturing Dziewanna is some attempt to change that."

I raised a brow. "You don't know?"

"There are many secrets among the Three Realms," he wheezed. "I need you if there's any hope in stopping her, and yes, saving Dziewanna. Ensure I control all twelve Moonstones and I will grant man eternal rule over Jawia. I will direct my power so that crops are bountiful, your people are freed from the dark days of winter, and Marzanna's Curse will never kill the innocent again. Every day shall be a feast! They will celebrate *your* name for freeing us from Marzanna's wrath. I can make you the most praised of goddesses!"

"How could I even help?"

"You are the first child of Weles. When you Ascend, surely you will wield a force strong enough to face Marzanna. With you by my side, we will be unstoppable."

A discomfort strangled my stomach like a boa constricting its prey. Behind his desperation was another obvious truth: He was lying. Jaryło's cockiness from the beginning had shown how little regret he had, and he had betrayed me already. The story about Dziewanna was embellished as well. Some element was missing, but even if I believed him, he would never share fame.

In fact, the offer itself revealed that he hadn't bothered to pay attention to me. I didn't want power or worship. Revenge against Marzanna was enticing, but that could only happen once I rejoined with Wacław and saved Mother.

"I'll find my own way," I replied, approaching him with a glare. "But tell me something before I go."

"You will change your mind when you realize you need me. Ask your question."

Snatching his arm, I whispered in his ear, "How much did it hurt when Wacław killed you?" before slipping out the door.

I clenched my fists with every step. But a smirk pulled at my mouth as I turned the corner, the muffled cry of a fallen god echoing through the halls.

22

Wacław

How could Bidaês ruin everything?

SOMETHING LICKED MY FACE.

The sun pierced through my eyelids, followed by excruciating pain. I cried out as Sosna yapped and grabbed my soul-form's tunic with her teeth. With her help, I attempted to stand, but my wounded torso and battered legs refused. I collapsed to the ash.

"Wacław!" a voice shouted.

Xobas...

"I'm here!" I called back through my scratchy throat. Even swallowing hurt, but when I reached for my canteen, it was empty.

Above me, the Thunderstone dagger still stuck from the oak's trunk. The night's memories slowly returned as I rubbed my palm against my head, fighting the headache that came with them. Bidaês was Frostmarked. He'd worked with Boz to weaken the clans, using the king's hatred of the Zurgowie to clear the way for the Horde.

I had trusted Bidaês too easily. He'd been Marzanna's puppet—the supposed wolf attacking the Zurgowie camp during our travels—and he wasn't dead yet. A wilkołak he'd called himself, but I'd never heard of such a thing before. Nor had I met another living demon. At least he hadn't stolen the sword.

The sword!

Panic struck me. I swiped at my back, letting out a relieved breath when my fingers touched Kwiecień's hilt. *Phew. Still there. Something* hadn't gone wrong.

What had happened to the rest of the clan warriors? I scanned the woods, but only Sosna's bright orange fur and a sea of corpses were in sight. My stomach turned at the stench, and tears came with the bile as I vomited. So many dead…

Boz had planned the ambush well. In the chaos, it had been hard to estimate the Astiwie numbers. I was certain, though, they had done plenty of damage to our ranks with far fewer men. *I couldn't save them.*

A bay horse broke through the trees at a canter, sending ash flying into the air behind it. On its back, Xobas rode with a cavalry sword ready. His eyes were reddened by fatigue, and what remained of his brown commander garb was slashed and bloodied. Gray ash covered his black curls, making him appear older than his age.

I offered him a weak smile as he stopped and leaped from his mount. "Wacław!" he exclaimed. "I had feared you were dead or captured, but it seems Sosna would never let that happen." He knelt and examined my many cuts and bruises. "These are not wounds caused by the weapons of man."

"Bidaês," I sputtered, descending into a coughing fit as the lingering soot worsened my dry throat.

Xobas returned to his horse. "You've seen him?" he asked as he grabbed his canteen and handed it to me. "He's been gone since the battle began."

I downed the rest of his water and coughed once more before replying, my voice cracked, "He attacked me."

"Why? I don't understand."

My Frostmark burned as I unwrapped it from the bloodied cloth. "He's a Frostmarked wilkołak—some type of half wolf and half man. He told me Marzanna had offered him rule of the Simukie if he helped her use Boz to start a war between the clans and the Astiwie. The assassination against Katiôn and Zakir wasn't Rasa's plot but his way to split the clans."

Xobas sighed and took his canteen. "I do not expect this will bring joy to the marzban."

"Nor should it. Marzanna controls him, and he's succeeded at weakening us. Without the clans united with the tribes—"

"There would be little hope against the Solga and the Frost-marked at once."

I rested my head against the tree and shut my eyes, defeated. "Exactly."

Yapping, Sosna nudged me before rolling her entire body into my lap. A smile slipped through my guard, if only for a moment.

Xobas rose and examined the Thunderstone blade, though I doubted even he could remove it from the tree. "Where is Bidaês now? Dead?"

"No. Otylia impaled him with Kwiecień, but he survived that. When I managed to get the sword away from him, I leaped on his back and shot lightning directly into his head. I thought it had been enough." I nodded to the pool of dried blood in the ash. "Apparently not."

"Otylia? How did she come to possess Kwiecień?"

My cheeks flushed. "She came as a vision of some sort. Let's just say that when she appeared, I got distracted. Bidaês attacked during our conversation, and she disappeared during our fight—probably back to Nawia."

He tore the dagger from the tree. *Guess I was wrong.* With a smile, he held out the hilt to me. "Even a minute with the girl and you're blushing after a battle? Ha! You are still that boy I knew. However, such laughter must wait. There is much more to last night than I'd thought, and the marzban will want to know what has happened. Where is your body?"

"I don't know," I said, sliding the dagger into its sheath. "During the fires, I had Zakir move it before I burned alive." I surveyed the charred forest. "What happened to the clansmen?"

"Here." He helped me up, throwing my arm over his shoulder as he guided me to his horse. "There will be plenty to discuss when we return to the camp, but know that our friends are safe, as are the marzban and Commander Andrij."

With some effort and a lot of complaining, I mounted the horse with Xobas's help. He jumped on in front of me, and we galloped up the slope, spraying up a cloud of gray behind us as I clung to him and hoped not to die. Sosna ran alongside with her mouth gaping.

Soon, the smoldering camp came into sight. Women huddled with children among the carts and collected what little food remained unburnt. Few tents stood, but it appeared many of the horses had survived the flames.

Clansmen in ripped and charred clothes guarded the trails, but only fifty were on patrol—far less than the twelve hundred who had ridden to battle last night. Though I assumed most were simply resting and mending minor wounds, cries rang from throughout the camp. Mothers were hearing news of lost sons, wives of husbands, and sisters of brothers. Both clans had female warriors as well, and my heart sunk knowing many children would have woken up without one or both parents. *Gods bless them.*

I forced myself to watch the weeping families and bleeding warriors. From the ruined forest to the burned corpses wrapped in spare cloth, I needed to remember the sights of war. Father and his chiefs had spoken of spoils and honor for the gods, but here, among the weary, heartbroken, and dead, there was only despair. I hung my head.

Simukie offered Xobas their traditional greeting as he rode past but gave me no such attention. It was odd to be invisible during the day. I looked forward to returning to my body, both out of worry for the *żityje* my soul-form consumed and out of want to escape the winds' sensations. Through them, I heard every whimper, sensed every tear. It was too much.

"Zakir!" Xobas yelled, guiding his horse around the carts to Zakir's makeshift alchemy station—a blanket and a few clay jars on top of a small, secluded cart.

Zakir didn't look up until Xobas stopped near him. Even then, he did so only because he winced at the horse's breath. "Oh, hello

Xobas." He leaned away from its mouth and looked to me. "And Wacław, glad to see you're alive."

"Same to you," I said with a nod, figuring that was as sentimental as Zakir got. "Do you happen to remember where you put my body last night?"

"Yes…" He considered that for a moment, as if creating a map of the mountainside in his head. Sosna jumped into his cart and rattled his supplies, but he didn't flinch. "It is seventy-three strides from the southern edge of the trail. Begin at the pine split by a bolt of lightning not far west of camp. I placed it in a nook among rocks where no one wandering by would see."

"That's oddly specific." I glanced back to the forest, admiring the view of the hills beyond the ashen trees. "Thank you, Zakir. Truly, I owe you my life."

He shrugged. "It's good to be useful. You extinguished the flames and stopped the Astiwie attack." Then, he cocked his head to the side and scrambled for a bag across the cart. I chuckled. *Never seen him move so fast.* "Here," he said, pulling a clay vial and approaching us. "This should help your pain, a little."

I closed his hand around the potion. "You are kind, but no matter how much pain I'm in, there are others that need it more—even if it is only to provide comfort in their last hours."

His thumb ran along the vial's mud seal. "It seems a waste, but I'll find someone who fits that description."

"Good, and thank you again."

He offered no reply as he climbed back into the cart and continued fiddling with a variety of substances, each that reeked of a different odor. *What an odd boy.* While Xobas and I rode silently to the place Zakir had described, Sosna stayed next to his supplies, watching him. The fox had been right about Bidaês. It was reassuring she liked Zakir more.

I hadn't the heart to tell Zakir about Bidaês, not until I spoke with Katiôn first. The brothers had never seemed all that close, but there was a pain in seeing your sibling hurt, no matter the distance between you.

"Whoa!" Xobas exclaimed, halting the horse when we reached a semi-circle outcropping of rocks.

Away from the trees, only a thin layer of ash coated the ground and my body laying upon it. He helped me limp along until I dropped to my knees next to its head.

"Gods, I used to think this was nothing more than a nightly wandering," I muttered, biting my lip to ward against another stream of tears. "I never wished for war or power."

He huffed and knelt beside me, resting a hand on my shoulder. "It's better for you not to want it. That desire consumed Bidaês if what you say is true. I do wonder, however, why you return to your body at all."

"Besides my responsibilities in reality?" I asked with a half-hearted chuckle. "My soul-form tires, similar to a body. I've almost never stayed in it past the night, but I think not all of the weakness I'm feeling is because of the battle. Jaryło said my demonic soul drains my human one of *žityje*. Maybe, if they're separated for too long, I have nothing to live on—like the undead demons. I would have to drain other creatures, like Bidaês did."

Xobas's eyes widened. "He *drained* the life from something?"

I nodded. "A corpse he'd killed a minute before. It's how undead demons survive without a human soul. Maybe, they aren't that different from me after all…" With a shudder, I placed a hand on my body's chest. "I would rather not consider that possibility further for now."

As he backed away, I rejoined my souls and awakened to a screeching that tore through my mind. Every scrape, every bruise, intensified ten-fold. I yelled and clutched my head, wishing for the winds to take me away, but there was no escape. The torture continued for what seemed like hours as Xobas held me and pled for me to respond. I couldn't. My thoughts were terror and my existence pain. Things writhed within me as if my organs were finding new places, and when I no longer had the voice to yell, I cried in silence.

Then it stopped.

Reality crashed into me at once. The searing pain was gone, but still I gasped, trembling with each breath. The sky spun above. My stomach churned as I stared up at the drifting clouds of white and gray. Under my control just minutes before, they were distant now, strangers to the humanity I'd returned to.

"Wacław?" Xobas asked. He held my face in my hands as tears cut through the ash coating his cheeks. Though he was a warrior who had seen death and destruction, he wept for me.

"I'm here," I said, grabbing my straw płanetnik hat. Like my clothes, it was covered in soot, and I coughed on the smell of smoke that lingered on me.

Xobas sighed and wiped away his tears. "Everything is a surprise with you. What just happened?"

"I… I don't know. Maybe punishment for leaving my body for so long?" I placed my hat on my head and forced myself to stand, ignoring Xobas's offer to help again. Though I was shaken, Xobas had enough to worry about already without my pain. "Whatever it was is over now, and I doubt my injuries are worse than those of your men."

He eyed me, obviously not convinced, but he allowed the diversion. "It was a brave thing for you to give Zakir's potion to a dying man, especially after what I just saw."

I gripped the twin amulets of Dziewanna and Mokosz at my collar. "A brave man would ride across Jawia to reach Dwie Rzeki, no matter what he had to leave behind. In truth, I'm too afraid to ride west alone."

"And why is that?"

"More than Frostmarked demons or Solga warriors, I fear returning home. Father's death was because I chose Otylia over him, yet when I reach Dwie Rzeki, I somehow have to explain how I lost both of them. Natasza, Mom, Nevenka, Mikołaj, Gośka, Seweryn, Maryla… My entire family will hate me for killing Father, and Dariusz will shame me for stepping near Otylia, let alone allowing her to be taken. Gods, the tribe will shun me. And that's before they learn I'm a demon."

He hopped onto his horse and pulled me up, pondering as he pushed into a trot. "The bravest thing of all is to reveal the darkness within ourselves. I don't fully understand your demonic soul, but I can tell you this: You are not alone. Even if the tribe were to turn its back on you, you have friends who will stand by your side *because* you were honest with them in the end. I wish I had ones like that when I was your age."

We neared the camp entrance to see Narcyz scrambling toward us. Out of breath, he stopped with his hands on his knees as Xobas reined in his mount. "What has you in such a haste?" Xobas asked, sarcasm slipping into his voice.

"Katiôn wanted me to find you," Narcyz huffed. "Boz sent a messenger, and the commanders need you both right now."

"I don't understand the rush," I said. "Surely we have time to recover before engaging with Boz's men?"

He bit his cheek. "He's offered Rasa and free passage for the clans."

"At what cost?" Xobas asked.

Shuffling his boots in the ash, Narcyz swallowed. "You're not gonna like it…"

"Five hundred horses in exchange for the high priestess and the lives of all our riders is a gift!" Zhaleh slammed her fist into the wooden table in the center of the tent. Clay pots rattled, and one rolled to the ground, shattering as she scowled. "Mounts can be replaced."

Warriors murmured across the tent. We had gathered the clan commanders and most experienced warriors in one of the few remaining structures. Katiôn's personal tent had been burned down, and this one had little but the table, a stool, and a cloth cot in the corner. With a dozen people, though, we needed the space. I just wished for some time alone to think through what we faced.

Katiôn crossed his arms and glared at the Zurgowie priestess.

"For a group so faithful, you are quick to hand over creatures holy to our people. We defended ourselves last night. Commander Andrij has riders sent to nearby Astiwie villages for aid. If we counter now, Boz will be defeated by nightfall."

Zhaleh huffed. "Hope does not free the high priestess. Nor does the death of our warriors grant us lands in the west. Do you hope to weaken my clan, Katiôn, so that your Krowikie allies can control us when we arrive?"

They plunged into a shouting match as I hid behind Xobas, unsure. Freeing Rasa would prevent another battle and her death, but that was useless if the clans ripped themselves apart. The Simukie would never surrender their steeds, and there was no way the Zurgowie would sacrifice all five hundred to Boz. That would mean losing nearly all of their cavalry. What was their army without it?

"Calm yourselves!" Xobas stepped into the middle of the circle with his hands raised. "Calm! We are allies here."

Zhaleh spat. "I will be calm when the high priestess has returned. It was *your* marzban who let Boz take her."

Katiôn sighed. "We were led to believe she had plans to assassinate my grandson, Zakir, and myself. Regardless, our attack would have saved her in less than a day if it were not for King Boz's ambush. He never intended to allow any of us through his lands: Simukie or Zurgowie. Why would this time be any different?"

The Simukie men nodded as Zhaleh glared at the marzban. "Hundreds of their warriors survived the battle last night, more than we thought they had in the first place. Otlezd save me, I will not let more of my men and women die because *you* were too frightened to give up horses!"

"Such a move would only bolster his army's strength," Andrij said, his ripped blue cloak sweeping behind him as he paced. "The few horses we have are ill-trained for battle, and we lack those saddles and stirrups you ride with. Agreeing to this deal would be handing King Boz the means for your death."

"I do not trust the words of a traitor," Zhaleh said flatly. "You could switch sides again as easily as you did the first time."

Andrij scowled. "Seventy of my men died defending your people, priestess. What else must I lose to appease your bigotry?"

"That is enough!" Xobas jumped onto the table, spurring both Zhaleh and Andrij to back away. "There is more to this than it appears."

Andrij raised his brow. "What are you implying?"

Katiôn glanced at me, and I nodded, confirming Xobas's comment. Because of the rushed meeting, I hadn't spoken with the marzban yet about Bidaês.

"There is a war brewing far bigger than any tribe or clan," Xobas began. "We have seen the forces of the Krowikie winter goddess, Marzanna. The 'Frostmarked' we call them, for they bear a symbol like that of shattered ice on their skin. We thought before that the Horde was the vast majority of her army, but there are others working for her as well. Each minute we spend arguing, her servants rush toward us, growing stronger."

Zhaleh waved him away. "You speak the words of Alunam. I will not hear demonic blasphemy!"

"It is true, Zhaleh," Xobas said with a fist pressed over his heart. "I did not believe it at first, but I have experienced her power with my own eyes. Have you not seen the death that still grips the world? Did you not feel the bite of winter weeks beyond its usual breadth? This is not about faith! We face very real forces far more powerful than us."

"He tells the truth," Andrij said.

"How—" Xobas started.

"The firebird saved me on my journey to Dwie Rzeki." Reaching into his bag, Andrij pulled out a flaming feather. "It warned me about Marzanna, but I didn't understand until now how bad things really were."

Zhaleh scoffed. "You're the least trustworthy of all, and now, you bring western sorcery into our presence?"

They descended into another spit of yelling until I sighed.

"Marzanna seeks to divide us," I said.

The room silenced, not because of my strength of voice but because with my head spinning and my body exhausted, my words were little more than a whisper.

"She tempts us all," I continued, "and she knows the high priestess's death would drive a wedge between your peoples. For only together are we a threat to her Frostmarked—Krowikie, Astiwie, Simukie, and Zurgowie. That's why she sent a demon last night to start that blaze and alert the king to our assault. She's using his hatred of your clans to shatter our alliance." I pursed my lips as I fought the sorrow in my heart. "We have lost too many already, both warriors and innocents. I know Boz's demands are heavy, especially for the Simukie, but if we can avoid more death, we must."

Xobas offered me a smile. "The boy speaks wisely."

"Ay, he does," Katiôn replied, "but our people will not part with their mounts easily. Such bonds are sacred."

With a deep sigh, Xobas held out his exposed forearm, bearing the tattoo of a horse over his gruesome scar. "Few besides Katiôn know why I left my clan in shame. It was many years ago now, but it haunts me each night."

"Xobas," Katiôn gasped. "You need not do this."

Xobas furrowed his brow. "Yes, I must. This has remained a secret for too long, my dear friend, and my failure on the battlefield that day is why I believe I can stand before you now and say Wacław is right. It is a warrior's instinct to charge recklessly into battle, as I did. But like a sole cavalryman charging Ushtazie spearmen, our fight is hopeless alone." He stared down at his muscled forearm and traced the tattoo. "My horse, Seimeikos, died because of my impatience. Many other warriors and mounts did as well because I charged before my commander said so."

He looked from Zhaleh to Katiôn and then me. "You may wonder what this has to do with the decision we face. You may wonder why I'd surrender hundreds of more horses after losing my own. I speak because of this: I have seen what unbridled aggression can bring. Thousands more will die when the Horde arrives. That is why we must keep our clans as strong and united as possible, no matter the past hatred we bear for each other."

My heart ached at the pain on the faces of the Simukie commanders. We were asking them to surrender their holiest animals, bound to them for life.

Despite there being no equivalent among my tribe, it felt as if I was watching them come to terms with the death of a child. I hated myself for that. Otylia's voice in my mind insisted there was no other way, but I couldn't help but wonder what she would do if a king had demanded she sacrifice her amulets and offerings for Dziewanna.

Katiôn watched their reactions as well. A shadow hung over his face, and when he spoke, his words came out mumbled, "Very well. We will fulfill half of the requested number. Commanders, begin the collection process until I can rouse myself to speak with the people. Bring my horse."

"But my marzban!" Xobas exclaimed, hopping from the table.

"No, my friend." Katiôn put an arm on Xobas's shoulder. "I will not ask our clan to suffer a pain that I cannot endure myself. If our bonds must be broken, let mine be the first."

23

Wacław

He doesn't deserve this.

KATIÔN SAT, STUNNED, ON THE SOLITARY CHAIR within the now emptied tent. It was quiet except the occasional cry from the camp beyond as he stared down at his trembling hands.

Once the clan commanders had agreed to hand over the horses, they had left me alone with Xobas and the marzban. I had reluctantly told Katiôn everything that had happened during the battle. For minutes after, he hadn't spoken a word.

"I could accept him being like you," Katiôn whispered, finally breaking the silence. "But for him to turn against his family, against me…" He shook his head. "Bidaês helped the Astiwie slaughter our warriors, our people, because he wanted to rule? Why? He was to be our next great commander…"

I felt his sorrow as I knelt beside him and uncovered my Frostmark. "Marzanna has corrupted many, and even I fell for her temptations at first. Bidaês bore a Frostmark. Who knows how long she's whispered to him, manipulating him slowly? When we fought, he seemed to actually believe siding with Marzanna would save both him and your clan."

"The goddess used him, my marzban," Xobas said. "Don't blame yourself for the boy's error."

Katiôn's lip curled as he looked up. "I trusted him… I gave up High Priestess Rasa to that lunatic of a king because of Bidaês's word, and now, my clan will suffer for *my* error. This journey west was supposed to bring safety. Instead, I have led my people into a trap."

"That safety can come when you have passed Kynnytsia," I replied, rewrapping my hand. "Your clans have lost many, but I wasn't lying when I said you will form the greatest army seen for generations. Never before have tribes from both west and east of Perun's Crown united. That success will be because of you."

"Is it a success if we sacrifice our holiest creatures, if I lose my eldest grandson?" He studied me, tears welling in his eyes. "Who are we without our strongest beliefs?"

With a deep breath, I rose and moved to Xobas's side. "Everything I believed in has been shattered in less than two moons. All I have left are the people I love and the allies that protect them."

"I understand… It seems, however, that I am incapable of protecting those I love. Bidaês slaughtered my son, my only son, years ago." Katiôn cursed beneath his breath. "How many died because I was too blind to see the truth? How can we have hope?"

"As long as we remain united against the Horde," Xobas answered, "we will fight to the last man and woman."

My heart ached knowing more would be lost, but this was war. We had to fight to win. "And when we bring back Otylia, we can stop Marzanna for good."

"How can one girl turn the tide?" Katiôn asked with a shake of his head.

"I ask you to trust me on this, marzban. The last thing I want to do is ride ahead after all we've faced, but I have to reach her before the Maj moon."

He rose, stepping slowly toward me. "She means something to you, doesn't she?"

"The girl is his lover," Xobas said, blunt. "Or if she isn't yet, she was soon to be."

Heat rushed to my cheeks as I remembered holding Otylia in the woods… Gone so quickly. "You could say that."

"But," Xobas added, "what he says about her is true."

Katiôn nodded. "Then I honor the risk you are taking to travel to this place you call Nawia, Wacław. Bidaês may have brought me shame, but I am proud to have journeyed this far with you." He approached and gave the Simukie greeting. "May the lands of the next life be kinder to you than this one."

I bowed my head. "Thank you, Katiôn."

When I looked up again, he was still studying me with his wrinkled brow furrowed. "My people are making a great sacrifice because of my trust for you," he said. "Ride swiftly, and do not forget your promises to us."

With another bow, I moved to the tent's entrance. "I will do everything in my power to ensure your people receive the lands they were promised." *If only they were mine to give…*

I stepped into the chilled morning air. Shivering, I pulled my cloak tighter. Both it and my tunic were bloodied from the battle, but as the moans echoed through the camp and the smell of death lingered in the air, I thanked the gods I was alive—for now.

"It's about time you showed up!" Boz shouted from atop a large chestnut horse. From the way it fidgeted beneath him, the poor thing didn't seem honored to carry royalty.

Hundreds of warriors filled the path behind him. Even if we'd planned an ambush, it wouldn't have ended well, and I assumed Boz had more men in the trees too, just in case.

"We are honoring our side of the deal, King Boz," Katiôn replied, dismounting his own horse ahead of the clan warriors—both Simukie and Zurgowie—and the rest of the offerings. The warriors ushered the horses forward in twos until they were alongside the trail, halfway between the king and marzban. "Release the high priestess."

I waited beside him, doing my best to hide my discomfort as I looked for Xobas. For a few minutes, he was nowhere to be seen, but he soon pushed his way through the crowd and to my side. His jaw was clenched, and he had one hand on his sword's hilt. *What is he expecting?*

Katiôn and Boz stared each other down for a long time, neither moving until the king chuckled to himself and nodded to one of his generals. The man marched through the Astiwie warriors and returned moments later with Rasa. Bruises covered her face, and she spat blood as the general forced her to her knees alongside Boz.

"Your savage priestess is here, Katiôn," Boz said. "Unfortunately, she had rebellious habits and never stopped praying to that false god of hers. That had to be addressed." He cackled as Rasa opened her mouth, letting out a moan.

Her tongue was gone.

My hopes diminished, and I froze as the crowd erupted. Before Katiôn could stop her, a Zurgowie priestess sprinted to Rasa. Boz smirked at the ruckus, raising an open hand. When the girl was just strides from the high priestess, Boz clenched his fist, and the *twang* of a dozen bows filled the air.

The young priestess didn't have the chance to yell or even whimper. Half the arrows hit their mark, and she dropped to the earth, pierced in head and heart.

Next to me, Xobas cursed in the clan tongue. "Be prepared to flee with the others," he said. "They are waiting in the southern woods. These negotiations are important, but if this ends in battle, you have sacrificed enough time already. Otylia needs you."

My heart pounded. Had Xobas assumed the meeting would go wrong and planned for my escape? I didn't have time to wonder. I needed to stop this, to prevent a slaughter, but Zhaleh screamed from upon her mount.

The golden eagle leaped from her padded arm and dove toward Boz. As its screech tore through the air, Zurgowie archers surged forward, their bows ready as they cried out to their gods to bless them. There was nothing I could do. Their clan wanted blood. Neither Katiôn rushing in front of the archers nor Xobas's orders for them to stop changed that. If they wouldn't listen to generals, why would they listen to me?

A horse plowed into the gap between the armies, sending the offerings at the head of the line scattering into the trees.

Its rider gripped his spear and shield as his blue and gold cloak flapped behind him. He looked from the Zurgowie to his king. "War between our people will not solve anything!" Andrij yelled. "I say this as a warrior. If we fight, the Horde of the east will crush us beneath their ranks, and Marzanna will smile upon the destruction we allowed."

For a moment, the Zurgowie stopped, but it wasn't because of Andrij's speech. Boz had dismounted. He gripped Rasa by her hair and held a dagger to her throat, his eyes wild. "I don't fear death. Nor do I fear traitorous swine like you! You defy both Marzanna and your king. You are the servants of Weles, swarming our lands with cavalry and his demonic bears, destroying all that I've created! But decapitate the beast and the minions scurry away."

"No!" I shouted, joining the chorus as Boz slit Rasa's throat in one swift cut.

The mad king threw her body to the dirt and licked his lips. "Kill them and their corrupted mounts! They taint our land."

Astiwie bows twanged and arrows rained as the Zurgowie charged into a shield wall Boz's men had formed in seconds. The unruly advance left the flanks exposed. As the Astiwie spearmen struck down the Zurgowie warriors unfamiliar with fighting on foot, their axmen swarmed from the woods with deafening yells. Katiôn ordered the clan warriors back, but it was no use. The Simukie had joined the fray. Horses scattered everywhere, crushing both clansmen and Astiwie alike in their panic.

I stood frozen in horror as women grabbed their children and ran. But they didn't get far.

Astiwie cavalry swept from our southern flank and into their path. Women pushed their children away, throwing themselves before the riders. I hesitated in my shock before pulling Kwiecień and scrambling to them, but outside of my soul-form, I was too slow. The cavalry killed the fleeing innocents without recognition of woman or child.

Blood coated the ash. My ears rang from the cries. The cavalry charged up the slope at the crowd as the Astiwie footmen encircled the clan armies. I ran toward the slaughter, hoping to save whoever I could. But before I arrived, Xobas grabbed hold of me.

"You need to go!" he shouted as he dragged me away.

"I can't abandon them!" I cried, my eyes stinging from the tears. I had seen death before, but Bustelintin had been nothing compared to this. Thousands of innocents had traveled with the clans, and now, Xobas wanted me to leave them to their deaths.

Xobas held my shoulders. His gaze was stern, his grip firm. "You cannot save those who are destined to die, but you can live long enough to protect those who have a chance to live. I left my people once, but I will not shame them again. Go! Those who escape will follow you west."

He glanced over his shoulder as Andrij approached at full gallop, stopping quickly and reaching out a hand to me. "C'mon, Wacław. Your friends are waiting further down the hill. If we're going to meet them, we need to go *now*."

"No…" I murmured.

Women and children screamed less than fifty strides away as the cavalry arrived. Boz's men showed them no mercy, and hatred burned within me. *I'll make him pay*, I promised myself. Someday, I would return and end his reign. *Then you'll see a real demon.*

I took a sharp breath and looked to Xobas one last time. "Whether here or in Nawia, I'll see you again. May Perun bless your sword."

"And may Otylia bless your heart," he replied. "Now, go!"

After sheathing Kwiecień, I grabbed Andrij's hand, but as I pulled myself onto the horse, pain struck my chest.

My mind spun. My breaths caught. Sputtering, I fell to the ground and snapped the arrow that stuck from my ribs.

Andrij and Xobas yelled my name, but my consciousness was already slipping. I felt my blood mixing with the ash. Though I fought for each breath, it wasn't enough. The last thing I saw was a squad of riders bearing down upon me before I slipped into the darkness.

24

Otylia

You have done well with the Trials, Lady Otylia. Today will hold two more—the last Weles has planned for many moons—but fear not. We will assist you in those that remain. I will come to you tonight, after the fourth Trial. The key to your escape awaits.

- A friend.

MEMORIES HAUNTED ME in the days following the Trials of Isolation and Connection. Every time I blinked, I saw Illya's body ravaged by my fox form or Wacław fighting in the flaming woods. Even when I tried not to think, the absence of my goddesses' powers left me empty, alone.

I held my fingers to my lips as I paced across my room in my shift. That stupid kiss had glee and dread warring within me. What would a real relationship with Wacław mean? The idea of being *with* a boy had scared me for so long, and that was before I'd kissed a demon. Each moment in his arms made my heart race. It made me never want to leave, to forget reality. That was dangerous.

With a shake of my head, I sighed. Feelings meant nothing now. I had to pass the Trials of Ascension before Maj—anything else was a distraction. I'd shoved down my sorrow of Mother's death and Wacław's absence for years. The storm within me could wait.

My bare toes dug into the cool dirt as anticipation swelled in my mind. It had been a week since the last Trial—a week since I'd stepped foot beyond Weles's palace. But that note, readable in the mirror like before, gave me hope.

The doors swung open, and Sabina slipped through the crack, carrying a multitude of dresses. "You will love these, Lady Otylia!" she exclaimed as she laid them carefully across the bed.

I frowned. *What is Weles planning?* He had never allowed the excitable nymph to bring options before. I hoped it meant another Trial—just one with less blood. "What's the occasion?"

She beamed. "You don't know?"

"Obviously not," I grumbled.

"Oh, Otylia!" With a leap, she took flight, giggling as her wings beat the air like a swarm of bees. "Today, you are to be presented to the realm! Spirits and souls have traveled from all over Nawia to see you. Many are considered royalty, protecting Weles's rule further from the palace."

Presented? I huffed and stopped my pacing. One arm across my chest, I studied the excited nymph. "I'm just some pretty flower for Weles to show off?"

"Lady Otylia?" Sabina landed, worry crossing her face. "Are you all right? This is supposed to be exciting."

I spun away. "I'm fine."

"Dziewanna isn't lost forever," she said, "and neither are we. You passed two Trials already."

"But what about the next one?" I folded my arms and avoided the dresses as if not looking would make the day disappear. "The Maj moon will come in two weeks. If I haven't Ascended before then, Jaryło's full return will make our escape difficult." When I reached the wall, I turned back to her and groaned. "What?"

"Sorry, Lady Otylia." She sniffled, her eyes reddened. "You've been so full of sorrow since you arrived, and I had hoped that this day could at least make you smile. The guests and the next step toward our escape…"

"I'm an immortal trapped in the underworld, the boy I… care for… is fighting a demonic wolf-man and apparently the entire Astiwie army to get to me, and my mother is imprisoned by the goddess of death." I realized I was clenching my fists, and I tried to release the tension as I looked to the early morning light creeping through the roots above. "Finding more about how Vlatka's friends intend to help us escape is positive, but it's hard to smile when everything you know is falling apart."

She ran her long fingers across the bed frame, tracing each symbol of the old tongue carved into it. "You're still worried about your vision of Wacław?"

I nodded. After the Trial, Mokosz's appearance, and my confrontation with Jaryło, I'd been exhausted. Sabina, though, had pried out my thoughts in her oddly tender way.

Smiling, she swept across the room and gave me a hug—one I begrudgingly accepted. She said nothing else. No shy giggle or pep talk. Just her arms around me as I shuddered, remembering the fits of pain and anguish that had washed over Wacław's connection to me since Mokosz's vision. Each one threatened to break me, to make me curl up in bed and whimper for days. But I'd wept too much already. Marzanna, Weles, Jaryło—they each wanted to use me in their own way.

I wouldn't let them.

"So, what *is* this presentation then?" I asked as I pulled away. "The note said there will be two Trials."

Sabina raised a suspicious brow at my change of topic but complied, her giddiness returning. "The Trials I know nothing of. For the party, the visitors are just happy to see you. Oh, I'm so excited! Pick a dress."

How does she cheer up so quickly?

I huffed before examining the dresses. They were ornate for our tribe's standards. Each was a different color, and elaborate figures and symbols were embroidered across the trim, sleeves, and, on some, across most of the dress itself. My dress for the Drowning of

Marzanna seemed ordinary compared to them. Nothing, though, could match the care Ara's mother had put into it.

Sabina flew over the bed and landed across from me. She waved a hand over each dress as she described the stories its embroidery told. Some were battles, others tales both familiar and not, but it was the final dress that took my breath away.

To anyone else, it would have been little to look at. The others had vibrant colors on the dress itself, but this one was brown with an attached cloak made from an array of autumn leaves—red, yellow, and green. As my fingers traced the soft fabric, I knew why I was drawn to it.

"This was Dziewanna's dress," I whispered. "The one she appeared to me in after my initiation. But it's different. Mother's cloak was green, but this..."

My breaths caught. Weles's nymphs wore clothes of bark and leaves like this, but when I moved the dress, the cape's colors shifted on the bed, providing a new pattern at each angle. It was immaculate, finely crafted to somehow appear as both a simple bed of leaves and a mesmerizing display. There was something else, though.

"The embroidery is new," I said, tracing the silver symbols along the dress's skirt, neck, and sleeves. Most of them were foreign to me, except two: *kobyla* and *lis*. Mare and fox. "What story do these tell?"

Cocking her head to the side, she looked closer. "I don't know. Master Weles didn't tell me about that one's embroidery, but he did say you would choose it." She smiled. "If it was Lady Dziewanna's, I guess we know why."

How did he get it?

That question lingered in my mind, but Sabina was too excited to tolerate my pondering. In the end, it was just another mystery surrounding my elusive blood father. My plan was unchanged. *Complete the Trials, ask questions later.*

Sabina spent what felt like forever painting my face with traditional markings, helping me into the dress, and adjusting it so that it fit a little *too* perfectly. Typically, my clothes were loose to allow me freedom of movement in the woods or fights with demons. This wasn't. Though the cloak flooded behind me, sliding across the ground, the dress was tight around my waist and low-cut enough on the chest to reveal the tip of my scar and make me blush.

Mother had been a stunning goddess in it. I was just a girl.

I turned away from the mirror, back into the bedroom. "I'll pick another one."

But she caught my arm and, with more force than I'd thought possible from her, pulled me back to the mirror. "Look at yourself!"

"I did…" I clenched my jaw but complied.

What am I supposed to see? My heart hammered as I studied the girl in a goddess's dress. From the glimmering lines of silver and green along my cheeks and chin to my skin's contrast against the colorful cloak, I seemed more a priest's painting than a person. I'd never felt so beautiful. Part of me wished I could see Wacław's face with me wearing this.

Still, something seemed *wrong*. The girl in the reflection was me: the unruly black hair, the narrow face, the sharp green eyes, and the scars from battles against the Frostmarked, but I was the witch in the woods, not some piece of art to be easy on the eye. With awe would come worship.

I didn't want to be worshipped. I wanted to be free.

To be free, you have to play the part. So, I let myself enjoy the way it made me look. Mother was the wild goddess. If she could wear beautiful dresses and put fear into her enemies at the same time, then so could I.

"If only the village could see me now," I said. "Wacław would gawk, but the girls would flee. No more laughing, just running in terror." I laughed.

Sabina grinned. "See, I knew you only needed a little time, Lady Otylia. Nawia's beautiful things are often new to even we nymphs."

Eyeing myself in the mirror one last time, I spun toward the bed. "And horrifying."

"That is… another way to see it, my lady."

"If you call me 'lady' one more time, I'll show you why the girls were afraid of me."

Sabina's wings fluttered anxiously as she slid beside me. "I have surmised."

I took her hand, smirking. "Where was this sarcasm when I was depressed? Gods, you were shy."

"Perhaps you are quite the negative influence on me." She reached for my fox pelt. "One last touch."

I snatched it, but she softly held my arm. "Allow me to, *Otylia*."

"Fine."

Sabina finished preparing me in quick fashion. Her dainty fingers touched up my makeup—more than I'd ever worn—and ensured the fox's silver fur didn't interfere with the cloak's colors. *I would be lost without her.*

As she worked, I tried to keep my hopes up about Wacław. Our connection had been faint ever since the night of the first Trial, but I sensed him. He was alive. In what condition, I didn't know, but as long as he lived, Wacław wouldn't give up. I'd seen the desperation in his eyes, felt the passion in our kiss.

Mokosz was right. We needed each other on a level deeper than I could grasp. My initial fear was fading, though, replaced by an odd comfort.

Was it contentment that he loved me too? Or was there something else? I wanted to be afraid of how joined I was to him, but in my heart, I knew the truth.

That connection was the greatest gift I had.

25

Otylia

Today's Trial is patience, apparently.

We waited in the throne room for at least an hour before Weles, clothed in a simple woolen tunic and cloak of bear furs, shuffled through the doors. He leaned on his cane more than normal, and when his eyes met me, his face was tired and more wrinkled than before.

"You look so much like your mother," he said as I stood to the side, among the vines. "That dress confirms it—you are surely a daughter of the wilds."

I held my chin high. His compliment meant little, but it was best for him to believe he'd bolstered my confidence. "Witch or not, they'll always be my home."

He chuckled, sitting upon the throne of twisting vines. Behind him, the roots of the World Tree formed the Heart of Nawia. The route to Jawia was just strides away, but two-dozen nymphs of various types guarded it. Unlike most of the servants, they carried staffs, blades, and shields.

"Indeed." With a nod to the chair alongside his throne, he smiled. "Based on your pacing, I figure that you were aggravated by my absence."

"I don't sit well."

"Yes, I have noticed. As has Jaryło after you strayed into my blood altar, alone." He folded his hands, placing his elbows on the chair's armrests. "What did you intend to find?"

I can't trust him with Mokosz's vision. He would only constrain me more.

"Nothing," I said, blunt. "The first set of Trials had been a lot to process. Despite my… discomfort… with the blood drinking, that room represents a core part of becoming a deity. I needed to come to terms with that."

"Hmm." He studied me, the wrinkles on his brow deepening for a moment. "And did you?"

I pursed my lips. *Gods, why does he make me so uncertain?* "I don't know, but I'm sure I want to continue with the Trials."

"Do you?" The right side of his mouth flicked up. "That is good to hear, as you are set to face the next set this afternoon."

My heart jumped. *The note was right...* "What are they?" *Anything to get me out of here again.*

"Patience, Otylia." He raised his hand, and a servant brought him a goblet. The god gave the nymph a nod before taking a long drink. "These Trials are just as they appear—tests. Each is a crucial step in preparation for your Ascension, and they should not be rushed into as if they were the flame of youthful love."

I clenched my jaw. "That's none of your business."

"Is it not? You may believe you are independent by wearing your hair down, but you are my daughter. By right, I shall have the power to decide whom you marry, or if you do so at all."

"Mother was forced to wed. I won't be."

With a glance at Sabina, who fluttered silently nearby, he huffed. "Though among your tribe you may have been considered a woman, ready to wed and bear children, you are but a child among gods. That you survived the attacks of Marzanna's szeptucha, Yuliya, proved you have a strength within you. But she was nothing. There are gods, demons, and beasts far greater than her, and it will take time for you to be prepared for them."

I raised a brow, crossing my arms. "Is that a threat?"

He laughed louder than I'd heard from him, and he coughed on his drink as he tried to speak. Once he recovered, he bore a wicked grin. "I have no need to threaten you, child. You are my daughter, so it is in my best interest to protect you, but if I wished the Three Realms to be rid of you, I would make it so."

So it's a threat.

"I will tell you this, however," he continued. "Do not let your attachments as a szeptucha twist your perception of who you are and who you can become. Whether it is this corrupted boy, Dziewanna, or the Great Mother, they cannot define you. The Trials are meant to expose your core. If you are not ready, they will be uncomfortable."

Just like this conversation. "I will be ready," I replied, not offering him the complaints he surely expected.

"Very well." He nodded to a nymph behind us, who opened the great wooden doors to the room. "Today's Trial shall be a difficult one, but we will celebrate before then, for it is time to present you to the realm."

People flooded through the doors as I retreated to my chair. The dead souls wore their white tunics, nymphs in their colorful clothes flew above to get a view of me, and spirits shifted between animals of various sizes. Hundreds, if not thousands, of them filled the hall.

I swallowed and instinctively reached for Dziewanna's bow at my collar, but the amulet was gone. Every eye of every creature was upon me. *What do they see?* I wondered. *A girl out of place? A childish goddess impersonating her mother? Or the princess of the underworld?*

Sabina fluttered among them. For once, her giddy smile was a relief, and she approached with something wrapped with cloth. Even Weles held a look of fatherly pride as she landed beside me.

"A gift?" I muttered. "You should've warned me about this."

"But that would have ruined the surprise!" she exclaimed, holding out the parcel to me.

"I hate surprises…" I sighed. *This is happening no matter what, so might as well take some control.*

Taking the parcel, I stood and walked perpendicular to the crowd, sweeping my cloak behind me as I did. They gasped at its flowing colors. My skin crawled with them watching me, but I was a goddess now. If they were going to watch, better that they gawk than curse.

Muscles tense, I spun on my heels to face them again. The cloak only half-followed, draped over my shoulder and sweeping for a stride alongside me. It had been an accident, but based on their reactions, I was doing something right.

I glanced down at the package and took a sharp breath. *What does a god gift his daughter?* Perun had gifted Marzanna the Thunderstone dagger for her wedding, but as I pulled back the cloth, I prayed for it to be anything but a weapon.

It was.

A hollow cylinder of intertwined silver and willow-wood bands hummed with power. Each band was engraved with words in the old tongue that glowed at my touch, and the familiar power of channeling greeted me as I grasped it. *What is this?*

"You are a *księżniczka*, a princess," Weles said, drawing near, "and you deserve jewelry to mark you as such."

"There is power in it," I said, still studying its perfectly woven design.

He held my shoulders and smiled. "As I told you, words have power in them, as do the symbols of the old tongue the tribes weave into their clothing. This armband is no different." Softly, he took it and slid my left hand and forearm into it until the bands met at my wrist at one end and the tip of my elbow at the other. It fit perfectly. "It will offer you some protection, should you need it."

"Why must you always be so cryptic?" I asked as a shiver ran up my arm. The silver was cold against my skin.

"There is much you must learn in time. It is the way of the gods."

Before I could object, he turned back to the crowd, who stared in awe at the glimmering armband. "Come forward," he proclaimed, "and greet Nawia's princess."

I snapped my gaze to him. "I have to meet all of them?" I whispered.

Weles chuckled as he leaned against his staff. In that moment, it was hard to remember he was one of the most powerful gods and had imprisoned me in his realm. He *seemed* genuinely happy for once, and despite everything, I felt his care for me for the first time. *His ways are deceiving and odd, but he's trying to be a father. Is that enough?*

It took all my strength not to squirm as the souls and creatures of Nawia formed a line, coming to me one at a time. Most simply bowed and said how much of an honor it was to see their princess. Others offered gifts of food or various amulets, which were accepted by servants and quickly swept off. I met them as respectfully as I could, curtsying clumsily and saying what sounded like a goddess's blessings.

The visitors went on for some time. Not all of them had fit into the hall, and the process was incredibly slow. When the line was *finally* coming to its end, I relaxed.

Then the last man drew a bone knife.

I stepped back, remembering Mokosz's visions of the Frost-marked Horde and their weapons of bone. But Weles did not waver. So, I regained my composure and bowed my head to the man.

"To my goddess, I gift blood from my very veins!" the man exclaimed before slicing his forearm from wrist to elbow.

I screamed as he dropped the blade. His blood trickled down his arm and dripped to the floor. *Not now. Please, not yet.*

Trembling, the man looked from me to Weles, his eyes full of fear. The god held my arm. "You must accept the man's offering, Otylia," he said. "It is the Trial of Life. Take his blood."

Every muscle in my body screamed for me to run. A pool of crimson had begun to form at the man's feet, and I could have sworn his skin was looking paler by the second.

The third Trial… I have no choice. Did I ever?

My heart hammered my chest as I reached out my cupped hands. The man smiled and scrambled forward, allowing his blood to fall into my grasp. When I could hold no more, I pulled back and shut my eyes. *Do it for Mother, for Wašek.*

I drank.

Instantly, my stomach retched, but I forced myself to continue until my hands were empty. The crowd cheered. Then, the man's footsteps drifted away.

I trembled as I tried to think of anything but the blood coating my tongue and throat, dripping from my lips to my chin. I couldn't. The first Trial had emptied my soul. The second had been vile, animalistic. But this was so much worse. A man had slit his arm just so that I could drink his blood—as if it were an honor. To applaud a man harming himself… *Is this how we worship?* The thought alone made me gag, but another frightening sensation built in my soul.

I craved more.

Someone laid a hand on my shoulder. I opened my eyes, and Sabina's soft smile met me. Beyond, the crowd still lingered. When they saw me looking, they dropped to their knees and chanted prayers in unison.

They believe I can save them, even in the underworld. Why?

A new wave of *žityje* burst through my soul as I studied the bowing people, nymphs, and oddly human-like animals before turning to Weles. He nodded, a proud smile on his face. "What was that?" I asked.

"Do not ask questions you know the answer to," he replied. "You have passed the third Trial—Life—and you have accepted a sacrifice of blood."

I passed another. Nausea overwhelmed my senses. "His *žityje*… I feel it."

"Good. A deity's soul gifts them strength beyond all other beings, but it is only through these gifts of life that we can truly serve our roles." Weles gestured for the guests to rise. "You must overcome this hesitance. From now on, the Trials will only grow more difficult."

I nodded, but before I could reply, my stomach revolted. With guests bowing before me, I waved them away and grabbed Sabina, bolting through the crowd and the halls beyond until we were alone.

"What are you—" she began as I dropped to my knees in the hall and vomited. "Oh…"

Spitting out bile and dried blood, I glared up at her. "Did you know?"

"N… No, Lady Otylia," she stammered. "Master Weles only told me of the celebration, nothing more. The Trials are a secret, unique for each god."

Unique? Weles had said the ritual connecting me to the silver fox was the same bond as others. Was only the process different? I shook my head and stood. *Just more secrets.*

"Will you be all right?" Sabina asked, her head cocked as if she didn't understand I'd just thrown up blood from a sacrifice. "I will have this taken care of, but Master We—"

"I'll be fine." I wiped away what vomit remained on my chin. It wouldn't remove the blood, but that seemed to be the point. "This is my life now. Might as well get used to it I guess."

Taking a deep breath, I stormed back to the throne room and pushed open the doors. I stared at my feet, but the crowd didn't care. A chorus of cheers greeted me as I returned to Weles's side.

26

Wacław

Is this Oblivion?

I DRIFTED.

The black water swallowed me like a devouring swarm, filling my lungs and mind. At least, I thought it was black. In whatever void I had descended into, it was impossible to know if my eyes were open or shut or if I was even alive.

Was I ever?

My demonic soul sapped my humanity with each passing day. Jaryło had lied about much—his identity, his goals, his willingness to fight alongside us—but I knew he'd told the truth about me. I had felt it my entire life. Whether plowing the fields, wrestling with Kuba, or fighting make-believe monsters in the woods with Otylia, I'd sensed its desire. Undead or living, demons desired *žityje* to fuel our power.

Our.

Yes, I was like them. Though I had denied the signs, they seemed obvious as I drifted in the endless sea.

It wasn't a voice or a bloodthirsty lust. It crept like a snake through the grass, biding its time. Urges, tugs on my soul. Dariusz and his priests spoke of demons who could track the gods, identify them even when they appeared as mortals. That thirst for *żityje* pulled us to its most potent sources. From plants to the beasts of the earth to mankind, and then to the gods themselves. But no demon could best the gods.

Our greatest need killed us. Our greatest desire wrapping around our necks until it squeezed the life out of us—the very life we fought to protect.

Did that make us any less than animals, mortals, or even gods? Was it not the wolf's hunger that drew him to the sheep's pastures, only to meet the farmer's scythe? Was it not a man's thirst for power that drew him to battle, only to be slain by an enemy's spear? And was it not the great god Jaryło's desire to be worshipped that brought him to a mortal woman's bed, only to find Marzanna's wrath?

No, I decided. *We are no different. Hunger drives both man and beast rabid in time, forcing them to do what they must to survive.*

I shared the carnal desires of human and demonic souls. Yearning for love, for acceptance, for purpose. Craving a connection to my power, *żityje*, and to draw closer to the strongest among us—for what else could have driven me to Otylia?

Before I had fallen in love. Before we had made amends. Before we were even childhood friends. I'd been pulled to her. Had I simply sensed her soul of a goddess? Had my fascination with her been nothing more than my demonic instincts bringing me to the *żityje* it wanted, or had it been something more?

I forced away those thoughts. *Our connection is deeper than that, especially now.*

If I cleared my mind, I could sense her starker than ever as I sunk to the depths. From her heart beating like a shaman's drum to her sharp, shallow breaths like the breeze along my cheek, it was as if she were only inches away. *My Otylka…*

Everything she felt was vivid, clashing with my own senses, but I couldn't see her. She was afraid, no, disgusted—both? Sweet aromas both familiar and strange met her nose. The chill of a band along her arm caused her hairs to rise. The salty taste of blood coated her tongue, churning her stomach.

She opened her eyes as nausea overwhelmed her. A crowd prayed, calling to her as her chest heaved with every breath. At once, *życie* swelled within her soul, alien for only a moment, and her revulsion subsided.

What is this?

A single, powerful voice replaced the worshippers, but his words were lost in the void. Whatever he said disturbed Otylia. The pride she'd taken from this new power faded, replaced by her nausea once again. As she vomited, a more familiar emotion took over—anger.

Then she faded away in a flash, and I was left alone in that pool of nothing, alone.

It was the first time since I'd entered the void an immeasurable time ago that I realized I was alone. My thoughts wandered, clear of outside interference. They had led me into my demonic soul and shown me the pain within me that I had rejected for so long. Our battles with the Frostmarked and my relationship with Otylia had taken so much of my time, so those had been the first moments in what seemed an eternity that I could simply think.

Contemplating my demonic soul had scared me. At times, I had run from it, pretending to accept what I could barely understand. There was nothing to flee to here, and my conclusions brought me comfort more than fear.

I was a human. I was a demon. Both parts of me were flawed, lured to desires that could be my death. Yet that was life.

Dariusz had called demons the *założnye pokojniki*—the unclean dead—but to be dead was to be lifeless. How could beings so desperate for *życie* to sustain ourselves be considered dead? What was life without an endless pursuit? Was there something that made life for mortals anything more than those of demons?

The priests had never answered that.

Eryk had shown me that demons were capable of a deep, selfless love. Though he'd served Marzanna and possessed great power over blizzards and winds in the east, his goal was not simply to survive. He had a purpose—more than many people I'd known.

A soul is a life, whether mortal, demon, or deity, I decided.

Bidaês had asked me during our travels if I would give up my powers to become fully human, but as I spun through the waters, allowing my fingers to dance through the current I'd made, the answer was clear.

I could never surrender my power.

My demonic soul had crept upon me, urged me in directions my entire life, but it was no different than my human conscience. Just because one was unfamiliar to the priests did not make it evil. Nor did the familiar make the other good. They both pushed me forward, to keep me alive as I pursued my purpose—one that existed because they had *both* shaped me.

Bidaês had not become a villainous fiend because he was a demon. Despite my initial failures, I had resisted Marzanna's temptations in time, but he had accepted them, allowed them to become his purpose. His demise was the weakness of his soul, not its type.

A pain shattered my chest.

My calm fled. I couldn't breathe. From my toes to my waist was numb, and all else was aflame.

I screamed. Water greeted me, rushing into my mouth and down my throat in a tide. *I'm going to drown.*

I coughed and sputtered, but that only allowed more water to fill my lungs as I slid deeper and deeper into the dark sea. The pressure was crushing me. My lungs spasmed, useless as my mind demanded air.

Light flooded my vision as I wheezed, lying on a bed and figures hovered over me. I knew I should recognize them, but their faces were distorted and their voices distant.

What's happening to me?

My chest burned worse than any pain I'd ever felt. Each time I coughed, blood spurted from my mouth as someone turned my head to stop me from choking. Seconds were hours. I could feel my body fighting without me, but just staying conscious took all of my strength.

The world spun as one of the figures held my face, saying something I couldn't understand. They seemed sad. Or maybe I was. My mind was too confused to know the difference.

Soon, the darkness called me again. It was kind, gentle. I wanted to follow it away from this pain. The void had kept me safe. There had been no despair or confusion, just the tranquility of a clear soul—or two.

So I followed it. The world drifted, and the figures rushed around me as the light faded.

27

Otylia

Wašek?

In the aftermath of the third Trial, I hadn't noticed his presence, but a familiar sensation lingered as the last of the crowd left—his steady heartbeat. Our tether was tight. My soul told me Wacław was within a stride, but it lied.

Then why do I feel him?

He'd faded as quickly as he'd come, leaving me alone once again. In that time, though, his constant pain from recent days was gone, replaced by peace. With dried blood still on my lips and chin, that was a welcome surprise.

Our connection had been so distant, and our new separation hung over me as Weles led me through the winding halls of his palace. I hated the longing. We had been apart for weeks, but our moment in the woods, and now this, had me shaken.

Being alone was easier. I had done it for years without Wacław, without Mother. The constant reminders of them gave me hope, but I needed to focus on the Trials, not the foolish desires of my heart.

"Where are we going?" I asked as the vines parted, revealing the swamp behind. Weles hadn't allowed me to clean the blood from my face, and we'd left the throne room as soon as the guests were gone.

The gifts they'd brought had been taken before I could examine any of them. All except the blood and armband of silver and wood.

Weles shuffled on, the muck and undergrowth hardly slowing his advance—not that he was all that fast with his cane. "Patience."

So I followed in silence. My cloak slid over the ground, picking up foliage that only made it seem even more a part of the wilds. The trees rustled around us. Unlike in Jawia's endless winter, a sea of green leaves blocked the Nawia sky, and flowers blossomed in the few cracks of sunlight that reached the swamp floor.

Marzanna can't ruin spring everywhere.

If I'd been back in Dwie Rzeki, I would've scampered through the water, collecting fungi and plants for potions. No one else bothered to enter the swamps around the Krowik and Wyzra rivers, and Dziewanna's power thrived in the places untouched by man. It had been my domain. Boys wrestled and their fathers struggled to claim who was the strongest warrior. None of them could tame the wilds.

I smiled. Men feared what they couldn't control, and gods were no different. Jaryło had cowered when I'd pressed his wound. A great war god had been killed by a boy—a demon he'd mocked.

In Weles, I saw pride, but it was not in battle, appearances, or even power. No, his weapons were wit and deception. Like the shadows of the forest, he lurked, patiently waiting for his moment to take victory. He couldn't defeat Perun and seize Jawia by himself. Instead, Weles had stolen the thunder god's golden cattle, attacking Perun's vulnerable pride, before kidnapping Jaryło and turning him against his own father.

We reached a winding, dark tree. Its roots bulged from the ground, and years of insect attacks had left its trunk scarred—more holes than bark. Within the green of the forest, its blackened branches were a stain.

Death.

I sensed him as if he watched me. Yuliya's sorcery had killed hundreds of trees around Bustelintin, but she'd only been Death's servant. Maybe even Marzanna was. But this was Death himself.

Fear should've met me with that realization. I should've fled from the stench of mold and decay, the feeling of my crawling skin like a swarm of spiders. My curiosity was stronger.

Without a command from Weles, I stepped forward, the bands of silver and willow-wood burning at my arm. Awe filled me as whispers circled. They swirled on nothing, as the winds had ceased, leaving a cold emptiness. I barely noticed. All I saw was the tree and the soul trapped within—a force more powerful than any I'd sensed before—screaming to be released.

My breaths dissolved into fog as I approached the tree. Though my cloak snagged on its uneven roots, I didn't stop. The whispers called me nearer. I rejected their sway, deafening myself to the mirage of voices and continuing on my own accord.

"I don't care what you promise," I declared. "You will not control me."

"I am what rules all beings—mortal or not," the whispers replied in my mind. They were hundreds, each a unique voice, but they spoke as one. *"Men may deny me, flee me, or delay my coming, but I am inevitable. I am what gives life its meaning, what strips it away, and what is the end of all things. Even for you, little goddess. You may believe yourself immortal, but all life has its end.*

"I see the deepest depths of your fragile soul. I see those you love, whom you believe you would sacrifice anything to save. I see your most fervent desires and the truths you could not bear others knowing.

"You are selfish and weak. You seek your goddesses not out of reverence or worship but to fill an emptiness in your soul. You believe you are nothing without them. You seek solitude out of fear of what others believe about you, but truly, you cannot stand to be alone because you fear that void. Though you show strength to others, you are no different than the chiefs and kings who believe themselves greater than I.

"You claim I cannot control you with promises, Otylia. And this is where you are wrong. I need no temptations. I need no offerings or gifts to lure you. You are like all who live.

"I own you."

I wavered.

When I blinked, tears filled my eyes. Death had not hesitated to strike at my core, and I trembled at his words. *Is he right? Or is he just manipulating me like Weles?*

"Doubting me is a grave error, child. I am not your father nor the fickle winter goddess. I need no marks to control or command. If I wished, I could kill you now and take you as my own—another goddess to do with as I please."

I shut my eyes and thought of Mother with me in the woods at the spring equinox. Her hair flowed freely in Dogoda's west wind, full of life, and her smile banished the demons with her joy. Before I ever knew her to be immortal, she was a goddess. She was untamed. She was free, daring any man to challenge her.

That's it.

With a sharp breath, I stepped to the tree and laid my hand on its trunk. Power surged through the connection and burned my hand. The pain spread up my arm, searing against the armband and threatening to cripple me. But I did not step away.

"Then kill me," I said.

"You are bold, daughter of Dziewanna, but you are a fool."

I grabbed the tree with my other hand. A stabbing pain shot into it, but I gritted my teeth. "I'm not afraid of you!" I screamed. "Kill me, or *you* are nothing!"

The world went black.

A force threw me to the ground as whispers echoed in the darkness. They were different than Death's voice, more dispersed. They danced, circling me with their taunting words.

"You failed her," they said. "She withers away as you chase power and the love of a demon."

Cracks shattered the void. I shielded my eyes as light cascaded off towers of solid ice. They surrounded me, forming a ring that went on for fifty strides, all covered in snow that stung my skin.

What is this place? Why would Death send me here?

Far above, a ceiling of blue ice stretched to the sky. The light refracting through it split into brilliant colors that touched everywhere except the furthest part of the ring. There, shadows hung.

I stepped toward the shadows, studying the black shards of ice scattered across the ground. Dread emanated from them. Even without Mokosz's power, I could sense it—a thing as dark as Death.

The shards cracked beneath my boots as I held my arm across my body, nervously gripping my armband. Its protective symbols glowed. *What does it know that I don't?*

Then the shadows shifted.

I froze as the figure stretched across the entire end of the ring. *That wasn't ice…*

Jagged black scales covered every inch of the creature's wings, torso, and long tail that curled around its body. When its eyes had been shut, it had faded into the shadows, but now its three heads were raised, its gaze fixed on me.

Żmij. I'm dead.

Father's legends of the great shape-shifting dragons had been every child's favorite. They were ancient beings, some as powerful as gods, and even the bravest heroes stood no chance against them. Before Jaryło's story of the one that had captured Mother, I'd thought them nothing more than stories. I'd been wrong.

The żmij seemed to smile as it uncurled its massive tail and slammed it into the ice behind. The tower snapped, and I raised my arms, awaiting the pain as daggers of ice rained upon me. It didn't come.

Instead, my armband's glow intensified, pulsing with power as it deflected the shards without my command. The attack stopped seconds later, and I took a shallow breath, grateful to be alive.

It's just toying with me.

The dragon had nearly killed me without even trying. When I finally dropped my arms, it laughed before speaking with a booming voice, "You are a pitiful little thing."

I didn't reply. Something else had drawn my attention: a woman lying where the żmij's tail had been seconds before. The shadows covered her face and lines of black streaked across her skin, but I knew it was her.

"Mother?" I asked, my voice shaking.

"So, it is true," the żmij said as it crawled around her body. Its claws scraped across the ice with each step, sending a screeching through the air. "The lost child of Dziewanna has been found. The queen will be pleased."

"Marzanna is no queen." I stepped forward, my fists clenched. Dragon or not, I hadn't seen Mother outside of visions in four years. I *needed* to be closer.

"And you are no goddess," it replied. "That pathetic artifact upon your arm cannot save you, nor can Weles. You are not Ascended; I can sense it." It stalked closer, blocking the light with its massive frame. "Which means you were bold enough to confront Death, and he sent you here."

Death sent me here? Why? I edged around the żmij, but it blocked my advance.

"You fear her death, child," it hissed. "I will ensure she suffers, that every bit of *żityje* is drained from her before we send her to Oblivion."

"I'll kill you!"

It lunged, its heads striking at me from every side as I sprinted toward Mother. I couldn't fight it without her power, and even with the armband's power shimmering around me, the żmij was strong. Its teeth tore through the band's aura with ease and ripped cloak and dress alike. I screamed as its claws ran down my back, shredding both skin and muscle as I collapsed just strides from Mother.

The pain swallowed my mind. Blood soaked the ground, turning the snow into a pool of red that grew with each second.

Keep fighting. My back begged me to stop, to surrender, but I struggled to my feet, desperate to see Mother, to touch her.

The dragon's shadow swooped over me as it laughed. "I should kill you both, but it has been quite some time since I could play with two goddesses!"

Mother felt miles away, and each staggered step brought me no closer. Sweat and tears stung my eyes. I could feel the żmij watching me, entertained by my failure.

Maybe it's right. Maybe Death was too.

When the żmij dove again, I screamed at my body to dodge, to fight on. My energy was gone, though, drained by the pain and the sight of Mother's deathly body. I could only whimper as the żmij's jaws closed around my right shoulder and lifted me up. The joint cracked, and the dragon's wings pushed the air like a gale, battering me as I wept. *I shouldn't have hoped.*

But I had. Seeing Mother again had ignited something in my heart—a fire that was smothered as I looked down at her from the żmij's grasp. In that moment, I didn't care about pain's grip or Marzanna's dragon. I just wanted Mother's care and Dziewanna's spirit.

"Do you see now?" the żmij asked from one of its mouths. "Do you understand that you cannot stop me, that your mother will wither and be forgotten to the winds of time? You are nothing without her." We began to rise, its great wings outstretched.

"No…" I muttered, closing my eyes as I remembered every lesson Mother had given me, from potions to survival to the stories of the gods. She'd raised me to fight for myself. Her love had made me *something*, and by her side, I'd been the daughter of the wilds. Alone, though, I was untamable—the girl who loved the woods and swamps, the szeptucha who listened and learned the legends of gods and demons, the woman who fought to protect those I loved, and the goddess whose path was my own. Mother had made me strong, but because of her, I could never be nothing.

I slowed my breaths and focused on the pool of *żityje* in my soul. It rushed through me, as if it *wanted* to be used. And when I opened my eyes, my body glowed with its power. "I'm not afraid of you."

We neared the peak of the ice dome as the żmij flew higher. Its chuckle echoed over the sound of its beating wings. "You should be."

Searing heat flooded over me. An orange glow covered my shoulder and arm, still trapped in the dragon's jaws. Then, the beast flung his head and released, throwing me into the air as fire poured from all three of its maws.

My fear and rage faded, my desperation washed away. I drifted through the still air with the chill stinging my back and the flames barreling toward me. For a moment, I understood the joy Wacław must've felt when he flew—the freedom of it with the earth so far below. It was thrilling. To a mortal, this height meant sure death.

Luckily, we weren't mortals.

The flame raced closer, rolling over themselves like waves as smoke blackened the sky. I was inches from being burned alive, but I felt calm. Instinctively, my soul pulled on the *žityje* and channeled the armband's symbols. I held my uninjured arm across my chest as a single word came to my lips.

"*Prì!*" Push.

Žityje poured from my soul as I threw out my arm. A blast struck my chest, and I tumbled back, the flames washing over my skin. But they did not burn me.

I shot toward the ground, staring up at a shimmering silver shield that forced away the blaze. *What did I just do?*

The żmij growled and dove after me, its mouths burning as rage turned his eyes red. With its wings tucked, it plowed through the shield and closed the distance between us.

Now what?

I could feel the blaze burning in its throat as I glanced down at the ground. My *žityje* was gone already. Somehow, I had stopped the flames, but that wouldn't matter if I died from the fall seconds later. I reached into my soul, searching for some bit of strength. *Not now! Please, not now!*

How had I burned my entire *žityje* reserve already? Was that one spell enough to leave me empty, or had the armband's protection slowly used it without me noticing? With the ground rushing toward me, there was no time to figure out.

No words popped into my mind as I wielded the little *žityje* I had left. Some force had whispered one spell to me, but I couldn't call the power for another shield. My soul was empty, my body weak.

Then a rush of energy surged through me. *Wašek?*

Wacław's connection only lasted a moment, but all his *žityje* burned through me at once. I grabbed hold of it and spun, throwing out my arms as the dragon released his blaze.

"*Rìnoti!*"

My breaths fled and my injured shoulder popped. Two forces crashed into me as I extended one arm toward the flames and the other toward the ground. Beneath me, the shimmering shield pushed away the snow and sent cracks through the entire base of the rim. Above, the flames shot back at the żmij, who dove again as my *żityje* ran out.

My arms crumpled. The shields dissolved as I dropped to the ice in a heap. My shoulder seized in agony, and the arm beneath it felt no better. I'd never broken a bone, but the *crack* when I'd hit the ground had been unmistakable.

Wheezing for each breath, I rolled over as an oval of black formed in the air just three strides away, where I'd appeared minutes before. I stared into its depths. *A way out… What about Mother?*

The snow burned against my fingers as I turned toward the rim's shadowed section. Mother's body lay there, unharmed. A part of me pled to stay by her side, to suffer alongside her as Marzanna drained her *żityje*, but I remembered Death's taunts. *This is the Trial.*

With my shield shattered above, the żmij roared with anticipation as I tried to stand, to stumble toward the portal out. My legs failed.

Blood and tears streamed down my face. I crawled with my one good arm, flailing to pull myself toward the black as the pain demanded I surrender. My mind was slipping. I felt the gusts from the dragon's wings. *Just one more stride.* My fingers were so close to the portal, pulling with everything I had left to break its threshold.

The smoke stung my nose. The flames would follow soon, but I had to live. I had to fight. For Mother. For Wacław. For myself. I screamed and lunged, piercing the darkness just as the blaze struck.

28

Wacław

Am I dying?

AGONY CONSUMED ME IN THE DARKNESS, ripping through my flesh and mind as the waters grew heavy upon my chest. The void itself was the same as before, but this was no comforting escape. My thoughts were pain. My existence suffering.

Boz's trap returned to me, and I cursed myself for believing he had any honor. No matter whether we agreed to his terms or not, the lunatic king never would have released Rasa—nor would he have let the clans survive. Twice, he'd bested me. Twice, he'd slaughtered the clans because of my plan. And twice, he'd weakened the only armies left to resist the Frostmarked Horde.

Marzanna would be pleased.

I winced at the throbbing of my chest, where the arrow had pierced my skin. Based on the fact my heart had beat and my lungs had breathed when I'd awoken, it seemed that my ribs had stopped it from penetrating too far. *Then why am I dying?*

That was the only possible explanation—death. Wasn't it?

This void had entrapped my mind as I'd lost consciousness, and I had escaped for only a moment as someone tried to heal me. The faces had been blurred. Memories of Andrij pulling me to his horse returned, though. Despite my injury, had he actually brought me west with my friends? Why had they even been prepared to go? They must have hidden their plan from me.

Dread crept over me.

Otylia? Is that you? I closed my eyes and reached for our tether as the sensation grew. It pulled at my heart, adding to my agony, but I clung to her. Our bond was my only connection to reality, my only hope of feeling anything but the pain eating away my body.

"Stay alive," I whispered, my voice lost.

I gasped for air as my chest seized. Though the darkness swallowed my vision, I could feel the blood pouring out of me, staining the water as I continued my descent. *Not long now.*

That thought came with a sense of certainty, as if my body knew Oblivion's call.

After hours or days or moons of floating, alone, in the darkness, I embraced it. Death had scared me for so long, but I had already accepted dying at Boz's hand. Success or failure, my end was the same.

But Otylia's dread escalated with every passing moment. It turned from a pull into an unending tide, and soon, it was joined by flashes of pain arcing down my back and shoulder. Each new wound merged with the others and turned what remained of my sanity into torment. I could almost hear Marzanna's sinister cackle as I suffered, fighting just to breathe. It meant little to me. All that mattered was the suffering sweeping through my connection to Otylia. Was she dying too?

"She can still make it," a voice said in my head—one I assumed was my confused consciousness.

I can't save her, I told myself. *I couldn't save Father. I couldn't save Kuba. I couldn't save the clans. I couldn't even save myself.*

"Yet you saved all of the lands within the embrace of Perun's Crown from a płanetnik's blizzards, cured Otylia of Marzanna's Curse, and protected innocents from the fires at the Battle of Kynnytsia."

They died anyway.

The voice laughed. *"Boy, you have much to learn of battle if you believe one charge slaughtered two entire clans. Thousands remained at the clan camp, and among those who fought, many escaped."*

That brought me some relief, but I had seen the slaughter. Nothing could make me forget that. *Who are you?*

"Your people call me Strzybóg, lord of the winds you so often twist to your will. But it is not I who is relevant at the moment. You must be swift if you are to save the child of Weles."

My chest tightened. *How do you know that?*

"The winds carry even the softest of whispers. I know far more than many wish for me to, and at a time when Jawia is teetering on the brink, it has advantages. Finding you is among them." He sighed. *"You are connected to Otylia, and though only she can pull herself from danger, you can lend her the żityje that remains in your soul."*

I reached out to her. Her strength had faded. Like me, she was close to death, but she fought some threat larger than I had ever sensed, unrelenting even as her body failed her. *That's my Otylka…*

I searched my soul and found my little remaining *żityje*, its force struggling to sustain my body. *Strzybóg, why do you help me now and not when innocents are being slaughtered? Why save me, a demon?*

"I have guided you more times than you can know, Wacław. My grandchildren aid you because I let them to do so, but even gods have our limitations. It was a grave error of mine to abandon my responsibility and allow Jaryło alone to protect Dziewanna. All I have done since has been to make right what I have broken." His presence faded, and with his last words, a breeze wisped through the waters. *"It is not our failures that define us but what we do when we fail."*

As I spun in the waters and felt the pain tearing me apart, fear gripped me again—my own. I had thought myself prepared to die, but the weight of saving Otylia, of sacrificing all I had left for her, was crushing.

Tears welled in my eyes as I held the amulets of Dziewanna and Mokosz at my heart. They had come from the women I loved, but we would never meet again. I would never again see Otylia's striking green glare, hear her wonderful laugh when I did something foolish, or experience the joy of kissing her, of our souls dancing together with her in my embrace. I would never again taste Mom's warm soup, her smile and care greeting me as I returned from the fields or forest. I would never again join Nevenka's childish adventures, cringe at Gośka's sarcasm, or suffer Mikołaj's arrogant banter. I would never again fly among the clouds, feel the winds slipping between my fingers, or wield the power of lightning.

My life was over.

A panic struck my heart as I felt Otylia fall from the sky. I didn't know why or how she'd ended up so high, but it didn't matter. Her heart raced as she plummeted, her *žityje* burning away on some unseen power. She was helpless.

With one final breath, I reached into my dual souls and released my *žityje*, sending it through our connection as she had done for me once before.

It seemed too easy to do something so unnatural—gifting her the life force I had left—but our bond held tight. With each second, my *žityje* flowed away. My body became cold, my souls empty and numb.

Then, Otylia's fall stopped as a burst of energy shot from her. With it, hope surged into her heart. I smiled, and as my consciousness slipped, one last thought forming in my mind.

I love you.

29

Otylia

Remind me to kill Death.

The blaze seared my legs as the portal sucked me in. Death's presence lingered within it, but even facing the dark spirit's dread was better than burning in a dragon's flames. I hoped.

Beyond the threshold, a black sea poured over me and extinguished the blaze. But the water streamed into my mouth as I struggled for each breath. I cursed Death and closed my mouth, concentrating on survival. If this was a sea, there had to be a surface. So, I swam up with my injured arm drifting at my side.

The progress was slow. Mother had taught me how to swim in the Krowik's current when I'd been little, but now my body refused to cooperate. It took all my focus not to panic as my lungs throbbed.

Just keep going.

I pushed on, doubting whether I was even headed the right direction. There was no light anywhere, and the water was lifeless and cold. Either Death was playing another trick, or the portal had dumped me as far from the surface as possible. Maybe both.

It wasn't long before my air ran out. Everything from my mind to my legs screamed at me to surrender, to give into the pain. I couldn't. Mother was still lying in the żmij's den. I wouldn't abandon her again.

Death had other plans.

"Breathe, Otylia!" he ordered. *"You irritate me, but you survived the Trial. This is not your time."*

Stubborn, I hesitated before taking a breath. The water rushed down my throat, but air came with it. I sputtered, my lungs working so hard I had to cough. *He definitely waited as long as possible on purpose.*

"Why am I here?" I asked when I finally stopped choking on air. "I passed the test!"

"With assistance, yes," he replied. *"Your methods were unorthodox yet cunning. Stealing a demon's żityje and leaving him as an offering for me was so surprising that I had to give you the chance to watch him die."*

Wašek!

I dove. The tether seemed obvious the second I thought of him. A force had pulled me down ever since I'd left the portal, but I'd thought it nothing more than a current. *How could I have been so stupid?*

I doubted Death's words as I swam, but the emptiness on the other end of my connection to Wacław confirmed it. He was dying.

Why would he give up his żityje to save me? Whether I'd survived the Trial or not, I was still trapped in Nawia. Had Death tricked him, or had something happened? I forced away my questions and pushed harder. It didn't matter what had put Wacław in Death's grasp—I would bring him back.

My desperation numbed me to the pain striking with each stroke. I heard nothing but my rapid heartbeat hammering my ears as my eyes strained. Only darkness met me. If there had been light, I surely would've seen the blood pouring from my back, shoulder, and arm, but I thanked the gods for the blessing of blindness. I didn't need sight, just our connection.

"Wašek!" I shouted. It was impossible to know how far he was, but our tether tightened with every second. Without it pulling against me, I could actually pick up speed.

Soon, a faint glow appeared. I kicked with all my strength, gritting my teeth until they hurt too. *I'm coming, Wašek.*

He drifted, motionless in the still waters. My breath caught when I saw his blackened veins and the blood flowing from his eyes. "No!"

I cried, holding his head and shaking him. "Wake up! Wašek! I swear to the gods, don't leave me!"

His body was limp and cold in my arms, his face glowing a sheer white, shattered by cracks of black. I had been strong at the sight of Mother and in my clash with the dragon, but now, my heart broke. Without Mother, Wacław had been all I had. He'd cared for me, suffered through my critiques and tantrums, and he was gone. My Wašek was gone.

He died for me…

I wept, clutching his body as his blood seeped over my dress. It didn't matter. Nothing did. Not my Ascension, not Weles, not Marzanna, and not my ruined dress. I didn't want to be a goddess. I didn't want offerings. I didn't want worship. I didn't want power.

I just wanted Wacław.

My hands instinctively covered his wound, but my *žityje* was gone, barely enough to keep me alive. I didn't even have my herbs to make a potion. He'd suffered in this void for days according to the pain I'd felt through our connection—alone.

"Death!" I screamed, my voice shattered. "Death! You've made your point. Now bring him back… Please, just bring him back."

The spirit's dark presence returned. *"He is gone, Otylia. I told you. In the end, all who live are mine."*

"You *won't* take him!" I snarled. "I will destroy you. I don't care how long it takes or what I have to do. I've got an eternity to make you pay!"

As he laughed, a black fog spread through the glimmer of light from Wacław's skin. Death came with it.

He was a constantly changing beast, his features shifting from man to horrific, distorted demon. Each of his teeth were canines, ready to devour, and eight dark eyes watched me from beneath his brow. His hands were claws swarming with black widow spiders. And when he spoke, his tongue was that of a snake.

"You cannot destroy something that has never lived," he said with his deformed mouth. "When Life was born from the great egg,

I was her twin, necessary for the balance of eternity. I am not a being but the absence of existence, and Wacław will be a part of me."

Will. I narrowed my eyes, not daring to hope yet. "He's alive."

"But he *is* mine." Death drew nearer, his aura of dread tearing apart my hopes, but I kept his gaze as he continued, "There is nothing you can do, goddess—not even Marzanna can command me."

Death's hands reached toward Wacław, but I pulled his body away. "Then we'll barter! Take my blood, my *żityje*, anything!"

He hesitated. "No god has ever offered me such a trade. A promise of any gift I choose in return for the life of a cursed boy…" Cackling, he flowed closer, sending the stench of decay over me as his jagged teeth tore apart what little skin remained on his face. "You have a deal, foolish child."

My forearm burned as his hand closed around it. "I need no mark to invoke my claim," he hissed. "But the time will come when you will do as I ask. Refuse to honor our agreement and you both shall be mine for eternity."

"One promise," I insisted. "One gift."

His lip curled. "One."

Then he dissolved.

I winced at the rash he'd left on my right arm, but that was the least of my worries. Death held me now. Sometime in my immortal life, he would return and force me to do his will. I resented the destruction he would cause through me. As I cleared my tears and looked down at the boy who'd given everything to save my life, though, I knew I would do it again.

Pathetic or not, I needed him. I could be strong. I could be a goddess. But without Wacław, the world seemed empty and broken—especially after seeing Mother trapped in żmij's lair. All the power and glory in the Three Realms meant nothing if he was gone.

Gods, what have I become?

Less than an hour before, I'd fought a dragon and wielded more intense sorcery than ever. I had passed the fourth Trial against Death, but in the end, I'd fallen to his temptations. He'd brought me here to watch Wacław suffer. Weles would've told me to leave him, to let the demonic boy waste away like any corrupted soul. Instead, I'd sacrificed potentially everything for him, just as he had for me.

I couldn't stop crying as I held him. Death had promised Wacław would survive, but the trauma of the Trials hung over me, merging with the pain that devoured my body's strength. From drinking blood to seeing Mother, clashing with a żmij, and promising Death a gift for saving Wacław, it truly had been the worst day of my life.

The pain will fade in time, I told myself. Wacław was an immortal demon and I an immortal goddess. If suffering meant I could have him by my side, then I would endure it for days if I had to.

Just a few moons ago, I never thought I would ever say that. Everything had changed since the equinox. I had believed the biggest discovery I would make was that Marzanna was alive and using Wacław's powers. In the moon that followed, I discovered so much more: purpose, friends, Mother, and the truth about the sky-eyed Half-Chief's love for me.

Wacław had never abandoned me. He'd taken beatings to see me just once more, and even then, he'd only stayed away to protect me from exile in the Mangled Woods. From the beginning, he'd been by my side, caring for me when I had everything and nothing.

I despised him for so long.

I'd spat at him like the others, and he'd called me a witch in response. Maybe some of the resentment had been real. It didn't matter. I regretted blaming him for his father's brutality.

Wacław stirred, his eyelids fluttering for a moment as a shudder ran across his body. His veins remained black and his chest bloody, but the movement was enough. I clutched his hand, intertwining his frostbitten fingers with mine, and whispered a song Mother had sung to me when I'd fallen ill as a child.

It was the story of a doe who'd fled her family in search of adventure. Her father kept a close watch over the herd, but the doe fought free. Days before, she'd seen a great mountain in the distance and wanted to see its peak more than anything. As she stumbled through the woods, though, she felt no closer with each step.

Darkness soon fell upon the doe. Glowing eyes watched her from the shadows of the moonlight, and the howl of a wolfpack echoed from nearby. Yet, the little doe refused to be afraid.

"Just one more step," she told herself in the song. "Then I'll sleep my worries away. Then I'll search and fight another day."

Instead, the night lingered on as she continued her journey over the hills at the mountain's foot. She was weary and cold, but she had nowhere safe to rest. So, she walked on, never looking back at the home she'd left behind.

"I'll stand atop the world," she said to the sky, "and Father will see."

But the doe's legs began to shake. She was young, a stranger to hunger and thirst. A white powder covered the plants upon the slopes, and there was no vegetation low enough for her to eat. When Dadźbóg's golden warmth met her face, she could walk no longer. She collapsed beneath an oak and cried out for her father, begging him to forgive her.

A reply came from within the sea of pines beyond, "Who calls out?"

The doe shivered. The voice wasn't her father's. "I cry not for you."

"Then you are alone." A bear stepped from the foliage—its deep brown fur matted and its teeth as sharp as a hunter's arrow. "Or you are with me."

"Will you not eat me?" the doe asked, backing away.

"You are safe, little one," the bear proclaimed. "For I am king of this wood, and all who live within are under my protection. Come. I will show you to the mountain's highest peak and the realm's greenest fields. Then, you will have the strength to find your family and bring them to safety here."

The doe squealed in excitement and followed the bear up the mountain. He gave her food and protection from the lurking wolves, and she told him of her many brothers and sisters and cousins. The bear listened with glee.

At midday, they arrived at the summit. The doe gasped at Jawia in all its splendor as the bear showed her how far his realm reached.

He was king of far more land than her herd could ever need. Surely her father would forgive her when she showed him the rolling fields, untouched by man and creature.

She could've stood there forever, but the bear was impatient. "There is your family!" he exclaimed, pointing into the distance. "Go to them, and show them to my plains of wonderful grasses. But do not tell them I am a bear, for they will be unnecessarily afraid."

"You will be here when I return, though?" the doe asked in hopes her new friend would not be far.

"I shall be here for you," he replied. "Now, be swift!"

The doe ran down the mountain with all the speed of the eight winds, returning to her family in the valley below. For once in her life, she had wandered free, and she would bring the herd the joy of a paradise. That hope drove her clumsy legs on until she stopped before her father.

The alpha's great antlers towered over her. Her father had clashed with many others to claim his status among the herd, and he was the strongest among them. Shame came over the doe as she approached. Despite her discovery, she felt her father's judgmental glare, but she would change his mind.

"Father! Father!" she cried. "I have found lands with food and protection."

He huffed and kicked the earth. "You abandon us and then return with such stories?"

"It's true! I reached the peak of the mountain and saw the fertile valleys below. There is enough for all the herd to enjoy for years."

Her father thought as her mother approached. "It cannot be worse than here," she said. "The snow covers all that is green, and the winds will be frigid here come nightfall. The valley will provide us with food and shelter."

"It's true," the doe said. "Father, let us go and see!"

Though he doubted, the whole herd went to the place the doe had spoken of. They were cold and hungry, but the tiniest glimpse of hope made them quick. As the sun began to set, they reached the valley and feasted upon the grasses. The doe smiled, watching her family eat well because of her discovery.

That's where I'd thought the story ended as a child, but it continued.

The bear emerged from the trees, seeing the herd happy and fat. "You have honored your word, doe!" he called out. "I thank you, for now, *my* family shall eat well."

Horrified, the doe froze as five more bears charged from every direction. Much of the herd still ate, unaware of the danger, and when she cried out to them, it was too late.

The bears tore apart her family before her eyes. She wanted to fight, to save her mother and father, but her father fell to the bear king's mighty claws. What could a doe do to stop a bear? So, she fled, weeping until she was far from that mountain, far from the bear king's realm, and far from all she'd ever known.

I finished the song with tears in my eyes. It was a tragic tale—one I'd found fascinating—but more importantly, it reminded me of Mother, of how I'd left her with the żmij. Was I like the doe, letting beasts slaughter those I loved?

I sighed and wiped away the tears, which floated into the dark water. Mother had never told me why she'd chosen that song. Looking back, it had been a terrible thing to tell a sick child, yet something told me there was a lesson I'd yet to grasp, even years later.

A cough tore me from my thoughts.

Wacław smiled up at me. I yelped as he squeezed my hand, his grip weak but his eyes caring. "I've never heard you sing before," he said.

I blushed. "I'm sorry you had to hear that."

"No." He chuckled, wincing as he did. "Considering that I'm supposed to be dead, I thought it was the voice of some beautiful spirit coming to lead me to Oblivion. Instead, it was a goddess."

"Keep it up and I'll make sure you're dead."

His gaze wavered. Leaning his head back, he took a raspy breath. "Otylka, why am I alive?"

I held my hand to his cheek, clearing away the black blood from beneath his eyes. "Because I'm too stubborn to let you go that easy," I quipped.

"I *felt* the calm of death, as if my soul knew it was my time." His voice was barely a whisper. Pain filled every word. "An arrow struck my chest during a battle outside Kynnytsia. I think… I think Ara and Narcyz are trying to save me, along with an Astiwie commander named Andrij, but it wasn't enough."

"The wound is far too shallow for an arrow to have killed you." I examined his chest, but with the only light radiating from our skin, it was hard to see much. "Its tip must have been coated in poison. Who shot you?"

He opened his eyes again and glanced at my tattered dress. "The Astiwie, but I know you are trying to avoid telling me how you saved me."

I raised my brow. "How do you know *I* saved you?"

Smirking, he shrugged and repeated my answer, "Because you're too stubborn to let me go that easy. Tell me your story, then I'll tell you mine. Talking hurts, so take as much time as possible."

He'll hate me for this.

I told him all that had happened in Nawia—from the moment Jaryło had killed me to his return from death. Time didn't exist as we drifted, and I talked for what could've been minutes or days. He didn't need to know what dresses I'd worn or the worries I'd dealt with each day. I told him anyway.

And he listened to all of it, his soft eyes never leaving my face. Without complaint, he tolerated my tangents about the taste of oranges, the moving vines of Weles's palace, Kyustendil of the northwest wind, Sabina, Ivan, and even the snakes. There was awe in his gaze. I didn't know whether it was because of me or the stories, but it felt *good* just to be able to talk about everything without judgement. Wacław offered no critique of my choices or disgust at my blood drinking. He just listened. Why did that make my heart race?

His eyes widened when I reached my fight with the żmij, and he embraced me as I wept for Mother and for him. I told him how I'd felt all his pain, how it had kept me fighting in the darkest moments.

I couldn't admit my deal with Death—not after all I'd seen and all he'd suffered. No, that was my burden to bear alone. "Death lured me here to watch you die," I said instead, "but you started glowing when I got here. It must've been part of the Trial…"

When I finished my rambling, Wacław's grip loosened on me, but he didn't pull away. Tears streamed down his face. This close, his heart pounded through our connection and his mind spun with all I'd said. I never wanted to leave. Despite the pain torturing both our bodies, together, we were stronger than any mortal wound. *Mokosz was right.*

"Apparently, we are both too stubborn to let go," he said. There was love in his eyes, but as I studied his face, there was something different about him. It wasn't the blackened veins or unruly hair from his travels. There was a hardness that hadn't been there before, like his heart had been taken from him and only pieces of it returned.

"Apparently," I said, resting my head on his shoulder. Fear gripped me as I did. How had I allowed him to know all of this? How could I let him become so important to me?

He stroked my head, his fingers running through my free hair. It calmed my mind, and I shut my eyes as he spoke, "You shouldn't be sorry for me, Otylka. All I have suffered has been because of my own decisions… my own failures. I've been with our friends while you were forced into isolation in the underworld, and instead of fulfilling my promise to find you, I've lingered with the clans. Each day, I knew I was wasting time to reach you. It's just…"

"I know," I whispered. "You're trying to protect them. They needed you."

His hand clutched mine as he groaned. "They died *because* of me. When they should have been safe in our lands, they were slaughtered at the end of the Narrow Pass by men I thought to be allies. King Boz is insane, tyrannical. Bidaês, the brother of the Simukie heir, turned out to be a Frostmarked demon—the one you saw attack me."

He told me about his plan to save the Zurgowie from slaughter and the fiery battle I'd seen. It amazed me that, in a few weeks, he had found a whole new world with the clans, just as I had in Nawia.

Bidaês being a wilkołak was the most shocking part. If he was another living demon, there had to be more. *How many has Marzanna marked? And what does it mean that living demons have returned, beyond just him?*

"We were ambushed again when we were about to trade the horses for Rasa and free passage," he continued. "That's when I was hit with an arrow, and though Andrij tried to get me to Ara and Narcyz, I don't know if he succeeded." He paused with pain in his eyes. "Marzanna's manipulation led all those people to their slaughter. She's been steps ahead of us every single time, and I can't help feeling responsible…"

Nuzzling my head into his, I ignored my fears and doubts. *He needs me more than I know.* "There was no way for you to know that Bidaês had used the Astiwie king for Marzanna. All your life, you've done what you believed to be right—not for yourself but for others. Those clans would have been slaughtered by the Frostmarked Horde if *you* hadn't convinced Jacek to offer them a new home. We knew it wouldn't be easy. We knew crossing tribes and facing gods could kill us. But you did it anyway, because you *care*. Gods know that's rare enough among the living and the dead."

"I love you," he breathed, wrapping his arm around my waist and pulling me tight against his side. I sensed his agony, his suffering, but beneath it was elation. "I tried to say it in the forest—which was probably a foolish time to—but I love you more than life, Otylka. When you were fighting the dragon, Strzybóg came to me. He showed me how to give you the last of my *żityje*. I knew it would kill me, but sacrificing that last bit of my strength to keep you alive was worth more than a thousand years without you."

I love you.

My heart skipped finally hearing him say it. I'd known, but his admission tore down every barrier I'd ever built between us. When we were alone, together, his care forced me to be vulnerable. Part of me wanted to flee, to hide from the emotions stirring within me. Who was I to feel joy amid this pain?

"I hate that," I said, fighting away my sniffling. *He said he loves me, and I tell him I hate that? Wonderful.* "You should be happy, with or without me."

He sighed deeply. As he rested his head against mine, I cursed myself for not being able to return his admission. "With every day that passes," he said, "I'm starting to think what *should* happen and what does are rarely the same. Every bit of my instinct tells me to fight for what's right… If only I knew what that was anymore." His voice cracked, and though he coughed, trying to clear his throat, his words were broken. "Little makes sense to me after all we've seen—except you."

We were silent for a long time. Being with him stole my need to fight, so I just focused on the sound of his breaths and the ache of his bony shoulder against my face. He had become a warrior since we left home. Those little things, however, reminded me he was still that little boy who'd run with me in the woods, who'd hesitated at every moment, making sure what he was doing was *right.*

There was no justice in the Three Realms. Father called Swaróg the god who judged. Other priests claimed it was Perun. But if a boy like Wacław could be cursed from birth with a corrupted soul and *still* be obsessed with being good, how could he be doomed to Oblivion, never to see the paradise of Nawia?

"So, Dziewanna has a plan?" he finally asked, brow raised. "How's it make you feel knowing your mother conspired with an actual witch to plan your future escape?"

"It makes me feel less alone." I offered a small smile. "I hate not knowing what's ahead, but at least I have someone else to fight for. There are souls and nymphs trapped here too. Maybe, I can be their chance at freedom."

He chuckled to himself.

"Why are you laughing?"

"Because you're more of a goddess than you realize. Dziewanna would be proud to see you saving people from Weles's grasp."

"Maybe…" I muttered before pulling away. The reality of our situation returned to me as I held his frostbitten fingers. This softness was a distraction. One I couldn't afford… *How did I slip so quickly?*

"Death tricked you, Wašek," I said, remembering how he'd described the wind god's directions to help me. "He impersonated Strzybóg to convince you to sacrifice yourself. I can die, but Weles would bring me back—he's done it twice already."

"Then it was just part of the Trial..." he replied, dropping his head. "Using me to teach you more about your power."

"Yes."

Despite the distance I'd put between us, he grabbed hold of my arm. Gentle, yet firm. "If it gets you closer to Ascension and the freedom you want, then it was worth it."

"Don't say that." I turned and laid a hand on his neck. Sharp bits of stubble met my fingers. *He's been worried for longer than he's admitting.* Despite our moon of travel together, he'd kept himself clean-shaven, unlike his father and many other warriors. If he'd forgotten... *Gods, we're a mess apart.* "I'd like to talk about anything but Death or the Trials," I said. "Anything."

Sorrow filled his eyes, but he offered that smile—the one he always gave to try and cheer me up. "Very well. Who am I to refuse a goddess?" His free hand ran through my hair again. "I see why the priests require girls to wear braids."

I raised a brow. "If my hair is too tempting for you, maybe you are a demon."

"Or maybe I like seeing you truly untamed."

With his hands at my waist, he pulled me close and kissed me. I resisted at first, but all his uncertainty from before was gone, replaced by a passion I'd never seen in him. I took pride in that. The hesitant boy who doubted his every decision didn't wait to kiss me now, and the connection of our souls washed away my pain. For a minute or ten, nothing else mattered. He was mine.

30

Wacław

She's hiding something…

WE KISSED FOR WHAT SEEMED LIKE FOREVER, drifting through the void with only the glow of our skin to break its darkness.

Admitting my love for Otylia had my head spinning. It was probably foolish to say it moments after I'd nearly died, but holding her, I forgot about Marzanna's plots, Death's tricks, and the slaughter at Kynnytsia. They had brought me to the edge, taken all my life.

Otylia had brought me back.

She hadn't admitted the same feelings and was obviously hiding something about Death's intentions. For now, though, I forced away my panic at that fact. This was my one time with her. Hesitance and fear had stopped me too often in life.

Neither of us knew what we were doing with love or our battle against Marzanna. It was all new and—considering the power in each of our souls—dangerous. Normally, that would have held me back, but with her, it was thrilling. My heart pounded my injured chest like Swaróg's mighty hammer as sweat clung to my skin. Her lips were locked with mine, her hands holding my neck and running through my hair. I never wanted to leave her.

Only when the water stirred around us did we part. Well, we

never *separated*, but our kiss ended as we stared into the abyss, still clinging to each other.

Not yet. Gods, please, don't take her.

I held my breath as light spilled into the void. It swept through the waters in a brilliant blue and revealed a sea that stretched beyond sight. Otylia spun to my side, clenching her fist while Weles's bands of silver and wood glowed upon her forearm. I held her back. Though her willingness to defend me was touching, her *życie* was nearly as drained as mine.

Smoke pierced the surface above, spreading down until it stopped in a vertical oval before us. My hope deflated. *It's time.* Surviving had been a miracle enough, and having a rare moment alone with Otylia had been a dream—one that must end.

Part of me wanted to lash out at the portal, to claim it was unfair. Other couples could spend their days and nights together without the weight of the tribe on their shoulders. They could dance from the fields to their beds, dreaming of spring blooms and a family of their own. If Mokosz was telling the truth—and I had no reason to doubt her—a piece of Otylia's soul was joined with mine, yet we couldn't have been further apart.

"Death is calling you back," I said.

"I know," she grumbled. "I passed the Trial, but if this is what it means to be a goddess…"

I offered her a futile smile. "Weles doesn't define who you are. Though you'll Ascend, I doubt he'll be able to force you to do so on his terms."

"You overestimate me." Her head dropped. "All I've learned in Nawia is that no one is telling the full truth—that and how to drink blood."

"And all *I've* learned is how much riding for weeks hurts your thighs," I quipped, rubbing her back in an attempt to comfort her, but she only spun away. It amazed me how she could go from the passionate girl I'd kissed to a cold, dangerous sorceress in mere moments. Though I loved being the one to break down her barriers, my heart ached when they came back up. Not that she ever dropped them completely.

"Demons take *żityje* from unwilling victims," I continued, "so I hardly think accepting people's honest gifts makes you like us. People need the gods to give us hope, Otylia. If accepting their strength allows you to serve them, then maybe that's what you're meant to do." I tapped the glowing bands on her arm—an accessory unlike any in our tribe. It suited her. "Plus, between the dress and jewelry, it looks like Weles has finally convinced you to wear something other than bones."

She jabbed my side and fought a grin. "Why do you have that stupid habit of making me feel better?"

As I opened my mouth to reply, a current formed around us. It pushed Otylia toward the portal, and though I grasped her hand, the current became a wave. Her hand slipped from mine. I cried out, reaching for her as she flailed and tried to grab hold again.

The current was too powerful. By the time I could swim with any speed, the portal had already swallowed her torso. I knew she was gone, that Nawia had taken her back. But I needed to say goodbye, to touch her once more.

Black wisps tore across my skin as I drew close, crying out for her. Pain had become too familiar to me. They were nothing but pricks compared to my days of agony. With every bit of strength I had left, I dove and my frostbitten fingertips graced her own for just a moment. Our eyes met as the void took her away, her bright green eyes piercing the veil until she was gone completely.

The world flipped.

I spun, my stomach flipping, as the waters dissipated into a rainbow in the sky. What had been up was now down, and I dropped toward the grasslands below. The colors danced around me. Against my blackened veins, they seemed infinite, full of life, and a song of spirits rushed past my ears as I fell.

What is happening to me? Otylia's success in the Trial had apparently saved my life, but could Death take it a moment later? Was I about to hit the ground at full speed, never to see Jawia—or Otylia—ever again? Or was my mind attempting to comprehend Oblivion, unable to understand what had become of me?

I fell regardless of the answer. The air tumbled past, and my body crumpled under the force of the fall. Instinctively, I called for the winds, begging for their power to save me. None answered, and as I neared the ground itself, I closed my eyes.

Make it quick.

The impact crushed my body—or so I thought. Every muscle, every bone, snapped at once, but then a light struck me as the pain faded.

I burst awake, coughing on blood and heaving for each breath down my dry throat.

"Wacław?" someone exclaimed.

Sputtering, I tried to roll over until they held me back. My ribs ached and my entire body was sorer than I'd ever felt before. After all I'd seen in that void, I needed to get up, to stand again.

"You're too weak, Wacław," Ara said as she gently guided me back onto a mattress only half-filled with straw. Sosna yapped and circled my feet, making the trip more difficult.

The room smelled of burnt herbs and violets, so strong that I coughed on the scent alone. "Where are we?" I asked. My voice was raspy, talking painful. It felt as if my tongue were non-existent, and as I stared up at Ara's face, sweat dripped from my chin to my chest. *Am I shirtless?*

I was, possibly because of the overwhelming heat wafting through the space. *Gods, dehydration alone could've killed me.*

My fingers traced the arrow wound at the center of my ribcage before moving on to the black veins spread across my entire body. *Death brought me back, but I'm still on the edge.* Exhaustion already crept over me. Both my souls were drained, and I doubted my mortal one would sustain the other for long.

"A village called Małe Wzgórze," Ara said. "Andrij led us here. He said the people here owed him after he helped them fight off a band of raiders."

We're that close to home? "You carried me all the way to Małe

Wzgórze?" I asked, stunned. "What about the battle? How did you cross the Wyzra? How long have I been out?"

"No *thank you*?" a sarcastic voice said from the doorway.

I bowed my head as Narcyz marched in. "Truly, I am grateful," I said. "A journey that long couldn't have been easy, especially with my injury."

"No, it wasn't," he replied, stepping to the bedside, his gaze intense. "Boz wants us dead, Half-Chief, and he sent a lot of warriors. Been six days of constant running."

Six days? Our time is running out before Maj…

"Father never warned me what Boz is capable of," I said. Pain shot across my chest, and I eased back onto the bed. Even my Frostmark pulsed. "What did they coat that arrow in? Otylia said it had to have been some type of poison?"

Ara's eyes brightened. "She spoke to you again? How?"

I blushed, remembering our time in the void. In retrospect, it felt silly, but I wouldn't have given it up for anything. "Let's just say we both had an encounter with Death, and without each other, it would've ended poorly. She told me everything that had happened in Nawia—about her Trials of Ascension."

"Oh!" Andrij said as he shuffled into the room, his torn Astiwie cloak draped over his shoulders and a fresh brown tunic replacing his commander garb. "Glad to see you're awake. What was that you were saying about some sort of trials?"

Ara and I traded glances. "You can trust him," she said. "We've told him basically everything, except about Otylia. You would be dead if he hadn't given us the antidote to the Astiwie poison on top of breaking through the Astiwie lines to get you free. Well, we'd *all* be dead if he hadn't helped us prepare an escape."

"How did you know?" I asked Andrij. Before revealing anything, I needed to know he wouldn't betray us like Bidaês. With every day that passed, it was harder to trust anyone, even those I had seen fight by our side.

Andrij paced, taking a wide berth around Narcyz. "I didn't know King Boz's plan, but I know him." He paused at the wall of the room and ran his finger along the wooden boards. "He's paranoid, and he believed that releasing the high priestess would ensure her wrath continued. My guess is that Bidaês returned to him sometime after I'd left for Dwie Rzeki. Boz had called warriors from the villages for weeks before your arrival—he knew something."

He knelt on one knee next to the bed, leaning on his front leg. "Marzanna probably used Boz's irrational fear of Weles, somehow leveraged it to earn his trust. Regardless, when Xobas told me what had happened with Bidaês, I knew something was awry, so he and I hatched an alternate plan in case Boz tried something." With a glance at Narcyz, he nodded. "Thanks to some help, it worked."

Xobas helped save me… I swallowed. "What about the clans? Xobas? The warlords?"

Ara shook her head. "No way to know. We're lucky we got you out without being surrounded."

"And Zakir?"

She smiled, failing to stop herself from smiling *too* much. "He's in the main room with Beáta, the village healer, and Andrij's old mentor Valentyn."

"Don't mess around with that woman," Andrij added. "I've seen her send a sickle through a man's neck and then keep slicing until his blood covered her. Valentyn's tough, but she can handle him."

Ara rolled her eyes. "That's a *wonderful* thought, Andrij. Thank you." She rose and walked to the doorway. "I'll grab Wacław some food. He'll need it."

"Thank you," I said.

Narcyz huffed. "He needs more than food. His veins are *black*!"

"*Žityje*, Ara had called it, right?" Andrij asked, looking from me to Narcyz.

I nodded. "I assume they already told you I'm a demon."

There was sorrow in his eyes when he replied, "Yes, though, you're nothing like the other demons I've seen."

"I'll take that as a compliment," I said with a chuckle. "*Žityje* keeps all things alive, kind of like a life force—at least, that's what Otylia called it. Most people have a bit of it in their soul, but demons never regenerate ours, not without draining a living thing of their *žityje*."

He cocked his head. "Then how do you live?"

"Jaryło claimed my demonic soul drains just enough of my human one to survive but not enough to kill it… At least, not yet. This isn't the first time my *żityje* has been drained, but this is the first I don't have Otylia or the golden egg to save me."

"Otylia," Andrij said, tapping his chin. "You've mentioned her a few times already, and the others have been pretty quiet about her. I know you were trying to find her. Is she a friend?"

Narcyz huffed, and my grin exposed me. "She and I are… I'm not sure what to call it, but we're close."

"Understatement of the year," Narcyz muttered. "Half-Chief and the witch have as much sexual tension between them as two rabbits in separate cages during mating season."

I shot Narcyz a glare as Andrij faked a cough and stood, rubbing his neck. "Uh… That's oddly specific," he said.

"What Narcyz *meant* to say," I said, "was that Otylia and I have known each other our entire lives. When we were twelve, my father, our high chief, barred us from seeing each other after she saved me using sorcery before becoming a szeptucha."

"How?" Andrij asked. "I've never heard of a witch that young."

"Exactly," I continued. "We were reunited when Marzanna made me Frostmarked and tried to recruit me to her side. Otylia saved my life and protected me from the goddess's influence, somewhat. And, well, after we got over the resentment between us, we realized we… cared about… each other."

Narcyz made a gagging noise as Andrij chuckled and patted him on the back. "A demon and a szeptucha," Andrij said, "That's new."

"Actually, it's a demon and a goddess."

He stopped, his body growing rigid as he returned his gaze to me. "A *what*?"

"Otylia is a goddess. She's the daughter of Dziewanna and Weles, but Dziewanna fled when she realized she was pregnant with Otylia. We didn't discover the truth until we went into the Lake of Reflection."

Andrij still hadn't moved. "So," he stuttered, "you walked into a lake and saw that the girl you're courting is the daughter of the god of the underworld?"

"Effectively, yes." I shrugged. "Though, there is a lot more to it than that."

"Gods…" Shaking his head, he rounded the room as he flicked his hands at his side. "And I thought *my* experiences were exciting. You all have seen more in two moons than most men see in a lifetime!"

"Sometimes, I wish I hadn't. But someone has to stop Marzanna, and only Otylia can free Dziewanna from her grasp."

Narcyz pointed at me. "And only Wacław can save Otylia from Nawia according to Dziewanna. Pretty convenient if you ask me. You get to see your woman again while the rest of us get dragged around by our—"

Ara entered the room, holding a steaming bowl of some type of food that smelled wonderful. "Dragged around by your what?" she asked with a wicked glare.

"Never mind," Narcyz grumbled.

We all laughed as Ara handed me the bowl. "That's what I thought. Did you tell him about Otylia?"

I eagerly accepted the bowl, but its heat only added to the warmth of the room. *How much wood are they burning?* "I did, and he was just getting past the shock of hearing she's a goddess."

"So all of this…" Andrij said, still catching his breath. "We're going to the underworld to save a goddess from her father? I don't understand."

Ara nodded to me. "Rest. I'll take this one."

I smiled, grateful, and ate my soup as she answered Andrij's questions. There was something more to him than met the eye. The commander had been threatening at first, but ever since, he'd gained my respect. Not only did I owe him my life but he had sacrificed everything to help fight beside the clans. Why? And how did he earn the firebird's feather?

Those were questions for later. For now, all that mattered was that I was alive and so was Otylia. My hopes of finding her before the beginning of the Maj moon were dwindling, but she was well on her way through the Trials of Ascension. Weles had no idea who he was dealing with. I wondered if even I did.

It was hard to imagine Otylia, or any deity, drinking the blood of offerings. Then again, it made sense considering our sacrifices of sheep, cattle, and… well, those the priests decided should be given to the gods—Dariusz had believed me to be one of them as a baby.

Father kept me alive just long enough to abandon me.

"Ain't that right, Wacław?" Narcyz said.

I shook myself from my thoughts and glanced down at my soup, now cool. The spoon found my mouth anyway as my stomach rumbled. "Sorry, Narcyz," I said when I was done with the scoop. "I unfortunately have a habit of not listening to you."

We traded grins. "What happened to you while you were out?" he asked. "Been a long time since I've heard something like that from you."

"Maybe I finally decided to accept my demonic side." I hid my wince at that comment. Though I *had* accepted I was a demon—and what that meant—I wasn't ready to admit it to the others. They hadn't experienced days in that void.

"Yeah…" Narcyz said. "Speaking of that, how are we going to get rid of those black veins. Not sure the people around here are going to like them."

Eyes shut, I remembered how Bidaês had drained a corpse of its *życie* by eating its heart. Had the zmora been trying to do the same to Tanek when I'd found it in the pasture? "Demons get our *życie* from other sources. In my case, my demonic soul feeds on my human one, but I don't know if that's going to be enough to keep me alive."

"What's the alternative?" Ara asked.

I set aside the bowl and slid my legs over the edge of the bed. "I need to take something's *życie*—apparently by eating its heart."

Andrij groaned as he leaned his head back against the wall. "Every time any of you reveal anything, I ask myself how I got into this mess.

My entire tribe will be out to kill me, and I lost almost all of the warriors under my command. Now, I have to help a demon kill something and consume its heart. Wonderful."

"Welcome to the team," Ara quipped. "Wacław, do you have to kill the animal yourself? Is it really any different than hunting?"

I shook my head. "Bidaês killed those warriors, but I don't know. Eating any meal I *think* gives my soul some *żityje*. Each time I use my power, though, I'm drawing so much of it… I'm going to need to get used to this if I don't want my human soul to be drained completely. Best I come with you and do it myself."

Ara reached out for me as I tried to stand, wobbling as I did. She caught me and threw my arm over her shoulder. "Let your body rest. Your soul-form might handle it better."

"Right…" *Why didn't I think of that?*

She laid me back onto the bed as Zakir entered the room and proceeded to lurk shyly in the corner. "Ara?" he said.

"You're not intruding," she said, glancing back at him. "What do you have to say?"

He wrung his hands as he shuffled forward, his gaze down. "I think there's another way to get the energy he needs."

When he paused, Narcyz huffed. "C'mon. What is it?"

"The Moonblade," Zakir replied. "The one he carries."

"Kwiecień?" I asked. "Of course… It allows Jaryło to return during the moon. Maybe it has a reserve of *żityje*? I knew I felt something in the sword when I held it."

"Perhaps," Zakir said as Narcyz drew Kwiecień, its blade shimmering in the candlelight. He must've kept it as they'd traveled. "Much of this is quite new to me, but it appears that the Moonstone draws power from the moon itself. In theory, anyone should be able to access that."

Narcyz eyed the golden Moonstone in the hilt. "Anyone?"

"The question is how," I said. "Zakir, if you want to hold onto the sword for a while to try and figure that out, you're welcome to. Until then, I'm not risking my life on it just hours after dying the first time."

Ara nodded. "Okay. Try to sleep, and then meet the boys in the main room. I'll scout out a good-sized kill. Doubt a rabbit has enough *żityje* for you."

Hopefully a deer does. "Thank you, Ara. And thank you to all of you. I know this hasn't been easy."

"Gods know it hasn't," Narcyz muttered.

When they left, I took a deep, raspy breath. It was my first moment to think since waking up, and I tried to comprehend what was happening. I had accepted I was a demon—that wasn't new—but now I must do what was required to live as a demon. That was unsettling. Eating an animal was one thing; consuming its heart to drain its life force was another. But if it kept me alive, that was all that mattered. Otylia had to drink blood to become a goddess, and I would kill to become a demon.

I just hoped my demonic craving stopped at animals.

31

Otylia

I don't want to leave.

My time with Wacław had been too short. I'd needed the respite from Nawia, but all my worries returned as Death's portal pulled me away from him.

I collapsed when my feet hit solid ground, each breath burning my lungs in the wet swamp air. It coated my throat and drowned my nostrils. That dampness mixed with the stench of rotten eggs as Death's presence surrounded the tree's base.

"We will meet again," was all he said, his whispers piercing my mind.

The darkness retreated, and soon, the tree was nothing more than a large weeping willow. With him gone, I could finally breathe—not that the air was any more inviting. Neither was Death's servant.

"You saw him, didn't you?" Weles asked, his cane thumping against the dirt between his sloppy steps. "And you saw *her.*"

I spat at the tree. "Death can go to Oblivion."

Weles stopped beside me and chuckled. "I would say he is probably fond of it."

"Stop acting like I'm a child," I snapped, sweeping to my feet. My cloak and dress were tattered and my body bloodied, but what remained circled me like a viper ready to strike. "Mother is trapped by a żmij under Marzanna's influence. You should've told me!"

Despite my aggression, his eyes softened as he leaned on his cane. "I did not know what Death would expose to you, nor did I know how Marzanna had trapped your mother, but I had my assumptions. Each of us faces what we fear most when we confront him. It was only right that you saw Dziewanna."

And Wašek. "I could've died! I almost did…"

"Yet you passed the Trial, my child."

"I left her!" I hissed. "Death made me choose, and I left her in Marzanna's grasp."

His face grew solemn. He turned away, his brown beard rustling against his furs. "That is what we must do—overcome the decision we are afraid to make. It would not be a Trial if we did not."

"You act like this is normal." I hugged myself as the wind slipped through the slices in my dress. "What did you see during your Trial, then? Who did you abandon?"

No reply came. He followed a patch of grass through the swamp, heading back toward his house. I watched him until he stopped across a muddied pond. "Come along, Otylia," he said with a simple wave. "Let us tend to your wounds, and then, come morning, I will answer any questions you have. Now that you have passed the first four Trials, you deserve to understand what comes next."

When I refused to follow, just gritting my teeth long enough to make my jaw hurt, he sighed and shuffled away. Every slice on my back stung as my shoulder throbbed. I'd left too much in that Trial: Mother, Wacław, and a piece of me I'd never get back. The child who'd clung to her mother, desperate, was gone. I would save Dziewanna, I promised myself, but my soul no longer felt empty without her presence.

Was Weles right? Had the Trial forced me to let her go?

I exhaled a breath I hadn't realized I'd been holding. *No,* I decided. *Nothing's changed. I'll pass the Trials, escape with Wacław and Sabina, and find Mother.* That was that.

A chorus of frogs filled the air as I found my own way back to Weles's palace. Without Dziewanna's power connecting me to the wilds, even the swamp's vibrant life felt deadened, dull. I no longer sensed the birds, insects, or trees.

My fingers ran across the missing brandings on either side of my neck—the marks of a szeptucha. While I'd served both Dziewanna and Mokosz, my bond with Wacław was different. It had been unintentional, but he was more than just the boy I was courting. He was my grip on reality. Even before the *żityje* ritual, everything changed whenever I was around him. It scared me knowing that I would've given Death a hundred gifts to keep Wacław alive.

Is that why we need these Trials? To remove any weakness, anyone who could be used against us? Is that why Weles hasn't gone after Mother?

Maybe I'd know soon. Weles had promised answers, but I had little hope he'd give real ones. The "friend" who'd sent the note was my only hope of finding the truth.

"There you are!" Sabina exclaimed, fluttering to me from the double wooden doors at the palace entrance.

How long did I keep her waiting? Her role was to cater to me, and a twinge of guilt struck me at that thought. "Sorry I took so long."

"It doesn't matter!" She took my arm and led me into Weles's halls. "You passed another Trial."

"Your unbridled optimism is a rare breath of fresh air—one I definitely didn't get in the swamp."

"I do my best!"

I chuckled as she dragged me back to my room. The nymph was so much more outgoing than when we'd first met. It amazed me that the frail serving girl who had stuttered at nearly every word had become the odd, sometimes unwelcome, ray of sunshine I'd needed in Nawia. Without her glee, I feared I would've fallen into a depression in days.

The doors to my room opened, and she swept inside, flinging me onto the bed. As she flew to the gawking male nymphs guarding the hall and waved for them to shut the doors, she squeaked, "I am so sorry to see that beautiful dress ruined. We'll fix it, but first, are…

are you okay? Do you want to talk about what happened in the Trial? Who do you think the writer of the note is?"

"Sabina, I'm fine," I said, wincing as her rambling added to my growing headache.

"Is… is that?" she stuttered. *Not* everything *has changed with her.* "Yes, that is certainly blood. I will fetch a healer!"

"No!" I shot off the bed and grabbed her arm. "I'm a healer. Just let me tell you the ingredients and utensils I'll need. Then I can make the salves."

She cocked her head. "Why don't you want someone whose sorcery could fix your wounds in less than a minute?"

I stood up straighter, imagining what I thought a princess's posture would look like. "I've spent my life so far fixing my own wounds. After what I just saw, I'd rather not deal with anyone else right now."

"Oh…" her wings fluttered as she curled in on herself. "I am sorry, my lady. I can leave if you would like."

"No. As independent as I'd like to be, I need you Sabina—not just for getting those supplies. You give me hope every time you come through those doors. I have no idea what I'm doing, but I refuse to give up on the promise I gave you. We *will* escape. Between you, Vlatka, all the souls Weles has forced down here, and me, we could have an army to force our way out even!"

I cursed myself when I stopped. *Exhaustion plus a few moments with Wašek and I'm suddenly spewing my feelings?*

"An… army?" Her cheeks burned red. "I've never rebelled before. I just help with dresses and food, my lady. To find enough nymphs and people and spirits to oppose Master Weles…" She swallowed. "I don't know how to help, but I'll do it for you. You've earned my worship, even if you don't think you deserve it, and you'll earn others' worship too."

"Once again, you inspire me," I said as another spurt of pain struck my shoulder. "Now, go get these ingredients so I can make a poultice and not be in agony when I see whoever sent the note."

Once I was done listing the things I needed, she curtsied, smiled and fled the room in a single, awkward motion. *How does she stumble so much with wings to steady her?*

Alone, I shed my dress and left it in a shredded pile on the floor. It rubbed the cuts sliding off, and I bit my cheek to avoid whimpering. *Be strong.*

My shoulder made that incredibly difficult. It cracked with each movement as I held my good hand to it. Tears welled in my eyes. I'd fixed a few boys' dislocated shoulders when they'd injured themselves wrestling but never my own. Based on their cries, it wasn't a pleasant experience.

I shut my eyes and pictured Wacław, the desire in his eyes as I'd pulled him close. It was too easy to just enjoy kissing him, forgetting about our pains even as our bodies suffered. I'd never thought about romance beyond catching a boy's eye or what would happen if Father had forced me to marry one. With him, though, every brush of his skin against mine was intoxicating, his warm breaths against my neck taking away my fears.

The shoulder snapped into place.

I cried out and dropped to my knees, shaking as a cold sweat clung to my skin. Blood from my wounds dripped to the dirt. I didn't stop it. My breaths were too heavy, my heart too weak as I fought to stay conscious.

After a few minutes, the pain subsided enough for me to stand and limp my way into the bathing pool. The steaming water hugged my toes as I soaked in the sunlight streaming through the roots dangling above. My wounds burned the deeper I went, but the warmth soothed the pain in time. I let myself drift from shore.

Why do I let Wašek make me weak? Why can he slide past every wall I put up? Why do I like it when he does?

Those questions hung over me as I allowed my free hair to flow around me. It was tempting to sleep in the water's embrace, the trickle against my temple taking away the headache. I couldn't afford to sleep now, though. Escaping wasn't going to be easy, and I needed to keep working. If Kyustendil, Vlatka, and Ivan were working under Weles's nose, there could be others.

I dipped my head underwater. Answers would come soon, and I

had to be prepared when they did. Weles and Jaryło saw me as a child. It was up to me to prove them wrong, to pass the Trials of Ascension on my own terms. Each of them wanted whatever power I would have when I Ascended. For now, I would let them assume, but *I* would determine what path I took, not them.

"Otylia?"

My head broke the surface. Sabina hovered at the water's edge, struggling to hold an armful of herbs and supplies. "You can set those down in my room, you know," I said.

Her cheeks flushed. "Right, of course."

She slipped into the other room and dropped the things on a table I'd had brought in days before. Weles apparently believed a woman needed just a bed and bath. I didn't expect much, but a place to sit and eat seemed fairly basic in a *palace.*

When Sabina returned, I had already wrapped a towel around myself. I would examine the wounds in the mirror later. My mind was shaken enough, and I didn't need to see my newest imperfections. Wacław's worried glances had told me how bad it was. *At least scars don't scare him away.*

"You're bleeding through the towel," Sabina said. "I don't want to insist but—"

"I'll finish the salves, and then you can touch-up the wounds," I interrupted. "I promise I won't bloody more dresses as long as Weles doesn't send me to fight another żmij."

Her eyes widened. "You fought a żmij? Like, a fire-breathing one?"

"With three heads."

"I… I guess I understand your frustration with the master."

I feigned a smile. "That's not the least of it. C'mon, I need you to help me mix the poultice. Maybe I'll tell you more about the dragon and Death himself if you're any good at it."

32

Otylia

What would I do without her?

SABINA WATCHED FROM MY BEDROOM DOOR as I paced around the bed, staring down at my bare feet in the dirt. Few things unnerved me, but that day had. Nothing offered enough of a distraction: not pondering my relationship with Wacław and definitely not remembering my experience with Death.

Sabina had proven more useful with the poultice-making than I'd expected. Her nimble fingers moved quicker than mine, and we'd quickly prepared the salves as I told her much of what had happened with Death, leaving out the details of my time with Wacław. She didn't need to know we'd kissed—a lot—in spite of our battered and bloodied bodies. Nor did I want to share what I'd sacrificed to Death to keep Wacław alive.

The salves had stopped the bleeding and dulled some of the pain, but only time would heal the deeper wounds. I'd faced a dragon and survived, barely. Of course basic herbs wouldn't fix it.

"Where is the messenger?" I thought aloud as my stomach rumbled. The sunlight had faded by now, but I'd yet to eat. Even dinner hadn't sounded appetizing to my overtaxed mind.

"They should be here soon… I think," Sabina said, peeking into the hall again.

In the hours since my Trials, Sabina had exchanged multiple more notes with Vlatka's messengers—nymphs and souls. Apparently, my inclination had been right. Her allies had gained the loyalty of quite a few mortals and nymphs. Most had likely been taken from Jawia like Sabina had, but we had no clue how many of them there were. Still, it was nice to be included in the plan for once.

"I never realized people don't admire Master Weles," Sabina said, her wings folding and unfolding as she hid yet another note in the desk. "Nawia is supposed to be a paradise… so how can we rebel against its king?"

"Simple," I replied. "Weles tricks anyone he can to gain allegiances that make him more powerful. He did it to kidnap you, Jaryło, nymphs, mortal souls, and even me. He probably uses dead souls too."

I stopped and pulled back the sleeve of my dress, exposing Weles's armband. It shimmered in the hint of moonlight from above. "He gives us gifts and claims to grant us paradise while locking us in his palace. When we demand to know more, he gives half-truths. Weles may not be evil, but he's built himself up on deception. That has to run out eventually."

With a sharp huff, I threw my silver fox pelt onto my head. "I've been patient enough. Weles wants to wait, but I need to face the rest of the Trials soon. He's waiting for Maj to come so Jaryło can control me."

Sabina opened her mouth to reply, but a knock came at the door. She dashed to it and flung it open.

An unnaturally pale man stood in the doorway, a flowing navy cloak and tunic covering his body. His black hair was flattened against his head, as if he'd just emerged from the rain, and a smell that reminded me of the Krowik in spring swept into the room with him.

I crossed my arms. "Made me wait long enough, Kyustendil."

"It is difficult to distract the master of deception, my lady," the god of the northwest wind said with a bow, sweeping his cloak out behind him. "Ivan is keeping Weles for now, but I do worry for your condition. We have heard of your encounter with Death and do not wish to weigh too heavily on you."

Every cut and bruise throbbed at his reminder, but I held my posture. *Be strong.* "I'm fine, thanks."

"Very well." He smirked with just the right side of his mouth before winking and turning to the doors. "Let me show you what is to come."

Sabina and I traded glances. By the time I looked back at Kyustendil, I needed to run to catch up. The god kept a brisk pace, walking on the balls of his feet like he was about to jump. Each nymph we passed bowed to him, but he paid them no care. On he went, humming a cheery tune.

I assumed based on his previous appearance that the god just preferred to be eccentric. The longer I spent with him, though, I wondered if it wasn't necessarily a choice for someone as odd as him.

The nymphs guarding palace doors nodded as we passed. I still didn't understand how they were guards, considering that most beyond the throne room bore no weapons, but Sabina hadn't wanted to answer much about nymphs' powers. It was rare that she kept something from me now that we were friends. Against my instincts, I'd let it go.

"I see you earned Weles's approval to leave," Kyustendil said as we traversed the swamp. The waning crescent moon shed little light through the canopy, but the pond shimmered beneath the streaks of silver.

Maj is so soon…

Wacław wouldn't make it before then. I'd held onto *some* glimmer of hope after our first vision together, but after the second, he was lucky to be alive at all. Crossing Krowikie lands in time to reach Father was hard enough. Reaching whatever route to Nawia Father knew of—if one existed—was another ordeal entirely.

"I did," I said, finally responding to the wind god. While he followed a dry path, I stepped my bare feet into the shallow waters. They were lukewarm, like they should've been in Jawia's spring. That calmed my thoughts for some reason. "Where are we going?"

He glanced at Sabina, who fluttered behind, apparently too afraid of a little muck. "To a place far from the roots of the World Tree where Weles has not strayed for years."

Years? Kyustendil got further ahead with the water slowing me down, so I hopped back to land and jogged after him. "Nawia can't be that large, can it?"

He spun to face me with a grin as he walked backward. "Nawia is indeed smaller than Jawia, but it is large enough for there to be lands beyond Weles's control. All those dead who aren't the special ones chosen for Prawia—or cursed for Oblivion—come here, so there is plenty of space for plenty of souls."

"But Weles said many souls return to Jawia."

With a shrug, he hopped back around and fell into stride beside me. "Many do, but ancestors have influence over their families in Jawia. Without strong ancestors, they crumble."

"Then why go back?" I shook my head. "Why abandon those they loved?"

"Perhaps it is too much to watch their family live on without them?" He swiped aside his cloak as it caught on a root. "Many also never bear children. Nawia is a paradise, yes, but for those who choose not to serve Weles or join in Nawia's battles in the outer reaches, there is little purpose I imagine. With no descendants to protect, well, starting over sounds better for some."

"They'd choose death over paradise?"

He waved his hand as we emerged from the trees into a meadow of high grasses and sweet-smelling flowers. Bees zipped among them, their wings battering the air in a constant hum. "Nawia can be quite wonderful, but for mortals, Jawia will always be home. Well, even for me it is. The majority of those who leave do so after many years—once that yearning to return has become too strong. Can you not relate to that desire?"

I dropped my gaze. "To go back to Jawia, yes, but I don't intend to die anytime soon."

"If rumors are true, you already did so quite recently."

When I scowled, he continued down the steady slope into the

meadow with a skip. The winds caught him on the second one, and he floated above the tips of the tall grasses with his arms extended and head back. *Was I chosen by the only gods who aren't strange?*

Sabina drifted by with a giggle. "How is the view down there, Otylia?"

"Playful sarcasm is new for you," I said, grinning up at her.

"I thought I might try it."

"And?"

She cocked her head to the side. "I don't quite understand sarcasm enough. I'll leave the quips to you, my lady."

"At least I can claim to be goddess of *something*," I said with a smile.

We traveled through that meadow for a long time. Kyustendil blabbered on about music and poems, occasionally playing his flute and waking up the animals who gathered around him as he flew. I stopped responding to him quickly. My feet were sore and my back's wounds screamed with every movement, so I just bit my cheek and walked. Wherever Kyustendil was taking us might hold the key to my escape. I couldn't afford to wait.

My patience wore the further we went, but soon, we reached the top of a ridge and stopped at the cliff's edge. Beyond, the moonlight exposed a place unlike any in Jawia.

Deep gray channels split the islands of spiraling willow, birch, and apple trees even larger than those I'd seen outside Weles's palace. A river flowed at the cliff's bottom and wound its way through the gorges. Despite barely climbing, I felt higher than I'd ever been as mist rolled from narrow slits in the cliff across from us, giving the air a dampness. It was deathly quiet. The birds slept and the winds slowed, and as I knelt along the edge, I could just hear the water rushing against the rocks below.

"Stupendous, is it not?" Kyustendil said, landing next to me. "Hardly the grim underworld the Anvoranie believe it to be."

"I wouldn't know," I whispered. To speak any louder seemed unholy at the edge of something only gods could have made. It took my breath away each second.

He held his chin up as the breeze flicked his cape into me, forcing me to move further away. "Oh yes," he said. "I often forget how little you Krowikie know about the people south of the mountains."

"Not all of us can fly." *Nor, apparently, can all of us shut up.*

His grin widened. "How else do you think we are to cross this chasm?"

"Ask me one more rhetorical question and *you* won't be crossing it."

With a spin, he took flight, hovering just over the cliff's edge and reaching out for me. "Step onto the air. You can be certain I won't let you fall."

I sighed and wished for five minutes of silence on that ridge. There was a peace there, one I would've enjoyed alone. But that was a luxury I couldn't afford.

I stepped from the ledge, remembering the sensation of Wacław's winds spiraling around me within the Lake of Reflection. In his power was passion, a desperation to save me. Kyustendil's northwestern wind, on the other hand, was like the hands of a skilled weaver. It caught my body and led me behind the god and Sabina with precision. It never applied too much force in a direction or battered my bruised body as we flew around the first island.

"You said we just had to cross the chasm!" I called up to Kyustendil.

He gave an exaggerated shrug and sped ahead. "There are many chasms to cross, my goddess."

Never direct. Gods…

Sabina's fluttering wings approached beside me, and I chuckled at the joy on her face. "You enjoying yourself?" I asked.

"Very much!" She rolled to the side, giggling before catching herself. "Isn't it fun to fly? You look so majestic with the winds rushing through your dress like that, Lady Otylia."

My cheeks flushed. *Is it possible for me to look majestic?* I decided it was unlikely, but Sabina was having too much fun for me to ruin. So, I closed my eyes and took in the sensation of the mists flowing over my face. They were chillier than the air, but their tickle made me smile as I held out my arms and did a spin of my own.

Sabina clapped, her eyes alight. "Like I said, majestic!"

Many of the other islands were like the first: mist-covered and cut as if by a straight blade. Within one cliff, however, I caught sight of a cave behind a waterfall, larger than the holes I'd seen before. *What lives in there?*

When we reached a patch of smaller islands topped with colored short-grass prairies, three creatures became visible. Scales covered their long bodies, matching the color of their respective island: red, green, and silver. My heart stopped at the sight of them.

"I did *not* want to see more żmije today," I muttered.

"These are hardly dragons," Kyustendil said. "Look, they are smoki, serpents! Weles keeps them on these islands, where they are unable to escape until they grow into żmije."

"How long does that take?"

Holding his arms before him, palm up, he beamed. "Hopefully not soon."

Then he dove.

The winds released me, and I tumbled toward an island beyond the dragons with no control. I cursed Kyustendil's humor. Only his wind could stop my fall, and he surely got amusement out of making me flustered. That suspicion was confirmed when he landed and smirked up at me from the island.

I'm going to kill him.

"Done gawking at me, or should I ask a smok to bite you?"

The god stepped aside without a reply and let me drop to the ground. My legs throbbed from the impact, but I shot to my feet as Kyustendil opened his mouth. "Smoki are not venomous, Lady Otylia. Besides, you—"

I was already gone, stomping past him to where Sabina danced among the grasses. *Oh,* now *she's graceful.*

"Lady Otylia!" Kyustendil called after me. "It was only a jest. We are not far from the place I wished to show you now."

"Where is it?"

"This way!" He leaped forward, spinning through the air before landing with a childish grin.

Sabina held my arm, trembling. "I'm not accustomed to interacting with so many secrets. Maybe I should stay back and keep watch in case we were followed?" Her eyes begged me to let her.

"Okay, I can go alone. All you need to do is make sure it stays a secret," I said as Kyustendil parted the grasses. His singing in the old tongue guided the plants out of the way, and I tried to remember each word for later.

Soon, we came to the western edge of the isle. It was higher than the surrounding ones and offered a seemingly endless view of forests, plains, and an odd sea of orange encircling a mountainous island—-even more stunning than the sights from the ridge before these chasms.

"Enough," I insisted, stamping my foot into the dirt. "Tell me the plan. Why are we here?"

Kyustendil pointed toward the orange sea. "Our friends are gathering around the base of the volcano on that island. A power alien to Weles dwells within it, disguising their presence until you complete your *essential* task."

"Again with the riddles!"

"My apologies. Immortality has granted me the chance to be more poetic, but perhaps urgency is more important now." He reached up his sleeve and pulled out a glass vial full of a deep blue liquid. "Your mother never wanted you to endure the pain you have. Nor did she wish for you to have to poison Lord Weles, but things have escalated quickly since your arrival."

Poison? I examined the vial, its contents unlike any potion or poison Mother had taught me. "How will a poison help? Weles is a god!"

Closing my hand around the vial, he raised one brow. "Though poison couldn't *kill* him, this is a sleeping draught that can render any mortal unconscious for a moon. Luckily, we only need it to work for a few days—long enough for you to complete the final Trials and Ascend. All you have to do is reach his blood altar and pour it in."

Can this work? A cautious hope rose within me as I sat on the ledge and stared down at the winding river below. Even in the moonlight, it was the clearest blue I'd ever seen. Contrasted with the sharp gray ridges along the cliffs, it seemed confined as it rushed to escape the maze of gorges. "I don't like this," I stated plainly.

"Nor should you," Kyustendil replied. "You will be risking your relationship with Weles until the end of time, yet that shouldn't matter if we succeed. Both of us will be free."

"Yes, *if*." I kicked my legs through the misty air. "What makes you think he won't see right through our plan? And why the blood altar? Wouldn't it be easier to have one of your allies pour it in his wine?"

"The draught would work far too slowly. He visits the altar at least once a day, and when he does, the *żityje* within would heal him of the potion. No, the only way is to pour it in the altar bowl itself. Tainted, the blood should not counter its effect."

"But why me? No one guards the blood altar, and even if I succeed, can't he just drink blood somewhere else?"

Kyustendil held my shoulder, his eyes wide. "No one guards it that *you* can see. Sorcery guards it, and only Weles, you, and Jaryło can enter. Gods, dragons, spirits, and even the most powerful demons are attached to places that hold some fragment of their soul. When we are defeated, these altars give us a reserve to survive with. A god as powerful as Weles has many, but poisoning his primary one will be enough to put him to sleep before he realizes what has happened."

"Soon," Kyustendil continued, stepping back, "you too will become a goddess worthy of mortals making offerings to."

I scoffed before rising to pace along the ledge. The concept of certain holy places holding power wasn't foreign, but I'd never realized a piece of Dziewanna's soul was within that willow in Dwie Rzeki's swamp. *No wonder Marzanna cursed it…* "The priests never spoke of this."

"Why would the gods tell their priests such a thing? Can you imagine what power-crazed kings would do if they knew where to find pieces of a god's soul?"

Fair. I glanced toward where Sabina waited. "Do nymphs have altars like this?"

"In a way." He sighed and held his hands behind his back, looking over the ledge. "A nymph, like a leszy, is a protector of its realm—either cloud, mountain, water, or forest—though, nymphs are more the embodiment of a particular element of that realm. So Sabina, for example, cannot choose her connection to a tree, but she does have one. No matter the being, they tend to protect their altar with force, as it represents their most vulnerable location."

"What are the chances this succeeds? Even if he sleeps and I Ascend, how will we escape with those he has taken from Jawia?"

"Once you put him to sleep, we will bring you to the island with our allies. There, you will be hidden and can complete the final two sets of Trials. Upon the beginning of your Ascension, however, Weles's warriors and nymphs will know where you are. They will attempt to stop it. Between the souls and nymphs on our side and me, we should be able to hold them off until the ritual's completion."

"What Trials are left?" I cringed at the thought of confronting something worse than the Trials of Life and Death. *Nothing could be worse than that...*

He gave a knowing smile. "Upon our return, Ivan will have hidden a book in your room that explains them. They will be difficult—and their exact form differs for each of us—but you must Ascend if there is any hope of us escaping through the Heart of Nawia."

"You want to go through the World Tree? Are you crazy? Weles guards it more than anywhere else in the palace."

"This is why you must Ascend and gain your power. It would also be helpful if that corrupted płanetnik of yours makes an appearance, but we won't have to fight Weles himself if you do your part."

"I still don't get why *you* are helping me. What did Mother offer you?"

His head dropped. The winds brushed against his hair, knocking a few hairs free, and for the first time, I saw him as just a person: broken, mourning. "I have little against Weles," he said, "but I have no will to continue furthering his plans. It has been too long since I have walked with the people of Jawia and flown among their skies. Unfortunately, he will not allow me to leave." He gazed at that distant island. "Dziewanna argued for my freedom, and though she failed, no one else has fought for me like that. If helping you escape leads to my escape and then her rescue from Marzanna, then it's worth it."

I offered a solemn smile. "Mother was always a fighter."

"She is," the god corrected. "Dziewanna and I are very much alike. Despite all we have done to provide for Weles's people and bring life to the wetlands of Jawia, Weles often sees us as the servants of Perun. Grandfather Strzybóg isn't particularly close with Perun, and neither is your mother. Unfortunately, Weles refuses to see the truth."

"So you've had enough mockery."

"Indeed."

Sounds familiar. Dwie Rzeki had never been kind to me. That disdain had forced me closer to Dziewanna and Mokosz, driven me into the wilds to learn about herbs, fungi, and the flow of nature. Most of all, it had bonded me to Wacław—even if Jacek had torn us apart for a time.

"You are thinking about your lover," Kyustendil said with an eyebrow raised.

I wrinkled my nose and released a sharp breath. *Focus.* A feeling in my gut told me we'd need Wacław's help against Weles, but his fight would be worthless if we weren't prepared when he arrived.

"That's not for you to know!" I muttered.

He smiled. "It was not meant as an insult, Otylia. The boy uses my wind against my will, but I am fond of him. If we are successful, he will be a powerful companion."

What if I don't care how powerful he is?

"I can see, however," the god continued, "that such a topic is upsetting to you. So, I will finish with this: We have until the end of the moon if we are to escape. It is a heavy risk with Weles already, but with Jaryło's recovery with the Maj Moonblade—"

"We're doomed," I finished. "Don't worry. I'll do my part."

"Good. Then let us find Sabina and return to the palace. Weles has an uncanny knack of finding me when I wish to hide, and I would rather him not know we spoke in length."

33

Wacław

Oh, how I missed you.

The winds danced through my outstretched fingers, their power swelling in me. Without *żityje*, though, they were of little use as Ara and I crept through the moonlit woods.

My only weapon for the hunt would be Marzanna's Thunderstone dagger. Its dark blade hummed in my grasp. As much as I wished I held Kwiecień instead, the dagger always drew me in. It *wanted* to be used. I didn't know how I could tell, but combined with my demonic soul's desire, my heart raced in excitement for the kill.

That frightened me. Though, with the black veins still covering my body, I had little choice anyway. I needed the *żityje* to live. If it meant eating an animal's heart, so be it.

"Why is it so dead out here?" Ara asked, crouching with her bow and quiver strapped to her back. In the shadows, her brown hunter's tunic meshed with the darkness. This was her element, and I could sense her excitement as she looked for tracks.

Ahead, Sosna sniffed around trees and dead undergrowth. After a few minutes, she returned, her head low. "Even Sosna can't find anything," Ara muttered.

I sighed, my breaths causing puffs of fog in the cloudy and oddly cold night. My soul-form's eyes had adjusted to the lack of light, but I could barely see four strides ahead. "Marzanna's extended winter has probably interrupted the wildlife already. Without Dziewanna and Jaryło, plants aren't growing, so I doubt the deer and elk have much to eat."

She rose with a groan. "I don't know about you, but the forest feels awfully dreary."

"Everything feels dreary lately."

"We'll get Otylia back." She clenched and unclenched her fists, staring through the trees as Sosna took off. "But first, we're going to kill a boar."

Without another word, Ara sprinted after the fox.

"Ara!" I yelled, stumbling after her with my chest throbbing. Even my soul-form felt exhausted, and I fell behind.

"Shush," she said once I caught up. We crouched next to an oak alongside Sosna, and Ara peeked around it, slowly pulling her bow from her back. "Sosna smelled a boar. Just one of them."

"A boar? You couldn't have picked something that's less willing to fight back?"

"Blame the fox," she hissed. "It's all we've got, so take it or die in Oblivion. Your choice."

"All right." I patted Sosna's head before sneaking around the tree. The boar was in a patch of moonlight no more than ten strides ahead. Its brown fur was patched with fallen twigs that it tried to shake from its back. As I backhanded the dagger and drew near, it huffed in frustration.

Just a few more steps. My steps were heavy, but they didn't alert the boar. My yelp did.

The boar spun as I slipped on a muddied log and fell on my face. I scrambled to stand, but it charged and struck me in the gut, sending me to the ground. With my breaths fleeting and pain searing my stomach, I turned as it swung around, sprinting toward me again.

"Signal if you want me to take the shot," Ara called from behind her tree.

I waved her away and prepared a fighting stance. Xobas's lessons had included how to fight with a dagger, but those were against another man, not a charging beast. Hunters had told stories often of their struggles with boar, and the agony I felt with each breath wasn't helping. It didn't matter. Pain or not, I had to make the kill.

I dodged when the boar lunged. Its body skimmed my sleeve before it landed with a snort. Skidding for a moment, it readied another charge, but its stumble slowed it down long enough for me to duck just out of the way and anticipate its next move. As the boar jumped, I stabbed. The dagger sunk into the beast's neck, sending blood spewing over my tunic.

Satisfaction filled my demonic soul as the beast collapsed. Though I winced at the blood covering me, the relief of the kill was greater, and I knelt next to it as Ara slipped from the trees and jogged to me.

"Well done," she said. "Sloppy, but you did the job."

Sosna gave her own thanks, tackling me and licking my face with an excited yelp. I pulled the dagger free with a chuckle and wiped it clean against my cloak. My chest was aflame. Even without an orange streak of fur knocking me over, it was hard to stay balanced as exhaustion took hold. "Let's get this over with."

"That's abrupt, coming from you, but okay. What do we need to do?"

"Honestly, I'm not sure." I held my hand to the boar's hide, its warmth thawing my frigid fingers. "Bidaês just devoured the corpse's heart. It was quick, easy for him."

She swung her bow over her back and crouched next to me. "I don't know how your power works… or Otylia's really… but you've said before it feels like you're reaching for the winds. Can you reach for the boar's *życje* instead?"

"I can try."

Taking a deep breath, I closed my eyes and focused on the power within me. The winds were there, loud and dominating, but there was something else too. I deafened myself to the call of the gales and reached for that quieter hum. No, not a hum. It pulsed, growing weaker with every second.

The boar's heart.

It had stopped beating, but the life force within it lingered. Silently, my demonic instincts instructed me to take it and absorb its power, as if I'd known how to for years. My stomach retched at the thought. Hunger was stronger. Not for food. Deeper, more demanding. It tore at my soul, and without another thought, I drove the dagger into its chest, carving open a hole.

"What are you doing?" Ara called out. Her voice was distant, as if she were back in the village.

My soul's desire pushed me forward as I reached into the boar's chest cavity and ripped the heart free, cracking its ribs further. Remnant life hummed within it, drifting away with each moment of hesitation. My hands shook. I knew what I had to do, but disgust and horror gripped me. *There must be another way.* But the demon within me knew there wasn't. For so long it had been merely urges, but now, my soul's craving wouldn't relent. It *needed życje* like my lungs needed air. And as I rose, fighting the demon's desperation with the heart in my grasp, it felt as if I was drowning.

The boar's *życje* tickled my fingertips. All I needed to do was eat it. I knew this, yet I resisted, fearing what door doing so would open. More importantly, I feared whether that door would shut behind me forever if I stepped through. But that hunger… Devouring, endless, cold…

Closing my eyes, I bit into the heart and instantly gagged.

Blood covered my hands and mouth. Its taste choked me, but the demon's pull was stronger. Desperate to calm its enraged screams, I listened, taking another bite of the heart. Then another.

Gods, what have I become? I asked myself as my teeth tore through the heart against my will. I remembered my thoughts within the void. Mortals, beasts, gods… we all did what was necessary to survive. Was this truly the same? Would my friends abandon me when they saw what I had to do? What would Otylia think? She'd said the gods drank blood from offerings to regain *życje*, but there was a ritual to that, an acceptance of a *willing* gift. This was nothing but carnal desire.

When I finished the heart, its blood trickled down my arms as its *życie* pushed back my blackened veins. It was alien, odd compared to the life force within me, but instantly, my exhaustion faded and my pain dulled. My blackened veins vanished in seconds. Though I could sense the energy wouldn't be enough for me to use much of my power, for now, that wasn't important. I was alive, and the demon's cry was gone.

"Wow," Ara said, watching me from the trees. "That was… something."

Staring down in horror at my blood-soaked hands, I mumbled, "The demon took over. I tried to fight it, but taking the *życie* was easy, *natural.* Gods… I'm a monster."

She swallowed and stared aimlessly into the woods. "If that's what demons do to survive, then I guess it is natural."

"You're acting oddly normal considering you watched me devour a heart." I took a shuddered breath as Sosna nudged my arm.

"All of this is so messed up, but it's not your fault. There's a small stream further north that you can use to wash away the blood. We'll leave the boar and let the villagers know where it is. Maybe, that can be some token of thanks." Her gaze flicked back to me. "Why are you looking at me like that?"

"Nothing," I mumbled, quickly looking away.

When the demon had spoken to me, I'd sensed another source of *życie.* Every tree had its small amount, as did insects that fluttered around, but the aura around Ara had been stronger than any of them. I had never listened to the noise beneath the winds' powers. Now, I feared I wouldn't forget those sources my demonic soul craved.

How long does my mortal soul have?

Ara explained what she'd learned about Małe Wzgórze as I washed in the stream before heading back to the village center. I let her talk. After the demon's anger ruling my mind, I needed the distraction.

Małe Wzgórze wasn't all that different from Dwie Rzeki at first glance. Just smaller and without a wall. The village center rested on a decently sized slope that had given it the name of *little hill.* Cottages circled a wooden well in the clearing. One was clearly larger than the others—Chief Wandelin's house. I assumed on lower terrain there would be fields nearby. In the darkness, though, there was little to be seen.

Małe Wzgórze couldn't have housed more than half the people of Dwie Rzeki, but it was an important village. Father had nicknamed Chief Wandelin the "Spear of the East" for his exploits in battles of the past. Years later, it was now the largest village close to the Astiwie border and would form a rally point for nearby warriors if Boz ever invaded.

Or when the Frostmarked Horde crosses the Wyzra River.

It was inevitable now. With the Battle of Kynnytsia and then the slaughter of the clans by Boz, we were divided. The Astiwie had far fewer warriors than our tribe, but Chief Mieczysław had swayed the other Krowikie chiefs into a war against the Kingdom of Solga. We needed the clans' cavalry to defeat our western rivals, let alone survive the Frostmarked invasion.

Everything had fallen apart so quickly at Kynnytsia. If Boz had just let us through, we would have been near the southern hills by now. Instead, hundreds—if not thousands—of men, women, and children were dead because of his hatred.

I clenched my jaw as we reached the house of the woman Ara had called Beáta. She was asleep already with the warrior called Valentyn—we'd checked before sneaking out—but I intended to give her as much thanks as I could. By providing her home and her healing skills, she'd likely kept me alive long enough for Otylia to reach me.

I owe everything to a woman I've never met.

This war against the Frostmarked was only beginning, yet I felt guilty for dragging more people into it so soon. They were villagers who wanted to protect their lives and crops, not fight a war against an invading army.

Unfortunately, none of us had a choice.

Zakir was studying Kwiecień when we entered the side room. His hair was ruffled and his eyes sunken as he traced the Moonblade and the symbols upon it. To a boy so interested in Jawia's secrets, the sword must have been better than a harvest crop. After all I'd seen, I wished some things had remained secret.

"It went well?" he asked with an eye on my bloodied tunic.

"It was unexpected," I said, flexing my Frostmarked hand. "Might need a new tunic, but at least I'm alive."

Andrij, who had lingered near the back wall in thought, smacked a snoring Narcyz and nodded. "What was it like, draining the boar?"

I winced as Narcyz swore and rolled over to face us. "It was as if there was another layer to my power, quiet but hungry. I could sense its *žityje* as it began to fade, and when I reached for it, the demon's call grew louder. It demanded I eat the heart… I did."

"Huh." Andrij said. "Draining an animal of its life was easy for you. Gods, what have I gotten myself into?"

"As long as you aren't draining me," Narcyz grumbled. Despite his exhaustion, he watched me with curiosity. "Touch my heart and I'll kill you."

Zakir raised a finger. "I believe if he were to take your heart then—"

"It was a joke," Narcyz said.

Ara scoffed, glancing at me out of the corner of her eye. "I saw it. There were dark streaks spiraling around him and obviously blood covering his hands and mouth, but if draining the animals we hunt keeps Wacław alive, I say it's worth it."

I smiled in thanks, but even with their acceptance, I feared what I'd done. The płanetnik instincts within me had just taken over. Would it happen again? "I just hope it won't prevent all of you from getting whatever *žityje* you need from food. Every soul relies on it, but I have no idea how much a mortal one needs compared to a demonic one."

"We'll deal with it," Narcyz replied, finally getting out of the bed. "We always do. And Andrij will suck it up."

Andrij scowled. "I'm just trying to figure all this out! I don't hate Wacław for being what he is, but all of this has come so quickly. If only the firebird had warned me of *this*…"

I stepped toward him and softened my tone. "You spoke of it before. That flaming feather—it's from the firebird, right?"

"Yes." He held his arm across his body and leaned back against the wall. His face drooped as he did, and he stared at the ground. "A lot happened on my journey from Kynnytsia to Dwie Rzeki."

"Care to tell us, or just gonna mope about it?" Narcyz mocked.

Ara sneered at him. "Go back to sleep if you're going to be an irritating little worm."

"Andrij can tell us if he wants," I said. "Gods know we have plenty of secrets of our own."

Silence answered me. Sosna plopped herself down, staring up at Andrij as he rubbed his boot into the dirt. "I'll tell the full story another time," he said, "but you can know the basics. Three of us left Kynnytsia to bring the clans' message to Dwie Rzeki: Valentyn, Mykyta, and me. All of us were forced into Boz's personal guard as a way to repay family debts. It should've been an easy trip, but Marzanna attacked us too—or, at least, her demon did. A nezhit I think it was called."

"Describe it," I said.

He shrugged. "Dark, decaying skin with black spiraling from its eyes. Looked like a walking corpse that'd been in the sun too long."

"Could explain why Jacek got sick," Narcyz said.

"That is how your high chief died?" Andrij asked. "Marzban Katiôn's commanders told me that he had, but if Marzanna killed him too—"

"She's planned this for a long time," I interrupted. "Every step of the way, she's sought to weaken our leaders and armies. Even our war with Solga was instigated by her, but it doesn't matter. Dziewanna believed Otylia was our only hope. With the slaughter we all saw, I believe her." I paused and met Andrij's gaze. "Sorry, I didn't mean to stop your story."

He offered a weak smile. "You're fine. It's just… I didn't realize how bad things were about to get when we left Kynnytsia. Bidaês and Zhaleh had spoken of the Horde, but King Boz didn't seem to care. He was determined to kill the Zurgowie for raiding our north-eastern villages. I didn't want war, but I didn't have much of a choice. We rode as fast as we could until the nezhit found us at the Wyzra. A blizzard had hit, and the demon swarmed Mykyta when I couldn't see him."

Ara and I traded looks. "A blizzard that late in winter?" she said. "Reminds me of your friend."

"Friend?" Andrij asked.

"Eryk," I said. "He was a Frostmarked płanetnik who had fallen under Marzanna's sway and caused storms even after the equinox. Whether it was the equinox rituals, her lack of control over the Moonstones, or Jaryło's presence, she was too weak to maintain the winter herself. We killed the cultists and demons protecting Eryk, but he told me about why he'd become a demon. I felt pity for him and gave him my mark. He's our ally now."

"Mark?" Andrij shook his head. "Like the Frostmark on your hand?"

"Right. I don't control him, but I can contact him when I need to. Last time I saw him, we rescued his daughter from the man that killed him."

His eyes widened, and he pushed off the wall. "Wait, so you can *recruit* other demons?"

I rubbed the back of my neck, not exactly proud of what I'd done. "Apparently, though I don't plan on making a habit out of it."

"We could call an army of demons on our side! Valentyn would be excited about this. We must—"

Narcyz huffed and threw up an arm. "We're not telling another stranger anything. Besides, the last thing we need is *more* demons. Hurry up. It's late."

Andrij sighed, pacing once again. "After we fought with the nezhit, the firebird appeared and protected me from the storm. Through it, Dziewanna spoke."

"She spoke to you?" I asked. "Why not Otylia?"

"I don't know, but she said I'd saved Valentyn's life by drawing the nezhit's attention. Then, she told me that Marzanna was planning something, that her sister hoped to survive, and that only a pair in Dwie Rzeki could stop her. I wasn't important, but my mission was. It would send the pair east."

"How did Dziewanna already know and not tell us?" I asked, drumming my fingers against my leg. "When I talked to Otylia in Oblivion, she said Mokosz believed there was a stronger force pushing us together, more than even the ritual that connected our souls. What in the Three Realms are we missing?"

Narcyz huffed. "I preferred it when I thought the gods never stepped foot on Jawia."

"And *I* preferred it when I didn't have to travel for moons with boys who haven't bathed in weeks," Ara quipped.

"Fair."

We all chuckled before the weight of what we faced returned to us. "So, Dziewanna's firebird gave you the feather to help your journey?" I asked, bringing the conversation back to Andrij. There was something in his story—a few more threads woven into a tapestry I couldn't see yet.

He nodded. "I'm not sure if she knew what would come or if she just thought I was hopeless. Regardless, Valentyn and I continued west to find Małe Wzgórze in the middle of a crisis. Raiders had been stealing the little they had. That night, they were supposed to return again, but we helped protect the village with the feather's help. That's why Beáta allowed us to stay here."

"How'd you stop the raiders with the chief and warriors gone for the equinox?" Narcyz asked.

Andrij crossed his arms. "We didn't have many people who knew anything about fighting, so I had to get creative. We poured the oskoła they had left along the path up the hill. When the raiders arrived, I dropped the feather and set them alight. The fight wasn't over, but it was enough."

"I like it!" Narcyz exclaimed, only to be shushed by Ara, who pointed to the other room where Beáta and Valentyn were sleeping. "Sorry. It's just a cool idea. Never would've thought of it."

"Leave him be, Ara," I said. "This is the first time I've heard Narcyz say something positive in a long time."

He sneered, but before he could reply, Andrij spoke up, "I'll finish so we can all sleep, if that's all right?" Ara waved for him to continue, and he paced, fidgeting as he did. "Valentyn stayed back in the village, wounded from the battle. It seems he's pretty fond of Beáta, so it was probably for the best. After that, I rode alone to deliver the message. That part you obviously know already."

Andrij slumped onto the bed across from mine. "Boz had promised me freedom from my service to him if I succeeded, but he lied. Instead, he thought promoting me to commander would be a great reward." He held his head in his hands. "All I wanted was to see my family again after so long. Now, I doubt I ever will after defying Boz."

"There was honor in your actions," Zakir said, not looking up from the Moonblade. His voice was flat, nearly emotionless. "Our clans would be worse if you had not warned us. Thank you."

"It didn't matter in the end," Andrij mumbled. "They died anyway. I'm useless."

I crouched in front of him. "No, Andrij, you're the one that has given us hope. Marzanna tried to stop you for a reason, and if she had, the clans would have never escaped the Horde. You protected our tribes' people despite having no connection to them. You were chosen by Dziewanna to bear the firebird feather when she can no longer fight. All of us have stumbled into or been born into this mess. Some surrender to temptations like Bidaês, but you have the heart we need to show people we *can* win this fight. In times like this, that'll help remind us what it means to be human."

Narcyz gave me a cold glare. "You act like any of us without powers actually matter."

"Grandfather believed simple men doing great things was all that mattered," Zakir said before continuing without an ounce of irony in his voice. "I think he misunderstood how important my research is, but the sentiment appears to be relevant here."

"Right…" Narcyz muttered. "Thanks."

Ara rested a hand on Zakir's shoulder, and for the first time, he looked up from Kwiecień. If only for a moment, I could've sworn that tears welled within his eyes. "Don't give up hope for Katiôn. He led your clan through many wars."

My heart ached as I remembered Xobas's last moment with me. In his gaze, I'd seen the shame for failing his clan so many years before. I wanted to believe he lived, but it had *felt* like he'd been saying goodbye forever. Knowing that hurt more than Father's death, because unlike Father, Xobas had bothered to love me like a son.

I miss you.

Ara must have noticed my sorrow, since she rose and offered me a smile. "Either Xobas is leading the remnants of the clans west, or he's found a faster way to Otylia. No matter what, you know he's not done fighting."

"No, he's not," I said with a forced grin. A tear slipped down my cheek as I returned to my bed. The pain from my wound was a welcome distraction from the abundance of it in my heart.

Andrij looked across the room at me, sorrow still clinging to his eyes, but there was something else now. A fire. "I'll fight by your side, and when you need him, I know Valentyn will too. Boz was raving mad, but because of Marzanna using him, I've lost my family forever. Promise me we'll make both of them pay."

Narcyz punched the air. "That's more like it!"

"I swear it," I declared, holding up my fist as well. Though I didn't feel strong, it was good to know I had brave people beside me. "But in the meantime, your family doesn't have to be at Boz's mercy."

The Astiw's eyes widened.

"I'll call to Eryk," I said, hesitating as I remembered the chała flying away with his daughter. I hadn't heard from him since, and this would mark a good opportunity to get an update from the other płanetnik. "He's been searching for his daughter and probably has a better view of what's east of the Wyzra at this point. Hopefully, he can bring your family at least further from danger, where the lunatic king can't find them."

Zakir nodded in recognition as Ara beamed at me, holding one hand over her heart.

Across the room, Andrij just sat in stunned silence. His breaths were labored, and it was a minute before he rose and grabbed my forearm. "Thank you, Wacław, son of Jacek. Between Father's debts and Boz's commands, I've never chosen where I stood. Because of you, that changes now."

34

Wacław

For days, I hovered at Oblivion's edge. Yesterday, I rose. And today, I leave for home. I do not understand it…

MAŁE WZGÓRZE GAVE US A STALLION for me to ride the morning of our departure. One last offering to Andrij after he had saved them from the raiders.

I wished there was more I could do for the village and Beáta specifically. She had sheltered us for two nights, given me treatment for my wounds, and kept us fed without question. When I offered my thanks, though, she smiled at Andrij and said, "Thank the Firebringer."

The poise and generosity of the woman had me in awe. Brown curls slipped from beneath her headscarf as she slid food into our packs for the rest of the journey. "Weles's blessings from the valley below," she called the offering. I grinned at the irony of that, but by her own smile, she believed my reaction genuine.

Near the well at the village's center, Andrij shared a hug with his stout mentor Valentyn before the two joined us. "Wish I could go with ya," Valentyn said in his thick mountaineer accent, nodding to me, "but Beáta needs me here. This Horde of yours would burn this place in a blink."

"You can't stop an attack yourself," Andrij replied. "The Krowikie army could use your help."

Valentyn shook his head. "Go on, boy. I've taught ya all I can. My days of adventuring are over, and it's about time I settled down for once."

With a laugh, Andrij looked to Beáta. "What have you done to him?"

"I simply gifted him some sense," she replied. Her smile faded quickly as she turned to me. "Ride on to Dwie Rzeki. The chiefs are gathered, and we've heard stories of a demon threatening the farms."

My heart stopped at that. "Let's go," I mumbled to the others. "It could be nothing, but if it's one of the Frostmarked…" Marzanna had threatened my entire family because of my betrayal. I couldn't bring myself to think of Mom in danger.

Many from the village whispered prayers and condolences for Father as I mounted. The dawn had brought an extra chill, and I was grateful for the horse's heat beneath me and Sosna's fur curled against my back. Despite the unusual cold, the lack of snow was a good sign. I clung to that small hope after weeks of nothing but bad luck.

As we began riding, though, I bit my cheek. *Mom has mourned Father alone, probably wondering if I died too.*

I imagined her thin frame weeping over his cold, pale corpse. No one would console Mom as they would Natasza and her children. Father had cast her out from the longhouse and village walls. She had been rejected, just like me, but Mom had never stopped loving him. I'd found it difficult to start.

My heart ached anyway. For Mom, for all my siblings—Nevenka, Gośka, Seweryn, Maryla, and even Mikołaj—and for the tribe. Father had united more chiefs than any before, and without him, there would be strife. He may have never been the perfect father or leader, but he had protected the tribe until now.

What will happen without him?

High Chief Jacek Lechowicz, uniter of the Krowik and defender against the Solgawi, had perished. Mikołaj was not strong like him. The wolves would circle if they had not already.

Based on the rumors from Beáta and the Małe Wzgórze villagers, the chiefs would vote on a new high chief soon. It had taken weeks for the news of Father's death to reach the outlying villages, and since Chief Wandelin had not returned to Małe Wzgórze, it was likely the debates had yet to end.

"Think Chief Mieczysław is going to try and take your father's spot?" Narcyz asked when we were clear of the village and on the trail west. Małe Wzgórze was one of the few settlements connected to Dwie Rzeki, and I thanked the gods for the steady dirt path.

"He's always wanted it," I replied, pulling my cloak tighter as the wind slipped between the trees. My clothes were new—yet another gift from the village I couldn't repay—and they kept me warmer than the thin, tattered ones from the clans.

"I find this odd," Andrij said. "Chiefs electing the high chief or king." He rode beside us on a dark horse called Oleh with white patched upon his shoulder. The two seemed to have a bond, and if my memory served me well, it was the same stallion he'd arrived on during the Drowning of Marzanna.

Ara huffed, never taking her eyes from the woods. "Better than the clans. We just anoint the strongest warlord and give them whatever title we please."

"Many are like that," Zakir said quietly from behind, "but Grandfather is not."

"Maybe not Katiôn, but he hasn't ruled that long," Ara said. "The marzbans before him caused the wars that drove my family away from our own clan."

I glanced back, questioning whether it was best to challenge Ara. The topic was close to her heart, so I softened my tone. "It seems there is disagreement among the clans about who started the wars. According to Xobas, both Simukie and Zurgowie broke their fair share of treaties."

She nodded. "That's true. Rasa was never one to let an opportunity pass, but she didn't deserve to be cut down."

"You're right." My stomach churned at that. If I hadn't trusted Bidaês, Katiôn wouldn't have turned the high priestess over to Boz. How had it all gone wrong so fast?

"Don't blame yourself," Andrij said, riding closer and laying a hand on my shoulder. "Boz has given himself to madness, Marzanna or not. Better to understand you couldn't stop him than to doubt."

Could I have stopped him? I was a demon with the power of winds and storms at my back. The clans possessed a thousand warriors and riders, ready to strike, yet I had preached a cautious approach, granting the Astiwie enough time to ambush us twice. No, I couldn't move on so soon after watching hundreds of innocents be slaughtered. My only choice was to carry their lives on my shoulders and make it right—if that was even possible.

"What is the distance to your capital?" Zakir asked when I didn't reply. "I find it hard to measure how far we have traveled with so much vegetation."

"Based on my ride," Andrij said, "about two days if we keep a pace faster than this. Three otherwise."

I cursed my injury. The moon was waning quickly and would end in just five days. By the time we reached Dwie Rzeki, we would have little time to find the place to enter Nawia before Maj. And that assumed Dariusz even knew of such a way.

"Kwiecień's end is coming too soon," I said with a sigh. The sword hummed on my back, as if it recognized its associated moon.

Narcyz eyed the Moonblade. "Learn anything about the sword? It's the best crafted blade I've ever held. Shame to let you wield it."

We both chuckled at the jab. Before the journey, I never would have expected to develop a friendship—albeit an occasionally awkward one—with the cocky warrior, but I was glad to have him. Kuba's loss still made my heart ache. I doubted that would change. With Narcyz, Andrij, Zakir, and Ara, though, I had hope of healing through new friends.

"There is much to the blade I don't understand," Zakir said. "Etchings that are unfamiliar to me cover it, and its material is odd—gold mixed with something I cannot identify."

"Moonstone," I replied. "Jaryło holds, well *held*, a Moonblade for each of the seven moons he rules over. Apparently, Marzanna has five Moonstones too. I'm not sure what form they're in."

His forehead wrinkled as he tapped his fingers against his reins. "Is Nawia not your underworld? Shouldn't trapping him there be the equivalent of death for a god?"

"Then he's haunting us," Narcyz grumbled.

I shook my head. "Moonstones allow their holder to recover during the related moon, so if he hadn't dropped Kwiecień when I killed him, then he could've returned faster. Unfortunately, I have no idea how to use the sword's energy myself."

"The force you call *żityje* appears to be involved." Zakir hummed to himself. "If only I could measure its potency."

"That would be helpful," I replied. "As you've seen, losing *żityje* isn't fun for me. It's hard to know how much of it I have left in a fight. Though, I have gotten better at tracking it."

"I will ponder this and the sword."

"Thank you." I turned forward again, staring down the trail as our horses lumbered on. "The horse you ride, what is his name? Xobas has told me a little about your religion, but I don't know much besides your worship of horses."

No response came. Ara giggled as I checked over my shoulder, only to see Zakir's distant gaze as he whispered to himself about *żityje*. It was amusing, and if it got us some answers, then it was worth letting him think.

We continued in silence for a good while. Both the fervent winds and chill stung my exposed skin, so I raised the hood of my cloak to protect my face. It had been a long time since I had seen my reflection, but I felt the dead, flaky skin on my cheeks and nose. With all I had seen since that arrow struck me, though, a tarnished face was the least of my problems.

Dusk came sooner than I would've liked. It seemed as if we'd gotten no closer to home, but I trusted Andrij's word. In two days at most, I would see Mom. I could feel the warmth of her smile and taste her soup. I could swing Nevenka through the air with willow catkins around her neck.

If only so. We would enter Dwie Rzeki in a time of mourning and contention. Politics between men far more influential than me would rule the day while Mom and others wept in the shadows. Hopefully, the sickness Beáta had mentioned wouldn't make things worse.

I tied off my horse on a tree and removed my pack. Zakir and Ara did the same, chatting as they strayed a bit further from the group with Sosna to chaperone. Andrij lingered on Oleh's back as he watched the setting sun, its light shining upon his boyish brown hair and narrow face.

Narcyz dismounted next to me. "You ignored me earlier about the vote."

"One can hardly ignore you, Narcyz," I quipped, rubbing my sore inner thighs as I sat with my back against a birch tree. As he smirked and sat at a tree across from me, I picked at the white bark. "To be honest, I don't know what will happen, or what *has* happened if we're too late. That scares me."

He huffed. "Takes a lot to scare a demon."

"It's a different type of fear." I twisted a piece of bark in my hand and felt its rough texture as bits scraped away. "I was never anything to my father or the tribe. They don't know that Father's death was my decision, that I chose Otylia over him."

"Yeah, but Marzanna tried to kill Otylia anyway. The choice didn't change anything."

I threw the bark deep into the woods, listening for the resulting *thud* and skid. "Maybe it did, maybe it didn't. I wouldn't change the decision, but that doesn't mean I don't feel guilty for it. Some part of me clings to the fact he was supposed to be a father to me. It doesn't matter that he wasn't. The man whose blood runs in my veins is dead because I let him. My ancestors would surely send me to Oblivion if I wasn't doomed to end there regardless."

"Not like any of our ancestors have been much help." He picked a stick from the ground and began whittling. The knife slid with each cut, far too dull to be of any use.

"I wondered about that," I said. "The priests were so vague when they spoke of ancestors' roles. They are supposed to protect us, but how? Why would they bother with us when they're in the paradise of Nawia?"

He shrugged. "Probably for the same reason Otylia's willing to fight two gods and more to get back."

"Love is a foolish thing, isn't it?" I asked, laughing to myself despite the hole inside me. *Otylia couldn't say the same to me…* "It drives me across all of Jawia to the underworld, leaving behind clans and tribes. It pulls me to Dwie Rzeki, to see Mom one more time. Why? I tell myself everything I'm doing is to stop Marzanna and protect the tribe. Is it?"

Narcyz's knife cut into his whittling stick and stuck there. Scowling, he yanked it free before snapping the twig in two.

"You all right?" I asked.

"Yeah…" He tucked his legs in, glancing toward Andrij for only a moment. "I don't think you're stupid, Half-Chief. The whole goddess and demon thing or whatever doesn't matter."

"It doesn't?"

"Nah. We've hated each other since we were little, but I've seen it for years. Didn't matter that Jacek could take you away from her. Pretty sure you loved her before you knew how to bed someone."

"I…" I chuckled. "Not sure anyone could have said that quite like you."

He grinned. "Ironsmiths can do more than handle metal."

"Please don't become a poet. The last thing I want to hear is endless tales of beasts and women you 'impaled with your spear.' "

"I'll stick with smithing and fighting, but not sure I'd ever have any tales of women anyway. Might be better that way." With a crack of his knuckles, he jumped to his feet and slid his knife into its sheath. "We're going to make it through this, right?"

"I would say only the gods know, but I'm not sure even they do." I sighed and thumbed Marzanna's Frostmark on my palm. "If we survive, we'll be legends, spoken of by priests for centuries until our story is forgotten. If we don't, then at least we'll pass knowing we did what we believed to be right. Either way, the gods have blessed me by ensuring I'm not alone."

With a single huff, he headed over to Ara and Zakir, probably to poke fun at them. *There's something more there.*

I didn't know how, but Narcyz had proven me wrong. Beneath his brunt exterior, he cared, and if he of all people was capable of it, I concluded anyone was. His father had tried to mold him like a blade. That heat had melted away parts of him and hardened others, but our souls could not be destroyed by the vices of our fathers or the words of our peers.

Over the past moon, Narcyz had finally had the chance to reach inside his own soul. We all had. I hoped he liked the part of him he'd found. Though friends and rivals alike came and went, we were stuck with ourselves and, if we were lucky, at most one other who pledged to stand by our side.

I'd found my companion. Soon, maybe Narcyz would find his, but first, I had a feeling he needed to convince himself he was worthy of that love.

Accepting love shouldn't have been hard. Yet, every moment I thought of Otylia, I remembered her unwillingness to say she loved me too. *Is it because of me?*

Every one of my wrong decisions flashed through my mind—the years I'd been too weak to tell her the truth of Father's threats, how I had failed to save her from Jaryło's blade, and each time I'd mocked her as a witch. Maybe I wasn't good enough. She was a goddess, after all. Could I be anything more than a płanetnik to her as my demonic cravings slowly ate away at my sanity? What if she saw me absorb the heart of a beast or worse? We'd kissed multiple times now, but no matter how I tried, she couldn't let down her walls with me. The fear of why was a rope around my neck, tightening with each passing day.

Leaning back, I stared at the sky and the twinkling souls surrounding the moon. *She cares for you,* I told myself. *There were a hundred other things on her mind at Oblivion's edge.* Yet, I doubted anyway.

Why was there a voice in so many of our heads that told us we were nothing? Was it our fathers' fists, a demon's whispers? Or had our hearts decided those we loved deserved more than us—people too broken to realize what parts were missing?

Part 3
Will & Destiny

35

Otylia

Will Weles actually give me answers?

THE SOFT DIRT FELT SATISFYING beneath my bare feet as I wandered the halls of Weles's palace. Apparently, I was to meet him in some place the messenger nymph had called a library, whatever that was. Despite weeks in the palace's vined walls, I still knew little about its actual layout, and I found myself walking in circles.

I stopped at a four-way intersection with a huff. My body was exhausted from my fight with the żmij the day before, and the meager *żityje* I had left wasn't helping.

What now? I asked myself, glancing down each of the halls.

The palace was a maze. I was becoming ever-more convinced that the vines not only moved but also changed the palace's arrangement. Perhaps Weles had some connection with them and wasn't bothered. I very much was.

I ran my hands through my skirt as I pondered what direction to take. Unlike Mother's dress that I'd worn yesterday, it was a simple thing—bone gray like my traveling dress. Green embroidery wove across its edges with symbols from the old tongue. If those symbols were as powerful as Weles had claimed, I couldn't rely on him to teach me their meanings. He would give me what was convenient to him, nothing more.

I shut my eyes and breathed deeply as I tried to sense Weles's location. Dziewanna could've shown me the way, but after the Trial of Isolation, I was supposed to discover my own power.

No answer came. No sensations of nearby spirits or gods. The world was dead to me and I to it. Maybe that was the way it had to be, or maybe I just needed to be patient. Unfortunately, patience was not one of my strengths. I went left.

The occasional doorway broke the vines on either side of the hall as I walked. I tried each, but they were all clasped shut from the inside. So, I clenched my jaw and went on for at least another hour with no success. Anger steamed within me as I thought of rebuke after rebuke I'd give Weles for sending me on a wild chase through the palace.

Focus on the book, I told myself.

As Kyustendil had claimed, a collection of sheets—similar to the notes—bound in leather had lain hidden beneath my bed upon my return. Its first page labelled it *The Trials of Ascension*, and Ivan had marked pages of interest.

I'd flipped through much of it last night. After hearing Kyustendil's plan, sleep had been a stranger anyway. Not that the book had been all that interesting.

My lack of knowledge of the old tongue made reading it difficult, but it seemed to be a priest rambling about his ideals for gods. Fascinating to Father… Dariusz… perhaps. Useless to me. One of the marked pages, however, gave me an insight into the Trials:

To become a god is to accept the inevitable opposites of life:

Isolation and Connection

Life and Death

Will and Destiny

Love and Loss

Ascension is the completion of these Trials. With it comes understanding, power, and completion that only a god can possess: divinity. While mortals possess life and demons consume it, gods must receive žityje through willing offerings. Because of this, only they hold the ability to create life for the Three Realms. Only they can truly wield the powers of nature. This is good.

Two sets of Trials remained: Will and Destiny and then Love and Loss. I didn't know which sounded worse.

The idea of Destiny disgusted me. Mokosz had implied the existence of such an entity during my vision in the bathing pool, but I hadn't wanted to accept it. If Destiny were a person who shaped our paths, did our decisions really matter?

I shook my head. *My choices are mine. Not some entity's.* Death had tricked me, controlled me. Destiny would not.

Pondering the third set of Trials had my skin crawling, but I had no desire to confront the fourth. *Love and Loss.* One seemed a hostile stranger, the other a familiar evil—not the romanticized tale of how gods earned their powers.

My thoughts returned to reality as I neared a large pair of doors at a dead end. A water nymph in a deep blue tunic stood to the side, nodding off as he leaned against his spear. *Don't mind me…*

When I slipped quietly through the door, a vast candlelit room met me. Where the palace's other rooms stopped among the World Tree's roots above, this one continued for as high as I could see. Shelves along the walls stretched toward the World Tree above while shorter ones zig-zagged with no clear order through the room's center. Dozens of colored books sat on each level. In fact, *nothing* filled the space but shelves and those books as I stepped into a narrow aisle.

Dust covered much of the space, and I sneezed when I reached for one of the books. It was brown and thick as four of my fingers. Unlike the rough, worn leather of *The Trials of Ascension,* this book's binding clung to my hands at first touch, as if it was desperate to be read. I pulled it free and groaned at the weight of the thing.

What is this?

I held it in one arm and flipped back the cover to reveal thin sheets of a light tan. There were hundreds of pages—far longer than *The Trials of Ascension*—each covered with words of the old tongue. Many words were unfamiliar to me, making reading difficult, but I could make out some sentences. Little of it made sense until one line caught my eye.

It was only then that the Luliowie people tamed the desert, bringing water and crops where there once were none.

What followed was gibberish to me, but I recognized Dziewanna's Bowmark a few lines later. My fingers absently traced the symbol that had been so close to me for years. I fought back the tears that threatened. *Mother.* Memories of her body lying beneath the żmij flashed through my mind until shuffling came from down the aisle.

I spun, clutching the book to my chest, as Weles appeared. His long beard and hair were darker than usual in the shadowed torchlight. "Taken up an interest in reading about ancient irrigation practices, have we?" he asked, a hint of amusement in his voice. "Do not worry, my child. Books are for the wise."

I glanced down at the book for a second before returning my gaze to Weles. "What are these? I've seen the old tongue painted or carved, but never like this."

"Words have power, as I have said before." Weles shuffled slowly toward me, admiring the books as he did. They were beautiful. From vibrant reds to deep blues, browns, and even blacks, each was unique. "Perhaps the most important element of their strength is one Perun foolishly believes is trivial—the storing of knowledge. Ink and paper are more capable of raising tribes or *razing* tribes than most sorcery or witchcraft."

"This book," I said. "It mentions growing crops in something called a desert, where there hadn't been water. What does it mean? Did Mother grant them that power?"

Weles chuckled. "It has been so long since I have met a young deity, and this is the first time there has been one raised on Jawia, acting as a mortal. There is much you have to learn." He stopped before me and leaned upon his cane. "First: We may be gods, but the finite nature of our power is for the best of mankind and all of the Three Realms. In some cases, miraculous events may have been put into motion by a god. Most, though, are simply made possible by our presence."

"I didn't expect you to claim gods should be limited."

He sighed and turned to the books. This close, the smell of wet moss wafted over me as he spoke, "There have been many wars between the gods for good or ill, and many times, each realm has come near to its destruction. If we were truly all-powerful, then you and I would not be standing here."

"Near destruction?" I gasped unwillingly. Neither priests nor gods had ever told me of the world's demise. "How many times has Jawia been ruined? And what did you mean, 'made possible by our presence?' "

"Yes, *near* destruction." He shook his head to himself, as if remembering the events. "I knew you would have many questions. Come, let us find a place to sit and rest. You have certainly had a few long days, and I am older than you could comprehend. Those years wear on both body and soul."

As he passed, my thumb rubbed against the sleeping draught, tucked into my wide belt. *After the meeting.* This would likely be my last opportunity to get answers from Weles. I needed to take it.

A thousand thoughts circled my mind as he led me through the rows of books. Their colors and the golden and silver lettering along their spines were a welcome distraction. Whenever anxiety threatened to halt my steps and choke my breaths, I would focus on the symbols, imagine what they meant.

If the old tongue's symbols are words with power, are gods' marks any different? I wondered. Dziewanna's Bowmark had appeared the same as others on the page. If I hadn't been familiar with each of the gods' marks, I would've skimmed right over it, just as I had the other, unfamiliar symbols. Did every word in the old tongue have a connection to a god's power? Was the word that had appeared to me in my battle against the żmij one of them—*Rìnoti*—or any of the other old tongue words I'd used to channel?

I gritted my teeth. This room held more answers than I could possibly need, yet I understood so little of it. When I did get an answer, it only seemed to make me question things more. It was an endless cycle—one I had to break if I was ever going to figure out how to be a goddess.

The bookshelves soon gave way to a sitting area with a low table, two plush benches covered with bear furs, and a wide leather chair.

I hesitated. *What is all of this?* Dwie Rzeki was our tribe's most populous and successful settlement, but even the high chief couldn't spare the resources to make such garnished furnishings. Though these weren't the vibrant colors I'd seen in the dead soul's village before my first Trial, they had obviously been made by a skilled craftsman. Not a single line was straight. Wood, leather, fur, and cloth flowed together in each piece like it were part of nature itself.

"This couch is most likely more comfortable than any bed you've felt on Jawia," Weles said, gesturing to the odd bench as he lowered himself slowly into the chair. It made a squeaking noise as he adjusted, but he didn't seem to mind. "There is much the Krowikie have not succeeded with. Finding a place to be idle in peace is one of them."

At first, I stood in defiance. Despite my exhaustion and dizziness from the swarm of new information, the entire situation felt *wrong*. Weles's mood, the books, the plush setting, and the slits of golden light streaming through the roots above—my instincts told me to run from it all. I was a girl meant for the wilds. The only thing wild here, however, was the dirt between my toes as I relented and sat at the furthest end of the couch, digging them into the earth. *He won't give me answers if I don't play along.*

"So, this is a library," I said.

"Indeed." Weles stomped his cane against the ground, and roots stretched up from what seemed like nothing. In seconds, they pulled the cane into a hole that formed between the god and me. While I watched in awe, he studied me. "If I must be direct—which appears to be the only way to handle you—I did not know what to do with you when I first sensed you passing from Jawia."

"Ironic," I muttered, "considering you were the one who sent Jaryło to kill me."

His gaze hardened. "Must we return to this topic every time we speak? Jaryło's methods were not what I wished them to be, but he brought you here to me, where you belong."

"I belong with Mother." I gripped the armrest, digging my fingernails into the pelt. "She died on Jawia because she was worried you were close to finding her. Now, when you take me to Nawia, you've lost her already. What kind of husband are you? How could you let Marzanna take her?"

"You do not understand what you are asking."

Fury burned me, and I felt the armband searing against my skin with the energy. "And *you* don't understand how much it hurts to lose your mother! She was everything to me. Marzanna's Curse took her, but she knew it was her time because you had almost found her. Mother fled you to protect me and then died to do the same."

I swallowed, trying to contain myself, but my heart pounded in my chest. I *needed* to say it. "You promised me answers, Weles. Give them, or I'll find them somewhere else."

"Otylia," he said, not raising his voice, "do you know why your mother rebelled against Perun and Swaróg, challenging their rule of Prawia?"

I shook my head.

He huffed. "You barely knew the woman you claim to love so much. Dziewanna is young for a goddess—the youngest of Perun and Mokosz's children—but we have been married for centuries. She despised me for so long…" His head lowered as he scratched his beard, grayer than ever. "In that time, though, I grew to comprehend your mother's complex mind more than I ever believed I could. Dziewanna was wild, yes, but she was also caring, strong. When she moved, it was with the grace of the forest's slightest breeze—until she struck. Wrong her and she could slice the most experienced warrior's throat without a blade. Demons feared her. Nymphs, at least the female ones, worshipped her. And every creature in the Three Realms answered when she called."

He gave a solemn smile. "I truly did love her, but I am not the almighty Perun or Swaróg. I could never be enough for my wife."

"You still haven't said why she rebelled."

"No, I haven't, have I?" Weles chuckled. "I got lost in memories, my apologies. Your mother lived for many years under Perun's thumb. As the god of justice, war, and thunder, I do not imagine he was a kind father for a child as free-spirited as Dziewanna." His gaze softened as he looked at me. "Perhaps it is not any easier for the daughter of Nawia's king, but regardless, your mother believed that there needed to be change. She saw my war with Perun, how his anger rained destruction upon Jawia and the souls of Nawia. She saw how it distracted Perun and how Swaróg stepped back, allowing his son to enrage mankind against itself.

"Both sides in our wars built great machines capable of destroying whole villages. Our chosen people erected massive walls, and our channelers—both men and woman alike—ravaged. In their rage, the tribes tore apart the wilds Dziewanna called home and slayed her animals. Trees became spears and siege engines, mountains were mined for iron and riches, and the rivers ran as red as rubies. That was the last devastation of Jawia."

She fought to save the wilds, to save Jawia. Pride pushed past my shock. "So, the legends are wrong. She fought to protect the Three Realms, not to selfishly control them for herself."

Weles nodded. "I regret so much I did in that war. Though I had no choice but to repel Perun's attempts to strangle Jawia, I did not wish to. Your mother's revolution may have failed, but it caused enough unrest in Prawia to force Perun to offer peace terms. Dziewanna became the bond between us. Despite the clashes your priests speak of now, Perun and I have not warred since because of her."

I scoffed at that. *Why is it that men are the same, whether they be gods or mortal? It's up to us to solve their problems.* "You claim the war was Perun's fault, but Father said your war with Perun began when you stole his cattle and escalated when you kidnapped Jaryło."

"That is a common belief, yes. But our wars had waxed and waned many times before I touched his cattle. Perun is my older half-brother, birthed by Łada and raised by Swaróg. I, having been born of Łada and a cow, was much less respected than him."

"Why did the goddess of love bed a cow?" I asked.

Weles waved a hand through the air. "Who am I to know my

mother's ways? I am ancient, and she is even older than I. Regardless, Swaróg favored Perun because of this and his affinity for the sky and storms, just as Swaróg was once known for." He smirked at my surprise. "Yes, Swaróg may be your god of fire and smithing today, but he is the one who rules the sky even higher than Perun himself. Perun rules Prawia because Swaróg lets him—I received nothing."

He rose with a scowl. Without cane or struggle, he circled the table, a shadow covering his face as his words sharpened. "Before me, there was no Nawia. Souls were granted an audience in Prawia or sent to Oblivion, but I created a paradise for those forgotten by Perun. People who lived their lives. People who fought and toiled in fields and valleys. I protected them, and in return, they worshipped me."

"Let me guess," I replied. "Perun was not supportive of his younger half-brother creating a third realm."

Weles reached a shelf and removed one book, opening it to a page near its center. "You catch on quickly. Do you see now why your mother and I connected, how we understood Perun's wrongs?"

"Somewhat." I stood as well, not willing to let him hold the more dominant position. There was some element of truth in his words. *Some.* But even now, he was telling me what he wanted me to hear and nothing more. In a way, it worked, bringing me into an understanding of his side of the story. I felt his pain of being forgotten. "I get why you loved her, but you still abandoned her to Marzanna."

"Then the Mistress of Winter rose from the ashes," Weles read from the book. "Like a beautiful snow stained by darkness, she brought disease and starvation, desperation and death. And when she came, none could stop her wrath."

He shut the book and slid it back onto the shelf. "Tymofij was a fine author in the days when the priests could write the old tongue. Little has changed about Marzanna since then, and I will not sacrifice my daughter to her as well.

"Your mother…" He sighed and raised his gaze to me, his lip curling for a moment. "She is no friend to staying in one place. Yes, she returned to me four years ago, but I had little control over her as she came and went. This past year, she sensed a change in the seasons. I did not believe her. After centuries of watching Marzanna seek revenge on Jaryło, I had grown accustomed to the routine. She knew her sister better than I, though."

"She left," I mumbled, realizing the only answer. "Mother went to stop Marzanna before the equinox, alone. Why?" Resentment crept into my voice again. "Why'd you let her walk into Marzanna's trap?"

"I did not know!" he shouted. I started, stepping back as his face burned red, his hand gripping the bookcase's edge. His fingers were long, gnarled like its wood. "Dziewanna is strong-willed, Otylia. It had taken many moons for her to recover after Marzanna's Curse took her. Ascended gods heal slowly after death without *żityje*. As you know, few worship your mother, so without a Moonstone or frequent blood sacrifices, her recovery took longer. She still wasn't at full health this spring. That did not stop her."

"Mother attacked Marzanna alone, weakened?" I asked, pacing as I pictured Mother curled at the base of the ice towers. "She was bold, but why not wait for Jaryło to be able to wield his Moonblade?"

Weles shuffled back to his chair and sat. This time, the leather's squeak was more irritating than amusing. "I do not know why she was so desperate to face her sister just days before the equinox. After she escaped my realm, I sent Jaryło to aid her, but she was too weak when he arrived. I am sorry, Otylia."

"*You* could've fought for her!" I snapped. "You make these claims about Perun, but when your wife is taken by Marzanna and slowly drained of her *żityje*, you do nothing. Tell me I'm wrong."

His glare returned. "Control your temper with me. Many of my szeptuchy have been searching for her ever since I learned of Marzanna's plan, but Jawia is the largest of the Three Realms. My power is needed not just to abate Perun's advance but also to sustain many bodies of water, the lowland plains, and the souls entering Nawia—of which there are many due to the Frostmarked Horde. Without Dziewanna—and after your corrupted boy killed Jaryło—it is only a few meager spirits and I left to maintain the forests of Jawia. Call to Perun, to Swaróg, or to Strzybóg, who was tasked with protecting Dziewanna. None of them shall answer."

"Wacław defended me," I said, resting my hands on the back of the couch and matching Weles's gaze. "And I believe him when he says Jawia is dying. Whatever you're doing isn't enough."

"You really are that desperate to return."

"I am," I said. "My connection to Dziewanna and Mokosz is gone, and I understand I need to be my own goddess, apart from Mother. That doesn't mean I'm willing to sit back and let her die." I paused, remembering Jaryło's offer to me. "Your son wants me to help him take all the Moonstones, to let him rule Jawia."

"I am aware of this, as it is my plan for him, but I sense hesitation in your tone—rare for you."

Slowly, I returned to my seat. My back had begun to ache again, but I concealed any sign of the pain. "Marzanna has no right to claim his seven Moonstones for herself, but I don't think Jaryło has a claim to her five either."

"Why is that?" he asked, raising his chin.

"He's the one who caused the divide in the first place. Marzanna became goddess of winter *because* he was unfaithful to her. Why should he be rewarded for that?"

"Do you believe the current cycle is best, then?"

I shrugged. "It's all I've ever experienced. Father always preached about the gods balancing the cycles of nature. You all still fight, sure, but the balance stops the destruction of the Three Realms. Destroy that and chaos reigns."

"Hmm." He pondered that for a second. "You may have some of my wisdom after all." I rolled my eyes, but he continued, "However, here I shall caution you: Do not consider chaos itself an evil. Too much order and you have tyranny, whether in nature, tribes, or gods. The untamed freedom your mother so fervently fights for is impossible with pure order."

"But life is impossible with pure chaos," I countered. "The plants, animals, and even the fungi and insects feasting on corpses are all part of the natural order. I've seen the chaos of the wilds. I've also seen what happens when its ways are broken by man and god alike."

Weles nodded. "Balance is a fragile thing, one that Marzanna's slaying of Jaryło destroyed many years ago."

"It was Jaryło's lust that destroyed their balance."

He huffed and threw a hand into the air. "It matters not. The current cycle is unsuitable, and it would be better for Jaryło to control the Moonstones and Jawia as a whole. You will finish your Trials in the coming years, and once you Ascend, you will wed Jaryło, becoming queen of Jawia."

"What?" I roared, shooting to my feet and glaring down at him. My whole body burned as my nails dug into my palm. "I will *not* marry Jaryło!"

Unfazed, Weles met my gaze. "Once you Ascend, your brother and my servants will be by your side at each moment you spend in Jawia. They will ensure you do as you are told instead of chasing demons whom you have so foolishly fallen for."

I crossed my arms, glaring at the god. *Barely veiled threats replace deception.* I had been right about him all along. He didn't care about Mother or me. Weles was just like the chiefs of man and Perun, the god he so loved to hate. I would not let him use me so that Jaryło could rule Jawia. And I sure as Oblivion wasn't going to wed that traitorous god.

I need to get out of here. Now.

"I fear that we have spoken for quite some time," Weles said after a prolonged silence, "and my servants will have become wary of my disappearance. I *am* thousands of years old, after all."

My heart sunk as my anger deflated into sorrow. Once again, I was left with even more questions—this time, about both Mother and the Three Realms. There was so much Weles hadn't said that lingered beneath the surface. Within this room was the history of tribes, spirits, and gods, but I couldn't read it without him. *That'll have to change.*

"Is that all you wanted me for?" I asked, gritting my teeth with each word. "Or are there any more ways you'd like to train me to wallow in service of Jaryło?"

He narrowed his eyes at my sarcasm. "Return to your chambers. After your encounter with Death, it will take time for your body to heal."

I winced and averted my gaze. "Fine," I muttered. "But I *must* be able to leave the palace without an escort. Leave me in here much longer and I'll go mad."

"Very well. You will not be able to stray far anyway without a thorough knowledge of these lands, but find rest tonight. Tomorrow, we shall continue your training, and for all our sakes, weave your hair, girl. You are not yet wed." He summoned his cane from the earth and walked back through the bookshelves, leaving me behind with my jaw clenched.

When the door closed across the room, I dropped onto the couch. I was done keeping up appearances. My head throbbed as I tried to comprehend all Weles had told me. It was hard enough to understand the cycles Jawia must've gone through if it had nearly been destroyed more than once, but the added complexity of Weles's deception made it worse. Could I trust his word about Mother or Perun? Considering his threats about Jaryło, I doubted it.

My muscles relaxed as I sank deeper into the bear pelt and rested my head upon the couch's back. "I miss you, Mom," I whispered.

With Weles delaying any further Trials or training, there was little for me to do except wait for him to be far from his blood altar. Any doubts I'd held about the sleeping draught were gone. Weles had made sure of that.

My skin crawled as visions of life with Jaryło flashed in my head. Girls in the tribe dreamed of what the god of war, spring, and fertility would be like. As far as I was concerned, they could have him. Handsome or not, Jaryło had betrayed me, *killed* me. It was his infidelity that turned Marzanna wicked. I had no interest in wedding a thousand-year-old god who carried the lust of a teenage boy.

I grabbed a pillow and screamed into it, releasing all my pent-up rage. Why couldn't I choose what to do with my life? Even as a goddess, people were trying to control me. Everyone had their own selfish plans for Jawia, and now it was even worse.

With a groan, I turned and lay down on the couch, staring up at the roots above. *I'm probably one of only a few to ever see the World Tree's roots like this.*

They were stunning from this angle. The fading light sliced across them, shadows layered on different branches as they twisted through the sky, reaching down into the palace and meeting the ground and random points. *Chaos or order?* To me, there seemed to be little reason to the pattern of the roots, but there was an elegance to it—an allure of the unpredictable.

I smirked to myself. *Allure of the unpredictable. Sounds like something Wašek would say when he's trying to be romantic.*

I like it.

My stomach flipped at that admission. I fought my discomfort, embracing the distraction.

Maybe it was okay to rely on Wacław. Maybe it was okay to stop resisting my feelings for him. Surely, it was better than wedding Jaryło, but just the thought of that *vulnerability* froze me. I'd seen so many people broken because they'd let down their guard, only to lose those they loved or suffer at their hand. That pain was all too familiar. I couldn't endure it again…

As I stared up at those roots, though, memories slipped through my defenses. The times when I'd surrendered, when I'd let Wacław in—partially—and when he'd been somehow strong and tender at once.

I'd loved those moments. They had been seconds of bliss, the rare times he'd put aside his hesitance and let me feel safe with him. A *demon* of all things. In his arms, I could imagine a normal life.

But our lives weren't normal.

I stood and wandered through the books, running my fingers along their spines. They grounded my thoughts as I made my way toward the doors and the inevitable conflict that lay beyond.

I pushed away those girlish dreams and swallowed my fear for Mother, for Wacław, and for the destruction that would come if I failed. Those emotions couldn't cloud my judgement. With gods, demons, and even Death himself standing against me, love could wait.

I'm sorry, Wašek.

36

Otylia

Soon, I'll be free. Whatever that means anymore…

MY HANDS BRAIDED MY HAIR WITHOUT GUIDANCE after years of doing so each morning. It had been part of who I was: an unwedded woman. That weave had signified to every man that I was yet to be claimed. He'd needed only to bring a suitable dowry to Father to take me away against my will.

In recent weeks, I'd broken that tradition. I'd worn my hair unbraided against the wishes of Father, of Weles, and of my tribe. It had been amazing. For the first time since I'd turned twelve, I'd been free.

That was over—for now. Weles had demanded I wear the braid once again, but instead of accepting that defeat, I smirked. His commands wouldn't matter soon.

Yesterday, after Weles had disappeared from the vines of the palace, I'd slipped into his blood altar undetected. Pouring the sleeping draught had been quick. All I had to do now was wait for the message from Kyustendil. Unfortunately, it had yet to arrive, and I would soon have to join Weles for my "training." Whatever that meant.

Just a few more days until Maj, I reminded myself. *The plan will work, Wašek will come, and we'll escape together.*

I finished the braid and groaned, holding my head in my hands. Everything had me irritated. My feet slid through the bathing pond's warm water as the morning sunlight streamed onto my face, but even that didn't improve my mood.

Why wasn't I convinced of the plan? Why couldn't I just accept the training for now, learn what I could, and then escape? It should've been simple, yet all I wanted to do was punch something.

I jumped to my feet and dried off as I stared at the mirror. My reflection had gone from a rare moment to something I saw at least twice a day. Part of me hated that. Why did I care how I looked? There were no eligible boys around, seeking girls they could parade in front of their friends—not that I'd ever paid attention to them. There were no priests or chiefs or gossiping women either. Just nymphs and the god of the dead.

My eyes found the reflection regardless. They studied every imperfection, both new and old, reminding me of them each visit. I scowled at the jagged scrapes and bruises on my shoulder. *Welcome to the collection.*

My back was worse. The żmij's claws had dug deep through both skin and muscle. Even after the ointments yesterday, the area beneath my shoulder blades looked like a child's first attempt at slicing herbs. Bits of discolored skin hung freely at points, surrounded by arcing lines of red. Luckily, none of the wounds seemed infected, so the treatments hadn't been *completely* useless. Their relief had been temporary, though, and any movement sent a jab into my mind.

And I thought the utopiec's claw marks were bad. They hadn't healed well—Father said wounds from demons never did—but the deep gray scars upon my mid-back were barely visible beneath the chaos above. It was a miracle I'd survived.

No, it was because of Wacław I survived.

He'd offered his life for mine: a deal I'd been unwilling to accept. I didn't know how to wrangle my feelings for him, but that promise to Death was a weight I would gladly bear to keep him alive. Did other people's relationship mean complete reliance on the other to live? Was that even what we had, a relationship?

Anger flashed through me. I clenched my fists and let out a scream at myself, at Weles, at Jaryło, at everyone who'd tried to control me.

The mirror shattered.

My heart pounded as I stepped back, gaping at the cracks that streaked from the mirror's smashed center. It looked as if someone had sent a stone into its face. But I was the only one here.

I raised my hands before me. They pulsed, glowing with *żityje* as the familiar sensation of power flooded through me. *I'll be free. No matter what.*

Clinging to that thought, I returned to the bedroom, grabbing what remained of the poultices. It would be a patchwork job on my injuries, but anything was better than my current pain.

By the time Sabina appeared with my dress for the day, I'd already slid on my shift and stuck the bone talismans in my braid. Weles could order me to weave my hair all he wanted, but I would do it my way. Besides, those talismans were a comforting bit of home in the land of the unknown.

The dress Sabina held was much humbler than Mother's autumn-leaf one from two days before. Layers of dark gray made up the skirt while a lighter shade tapered to the edge of each layer. Circular, black patterns swept down from the neck through its torso, meeting the wide leather belt at the waist.

"This one is ruffly!" she said, spinning with it in her arms. As she did, the skirts flew around her, and the two shades of gray rolled like storm-clouds in the night sky.

I leaned back on the footboard of the bed. "I like it. After the last few days, I don't think I could tolerate another colorful dress."

"I am glad you were the one to face Death and not me, Lady Ot..." she blushed as she caught herself. "My apologies. I didn't mean that to sound so dismissive."

"It would be hard for you to offend me, Sabina." I eyed the blue sheet of fabric draped over her arm. "What is that?"

After laying the dress on the bed and adjusting it to ensure there were no wrinkles, she held up an open-front coat lined in fur. "It's quite cold this morning, and I thought you might want to have a robe to keep away the chill."

"You never fail me," I said, taking the coat. Like everything Sabina brought, it was softer than even the comfiest gifts Mother had given me. It seemed wasteful to wear each outfit only once. Dress-makers like Ara's mother spent weeks, or even moons, weaving. That was when materials were plentiful. Sabina, however, had insisted Nawia had more than enough resources to spare and that each was remade into its base fabric afterward. That didn't make the daily dress any less odd, but at least I wouldn't have to feel guilty about it.

Sabina curtsied. "It is my responsibility and pleasure."

Without my clothes in her arms, it became obvious now that she had her own coat. It was thin and made only of leaves woven with what seemed to be bark, but it was reassuring to know she wasn't freezing while I wore the heavy furs. It didn't protect her face, though, and her narrow nose was bright red.

Why is it so cold?

The chill struck me as I spun around the bed and held the dress. Stuck in my thoughts, I hadn't noticed the change from yesterday, but it was significant. That seemed odd. Had the temperature shifted before during my time in Nawia? If it had, why was it getting colder during spring if Weles was protecting the realm?

Gods, am I really questioning the weather now? I'm starting to sound like Narcyz.

It *had* gotten colder, but it was far from the frigid temperatures of Jawia I'd left behind. Maybe it was Marzanna. Maybe it was just another element of the fickle spring. I would have to be careful regardless. Though I assumed even Dadźbóg alone could keep Jawia from freezing after Wacław had defeated the Frostmarked płanetnik, it was possible Marzanna had found another way.

"Please tell me this isn't silver fox fur," I said as I pulled the coat over the dress. Both covered my right arm down to the wrist but kept my left forearm, and the armband upon it, exposed. It felt luxurious against my skin, tempting me to curl up within it instead of facing Weles.

"I believe it is wolf fur, my lady." She held her hands in front of her, her face uncertain. "We… We would have liked to get you more silver fox fur, but it is a rare animal that—"

"Wolf is fine." I placed the fox pelt on my head, allowing my braid to stick out beneath it. "Better to kill Marzanna's beasts than my own, and I doubt it's a good idea for a goddess to hunt her totem animal out of existence."

Her eyes lit up, and her wings fluttered. "Oh! I'm so happy you like it! Master Weles instructed me to ensure you were pleased, and—"

I cupped her cheek in my hand. "You don't need to do anything more for me, Sabina. You're already risking your life to help me escape—especially after what I did with that potion. That's braver than most people would think a nymph capable of."

"Well, you offered me hope of finding my family on Jawia, so we're even."

"Fair enough." I slid on my boots and approached the door, stopping with my hand on it. "Pray that I'm strong enough to hold my tongue with Weles."

"To whom should I pray?"

My fingertips stung against the cold wood as I thought. "Mother, Mokosz, any goddess who understands what it's like to be deceived by men."

She neared, her wings beating the air and her breaths short. "Even Marzanna?"

"Sure," I huffed. "Even her."

Weles leaned on his cane with each step as we followed an earthen path past the village I'd seen during my first set of Trials. Robed in bear furs, he hadn't spoken a word since I'd found him in his throne room.

He'd been bent over his knees, staring at the ground on his throne. Even when I'd knelt on before him, he'd just looked at me with contempt. There was an age in his eyes I hadn't seen before. Eternity dwelled within them, and I'd ignited his anger. I was a tool for his son to rule Jawia, nothing more, but all I'd done since arriving in Nawia was rebel and find my own way. Apparently, he'd finally had enough.

The village was alive in spite of the cold. Women paraded about in colorful dresses, their hair adorned in matching kokoshniks that towered up to a foot above their heads. I stared in awe at the crowns and the intricate patterns upon them. They seemed something a distant queen would wear, not the souls of villagers in the afterlife.

Men, too, wore long colored robes with fur. They sparred in rings with dulled blades or gathered on horses for a hunt in Weles's woods. The eldest among them sat together with some kind of smoking pipe, laughing at boys who ran in circles with wooden swords.

Maybe this is a paradise for them.

Father had often told stories of souls visiting their families in the form of ravens, nightjars, and other birds. They flew free before returning to Nawia, full of luxuries they never had in life. Though I was a goddess, I had been raised as one of them—a mortal. Now, they soared while I flailed on the ground like a mighty falcon with its wings clipped.

Weles stopped when we were clear of the village. The trail seemed to wind on for some way still, but his focus was on me. "You envy them," he said, his voice rough.

I bowed my head, feigning submission. "Yes, Father." My tongue burned calling him my father, but I thought of Mother and Wacław. Words meant nothing. If it kept Weles's anger at bay long enough for the draught to work, then I would suffer it.

"You call me 'Father' now?" He raised his brow, but a smiled tugged at his mouth. "Perhaps I should have been sterner with you from the moment you arrived with my bloodied and dying son."

It took all my strength not to retort, but I kept my head down. Every muscle in my body was tense beneath his gaze. "I should've listened to you sooner," I said, resentment slipping into my voice.

"Look at me, my daughter." I met his gaze as he folded his hands atop his cane. "You have your mother's spirit. That makes you stronger than a goddess should ever be before Ascension, but it also means you have much to learn if you do not wish to be captured as well."

And if I've already been captured?

"Come," he said, nodding down the trail. "We are close."

This time as we walked, he stayed beside me instead of leading the way. His eyes remained heavy, but he seemed *younger*. The gray hair and beard were the same, yet he relied less on his staff and admired the surroundings more than staring straight ahead. Or was I just seeing things?

"Where are you taking me?" I asked when we entered a farm field.

It was early in the planting seasons still, so the flat plain was barren except for the horses pulling iron plows through the soil. Both mortal souls and nymphs drove them on from behind. These nymphs wore brown roughspun tunics and trousers, unlike the finely made clothes of leaves and bark for those in the palace.

"You will see soon," Weles replied. "I promise that it shall be far less painful than meeting Death."

It'd be hard to be worse. We crossed the untilled section of the field, but when we were halfway across, a commotion came from the workers.

Women with long staffs shouted at a female nymph, who flew overhead until one of the women slammed her staff into the earth. Instantly, vines shot from the earth. I gasped as they wrapped around the nymph's limbs and dragged her writhing body to the ground. The women surrounded her, their embroidered brown cloaks sweeping behind them as they chanted in the old tongue.

The power of their words swelled around me. I couldn't sense it like I had with Dziewanna and Mokosz's powers, but the sorcery was unmistakable. "They're szeptuchy…" I whispered to myself.

"Indeed," Weles said. "And it appears a nymph has grown restless."

The nymph fought as the vines engulfed her, but it was a futile fight. Soon, she disappeared into the ground, and I bit my tongue to stop myself from crying out. "Restless? They just killed her!"

Weles turned and continued through the field without another look. "Nonsense. Nymphs are soulless. They are merely manifestations of a place's essence—forest nymphs of trees, mountain nymphs for the earth, and so forth. When they return to that place, their *žityje* simply joins with it. We will bring other nymphs to assist those mortal souls choosing to work in the fields."

Apparently, nymphs don't have the same choice. But I held my tongue, eyeing the szeptuchy as the farmers went back to work. Part of what Weles said made sense. Sabina was very much alive, though, and I had no intentions of ever letting him *return* her. More importantly, I knew many of those nymphs were those stolen from Jawia in Weles's deals with their parents. *Power in exchange for a child… Disgusting.*

The field soon gave way to a meadow in full bloom. Flowers of every color stretched as far as the horizon, rolling with the hills, but our path swept left, away from the beauty and instead sloped into the ground. Roots held back the earthen sides as the sun disappeared behind us.

"*Svět,*" Weles whispered. The curled peak of his cane glowed with a harsh light, and I covered my eyes, committing that word to memory as we descended deeper underground.

Here, the sun's absence left me shivering. The fur coat was thick, but even it couldn't keep out the chill that encroached from the depths. I prayed that, wherever we were going, it had at least a fire.

Weles sighed when we reached a wooden door. He tapped the cane against it before stepping back.

"You're not going in?" I asked as he waved me forward.

He grinned—one I couldn't tell was joyful or devious. "I will follow, but I am not the one training you today."

Slowly, I nodded as the door swung open to reveal a ragged man with the skull of a raven jutting from beneath his black hooded cloak. In fact, everything about the man was black from his robes to his pants. Even his skin was darker than the light brown of the eastern clans, and he seemed to blend with the shadows.

The Raven Wizard?

Ivan's story before the first Trial returned to me as I studied the man. He'd said three wizards had revived him after Koschei the Deathless struck him down. The Raven Wizard was among them. But what was he doing here?

"The princess of Nawia has come," the wizard said in a deep yet crisp voice. "I wondered when this day would come."

Then he backed away, fading into the darkness. With a glance at Weles, I followed the man into a small room. There was a stone stove in the corner, but from the lingering chill, I doubted he'd fed its fires in some time. A stark smell of dirt choked the air as the roots creaked and held back the weight of the earth above.

The Raven Wizard swept his robes back and sat on a solitary stool by the stove. A candle hung from the ceiling by an iron chain, and its flickering light added to the man's mystery beneath his hood. He waved for me to approach. "Do you know why you are here?"

I shook my head.

"Hmm. Look at the pelt you wear."

"It's about my connection to the silver fox?"

He wagged his finger. "You hold more than a mere connection to the silver fox. It is an inseparable part of you now—one that must be honed if you are to survive."

"Survive?" I asked, raising my brow.

"Yes," Weles said as he entered the room and lingered by the door, the candlelight barely enough to see the outline of his face. "The silver fox has merged with you, and every piece of your soul defines who you are. Apart from its elements, your soul withers, reaching for what makes it whole. Many more forces will become a part of you during your Ascension. Shape-shifting to the fox is a crucial start."

Apart from it, your soul withers… What about Wašek? Is the piece of his soul in mine the only thing pulling me to him, or is there more?

I pushed away those thoughts and nodded. Whatever this man was supposed to teach me, I doubted it would be any easier while questioning my love life. "Then what do I need to do?" I said, blunt. "And who are you?"

"Tibês, I am called by some," the man said.

"That's an eastern name, from the clans."

His sharp eyes tore into me from beneath his hood. They were bronze daggers, and, standing before him, it felt like they were pressed against my jugular. "You speak of things you do not know, princess. There are many people beyond the tribes and clans you are familiar with. Within the cradle of Perun's Crown, your people grow complacent with their fertile lands. Only demons offer any real threat, and your szeptuchy are common enough to rid them without need of people like me."

"Sorcery," I said. "Ivan told me of the Raven Wizard. Is that you?" Witches and sorcerers alike were banned in Krowikie lands, as they channeled the powers of spirits and demons. If I hadn't lost my connection to Dziewanna and Mokosz, I would've sensed him before we'd even entered the room.

"I have been called such a title," the man continued. "In my people's lands, far to the south of the Anshayman Steppe, sorcerers are worshipped nearly as much as the gods. Some as gods. It matters not. You are here to prove you can become one yourself."

"Tibês," Weles replied, "she was born a goddess. What must happen in time is Ascension."

The man huffed. "One who has not Ascended is not a god. Her soul may claim her to be powerful, but it does not make her a goddess until she shows otherwise."

"Then show me," I said, stepping forward. The smell of rot and decay met me this close, but I swallowed my nausea. "Give me the chance, and I'll prove you wrong."

He spat at my feet. "I don't listen to little girls."

My cheeks burned. Throwing out my arm, I sensed every glyph upon my armband and sent my *žityje* into it. "*Meti*!" Sweep.

Tibês flew aside and slammed into the wall. *Žityje* rushed from me at the spell's use, but I grinned as he fell to his knees. Kyustendil had sung the word to brush away the grasses in the meadow. This had been entirely different. While his channeling had been light and repeated, I'd thrown Tibês as effortlessly as a leaf. It had used a lot of energy, but something told me the spell could've been even stronger if I'd let it.

Tibês scowled as he fought to stand. "What are you doi—"

I was already upon him. My foot met his chest before he could gain his footing, and he collapsed into the wall. "I don't care what you think of me, wizard," I said as I crouched before him, meeting the intensity of his gaze as my armband glowed with power. "And I'm sure you feel the same. So, you can help me and make this easy for both of us, or we can waste both of our *žityje* figuring out who is stronger."

The end of his mouth twitched, and I expected a strike. But a laugh came instead as he reached an arm out to me. "You have all the ferocity your father claimed."

"No more stupid insults?" I asked, brow furrowed.

When he nodded, I grabbed his forearm and pulled him to his feet. Dirt coated his cloak, but he didn't brush it away as he sat on his stool. "First lesson of shape-shifting: never do it without a way to change back. Many young sorcerers forget this and are never seen again."

"What do you mean? If it's a part of my soul, can't I switch freely?"

He let out a single laugh and pointed to a tree stump that sat at the room's center. "A skilled sorcerer or deity can shift without a ritual, but that takes time and *žityje.* This stump will be your gateway for now."

I examined the stump and the roots stretching to it. It appeared to have been an ash tree, and based on the charred bits around its bark, lightning had struck it. *But we're at least fifty feet underground…*

Tibês drew five knives from beneath his cloak. "Take these and set them upon the stump, blade up."

"Won't the daggers fall?" I asked, doing as he asked until the first rocked on its hilt and toppled over.

"Those words you whisper—or apparently shout—are part of channeling. Until you can manipulate inanimate objects without needing even thought, though, you have little power. Grand spells are easier than precision, but it is precision that is required to master sorcery."

I gripped the dagger and cocked my head. "Are you going to

mock me again or help?"

With a grin, he shook his head. "Focus upon the blade as you're setting it down. At first, command it with your power, your *žityje*, to remain still or to simply *be*."

He said that word for a reason. I knew it in the old tongue: *bǫdi.*

Clearing the stray thoughts from my mind, I set the first knife down again, focusing on the word and imagining the blade remaining still. It felt stupid, but I had no other choice with Weles watching.

After an eternity of ensuring the blade was straight, I let go. It wobbled, but I reached into my *žityje*, demanding that my power hold the knife upright. The energy trickled from my soul. I stared at the blade and bit my cheek so hard it bled. *C'mon…*

The knife stilled, and I grinned up at Tibês. Though its point tilted to the right by a few degrees, I'd done it. "That's oddly satisfying," I said.

Arms crossed, he shrugged. "It would be more satisfying if you had successfully kept the blade straight. Do it again if you want the ritual to work."

I narrowed my eyes but relented, letting the knife drop to the stump. *Don't let him get to you,* I told myself. *You fought a dragon. What can five blades do?*

So, I tried again. Then again. Then again. On the fifth attempt I fell onto my rear, sweat dripping down my face despite the cold. With exhaustion gripping me already, I didn't bother to look at the knife. Surely, I'd failed. Tibês would be proven right, and I'd whisper the word just to get the ritual over with.

"Get up, child," Tibês said without a drop of pity.

The dirt coated my fingernails as I dug them in, throwing myself back to my feet. My back ached from both wounds and stress, and blood covered my tongue from my bit cheek. But a surprise met me.

"I did it," I whispered. The knife stuck straight into the air, and my heart skipped a beat as I smiled. Despite struggling more than when I'd learned to channel, I'd made the stupid blade obey.

"Took long enough, but you did." Tibês nodded to the rest of the knives. "Hurry up and finish the rest. I might be dead, but I'd rather not spend an eternity watching you stare at a stump."

I shot him a glare but did as he asked. The second knife took another three tries. Each after it came quicker.

Within minutes, all five blades stood straight up on the stump. *Žityje* seeped out of me to keep them that way, but I took a deep breath and released my muscles. *One step down.*

Tibês swept past the knives and tapped each. None stirred. "Good."

"Why didn't my armband glow or channel my power this time?" I asked, running my fingers across its dark bands.

"Your father is better to answer about such a powerful artifact."

Weles shifted in the shadows behind me. I'd almost forgotten his presence, but the thud of his cane echoed through the room as he approached the stump. "The words of the old tongue upon it are those of protection, so it will draw from your power in combat. And even then, your own strength must guide you."

That's too simple. But I didn't push him. The god was frustrated enough with me already.

Tibês stood across the stump, the candle illuminating only half his face as he studied me. "You had many attempts with the knives, but you only have one chance to shape-shift. Succeed and you will land before me in the form of your silver fox. Fail and you may find yourself trapped in a form that you can never leave."

"That's reassuring," I quipped, stepping toward the stump. Sweat clung to my skin from focusing so hard on the channeling, so I slid the coat from my shoulders. A chill met me, but I ignored it. "Tell me what to do."

"So firm for a princess." He chuckled. "It is better than weakness. Come, approach the stump and close your eyes."

I followed his instructions. There was a power swirling around it that hadn't been there before. It darted among the knives as if it was excited to be released, and that thrill rose within me as I held my hands over the blades.

"Now focus on the essence of the silver fox within you. Stop smirking. You are joined with it, and that is no simple joke. You must believe the fox *is* you, and until you accept that, you will fail."

I won't fail. I can't. Each step toward Ascension brought me closer to Mother, and with only days left until Maj, I needed to take advantage of every second of training. So, I nodded and focused on the power I'd felt during the second Trial. That carnal desire had taken over so quickly. It had taken away my thoughts, replacing them with a hunger unlike any I'd felt before.

Now it struck again.

The silver fox lured me in before merging with me, but unlike during the Trial, it didn't take over. Instead, its predatory instincts appeared alongside my own feelings and sensations. Maybe Tibês had been right—the fox was part of me now, not an invader. That scared me.

"I'm ready," I said.

"Good," Tibês said. "Now leap over the knives."

I opened my eyes, and memories of my fire jump swarmed my mind. The Drowning of Marzanna had changed everything. Those flames were supposed to have marked me as a woman as I passed through them. They'd meant nothing compared to Wacław and Marzanna, but the fire jump now felt like it had been the end of my free childhood. I'd been fighting for Mother and, surprisingly, for my tribe ever since. This leap felt like another moment—one in which I would finally accept I was a goddess.

Clenching my fists, I stepped forward. Then, with one powerful lunge, I jumped the blades.

37

Otylia

Did the fox choose me or I it?

A FORCE TOOK HOLD OF ME IN MID-AIR. It twisted and mangled my body as I glided over the daggers, replacing nails with claws and hair with fur. Smells and sounds intensified. Colors dulled. And when I struck the ground in a pile of flailing paws, my instincts changed.

Tibês grinned down at me, his hand clutching a warped wooden staff. My resentment remained, but with him towering over me, my fear was stronger. I scampered into the dark corner.

"The fox's desires will attempt to suppress yours," he said as he stepped forward. He stunk like an unwashed boy, and that stench only drove me further away, despite his advance. "You must not let them consume you."

I slipped past him to the doorway. Running on four legs should've been odd, but it came easily, as if I'd done so my entire life. Even the sleek silver and black fur covering me felt *right*. "Stay away from me!" I snarled.

Tibês glanced at Weles. "Tame your daughter, or this is a waste of my time."

"Patience," the god replied. "This is only her second time in this form, and it is the first in which she is not being forced to hunt."

"That's not entirely true."

The wizard shifted. Without knives or a stump, he changed into a raven in an instant and zipped through the open door, right over my head. Each beat of his wings pounded my ears like an ironsmith's hammer, and my nose traced his scent as I took off at full sprint.

The incline was steeper than I remembered. My lungs and heart burned at the intensity of the chase, but hunger drove me faster until we burst into the sunlight.

Above, the raven fluttered through the wind. My vision was little more than a slit, and the raven's dark form was all I saw as I followed it through the meadow. I flicked my gaze from it to the path ahead for only a second at a time, desperate not to lose sight. My nose was strong, but fragrant flowers surrounded me. Without sight, only my ears could track the bird.

"Keep your composure, child!" Tibês shouted, sweeping over me.

Tibês. I'd already forgotten he was the bird. Only the hunt consumed my mind, but I clung to that piece of my consciousness and forced back the fox's desire to feed. "I'm here," I muttered, "but that doesn't make me any happier with this."

"I don't care about your happiness." He landed on my head, and I growled as he continued, "Shifting allows you to experience the world in a new way, but if you let your animal define you, you can become lost forever."

"What advantage does a fox have?" I asked. "I can't see anything, and I'd rather not smell every stench for miles."

Tibês sighed. "That ability to track keeps the fox alive. Use it right, and it can help you find any target while ensuring they are ignorant that a goddess stalks them."

"But I'm still a fox. Unless I'm hunting a rabbit, I can't fight like this."

"You will learn to channel in this form in time, but for now, turn away and count to ten. I will hide in the woods. Find me, and I will teach the rest."

His wings flapped against my back as he took flight. My patience waned at playing a child's game of hide-and-seek, but Tibês's bluntness offered answers. If earning his respect gained me greater access to my power, then it was worth the effort.

When the time was up, I ran to the woods in the distance. The trees were towering and tight, offering no clarity to Tibês's location. *Smell and sound it is.*

I stopped in the shadows and waited with slow, controlled breaths. Leaves stirred in the winds and twigs snapped in the underbrush, but the wizard's raven form would be more subtle. I ignored the loudest noises and listened for the flap of a wing or the scraping of his claws against a branch. Nothing came. So, I smelled the air, revealing a squirrel in the bushes, but no raven.

Another growl escaped my throat. Tibês couldn't have flown *that* far in ten seconds. I should've been able to sense a hint of him somewhere in the forest, even if he was high above.

That's assuming he's in the forest. I smirked. *Even a wizard can't outwit a fox.*

My legs carried me eagerly through the trees and back to the meadow, where I caught his scent once again. He'd ducked into the hole in the ground where we'd found him—the last place he probably thought I'd look. He was wrong. A thrill pulled me after him, my fox instincts merging with my joy of beating Tibês at his own game. Nothing could stop me now.

A *snap* filled the air.

I cried out as the ground gave way beneath me. Momentum carried me into a dirt wall, and my right front leg twisted in a fit of shooting pain. Then I dropped into a dark pit, striking its bottom head first.

My vision faded. Pain coursed through my body. Everything except the pain was dull, distant. All I could see was my broken leg, snapped from the impact against the wall, and I shuddered as a cold chill met my skin. *What happened?* Had this trap been part of the lesson? Had Tibês expected me to leap it, or had he wanted me to fall?

It seemed like hours before the flapping of the raven's wings approached. I tried not to whimper or cry out, but whether it was the fox's whine or mine, it echoed through the pit.

"What is this?" I asked Tibês as he landed on the pit's rim.

His dark eyes studied me, unblinking. "You thought you'd outsmarted me."

I snarled. "So you broke my leg?"

"Pain is a good motivator." In a wisp of black smoke, he returned to his human form, gripping his staff. "Fortunately, it is also quite effective at keeping one's target in place when she's betrayed your master."

"Send you to Oblivion!" I cursed as the Raven Wizard backed away. My chest seized with every breath, and my heart beat so hard it hurt.

Footsteps approached from the meadow. A slow shuffle, broken only by the striking of a cane against the earth. Fear clashed with rage within me. I had nowhere to flee and no *życie* left to fight Weles. Even if I did, he was too powerful to face alone. Yet again, I'd walked into his trap—but how had he discovered the sleeping draught?

By the time the god peered into the pit, my fur stood on end and my claws gripped the dirt. Words didn't come, so I just growled as the sunlight shone upon his deep brown beard and wrinkled face. "You have forgotten who is king of this realm," he said. "Each time I believe you have settled, you surprise me. I am sorry, my daughter, but you have proven you cannot be trusted with freedom."

"You led me into another trap to die!" I snapped. "How many times are you going to kill your *princess*?"

His gaze was stern as he leaned against his cane. Standing with his side to the sun, a shadow hung over half his face. "Perhaps it would have been best if I had thrown you into this pit when you first arrived in my realm. After all, it is this boy you are so fond of who slayed my only son. And now, you conspire against me with gods and servants. You poison my altar."

"Kill me then! I'd rather suffer Oblivion than be forced to wed Jaryło."

"Oblivion? You have a far greater role to play, my daughter, than wasting away. You are the catalyst for our freeing of Jawia."

"Why did I ever believe a word you said? You hid what I'd face in the Trials, and you trapped me in your palace!" I stopped, my anger making it hard to catch my breath. "Who told you our plan?"

The god shook his head. "That is a clever attempt to lure me into revealing my secrets, but no, I have little need to answer anything you say. Though I wished to train you freely over the necessary moons, you have forced my hand." He stepped closer to the edge, his face drooping and weary. "You will always be my daughter. I am sorry I have failed to make you feel so, but from the moment you entered Nawia, you feared me. Your mother was the same until she learned to love me."

"She'd *never* love someone like you!"

"So you persistently claim. It matters not, however. I know of Wacław Lubiewicz's mission to 'rescue' you, Otylia, even if your plan has failed."

The god laughed as I winced at that. *Wacław*...

"Yes, the corrupted one has made quite a stir in the realm above," Weles continued. "It would be quite hard for me not to hear the tales of the boy who let the Astiwie slaughter the Simukie and Zurgowie while he pursued you. But fear not, my daughter. When he arrives, I will do him no harm as long as you obey me. You will serve your purpose, and Wacław can live. Just not with you."

I shook my head. "Wacław won't give up until I'm free or he's dead."

Weles turned with a sigh, glancing over his shoulder one last time. "Then perhaps it is for the best that such a powerful demon will be cast into Oblivion. I truly am sorry."

When he stepped away from the rim, I leaped at the wall. I knew it was foolish. My leg was broken and the god too powerful, but I had to try.

A fresh wave of pain shot through my leg, dropping me to the ground as roots creaked above. I could only watch as they slowly stretched across the opening until vines and dirt engulfed it all. Only a small hole at the pit's center allowed any light through.

The crunching of Weles's boots against the dirt trailed away until even my fox ears couldn't pick up any sound. The pit would've barely been above my head in my human form, but with the barrier blocking above, the wonderful smells of the meadow were faint. Weles had trapped me in a world apart from the rest of Nawia.

Alone with myself.

Now, I could only wait in fear of what he would do to Wacław and Sabina for trying to help me flee. I would rot away, doomed to become Jaryło's bride as Mother succumbed to Marzanna's torture. Winter would reign forever, and there was nothing I could do to stop it.

I lay there in my misery for a long time, whimpering as my broken leg taunted me. Luckily, the bone hadn't pierced the skin, but that didn't lessen the pain. All szeptuchy were trained as healers—more than most women already were—and broken bones were well-known to be lethal. If the bone couldn't be easily set, you'd be maimed for life. But even in the best cases, the injury meant being unable to work, which was as good as death with how little most families had to survive.

None of that experience told me how to fix a fox bone—even with Dziewanna's power. I forced myself to try anyway.

Eyes shut, I focused on the pool of *žityje* within my soul. It boiled, ready for use, but much of it had seeped away to keep the daggers upright on that stump. How could I mend a bone when even szeptuchy couldn't?

Don't worry about anyone else. Not Mother, not Mokosz, not Wašek, not any szeptuchy or goddesses. Just you.

My heartbeat slowed as I steadied my breaths and thought of the old tongue, of the one word I knew that *could* work: *kostć*. Bone. Tibês had insisted I could channel without the old tongue, but my soul felt disconnected without my bonds to Dziewanna and Mokosz. It wasn't whole, so neither was my ability to channel. The word would have to do.

I opened my eyes and stared at the warped leg. My stomach churned, but I blocked the pain from my mind as I summoned the *žityje.* "*Kosté.*"

A pain slammed into me, knocking away my breath and my thoughts. My leg spasmed and cracked. I didn't dare look—not that I could. Wave after wave of the slicing, jagged agony forced my eyes shut as I fought to stay awake. I wouldn't pass out now. Weles was testing me, and to surrender was failure. I couldn't fail.

But it was all too much. The sharp stench of blood piercing the air. The snapping of my bone. And the torture that shook my body to its core. In the end, I was too frail to fight it. Darkness took me in its embrace, stealing my sorrow and fear until nothing remained.

38

Wacław

I see home today—Mom, Nevenka, Tanek…

ANTICIPATION DROVE ME FORWARD despite the dread hanging on my shoulders. On the third day of riding since leaving Małe Wzgórze, we'd reached the small villages at the outskirts of Dwie Rzeki. My excitement grew with every cottage we passed. *Less than an hour now.*

But as we neared the furthest edge of the settlement's woods, that excitement faded. This was the same trail Kajetan had led us down only a moon before, and the weight of our journey returned to me.

Everything had changed since the Drowning of Marzanna. We had faced cultists, wiły, zmory, a rusałka, a szeptucha, płanetnikami, and a god himself. I had sacrificed my father to save the girl I loved and channeled Marzanna's power to cure her of the goddess's curse. I had watched comrades fall and had held one of my best friends as he died in my arms. I had learned how to channel wind and lightning and had nearly died twice in the process. I had accidentally joined my soul with that of Otylia, bonding myself with a goddess for eternity. I had led two clans west through the Narrow Pass and into battle against Boz's Astiwie. I had been slain, and only Otylia's completion of the Trial of Death had brought me back.

Now, I returned home, not as a hero with two armies in his wake but as a survivor. The mission that had summoned us east had failed—I had failed. The clans would never reach the southern hills, and if they did, they would do so crippled and weak. Father had betted on their cavalry rescuing us from Solga's warriors, but help would not come.

Our secret quest had gone no better. Otylia and I hadn't found Marzanna or her cultists' base, nor had we discovered where she'd taken Dziewanna. Winter marched on, only deterred by me turning Eryk against his goddess.

Marzanna was still gathering her strength. Soon, though, she would surely strike, and her Frostmarked Horde would plow through the Narrow Pass, laying waste to all within the embrace of Perun's Crown.

How could I explain all that had happened to the chiefs and my tribe? How could I make them understand the true threat was in the east? And how could I do it without revealing what I was… what I would become?

A void opened in my chest. It pulled me in, suffocating me and drowning my thoughts with worries and doubts. Surely, my family would scorn me for my choice to protect Otylia by slaying Jaryło. The tribe, too, would throw me into the fires when I told them I was a demon. They would hear nothing but my faults. They would see the Half-Chief as a failure who had killed their high chief and their spring god.

No, I can't tell them the truth.

Then what could I tell them? What would convince the arrogant, battle-hungry chiefs that our war with the Solgawi had to end before it had even begun? Most of them were driven by pride, lust, and fear. Only the last was capable of changing their minds.

I flexed my palm. The Frostmark upon it remained a jagged, ugly gray beneath my hand wrap. It still burned at random—Marzanna's constant reminder of my surrender to her temptations. If they needed to fear, I would make them fear. *Gods forgive me.*

Andrij rode behind the rest of the group with his head low. Dark rings had formed beneath his eyes, and when he looked up, it was only to scan the woods. Fighting my own fear, I slowed and pulled aside him, offering a futile smile. "Why is it that whenever you come to Dwie Rzeki, it's when the chiefs are squabbling?"

He huffed and shook his head. "Perhaps I'm just doom's messenger."

I patted his shoulder. "Listen, Andrij. I can't thank you enough for what you did for me. Rebelling against Boz… that couldn't have been easy. I owe you my life."

"Gods send the both of us to Oblivion, then," he muttered, gazing over the lowland forest, his breath fogging the chilled air.

"What's worrying you? Eryk found your family and brought them to Likiec—far from the Narrow Pass. They'll be safe." Despite his daughter still being lost, the płanetnik had been eager to help after what I'd done for him. If only his search for Xobas and the clans had yielded results…

He offered a small smile. "I know, and I'm grateful, but I can't forget the Battle of Kynnytsia. How do I move on after losing so many of my men?"

"Marzanna has broken so much in just a couple moons." I dropped my head. "She's taken Kuba, Marek, Kajetan, my father, and others. Honestly, I don't know if we can ever move on. I'll make her pay, no matter what it takes."

Andrij held a fist to his chest and said nothing else.

We rode on in silence until we reached the familiar woods near Mom's house. A smile forced its way across my face, and I pushed my horse into a gallop, passing the others. By the time they realized what was happening, I had already burst into the clearing around our cottage.

The late morning light trickled through the trees and into the pasture, where Tanek, my chestnut gelding, was ripping the few remaining shreds of hay from his feed trough. Little distracted him from food, but his head popped up at my arrival.

I slid off my horse and ran to the wooden fence as Tanek did the same. He huffed, rubbing his head against me, and I patted his muscular neck and side. The zmora's scrapes had healed well—thanks to

Otylia.

An eerie sensation crept over me. I stopped and scanned the empty fields. *Where's Mom?* No plumes of smoke spiraled from the cottage, nor did the sound of iron striking dirt drift on the winds. It was rare that she ever strayed far from home, but maybe she had gone into the village center to trade?

The others approached at a canter, stopping at the pasture's edge. "Is this your home?" Andrij asked, the gales forcing him to push his cloak behind him as it flapped across his body.

I nodded without reply. Mom's disappearance was the only thing on my mind. With a sigh, I swung open the wooden door of our cottage and took in the familiar smell of wood and cloth mixing in the air. Unlike usual, though, a chill struck my skin. The stone stove was frigid to the touch. Mom never let the house get so cold, even when she was away, and my breaths turned shallow as I examined the dark room.

She's been gone for a while.

There were no tools about or water bucket ready to be boiled. Her bed was made, as usual, but two dresses lay strewn across it. She *never* left her clothes thrown in an untidy fashion. Anyone could walk in, she'd always claimed, and gods forbid they realized someone lived in the house.

"You okay, Wacław?" Ara asked, pacing to the far wall as Narcyz lingered with Andrij in the opposing corner. "You look like you've seen the mounds of a great sand worm."

Narcyz raised a brow. "I don't want to know what that is."

"Why not?" Zakir replied. "There have been some deep studies into their—"

Ara patted his arm. "Studies that we'll be happy to talk about *later.*"

"Mom's not here," I said, stopping at my bed as I fought the panic within me. "We should head to the village center, unless either of you want to see your families first."

Ara shook her head. "Father is likely on a hunt, and Mother will be trading her work in the village center anyway."

"My da's gotta be in his shop," Narcyz said. "I'd like to show him that sword while Ma is out."

I clenched my jaw but nodded. If I had the right to find my family, so did he. "Then we'll take a few minutes to do that."

"Don't let him look *too* close," Ara replied. "The last thing we need is the iron smith revealing we stole a god's sword."

Narcyz scoffed and stomped outside. As we followed, I couldn't shake the feeling that something was wrong. There was nothing off about the pastures or the fields—beyond their lack of life with the extended winter—but Mom rarely left home.

"Let's go then," I said, grabbing my coat and gloves from the chest beneath my bed before rushing out to Tanek. "Our families await."

39

Otylia

I don't care if Weles is my father. I'll kill him.

SUNLIGHT SPEWED INTO THE PIT for the second morning since my fall.

For hours, I'd hobbled from end to end on my three good legs. I'd muttered the spell each time I turned until dehydration and hunger shredded my mind and the repetition burrowed itself into my being.

"*Kostć*." Wince. Step. Step. Step. Step. Step. "*Kostć*." Wince. It was a tuneless dance where the only participants were misery and me.

I'd rather dance alone.

Rain had come last night—a gift from the gods who didn't hate me, whoever they were. It had matted my fox fur and chilled me to my core, but I didn't care as the few precious droplets slipped through the hole and filled my maw. I praised Mother for her water and Perun for his storm. Even in Weles's realm, he couldn't keep his nemesis away. Something about that gave me joy.

That was the only relief I found in the pit. Days of pacing and channeling had done nothing but leave my body exhausted and my soul drained. What little *žityje* I had left I would need to shift back to my human form. If I even could.

But that didn't matter with my leg being a mangled, bloody mess that twisted in more directions than should've been possible. My command had reconnected the bone successfully—just not how I'd expected—and as I lay on the muddied ground, I wondered whether disfiguration was any better than a break. *Probably worse.*

I groaned as yet another drop fell on my head from the pit's hole. Escape was impossible, I'd decided, so either I had to figure out my leg or hope one of Kyustendil allies found me. Option one had failed. Unfortunately, option two seemed unlikely.

Drip.

What had been the point of breaking my leg and trapping me in a pit? Had Weles wanted to ensure I stayed in my fox form while detained? Tibês had implied I could channel just as easily in this form, so why did it matter?

Drip.

Weles, I concluded, never intended for Tibês to teach me anything. Nothing else could explain how long it had taken me to do something as basic as keep a knife standing when I could deflect a dragon's breath with a single word. Tibês had given little instruction but vague gestures and sarcastic quips. I could've kept those blades quickly if he'd bothered to help, and I could've mended my leg days ago if he'd given me any hint of how to do so.

Drip.

I scowled and looked up at the droplets, but a laughed escaped my lungs as they became a trickle. I leaned back, allowing the water to stream down my parched throat, far more than had made it through last night. Memories of Mother's lessons returned to me as I drank.

In between lectures about potions, edible fungi and plants, and various animals, she'd taught me how to survive the wilds.

"The trees need nothing but food, light, and water," she said. "Why should we be any different? The first two are simple enough for even a drunk warrior to find, but the third must be pursued like a wolf does its prey."

"But how do I find it?" I asked, staring up at her in awe as the autumn sun formed a halo around her head. Even with her hair wrapped in a brown headscarf of simple embroidery, she appeared like a queen.

She knelt on the bed of scarlet and gold leaves, not worrying about the dirt getting on her dress. With a hand pressed firm against the ground, she grinned up at me. "The trees and brush send their roots down in search of it. That, then, is where we go too."

She took off downhill at a sprint, darting and dancing through the trees as if the two motions were the same.

Dogoda, the kind wind of the west, blew the falling leaves with her. Earth and air met between them, her brown clothes brightened by the lively colors. *Ironic, considering they're dead*, I thought as I chased after her.

We ran deep into the forest. I'd never dared to go that far alone, even years later, but Mother went with neither hesitation nor fear. Whenever she lost her way, she stopped and bit her bottom lip—just the left side always. Then she smirked at me and ran again.

The process continued for an hour until we reached a stream south of the village. But even then, she didn't stop, leaping into the shallow waters and laughing as she did.

I thought her ridiculous at first. Mothers were supposed to know everything and be models for girls on how to be an obedient wife, yet she swam through the water as if she were as free as a fish within. She wasn't supposed to sprint through the trees, know the art of woodland survival, or soak herself in a chilled autumn stream.

What the village said Mother was *supposed* to do didn't matter to her. And in that moment, eight-year-old me decided it didn't matter to me either.

The water was frigid, but I laughed and embraced her. With her dress clinging to her skin and her smile as bright as Dadźbóg's light, she smiled, pulling me through the current. It felt like I was flying as she held me up so just my toes skidded across the surface.

We stayed for hours until the sun neared the horizon, when Mother froze and looked to the woods. The waning light illuminated a tall, robed figure maneuvering through the underbrush with staff in hand. "Odeta, my wife, what are you teaching our child?" Father asked as deep lines embedded themselves above his brow.

"To experience the gifts the gods give us," Mother replied. Droplets fell from her hair—half-freed from the scarf in a tangle of brunette and earth brown. Her smile was gone, and a frightening glare replaced it. "One would think their priest would understand that."

Now, as I stepped back from the pit's hole and watched the steady flow, it seemed obvious. Water was found at the lowest point, so why wouldn't this pit be it?

I drank until my stomach felt ready to burst. After nearly two days of nothing to distract me from my pain, I needed every drop of the hope that water gave me. It wouldn't get me out or heal me, but at least I wouldn't die of dehydration.

What a way for a goddess to die.

The water cleared the fog from my mind, and I limped to the edge of the pit, closing my eyes. *Žityje*, dwindling but vibrant and powerful, still flickered within me. Was it enough to mend the bone if I got the spell right one last time? It needed to be.

I pictured the leg in its uninjured form, holding it until the image lingered, as if burned onto my eyelids. Whether it was the word or my execution of the spell that was wrong, I had only this chance—if that. I needed the spell to work. Perfect result or not, I would mend my leg and escape the pit.

I plunged all my *žityje* into the bone.

The spell needed neither words nor thought to execute my demand. It fed on my will, my desperation, and a *crack* tore through the hole as I collapsed. A sharp pain overwhelmed me. It shattered my drained soul, streaking through my body like the plunge Mother and I took in that chilled river.

Seconds later, it faded. I released a gasp, struggling for breath as my head throbbed from the shock. Even my vision blurred from the pain's strike, but when it cleared, I laughed in joy at the sight.

The bone was straight. The fur by the wound was matted and spattered with blood, but the leg itself *looked* right. Tentatively, I took a sharp breath and rose, smirking as it held, despite a remnant soreness.

It'll do. Now, how to get out of here and take a bite out of that raven…

I stalked around the rim and stared up at the small streak of light. The pit was as tall as Wacław—too high to jump, even without the roots. Tibês had implied it was possible to shift between forms without the knives, but I was already dreary with little *żityje*. I couldn't afford an attempt, especially if it was harder than placing the knives. I'd have to claw my way out.

Instincts took over as I dug into the pit's side. My claws ripped through the dirt, but small stones clipped at my softer paws, forcing me to slow.

I hated every second wasted. The chance at a tunnel out had given me hope, and I yearned to run free. Whether it was my desire or the fox's didn't matter.

It wasn't long before my legs tired. I was still weak after repairing my bone, and without food or water in the room, that exhaustion would only grow. So, I took shifts, digging until I couldn't anymore and then resting until my patience ran thin. Debris hung in the air during those breaks. It coated my mouth and throat, making my eyes water.

The hole was completely dark, but I smiled as I made steady progress upward. The pit wasn't *that* tall. Surely, I was close. My paws were bloody and my entire body exhausted, but rest could wait until I was in the woods, far from Weles's palace and Tibês's tricks.

After hours of digging, my heart skipped a beat as I swiped ahead and hit nothing but air. *It's there!*

I yipped in glee and pulled myself out of my hole. The waning crescent moon hung high above as I breathed in the sweet meadow flowers. Cover was thin here, however, so I sprinted toward the woods with all the energy I had left, my mouth wide open and my tongue flapping as I ran. It was ridiculous, but I didn't care. I was free.

With each stride into the dark forest, I listened for the beating of the Raven Wizard's wings. It hadn't occurred to me that Tibês might've been watching for a potential escape. *Too late to wonder now. Run.*

Nawia was a maze with its towering trees and vast, chaotic landscapes. I hadn't seen much outside the swamp near the palace, so I ran without direction. Where didn't matter as long as it was far from Weles and his wizard.

My legs ached as I reached a tree-lined ridge. Beyond lay the deep canyon I'd seen days before. The islands appeared as looming beasts in the night, powerful and mysterious. Exhaustion hung over me. I felt powerless standing before those shattered islands, unable to save nymphs like Sabina and mortal souls Weles had stolen from Jawia, let alone myself. I'd completed the first four Trials of Ascension, but I felt no more like a goddess than the moment I'd entered Nawia.

I lay down at the ridge, watching the moonlit fog roll through the canyons. Despite my desire to sleep, I couldn't fight the sensation that something was wrong.

My breaths turned shallow. My heart raced. As I staggered to my feet, a wave of sorrow and fear washed over me.

Wašek?

Our connection had felt so weak and distant recently. The waxing and waning of that tether between us made little sense to me. Why had he felt right next to me a week before and so distant now? And why was his sadness so potent?

Wašek? Are you okay?

It was a foolish attempt to reach him. I knew that. But the terror gripping him was enough to make me desperate.

Wašek, please!

No response came, and soon, the connection disappeared, leaving me shaking in a heap. The absence was worse than the anguish. All I wanted was some piece of understanding, a hint he was okay. Instead, I was alone again, and the silence was maddening.

A long time passed, but sleep was as distant as Wacław. Thoughts of his sorrow consumed me. When they relented, those of Mother and Sabina replaced them.

I had neither the energy to pace nor the *żityje* to change my discomfort. My mind was exhausted with the constant worries, and for once, I wished for the simplicity of home. The people of Dwie Rzeki either despised or feared me, some of them probably both, but they would come to Mother and me for healing anyway.

After Marzanna stole her, they'd still come. Some of them for the old reasons, others for curiosities they hoped Mokosz's visions could answer. Maybe that was why they hated me.

I knew their secrets.

Of course, most villagers had never come to the 'witch,' but those that had revealed enough. Wives suspecting husbands of infidelity. Men seeking to know the success of the harvest or if he'd ever find glory in battle. Boys and girls giggling as they asked whether those they were fond of felt the same.

Ironically, whenever someone came with worries, the person they were asking about often came soon after. It was an odd case of Destiny, Father claimed. But Destiny was a lie—only Death's grip was certain. *Well, for all except me.*

This wasn't the first time sleep had been fleeting in Nawia. Ever since I'd surrendered to Death's temptations in Oblivion, I'd woken most nights in a sweat after dreaming of Wacław's dying soul. My deal with Death would come due sometime in my eternal life.

So, too, would Wacław's demonic soul drain his human one in time. The process would only quicken the more he used his power. Considering he was fighting to rescue me, I doubted he was holding back.

Why is he such a fool for me? I shook my head and sighed, staring into the woods, where the trees swayed in the breeze. *And why do I feel so weak when I think of him?*

Wacław had acted oddly confident the two times I'd seen him in visions. With everything else, he was a hesitant mess, yet he'd shed that when showing affection. How? Why? During our first kiss, I'd deflected with a quip, and since then, *I'd* been the hesitant mess. The physical attraction to him was there, but… *Gods, am I really worried about our emotional connection right now?*

Our souls were bound. Shouldn't that have been enough of a connection? As I thought of our time since the Drowning of Marzanna, though, I realized we hadn't had time for much except saving each other's lives. Surely, most couples had more to their relationships than taking turns dangling on the edge of death. That meant vulnerability.

As I gritted my teeth and pawed at the cliff's edge, another feeling struck my chest—my own anxiety this time. It was paralyzing to think that, despite how little privacy we had with our bond, I would need to be more open with him. Where did that even start? I'd spent the last four years with festering resentment against Wacław only to find out a moon ago he had been protecting me from Jacek. There was so much left unsaid between us *still* as well as years of our lives that needed to be filled and wounds that needed to heal.

What would he say if I told him everything? All my fears and worries? How much I'd cursed his name and wept when he wasn't looking? The ritual had shown him the pain I'd felt, but that toll was only a part of it. Mother's death and Jacek taking Wacław from me had forced me to be resilient and independent—just like Mother had taught me. I'd clung to Dziewanna and Mokosz, but even they were gone now. How was I supposed to peel away four years of callouses and just tell him what I'd become?

That assumed *I* knew what I'd become during our years of forced separation. I wasn't the witch everyone thought me to be, but I was no longer the innocent, adventurous healer either.

What does he see when he looks at me? The witch, the szeptucha, the goddess, or someone else?

Wacław had changed too in those years, growing quieter and more reserved. Despite him not admitting how much his father had beaten him, I'd made my own assumptions. He mourned Jacek's death and blamed himself for it. I didn't. Jacek had torn away my best friend. He'd scarred his son beneath the skin—something Wacław was still trying to hide from me. The high chief had deserved to suffer, and if I'd seen him in Nawia, I would've happily sent him to Oblivion.

I cursed myself for ever calling Wacław the *Half-Chief*. He'd been cast out, just like me, and I'd joined in the mockery out of resentment. If I'd known… *We really do have too much unsa—*

Footsteps.

Breaths quick, I spun and sniffed the air. My fox senses had alerted me sooner than my human ones would've, and the approaching threat was at least fifty strides away. Plenty far for me to escape.

The creature smelled… nice? By the weight of its steps, it was a beast larger than a man, but that scent was familiar. I couldn't place why as I stalked through the shadows, searching for it from a distance. Somehow, it headed directly toward where I'd been resting. *Does Tibês have another form?*

My footfalls were far lighter than the creature's, so I snuck closer. Circling behind it, my fox eyes turned to slits and focused squarely on the furred beast. *What's with Weles and bears? At least it's not a snake.*

The bear walked two-legged as it reached the ridge. For a moment, it waited, sniffing the air like I had a minute before.

Then it turned.

I scrambled behind a tree, holding in a yelp as the bear approached. My fur—black with streaks of silver—would conceal me. If the bear's vision was even close to as bad as the fox's, the tree cover would be enough. I hoped.

But the bear lumbered closer still. No more than five strides away now, its smell became overwhelming. Fish mixed with mint. *A bear with a woman's perfume?* "Ivan?"

"Lady Otylia!" his voice said from the other side of the tree. A hearty chuckle came from the figure as he moved away the pine needles. "I am overjoyed to find you, but the Raven Wizard seeks you as well. It would be best for the both of us to be far away when he arrives."

I crawled free from the tree and smiled up at the smiling bear who had once been a king. "How'd you find me?"

"There is much you and I must discuss," he replied, his voice hushed. "Now is not the time for such an exchange, though. I understand the trust I am asking you to place in me is difficult after what Master Weles and Tibês have done, but I have been told by an old friend of yours that you would come at the mention of his name."

"Who?"

"A rather graceless soul called Kuba Piotryk. He has told us much about your adventure before his death. However, he seemed quite surprised to hear you were in Nawia as well."

"Kuba?" I smirked, remembering the clumsy fool who had rarely left Wacław's side. "But it hasn't been forty days. His soul should still be wandering."

"That is a story of its own, Lady Otylia." Ivan raised his head and muttered to himself before dropping to all fours. "You may ask the boy yourself when we arrive. Right now, though, you must come with me."

"Where are you taking me?"

He smiled. "To the place where you will Ascend."

40

Wacław

Where are you, Mom?

WHEN WE REACHED DWIE RZEKI'S WOODEN WALLS, six warriors guarded the eastern gate. They gripped their spears at the sight of us.

"What are you do—" one began, stopping as we rode closer. "Narcyz? Half-Chief? Gods…"

"You believed *I* died?" Narcyz huffed, puffing up his chest. "Think again."

The guard furrowed his brow. "Where are the clans? Kajetan?"

"Oh… them…"

I took a sharp breath and pushed Tanek ahead of the others. Nerves gripped me. If this many warriors were posted at the gate, something was wrong. "We were ambushed in Bustelintin. Only a small group of us managed to reach the clans, and though we negotiated a peace, King Boz betrayed us." I pushed away the memories of the battle that threatened to come, but the pain lingered. "Many of them are probably still out there, but we have to speak to Dariusz."

Ara joined me with her brow furrowed. "Now."

The lead warrior glanced back at the others, an uncomfortable look on his face. "Half-Chief… Have… Have you heard about the high chief?"

"Father is gone," I said, swallowing at the sorrow that came with that admission. "I know."

He let out a relieved breath before stepping to the side. "You better get inside. There's a wolf-man lurking outside the walls that's been grabbing people. Mieczysław will want to talk to you anyway."

My breaths caught, and I looked to Zakir. "Your brother apparently isn't done haunting us."

"Bidaês has never been one to give up easily," he replied, neither his face nor tone revealing any hint of emotion.

"Wait!" Narcyz grumbled. "What was that about Mieczysław?"

The warrior didn't give an inch as he glared up at Narcyz. "He's high chief now. The chiefs voted on it last night, and he doesn't appreciate annoying children trying to push around his guards."

"Then don't be so easy to push around."

Andrij grabbed Narcyz's arm, pulling him back as I sighed and led the way through the gate. Nothing the guards had said was good news, and I feared for Mom if Bidaês stalked outside the walls. "If Bidaês really is here," I said once we were beyond earshot of the guards, "then there's no time to stop at the forge right now. Dariusz has to know something."

Narcyz muttered under his breath but nodded as I pushed Tanek down the path to Dariusz and Otylia's house. It wasn't far from the gate, and anticipation swelled within me as I dismounted before it. *Time for answers.* If Dariusz knew of no way to Nawia, our journey would have been for nothing.

I hopped down the three steps to the door—as I'd done many times as a child—and raised my knuckles to knock. Something held me back. We'd come all this way, but I realized right then that I hadn't thought of what I planned to say to Dariusz. How would he react to me losing Otylia? Would he even want to help me, considering he'd tried to sacrifice me minutes after my birth?

Ara knocked instead, rolling her eyes at me before stepping back. There was no reply for a few moments, and I nervously pawed at the dirt as the breeze carried voices from closer to the village center. Just when I was ready to give up and look elsewhere, the door flung open.

"Gods save us," the high priest gasped before us, his gaze fixed on me and his long ashen hair draped over his crimson robes. "We thought you were all dead." He looked past me to the others, and a scowl replaced his shock as he snatched my arm. "Where is Otylia? Where is my daughter?"

Stammering, the Wacław from before the Drowning of Marzanna returned as I stared up at Dariusz's reddened face. I'd fought demons, cultists, and even a god. None of that mattered standing before Otylia's father.

"Answer me, Wacław! What curse have you brought upon us, and what have you done with my daughter?"

Rage burned away my fear. The demon's call merged with my resentment from years of Dariusz trying to tear me from Otylia. Though Father had done it for him in the end, Dariusz had hated me from the moment I'd been born. An ache struck my heart with those memories, but the demon fed on the anger within them. I owed Dariusz nothing.

"I've done everything I can to save her!" I spat, ripping my arm from his grasp. "We could've stopped Jaryło if you'd told us the truth!"

Dariusz's glare pierced me, but he turned and stormed into the house. "Come. Obviously, there is much to be said."

I followed with the others into the house's main room. Unlike ours, it had two separate bedrooms, blocked off by fabric embroidered with symbols of the old tongue. Wooden statuettes of various gods lined the walls as cattle skulls dangled from the ceiling. It felt like their eyes watched me as I circled Dariusz. *So many memories…* Otylia's mother, who I'd believed to be Odeta as a child, had fed me countless times here. I ran my fingers along the stone stove in the corner, letting its warmth pull me from the demon's grasp for just a few seconds.

As he leaned over the wooden table, Dariusz's wrinkles deepened on his brow. "How do you know?" he asked, his voice suddenly solemn.

"The Lake of Reflection." I removed my straw płanetnik hat. The lake's visions had forced me to admit what I was, but I wasn't sure I'd truly accepted what being a demon meant. "On our journey east, we found Jaryło fleeing from Marzanna. He took us to the lake and when Otylia and I entered, Dziewanna revealed the truth." I narrowed my eyes. "It also showed us that you wanted to kill me."

Ara scoffed. "How could you not tell her about Dziewanna?"

"I was protecting her!" Dariusz yelled, throwing out his arms. "It was Swaróg who brought Dziewanna to me in the first place. Her pregnancy had yet to become visible, and he tasked me to protect her and the child from Weles. This was my duty as a priest, and it is why I took the woman you knew as Odeta as my wife. When you, Wacław, were born mere hours after her under the blood moon, I considered it an ill omen. But, gods, you two were inseparable."

He paced toward me, looking me up and down. "That dagger…" His wrinkled and veiny hands trembled as he reached for it, stopping just short. "This is Thunderstone, and based on the *życie* pulsing from that golden sword, you possess Kwiecień too. How did a demon come to hold the weapons of two deities? And *where is Otylia*?"

Shame weighed heavily on me as I unwrapped my Frostmarked hand. "Marzanna came to me on the morning of the equinox, tempting me and demanding a blood offering with the dagger. I… I gave it to her."

"You fool!" Dariusz grabbed my wrist and examined the mark, shaking his head. "I sense Dziewanna's presence upon you. Did Otylia know? Is that why she asked to join this journey east?"

I dropped my gaze. "Otylia told me that night that I'm a płanetnik after the zmora attacked me and an utopiec poisoned Dizewanna's altar. Between the demons and Dziewanna's silence, she realized Marzanna had somehow survived. We decided finding her cultists in the Mangled Woods could bring us answers."

"Dziewanna is gone?" he whispered to himself, as if he couldn't believe the words. Stepping back, his breaths quickened as he caught himself against the table. "That explains the lifeless fields and forests. My love…"

"She had a plan," Andrij said, pulling forth the firebird feather.

"Dziewanna saved me on my journey here before the equinox and gave me this feather. Somehow, she knew Marzanna would survive."

I nodded and took a breath to regain my composure. "When Marzanna's cultists attacked us at Bustelintin, Dziewanna sent Sosna to save Otylia and me from a Frostmarked szeptucha." Sosna yapped at her name and slipped between my legs, but Dariusz didn't pay her any heed. "Jaryło claimed he tried to protect Dziewanna on the equinox. I'm not sure I believe him anymore."

"I don't believe anything that lustful idiot said," Ara said. "He killed Otylia!"

Dariusz spun toward the huntress, his eyes wild. "He did *what*?"

"You deaf?" Narcyz spat. "She said Jaryło killed Otylia. Ran that golden sword Half-Chief's got right across her throat."

I winced, my heart aching at the images slipping through my guard. Otylia's desperate gaze. Her eyes rolling back. *I'll bring you back. I promise.* With a hand extended toward Narcyz, I tried to calm my voice. "We fought Marzanna's cultists and another płanetnik in the Mangled Woods. It ended the blizzards the demon was causing in the east, but Jaryło grabbed Otylia when we were weak. He revealed his loyalty to Weles, and when I used the last of my *żityje* to send the Thunderstone dagger through him, he took Otylia with him. He dropped Kwiecień before he died."

Dariusz touched Swaróg's Forgemark on his leather headband. "I have failed you, my god." His mouth formed a narrow line when he turned to me again. "I should have never allowed my daughter to travel with a fiend like you. I should have never let you live!"

"I'd have given my life for her!" I shouted, grabbing his robes at the chest. "I would have died trying to save her if Dziewanna hadn't used the golden egg to gift me the last of her *żityje*. You hate me—I know—but Dziewanna said I'm Otylia's only chance of escaping Weles."

"Wacław!" Ara grabbed my shoulder. "Let him go."

I staggered back. My heart pounded, echoing through my head as I stared down at my hands. *Was that me?* The anger had come so quickly. All else but it had faded compared to it, and I found myself craving that sensation again. Power. "You need me, Dariusz," I growled. "Without me, Otylia is trapped, and without her, there's no hope of rescuing Dziewanna. So, unless you can convince Swaróg to come down from Prawia to fix things, stop blaming me for being born."

Fist clenched, he turned away and stared up at the hanging skulls with his hands locked behind him. "You seek to enter Nawia. There is a way, but no demon has ever crossed the divide between the realms before."

Zakir, who was examining a statuette of Mokosz in the corner, replied without looking back, "We have all experienced events in the past moon that none of us thought possible. No heir of the Simuk Clan has stepped foot in Krowikie lands before. No goddess has ever been raised among mortals. No winter has ever broken the bounds of the equinox. The world changes before our eyes. We must too."

My jaw dropped, awe replacing my anger for a moment. That was more than I'd heard him say at once since we'd met, and I couldn't have said it better. But before Dariusz could reply, a clamor came from outside. We swapped glanced as someone pounded on the door.

"Open up! Mieczysław needs to speak with Half-Chief immediately."

Dariusz mumbled to himself as he unlatched the door, revealing a sole warrior. "The high chief can wait," he said.

The warrior shook his head. "Wacław will want to come now."

My chest tightened at the pain in the warrior's gaze. "Why? What's happened?"

"It's your mother." He swallowed. "The wolf-man's taken her."

I never should've picked up that dagger.

It felt as if the winds themselves carried us as we galloped down the trail toward the longhouse. I was awake, so they couldn't have been connected to me, but they pulsed with my breaths, thumped with my heartbeat. The chill disappeared—as did the pounding of our horses' hooves. On Tanek's back, I flew on with the fury of Strzybóg's eight grandchildren.

The gales broke when we charged into the busy village center. Perun's Oak stretched to the sky before us, the animal skulls upon it rattling in the breeze and its many roots bursting through the earth for a dozen strides in each direction. People scattered at our hasty approach, but a sense of calm met me there. Though our cottage was home, so was the heart of our village. I hadn't realized until then how much I'd missed it.

I dismounted and tied Tanek up before taking a deep breath. This was where Otylia and I had stood a moon before when we'd entered the Lake of Reflection. So much had changed since then for us. Learning that both my parents and Dariusz knew I was to become a demon seemed like nothing, but it weighed on me as we approached the longhouse.

The warriors guarding the longhouse entrance moved out of the way as I plowed past them, throwing open the doors with my cloak sweeping behind me. Bidaês had gone too far this time. With each step, I tried not to think about his wilkołak teeth tearing her apart.

I'll kill you.

Torchlight illuminated the table stretching across the longhouse center and the carvings of gods' marks on the wooden pillars lining it. At the table's end, Mieczysław sat on Father's fur-covered throne. A cloak of wolf fur hung over his massive frame as he leaned his forearm on his knee. Unlike his long hair from the Drowning of Marzanna, he now wore it shaven on the sides with a tuft on top—the traditional style for a warrior marching to war.

"If it isn't Jacek's lost boy," Mieczysław roared.

"High chief," I said, advancing toward Mieczysław without a bow. "Where is my mother? Why was she not allowed within the walls?" Questions around Mieczysław's election as high chief still circled my head, but politics were irrelevant with Mom's life on the line.

"Dead," Mieczysław's deep voice rumbled. "No doubt that beast tore her to pieces already."

Red swarmed into my vision as I clenched my fists. "Why didn't you let her in the walls? Who saw her?"

"Calm, boy. Your mother was allowed into the village, but she refused my offer of hospitality. With our warriors marching into Solga, we don't have the men to protect every stubborn farmer who refuses to leave their home. That godsforsaken demon has already killed five of my own guards."

I cursed my father. Mom had avoided the village ever since he forced us away, and Bidaês had used that. Two moons before, Marzanna had threatened both her and Father. She'd taken one, but I swore I wouldn't let her take Mom too. "Who saw her?" I repeated. "Where is the beast?"

Mieczysław just waved a dismissive arm. "Some farmer beyond the northern gate. Ksawery, I think he was named. He claimed to see the demon running into the swamp north of his fields with Lubena a couple hours ago."

"Thank you." I turned sharply and led my friends out.

"You have no hope against the beast!" Mieczysław called after me.

If only you knew.

41

Otylia

How can I Ascend with such little time?

IVAN'S LUMBERING FORM LED THE WAY through the woods for hours. Our breaths fogged the air beneath the towering trees, but the cold wasn't my concern.

Despite escaping the pit, I had a dark feeling about what lay ahead. I wasn't keen on trusting one of Weles's most loyal servants. Ivan had saved me and claimed to be allied with Vlatka and Kyustendil, but everyone in Nawia shrouded the truth. Only Sabina had been transparent from the start.

Gods protect her.

The nymph had stood by me from the moment we'd met, but because of me, she was in danger. Surely, Weles knew she was part of our plan. What would happen to her?

I stopped, crossing my arms. "I'm not going any further until you tell me where we're headed. This isn't the way to the island Kyustendil showed me before."

"Our destination remains the same," Ivan replied with a smile. "Nawia is a vast realm. The moment you believe you know it it, locations shift and change, becoming new creations of this paradise."

"Then tell me *something.*"

"Very well."

Rising to his hind legs, Ivan uttered a phrase in the old tongue that I couldn't understand.

His body changed. Fur receded, replaced by skin and clothes, as his long nose flattened to that of a man's. Rich robes of vibrant reds and golds draped down his tall, muscled frame, and a bear fur cap covered his blond hair. Despite appearing over forty, he seemed as fit as Dwie Rzeki's most renowned warriors.

"You weren't lying about being a king," I said, hiding my awe. In sixteen years, I had never seen so much wealth, let alone all of it worn by one man.

Ivan bowed his head. "I hope you will find, Lady Otylia, that I have never lied to you. My master may be a deceiver, but that is not my way."

"Then why spend so much time as a bear?"

"I spent many years of my life cursed in that form." He waved his hand to his robes. "All this wealth may be how I was seen at the height of my power, but it was that suffering as a bear that molded me into the king I was to become. It was my wife who ended the curse."

That piqued my curiosity. Father had never spoken of such a curse. "How?"

"She showed me care when no others would. *That* is why I prefer my bear form. Anyone can easily show respect to a wealthy king, yet it takes the pure of heart to pity a cursed man." With another smile, he began walking again. "I saw that in you as well, young goddess."

Purity of heart in me? I huffed as I followed. Wacław was the one with the care he spoke of, not me. While Wacław possessed a child-like desire for peace and love, I wanted revenge—against Marzanna, against Weles, against Tibês, and against Jaryło. They had wronged me and hurt those I loved. The first I'd come to expect. The second was unforgiveable.

Ivan raised his worn face to the moonlight as he walked. "There are many of us who care for Weles but believe his desire for power has corrupted his mind. His rule over Nawia is good, just. As is Perun's over Prawia. Yet, Jawia is different."

"Father always said Swaróg rules Prawia," I said. "That Perun is only his enforcer."

He chuckled. "There was a time that such a thing was true, but as of now, it is Perun who reigns within the realm of the gods. This makes Jawia the essential middle between him and Weles. Prawia ensures order. Nawia allows change. Jawia, in turn, is the balance between these powers."

"Weles tried to explain to me why chaos was more important than order." I thought back to our conversation in the library. Had my anger revealed my intentions, or was there something else?

"Master Weles would make such an argument, as it is who he is. I've realized after far too much time, though, that Jawia must never be ruled by a single god. Without the cycles to protect balance, the eternal war among the gods would destroy all life."

We reached the edge of the forest, where the great orange sea stretched before us. The smell of salt was so strong it stung my nose.

My confusion at the orange water gave me pause. "Weles mentioned that too," I mindlessly replied before shaking my head. "He called it Jawia's last devastation."

"Yes, and only women have been allowed to channel the gods since. Men proved they were too greedy for such power." Ivan stared over the sea for a minute, not offering another word until he swept his robes behind him and continued to the water's edge. "Weles has told me of his peace deal with Perun: Neither shall directly influence the tribes of Jawia for either war or peace in order to solidify their own powers within the realm. They may strike or assist those they wish from the edge of their realms, but no longer can they seek to rule Jawia."

"Weles sees Jaryło as his way around that," I said.

He nodded. "That is why he delays your Ascension. Until Jaryło is powerful enough to control Jawia—with your help—you are less of a threat before Ascension." With a sigh, he stepped onto the water, his feet never dipping below its surface. "We, on the other hand, believe you are a goddess, not a tool for you to be used by Weles and his false son."

"You're standing on the water..." I looked from his boots, resting on the water as if it were dirt, to him. "Are you a sorcerer?"

His eyes were like Mother's when she'd showed me a rebellious trick—one Father would hate. "Nawia is a fascinating place," he said. "I have lived here nearly two-hundred years and have failed to understand most of its secrets. Come. The others are waiting."

I gritted my teeth as he walked across the sea with no hesitation. *The others. Who?*

There was only one way to find out, and gods knew I wasn't going back. Weles had trapped me already. I didn't intend to give him another chance.

My fox instincts resisted my approach, but I forced myself to step upon the waters. At first, nothing *seemed* different. When I put my entire weight onto the sea, however, it held, and I let myself be amazed by the fact I was standing on water.

No wonder Kuba's with these people, whoever they are. He'd have followed Marzanna if she'd let him do this.

I smirked and sprinted after Ivan.

It felt good to run because I wanted to, not because of fear. With the winds skipping across the sea and rushing through my fur, I was free. And in my fox form, I was incredibly quick.

Ivan laughed as I bolted past him and skidded to a stop, sending the orange water spraying through the moonlight. "I believe, Lady Otylia, that this is the happiest I have seen you."

"It's the happiest I've felt since I died," I said before circling him as quickly as I could. Initial shock gone, the fox within me wanted nothing more than to run for an eternity. If only life was that simple. "But why is the water orange? And why can we walk on it?"

"That I do not know." He scratched his stubbled chin. I thought it odd that a man who spent so much time as a bear bothered to shave at all. "Nawia is beautiful in that way. It would fail to be a paradise if we could understand each of its secrets. What is life without discovery and change?"

"Stagnation?" I asked, slowing to a walk alongside him. All the running had me panting, but the fox still wanted to sprint.

Ivan held up one finger with a grin. "Correct. Preventing this stagnation is much of Weles's job in Nawia. Many souls choose to return to Jawia for a new life, but to ensure his own power, Nawia must thrive."

"Isn't it odd for him to oppose Marzanna, then? She's the goddess of death."

"Yes, but she is not Death." Sorrow filled his eyes when he looked down at me. "I have heard about your encounter with him during your Trial. As you have likely realized, it is Death who is inescapable, not Marzanna. Such a force is more powerful than even the gods."

Waving an arm through the air, he chuckled to himself. "But you asked why he opposes her. Simple: Jaryło. There is little Master Weles would not do for him, even defy a goddess who is aligned with his interests."

My head throbbed thinking of the gods' relations. Jaryło's war with Marzanna had brought Dziewanna with him, but each deity was trapped between Perun and Weles as well. And surely, with the multitude of other gods, there were more conflicts I didn't know of. Mother had defied both Perun and Weles. She'd fought Marzanna and sought independence. Where did that put her among the hidden factions of the Three Realms? More importantly, where did that put me?

I groaned. It had been hard enough to know who to trust before. Now, it seemed everyone had their own secret plans to rule Jawia—even Mother with her youthful rebellion against Perun.

"You still call Weles your master," I said, pulling myself from my thoughts some time later. "Won't he kill you for helping me escape?"

Ivan raised his brow. "I have not said we are helping you escape, have I?"

A growl escaped my throat.

Defensively, he raised his hands. "It was meant as a joke, Lady Otylia, nothing more. I should have realized how desperate you are to leave after what Master Weles has put you through."

"So, you're going to help me?"

"That is our intention." He pointed, and in the distance, I saw the dark outline of an island. "It will be much simpler to explain when we have arrived, however."

I stopped baring my fangs, but after all I'd seen, I *needed* to know more. "Tell me everyone who will be there."

The end of his mouth flicked up. "You are just like Lady Dziewanna. Very well, if I must explain who and what you will find on the island, then I will. We have no secrets that you cannot know, my goddess."

As he began walking toward the island again, I followed, hesitant. *No one exposes all their secrets.*

"Kuba Piotryk, as you know, is the first," Ivan said. "The others who you have met are Kyustendil of the north-west wind, the witch Vlatka who showed you to the first Trial, and your nymph, Sabina.

"Sabina's safe?" I sighed deeply as a ball of tension released in my back. "Thank the gods!"

Ivan grumbled to himself before giving me a passing glance. "She is, but we barely managed to sneak out of the palace when we discovered that Weles knew our plan. Half the souls and nymphs we had recruited were captured or killed by the god's loyalists."

A chill came over me. "What happens to souls that die here?"

"Worry not. On this, Weles did not lie. A soul that does not pass through the Heart of Nawia returns to the land above with a new life and memory."

"A final death," I said, my skin suddenly cold. "Oblivion?"

"Oblivion is not a place to be seen," Ivan replied, his voice lacking the cheer it had held minutes before. "It is neither a realm nor an eternity but the lack of it. Mortal souls do not go there. We call it Oblivion because it allows us to comprehend a location beyond the Three Realms where demonic souls are destroyed. In truth, Nawia is the only afterlife. A soul comes from Jawia when its time is up, and once it decides it wishes to travel home, it returns to begin anew. This is another essential cycle."

"You're saying any memory of their old life is gone?"

Intertwining his fingers before him as he walked, Ivan stared into the dark sea. "Yes, but such is a choice some make. The role of an ancestor is important and powerful. Some, though, lack such an opportunity. That being said, it is fortunate that souls rarely perish here against their will. If another were to rule this realm—and there are many who fight at this very minute to do so—such losses would be more common."

I shook my head. "How can you call him master after he killed so many people he *stole* from Jawia?"

"Because every man has his flaws, every god his pride." He held his hand before him, studying them with sorrow in his eyes. "To be king is to make decisions that impact everyone under your rule. To Weles, protecting his realm, his daughter, and Jaryło's claim on Jawia are his duty. He is a good king on most days, but he fails to realize the peril he causes by choosing to exert Jaryło's authority and deceiving those who need his help.

"Weles will need advisors to temper his ambitions," he continued. "Though I am helping you escape, it is not out of disloyalty for your father but out of a desire to ensure you become your own woman and goddess. The Three Realms will need you free if we are to survive what is coming."

The winds picked up as we neared the island, sending waves crashing over my ankles. I resisted the shiver that followed. Within Ivan's words had been a hint of fate, the same that Mokosz had spoken of, but I refused to admit that I could be both free and confined by Destiny's command.

"I haven't even Ascended," I said, "but everyone watches me like *I'm* the one who needs to fix the gods' problems. Why can't Perun stop Marzanna, or Swaróg? Why do the other gods sit back and let Marzanna sweep across Jawia without resistance?"

Ivan smiled again, and I growled at the condescending look. "If only it were so simple," he said. "The miraculous thing about the gods is that they are the most powerful living beings in the Three Realms, yet they so often fail because they squabble amongst themselves. Weles and Perun's war you are aware of, but there are other quarrels: Jaryło and Dziewanna, Dadźbóg and Swaróg, and others.

Though most are far less severe than the one between the masters of Prawia and Nawia, they have had hundreds and thousands of years to fester."

"Mother and Jaryło?" I tried to remember any conflict between them in my parents' stories. "I know Dziewanna revolted against Perun, but why would she have a rivalry with her brother?"

"When you are the protector of the wilds and another god has claimed all the worship for spring, then conflict is sure to arise. Dziewanna was also quite perturbed on behalf of Marzanna after Jaryło decided to be unfaithful."

Wonderful. More secrets.

Ivan sighed. "There are enough of these conflicts to distract the gods. If Perun were to interfere against Marzanna, another god could threaten his reign. If Weles were to devote his strength to a fight before both you and Jaryło were strong enough, then Perun could destroy him once and for all. Or, at the very least, one of the many powerful spirits that inhabit this realm could take his throne. In a way, the very balance that ensures the Three Realms do not crumble is the thing that could allow them to fall to Marzanna. She defeated those who opposed her. Now, there is no one left."

"But me…" I whispered.

"Precisely."

The island loomed before us now. Despite being no wider than a thousand strides, a mountain stretched to the sky at its center. An odd crater filled the mountain's peak, and from the little light the moon offered, the island seemed to be made entirely of black rocks.

What is this place?

"Welcome to a rare island of consistency amid a realm of chaos," Ivan said, stepping onto the shore. The stones cracked beneath his boot. *How are they so brittle?*

With a smile, he waved for me to follow. "Come. The others await us at the volcano's base."

I stood in shock for a moment. *Volcano?* I'd never heard of such a thing. Then again, I had never seen an orange sea either, so I pushed away my awe and ran after him, excited to soon be free of my fox body—I hoped.

42

Wacław

Bidaês, what have you done?

A GUST OF WIND BLEW MY SOUL-FORM'S HAIR across my face as I rode through the northern gate with Ara, Narcyz, Zakir, and Andrij. It had grown too long, but cutting it had been the least of my concerns over the last two moons. I needed to save Mom. Then Otylia.

Despite my reservations about bringing Zakir beyond the walls, Ara had insisted he might be useful in convincing Bidaês to let Mom go—if she was still alive. I bit my cheek. *She's alive. She has to be.* From what I could tell, Zakir and Katiôn had been close, and I'd sensed his unease in recent days. He wasn't a warrior or a demon. He sought not to shed blood but to help those around him in his quiet, consistent way. To lose his grandfather like that…

I took a shaky breath and glanced over my shoulder at Ara, whose eyes were fixed on the shadows between the trees. She held her bow tight in her grasp. With an arrow already nocked, I doubted she would let anyone strike Bidaês before her. The Simuk had taunted and teased her for weeks. Like Otylia, Ara didn't take that well.

"I'll take flight and see if the winds sense him," I said. "We don't have time to wander aimlessly."

She nodded, and I launched myself into the air, letting the demonic thrill course through me with the breeze at my fingers. The sky had darkened since morning. Clouds of both white and gray drifted about like an unfinished quilt, the holes allowing Dadźbóg's light to trickle through.

Where are you, Bidaês?

The winds traversed the land. They darted among the trees and tickled their branches in pursuit of the wilkołak, and soon, they found something. Matted and covered in muck, Bidaês was just as I remembered him the night of the Battle of Kynnytsia. Now, he lurked in a section of rock south from the Wyzra, not far from the trail we'd been riding on.

I slowed to return to my friends, but my heart caught as the winds found another form. *Mom!* Her breaths were slow, weak, and my Frostmark seared when the winds neared. But she was alive. I clung to that fact as I dove landed before them, startling Andrij's horse, Oleh, as well as Narcyz himself.

"Gods, Wacław!" Narcyz stammered. "Maybe a bit of a warning next time."

"Sorry. I forget how odd it is for you to see me flying."

"Find him?" Ara asked, her deep brown eyes eager.

I nodded. "He's to the northwest, hidden in a rock outcrop in the woods, and Mom's with him—alive. The terrain will be difficult to ride in, so we should tie up our horses here."

Andrij slid down and hit his spear against his shield, his brow furrowed. "Let's encircle him. Narcyz and I will take each flank and Wacław the rear to the north. We'll force him away from your mother and into the path of Ara's arrows."

"Sure, send the demon straight at me," Ara quipped.

"It's a good idea," I said as I drew Kwiecień. "If he charges you, I'll be there, don't worry. Our best chance is to keep him confined to the swamp as much as possible. The uneven ground will slow him… hopefully."

"*Hopefully*," Narcyz huffed. "You rely too much on hope, Half-Chief."

"And you too much on hostility."

Keeping close to the trees, I flew in a curve to the west, trying to stay out of sight. I didn't know if Bidaês had a wolf's sense of smell and hearing too, so I kept further than necessary. The others would be slower on foot anyway.

The muck squished underfoot when I landed a stone's throw from the Wyzra. Despite the chill, the waters ensured the ground didn't harden here until deep into winter. Otylia had laughed as I'd stumbled through it as a child. She'd always been more sure-footed, but even I hadn't been as clumsy as Kuba. *Gods bless him.*

The gales escalated as I trudged toward Bidaês. They fed on my desperation to save Mom and my desire to make Bidaês pay for what he'd done. Revenge itself so often felt wrong, but now, it drove me on with the strength of a great tempest. I tightened my grip on both Kwiecień and the eight winds.

With the winds, I sensed Ara crouching on a slope that could barely be called a hill. Her breaths were shallow, short, as she watched Narcyz and Andrij advance behind their shields. Bidaês remained still.

I slowed, my breaths fogging the air before me. My steps were loud, so I floated on the winds just inches off the ground.

Not far now. The hammering of my heart pounded my chest and head. It demolished my hesitation, my fear. I let it, and the fire grew with its beat, spreading through my veins until only hatred remained.

Hidden in the narrow slit between two rocks, Bidaês's gray tufts of fur could have easily been mistaken for stone. Even I would have passed him by if it hadn't been for the guidance of the winds and my Frostmark. Yet, there he was, his chest rising and falling with each breath as he clutched Mom in his grasp. He likely never left his wilkołak form now. His demonic soul had taken control. Would the human one ever return?

Andrij nodded to me from across the rocks. Narcyz wasn't in sight, but it didn't matter. I would start the fight. If all went well, I would end it too.

Kwiecień hummed, pulsing with the winds as I stepped onto the rock. Bidaês was less than ten strides away now. A foreign rage poured over me this close to him. I no longer needed the winds to hear his deep breaths, and I held my own in preparation.

When I reached the crack, he stirred.

"You were slower than I expected, Wacław," he growled as he climbed onto the rock before me. Behind him, he pulled Mom by her bright blonde hair. My heart pounded at the sight of her trapped in his grasp. "Were you busy dealing with a little poison?"

"Let her go!" I spat, the winds whipping around me.

"Give me Kwiecień and she's free." He threw Mom to the ground, and I bit my cheek at her head hitting the stone. "That's all you have to do."

I glanced down at the blade. Its hum grew with each moment, as if it could sense the demon's hunger to fight, but that desire was no longer just the demon's. It burned through my veins, tempting me to kill the boy who'd betrayed me. But what would Bidaês do if I rejected the demand? *He'll kill her.* I knew it, and that fear paralyzed me as I raised my gaze to the beast before me. *I can't lose her too.*

With a shuddered breath, I held the blade out to him. "Take—"

A shout rang from across the rocks and tore me from my trance. As I stumbled back in shock, Narcyz lunged at Bidaês's flank with his spear ready, but the wolf was faster. He turned to meet Narcyz's strike with jaws wide.

"No!" I screamed, regaining my bearing and sweeping Kwiecień across my body.

It was too late.

Narcyz's wooden shield snapped as he slammed into Bidaês. The impact threw Narcyz to his knees, but the demon did not waver. His claws lashed out. Blood splattered the rocks. My sword struck Bidaês's arm, and he growled as Narcyz dropped into the crimson pool.

Stay alive, Narcyz. Please, just stay alive!

I pushed Bidaês back with an array of strikes that put me between him and Narcyz. With each movement he kept me from reaching Mom. Andrij had broken from his shock, and I pointed to our fallen friend. "Get him to the healers!"

"What about you?"

"I'll be fine," I huffed, deflecting another blow from Bidaês's claws. "Hurry! He's lost a lot of blood already."

Kwiecień found its mark and drew blood greedily. Black joined red at my feet as Bidaês whirled away, gripping his arm. I followed with the winds strengthening my strides, but he dodged my strikes before grabbing Mom and running north toward the Wyzra.

He's too fast.

I took flight and flipped above the tops of the trees. Though the mud slowed Bidaês, his four legs offered him more grip. Even with the winds at my back, it was difficult to keep up.

But he didn't know the woods like I did. In his haste, he'd chosen the one route that allowed me to corner him against the bank of the Wyzra. This was my home, and this time, I had both my sword and the *żityje* to fight.

He skidded to a sloppy stop just strides from the current and dropped Mom on the bank. Black spewed from his arm. It covered the shadowed ground, and as the sun emerged from the clouds, I dove.

Bidaês rolled aside with remarkable agility, his long arms stretching back to rake his claws along my shoulder. I cried out but held Kwiecień. The golden blade shone in the light with streaks of black coating its sharp edge. It pulsed with excitement, and I struck again.

We sparred back and forth. My speed matched his with the aid of the gales that stormed around us, but even with the sword's reach, he ducked free each time.

I sent wind blasts to distract him, then stabbed at his leg as he batted them away. This time, Kwiecień ripped through his thigh. I drew my dagger as he grabbed my sword arm. The move left his chest open.

His unscarred eye narrowed. Pain seared through my chest, still healing from the arrow wound, but I pushed myself forward on the winds. We tumbled to the ground with the dagger to his neck and my knees on his chest. "It's over, Bidaês. Let her go!"

He lashed out, throwing me through the wall of wind and escaping again. I skidded across the ground with blood seeping from three gashes across my chest.

But I felt no pain.

Heat rushed through me. It numbed my thoughts, dampened my fear. All that remained was fury.

"Marzanna will betray you too!" I shouted, marching forward with Kwiecień gliding over the ground at my side. The clouds above smothered the light once again, but the blade's glow formed a clear ring around me as the gusts hammered the trees.

Deep gray fur flashed in the darkness just beyond Kwiecień's glow. Fluttering debris filled the space between us as his growl rumbled the ground. "You're too weak to kill me. You were before and you are now. Give me Kwiecień!"

"No!"

He broke into the light. I dove aside, and Bidaês rammed across the circle. Teeth bared, he spun back as I brandished both sword and dagger. Thunder rolled in the east. The sky had turned a deep gray, all color smothered by winter and storm—all but Kwiecień. Bidaês kept Mom behind him, and my body shook in rage.

"Why let her win?" I yelled. "Why serve the woman whose Horde killed your people?"

"It was you who slayed Jaryło and freed her." He smirked, circling me with his dark eyes reflecting the golden light. "You and I were born to be powerful, to rule. But we cannot do so when our people are blind to the potential we hold. We could bring the Krowikie and Simukie into a new dawn with the eternal frost. Imagine! They will see us as gods in our own right, not demons and beasts to be scorned."

"We can't earn their trust through slaughter!"

Shaking his head, Bidaês stopped. Lightning cracked behind him and sent a flash over his scarred face. "Why do you choose to fight for those who despise you? These people cast you out before they even knew the truth of your birth. Imagine the scorn when they learn. Or have you still failed to admit you're a demon?"

I took a fighting stance and edged forward. With Kwiecień's glow in my right hand and the dagger's smothering darkness in the other, *žityje* drifted between. It flowed from right to left, as if the dagger fed upon Kwiecień. "It doesn't matter if they care for me," I said. "They are my people, my tribe, and I cannot abandon them."

"Then you have chosen her fate."

He snarled and dashed toward Mom as another bolt of lightning shot through the sky. I rushed after him with the winds at my back, but the wilkołak was too fast. He was upon Mom in seconds. She stood no chance.

I screamed into the storm as her body dropped, but my voice was lost in its torrent. Blood poured from Mom's throat at the river's edge, ripped apart by the beast's teeth. She was gone. Mom was gone. And as I stared across that muddied bank at the demon before me, hate burned within my soul.

I let the demon free.

My vision turned red as I tightened my grip around the hilts of my blades. The fight became a vision. Someone else—*something* else—took control, jabbing and slicing as we clashed. Bidaês was dangerous, even with his wounds, but with the winds screaming in my ears and lightning surging through me, he stood no chance.

I jumped, pouring my *žityje* into the winds. Bidaês leaped after me, and his claws missed my legs by mere inches as I landed behind him. His breaths were heavy when he struck again, the confidence slipping from his eyes. My dagger found his scarred cheek. Just a scratch. Black blood sprayed across my tunic and face, but the success pushed me faster.

For Xobas. For the clans. For Mom.

The entire forest glowed now. Each snap of lightning fed my luminescent veins, and Bidaês's jaw hung open as he staggered back. His cries merged with the tempest.

I rushed forward. Bidaês deflected my dagger-arm, but I dodged his counter-strike. The demon's call in my mind spurred me on, and he was too slow. Kwiecień slipped by his guard.

His howl tore through the storm and joined the chorus of thunder. Lightning cracked at my fingertips as I stared in horror at the blade—run straight through his sternum. Pleasure hummed within me, but I cracked, falling to the mud as Bidaês's eyes rolled back.

What have I become?

My anger had swept away my fear. With it gone, all I felt was pain as I stared down at the fallen wilkołak before me. Regret, sorrow. It came like a mighty river, and I was helpless before it. I had killed Bidaês out of revenge, but it was too late. He'd taken Mom from me, just as Marzanna had promised.

Rain slipped down my face as I rose and pulled Kwiecień free. For one moment, frozen in time, I just stood in the downpour, watching it drip from my nose and chin into the pool of black forming around my boots. It seemed a dream. A nightmare. I had defeated the beast. I had surrendered to my demonic rage. And as I opened my Frostmarked hand, that symbol, glowing with my veins of lightning, dulled with them to black. One part of me wept—another thirsted for blood.

If this is truly who I am, who I must become, then I am the monster they claim demons to be. I'm not better than the corrupted ones. I'm not the one who can save them from the damnation that consumes our souls. I'm not the one who can defeat Marzanna.

I'm just a weapon of the dark.

43

Wacław

She's dead…

I RAISED MY HEAD TO THE SKY, drowning in the storm as regret and dread seized my chest. I hadn't the strength to cry. Mom was dead. Though I'd slain Bidaês in revenge, my hope had vanished with her. Only pain remained.

Then I felt it: *žityje.*

It poured from Kwiecień, more powerful than anything I'd sensed before. Life. Vibrant and pure, its power joined with mine as a golden light swirled around me. The energy within it was intoxicating, and I breathed in deeply, letting the storm join with my soul. My dread dissipated. My pain pulsed in my heart as it fed the energy rushing through my veins. It was as if that hurt—that anger and sorrow I'd held back for so long—had ignited an unquenchable fire within me.

I can save her.

My breaths quickened as I rushed toward Mom's body. Blood pooled around her in the sea of swamp mud, but I clung to the hope of healing her. The Moonblades held the power to bring a deity back from death. Surely, they could do the same to a mortal. They had to.

Kneeling before her, I held Mom's head in my free hand as I

grabbed hold of Kwiecień's *żityje*. It had been unreachable for the entire moon, but now, it seemed *eager* to be used. I knew no spells of healing. I knew little of channeling or of the power I wielded. So instead of chanting in the old tongue, I plunged all of my strength into her and shouted through the storm, "Bring her back!"

Lightning struck.

Kwiecień slipped from my hand as the blast flung me into the river, my entire body searing in a blaze of pain. Spots filled my vision, but as I struggled to stand in the Wyzra's current, my now blackened veins were obvious. With Kwiecień's *żityje* out of my grasp, I had little left. Now, all I could do was pray: to Mokosz, to Dziewanna, to Otylia, to any god who would listen. *Please, let her live.*

When my vision cleared, I choked on my breaths. Mom stood on the riverbank with her bright blue eyes watching me—unwounded. "Wašek?" she exclaimed.

"Mom!" I rushed toward her, sweeping aside the river with the gales until I tumbled into her arms at the shore. "Thank the gods!" I held her tight as the torrent weakened to a trickle. Though my body trembled from the cold water, I let myself relax for the first time.

"No, Wašek," she whispered, her fingers gripping my ripped and bloodied tunic. "The gods abandoned me. You didn't."

"I thought you were gone…"

"Yet you saved me." She pulled back and held my cheeks in her hands, that familiar warm smile on her face. "I always knew the gods had blessed you."

Mud sloshed nearby, and I spun, dragging Kwiecień from the dirt. Black and brown oozed down its golden blade as its lingering power coursed through me.

"That you, Wacław?" Ara's voice asked from behind a willow. She ducked her head around its trunk, arrow nocked, but she lowered her bow when she saw us. "You did it? It's over?" Zakir emerged cautiously from behind her, gripping a clay jar in his grasp.

I nodded toward Bidaês's corpse and took a deep sigh. "It's over. I tried to appeal to him, but he was an entirely different person. He's probably not left his wilkołak form since he fled Kynnytsia. Staying a demon for that long… it changed him." I raised my gaze. "It's changing me too."

She huffed and cocked her head to get another look at the boy who had once tried to woo her. "He deserved it." When Zakir approached from behind her, she winced. "I mean… I'm sorry."

"No," he said, pursing his lips. For the first time since we'd met, his voice cracked, only for a moment. "Bidaês was born a demon, but there's always a choice. He made his when he killed our parents. The world is better without him."

"You knew that beast?" Mom asked with a gasp.

I took a sharp breath as the first beams of sunlight streaked through the clouds. "Yes, he was the grandson of the marzban of Clan Simuk, and he betrayed us."

"What exactly happened?" Ara said, still gripping her bow. "After Andrij took Narcyz back to your house, I tried to follow. There was a black mist swirling from you, and the heart of the storm formed over you when you fought." She nodded toward Mom. "How did you bring her back?"

I called the storm? "That's not possible. To call a storm like that from nothing would've taken an immense amount of *życie*—probably more than I had before using Kwiecień's to save Mom." I glanced down at the black veins covering my skin. "I'm mostly drained now, but I definitely wasn't during the fight."

"Would that explain it?" she asked, swinging her finger in a circle at the trees around us.

I was confused at first, but my heart stopped when I stepped closer to a birch nearby. The tree's white bark had been torn away, leaving a decaying, black mold behind. I ran a finger across the bits of bark that remained. It flaked off before shriveling into a ball.

My voice shook. "I did that?"

All the trees nearby were the same. I rushed between them, reaching into my *życie* to check for other sources, but each was lifeless. I stood in a ring of death with only Kwiecień's strong, pulsing life offering any break from the suffocating void.

"The trees kept me alive," I whispered, holding a hand to my temple as it throbbed. Why? How could I drain them so easily? I turned back to Ara, trembling. "I don't understand…"

A hint of fear flashed in her eyes. She stepped back, the rain soaking her hair, half-braided, half-not. It was the cut of a huntress, and the arrow remained nocked on her bow.

"Ara?" I asked with another step toward her.

She swallowed. "You just drained a dozen trees without even realizing it. Wacław, think what that's doing to your mortal soul."

I paused and shut my eyes. Before, my *żityje* had been a single pool with my demonic soul feeding on my human one. As I looked closer now, though, each had its own reserve of *żityje*. My demonic soul swelled with power. I felt it in my connection to the winds and how they seemed ready to respond at any moment, despite me not actively reaching for them. It was freeing, like my mind had awoken for the first time from a deep slumber.

Then I sensed my mortal soul: dwindling and fragile.

The shock tore me from my stasis. I dropped to a knee, clutching Kwiecień before me with its point in the mud. Jaryło's warning rang in my ears. He'd claimed I would eventually lose grip of my humanity. My demonic soul would someday destroy my human one. Someday.

No one, not even Jaryło had known when that day would come. I was an oddity of nature.

Demons were supposed to be just demons, their humanity lost upon their creation—their first death—but I had yet to die. Like Bidaês, I had been created from the circumstances of my birth. The blood moon had cursed me in life, but that sliver of light during the eclipse had allowed my human soul to live on. When would that sliver fade, drained completely?

With a raspy breath, I looked up at Mom as terror filled my chest. *I'm killing myself.* The process was slow, but each time I entered my soul-form, my demonic soul took control. It grew stronger every night, my use of its power only strengthening its hold as it stole more *żityje* from my human soul.

"Kwiecień only responded to my call when I embraced my demonic soul and the anger within me," I admitted. "My mortal soul is dying anyway, but my demonic one brought you back. I'm a płanetnik. Nothing can change that."

Mom held her hands close to her chest as she approached me. "Who you will become is up to you alone. Your father became a monster not because of his soul but because of his own choices."

"Some things aren't a choice." I took a shaky breath, feeling the demon's anger roaring within me. Unleashed, it was a part of me now, and I doubted I could ever cage it again. "This power is dark, but it's my only hope of saving Otylia from Weles. I won't fail her."

"Otylia?" she asked. "What has happened to her?"

I sighed and looked back toward the village. "A lot has happened in the last two moons."

Mom asked many questions as we traveled back to our farm. She rode with me on Tanek, and though he wasn't used to holding two riders, he walked on with an eager stride. My chest clenched as I explained my decision to save Otylia instead of Father, and Mom remained quiet for almost a minute before responding.

"I'm sorry you were forced to make such a choice…" She dropped her head. "I loved your father for so many years. He didn't deserve death."

I winced. "It's my fault. If I hadn't given my blood to Marzanna—"

"You mustn't think like that," she interrupted, her voice unusually sharp. "Marzanna is the goddess of death. Who she takes is not your responsibility, and I could not ask you to save my love before your own. Don't try to claim you don't love Otylia. I've seen it on your face ever since you were no taller than my hip."

Ara smirked at me when I replied, "I do love her. If only the feeling was mutual." My heart ached from memories and doubts about Otylia alike. We still needed Dariusz to tell us how to get to Nawia, but I felt more exhausted than I'd ever been.

"Asking Otylia to admit she loves someone is like convincing a stubborn horse to trot," Ara quipped. "That doesn't mean she doesn't love you."

Does it?

"And she is trapped in Nawia now?" Mom asked. "You said she is with Weles?"

I swallowed, but this time, I let the pain come when I recounted Jaryło's betrayal. That resentment pushed me forward, an unstoppable force that joined with my desperation to find Otylia.

We reached the northern edge of our barren fields by the time I was finished telling her about the Lake of Reflection and our battle in the Mangled Woods. Instead of asking questions like before, she listened in a stunned silence until we dismounted outside the pasture. Then, she just held a hand over her heart and stared up at the sun. "My son in love with a goddess…"

"If only it were as romantic as that," I mumbled. "All that matters is that I bring her back."

She embraced me again. "Then go to Dariusz and find the way to Nawia quickly so that you can rest. The day is nearly done, and if you want to leave in the morning, you'll need your strength."

"Yes, *matka*," I replied with a kiss on her cheek before stepping back. "Ara, can you and Zakir stay with her until I get back? If something were to happen—"

"We've got it," she said, raising her bow. "Besides, someone needs to stop Narcyz from complaining about his injury."

Zakir nodded. "It is the least I can do."

With the winds at my back, I mounted Tanek and rode for Dwie Rzeki's eastern gate. We'd left my physical body under Dariusz's protection. I wasn't looking forward to explaining to the guards why I had black veins covering me now, but admitting that I was a demon seemed less threatening with Mom safe. Something had changed within me during the fight. As I straightened my wide-brimmed płanetnik hat and stopped before the warriors, I knew what I was. And for once, I wasn't ashamed.

"The demon is dead," I announced to the guards. "Let me see Dariusz."

But they didn't move aside. Their leader raised a fist, and they approached with spears ready. "Nah, the demon's right in front of us," he said. "Dismount now and drop your weapons! Mieczysław wants a word with you, Half-Chief."

44

Otylia

Something terrible has happened.

AGONY WASHED OVER ME.

Ivan and I had been climbing the incline toward the volcano's base, but I stopped, struggling for each breath as pain and sorrow surged through my connection with Wacław.

Wašek? Wašek, are you okay?

No reply came.

A worried look on his face, Ivan rushed back to me. "Lady Otylia! What has happened?"

"It's Wacław," I groaned. It was paralyzing, and I collapsed onto the black rocks. "We're bonded, and when he feels pain…" I winced. "Whatever happened is horrific."

"This is an ill omen of Marzanna's actions. If you must rest, do so. You are our goddess, and the others will wait until our arrival."

I hated the idea of that. To be a burden on those trying to help me was weak, selfish. Clenching my jaw, I rose and forced my way up the trail. "Waiting won't make it any better." *Won't make* him *any better.*

Gods save him.

As we walked, I tried to distract myself by examining the island's sparse vegetation. Only small, bulbous plants poked up through the harsh rock, and I could have seen for miles if it were the sun and not the moon lighting the realm. Every few seconds, I had to dodge the spines that covered the round grasses. They weren't tall enough to cause Ivan any harm. A fox, however, was far less removed from the ground.

I admired those plants. With neither plentiful water nor fertile soul, they were strong. They almost survived in pure spite of the harsh terrain, adding their sharpness as an extra jab at the world that said, "Fight me if you dare."

Mother would've hated this place. She loved change and discoveries, but the island's barren landscape would leave her eager to return to the wilds. To me, though, there was something beautiful about its gleaming black rocks and towering core. I could've enjoyed the view if my heart stopped throbbing.

But it wouldn't.

Marzanna had threatened to kill Wacław's mother if he didn't serve her. Had she followed through on her omen?

Just the thought of that made me shudder. I'd suffered from Marzanna's Curse. Though Wacław had saved me then, if Marzanna brought her wrath again, he couldn't save everyone. Knowing Wacław, he'd try anyway.

A light flickered ahead, pulling me from my thoughts.

"Here we are," Ivan said with a smile. "Our little tribe."

When Kuba's head popped up from behind the flames, I let myself smile and rush toward him. Ivan must've warned him I'd be a fox, because he grinned and wrapped his arms around me as I arrived. "If it isn't the witch who stole Wacław!" he exclaimed with a laugh.

I chuckled. "You're lucky I'm happy to see you. He's not here to stop me punishing you for your stupid jokes."

He released me and held up his hands. "I've died enough times already."

More footsteps approached from across the fire. Ivan smiled as Kyustendil appeared with a band of at least a hundred other people. It was hard to make out their faces in the darkness, but there were mortal souls and a variety of nymphs—both male and female. Awe filled their faces at the sight of me.

"Lady Otylia!" Kyustendil said, hopping toward me on the wind. "It is *truly* splendid to see you free from Weles's grasp."

I looked past him to Sabina, who smiled shyly among the nymphs. "And I'm happy to be free from it," I said.

Fluttering on her forest nymph wings, Sabina swooped toward me. "I was so scared he'd trapped you."

"He had…" I muttered.

"Many others were the same," Ivan said, "but the threat has passed for now. Gather around, all, and let us introduce ourselves to our newest goddess."

What do they see? I wondered as Ivan's allies formed a circle around the fire, leaving me alone at its center. *A goddess? A tool to gain their freedom? Or just a girl hopelessly stuck in the body of a fox?*

One-by-one, they approached with a bow and gave their names. I forgot most—despite my best attempts not to—but I memorized each of their faces. I needed to consider all they were risking for me. If my escape failed, then I would take moons to regenerate enough *žityje* to recover. Their lives as they knew them would end.

When they finished, Kyustendil faked a cough and twirled his fingers in a little circle. I took a sharp breath. Wacław's pain and sorrow still gripped my mind, but for now, I focused on what lay ahead. But what could I say?

"Thank you," I began, my voice far too shy for a goddess. "I don't know each of your stories or why you decided to trust in me over Weles, but after weeks in his palace, it's good to know I'm not alone." My gaze fell on Sabina. "Not that I ever was."

Ivan waved to Vlatka, the witch from my first Trial, in the crowd. She stepped forward with her hands clasped before her, wearing the same deep gray dress of simple cloth that covered her short, stout frame. Smiling cheekily, she knelt before me. "Lady Otylia, my goddess, I will guide you in your transformation back to your human form—if you will allow me."

I nodded, and Vlatka rose, that giddy grin still on her face. "Shifting forms is a delicate art," she said. "Since you are bound with the silver fox, however, it should be easier to change you back."

"Should?" I asked.

She winced. "I am a witch, not a goddess. The channeling is often similar, but who am I to understand *your* power?"

Why does a witch speak about me with such reverence? Father's lessons had always said witches channeled dark spirits, but there was nothing dark about this woman. At least, not that I could tell without my connections to Dziewanna and Mokosz.

"How much *życie* remains in your soul?" Vlatka asked before catching herself. "I'm sorry. That was abrupt."

"It's fine," I replied. "And not much. It took a lot to heal my broken leg, and I haven't eaten in days."

"We will ensure that changes," Ivan said.

I shook my head. "Not until we're done. I need to get out of this form."

Vlatka held a hand toward me. "Then we shall begin." Laying her palm upon my head, she chanted in the old tongue, "From creature to goddess, shift."

The change struck instantly, twisting my stomach. A chill pierced my skin as fur retracted, and I gasped at the array of colors that greeted my eyes—even in the dark. Paws became hands. My nose shrunk and my smell dulled. My ears did the same. It was freeing to *feel* my body again, but then a realization struck me.

I'm naked…

I yelped and huddled against the rocks with my arms covering my body. Only Weles's armband remained of my previous clothes. Swiftly, Sabina swept a cloak over me, but I blushed at the sight of everyone watching.

Kuba, however, gave a sharp whistle, jumping between me and the crowd. "Give Otylia some space! How'd you like everyone gawking while your trousers were down, eh?"

My cheeks flushed again. I'd always thought Kuba to be a fool, but he brought a sense of familiarity. In a realm of chaos, I needed that.

"Away for the evening," Ivan ordered the crowd, never laying his gaze upon me. "Come morning, Lady Otylia will confront the remaining Trials, but she must rest."

I silently thanked him as the crowd drifted into the darkness. Fires flickered on the opposite end of the island. *Keeping them out of sight of the mainland. Smart.*

Soon, only Vlatka, Sabina, Kuba, and Ivan remained. Even Kyustendil, surprisingly, had allowed me privacy, leaving with a whisper in the old tongue that I couldn't hear over the cracking of the brittle stones. Something was still off about the master of the northwest wind, but I was grateful for him.

Vlatka knelt before me and pulled a dagger, holding it to her hand. I recoiled, but her joyous eyes calmed me. "You will need the strength from my blood, Lady Otylia. It is a sacrifice worth making for you."

There was an eagerness in her voice. *She* wants *to give it to me.* I couldn't understand why these people and nymphs would surrender so much for me, but the transformation had used my remaining *żityje*. The witch was right.

Reluctantly, I nodded as Ivan held a bowl beneath her extended hand. "Why are you doing this?" I asked. "You're a witch, not a szeptucha."

"Szeptuchy chain themselves to the whims of a god they don't choose," she said. "I, on the other hand, am free to choose my loyalties. The daughter of the wild goddess should understand this."

"But why me?"

"Like I told you before, I was close with your mother. Besides, there's little difference between Jaryło and Marzanna to me. They both want to control Jawia, control everyone. I'd prefer you stop them from taking it."

I raised my brow. "And if I try to take it?"

"Then you'll prove me wrong about you."

Without another word, she sliced open her hand. I recoiled as her blood poured into the bowl, my stomach churning. *This will never be normal.*

But when she wrapped her palm and held the bowl out to me, I took it. I needed the *žityje* to face tomorrow's Trials. More than that, though, I needed to accept who I was if I was going to Ascend. The words from that book burned my mind as I held the bowl to my lips.

To become a god is to accept the inevitable opposites of life:

Isolation and Connection
Life and Death
Will and Destiny
Love and Loss

Ascension is the completion of these Trials. With it comes understanding, power, and completion that only a god can possess: divinity. While mortals possess life and demons consume it, gods must receive žityje through willing offerings. Because of this, only they hold the ability to create life for the Three Realms. Only they can truly wield the powers of nature. This is good.

From what I could understand of the Trials, I'd completed half. Isolation had stolen Mother and Mokosz from me, leaving me without their marks or their power. Connection, in turn, had bonded me to the silver fox—a bond I wasn't feeling so grateful for at the moment. Life had forced me to accept a blood offering, and Death… I needed no reminding of Death.

But what would come next?

I forced myself not to close my eyes as I drank. There had been a weight in the priest's writings—a responsibility I bore. To be given the gift of even part of someone's life was sacred.

Žityje flooded into my soul. I hadn't realized how empty I'd truly felt, but the blood lit a spark within me, making the world look and feel clearer. Despite my stomach rumbling beneath it all, I finally felt myself again. *If only I had clothes I didn't need to hold shut.*

Once I gave Vlatka my thanks, she retreated into the darkness with the others. Sabina's wings fluttered behind me, and when I turned, she held a simple dress of white and black. "I'm sorry," she said. "It's not like the ones in the palace, but I tried my best."

"Thank you, Sabina," I replied. "I'm far more used to that anyway."

I sharply waved for Kuba and Ivan to look away. They did, and

Sabina helped me into the dress. I hated that I needed her help at all, but I was weak and sore from my time as a fox. How I would face the final Trials tomorrow, I didn't know.

When she finished, I flexed my hands, enjoying the feeling of a fresh dress against my skin and my free hair flowing with the breeze. It unnerved me that the silver and willow wood bands remained on my arm, but I figured the protection was better than not. Ivan would warn me if that guess was wrong.

"You can turn around now," I said to the men.

Kuba grinned as he faced me. Only my exhaustion restrained me from smacking it off. "I expected you'd look different, you know, as a goddess," he said.

Ivan chuckled, patting him on the back. "Much will change for Lady Otylia when she Ascends." I furrowed my brow at that, but he held up a hand. "Worry not, my goddess. I promised you answers, and now, you shall have them. So, ask away."

"I..." My voice caught. *Where do I start?* With Weles's riddles and secrets, I knew so little about what Ascension actually entailed. So, I dodged the topic entirely. "How long have you been planning this? And Kuba, how are you even here so soon?"

"Sit," Ivan said, gesturing to a bed roll nearby. "This will be the area for the four of us, and I will remain awake as long as needed to satiate your appetite for the truth."

"Speaking of appetite..."

Sabina's eyes widened. "Oh, right! I'll fetch some food for you, La... Otylia!"

I laughed as she burst into the darkness, far quicker than I'd ever seen her move. *I don't deserve her.* For the first time in days, I let myself enjoy the laughter. Even my connection to Wacław had lightened in the time since the initial panic. An anger lingered in it, but it no longer seemed that he was suffering. I took that as a good sign.

Ivan cleared his throat, and we sat as his eyes fixed upon the moon. "Master Weles told me of his plans to bring you back many years ago, Lady Otylia. At that time, he had little hope of finding you, but when Lady Dziewanna returned to us, I knew he was drawing close. Your mother consulted with Vlatka, Kyustendil, and me in secret. She hoped you would never come here, but she entrusted us with helping you escape if you did."

"Why you?" I asked. "Why would Mother trust a witch and one of Weles's advisors?"

"She is a woman of her own volitions, and perhaps she saw the same in Vlatka. I, myself, have found much more in that witch than meets the eye."

"And you?"

The old king waved his hand, his fingers almost dancing as he did. "Let us say that I have questioned Weles's plans from time to time. Lady Dziewanna and I had our disagreements, yet I choose to believe she respected my willingness to temper Weles. I do not take her trust lightly." He sighed. "To trust is to make yourself vulnerable, but to succeed against Masters Weles and Jaryło, we must trust one another."

"You don't seem confident. Are these people all we have? Hardly an army to face a god as powerful as Weles."

Kuba shrugged and tossed a black stone through the fire. It skidded down the slope, snapping with each roll. "We'll get him anyway. No way I'm letting Jaryło rule Jawia after he killed you."

"Oh really?" I smirked. "What makes you think that?"

"Last time I checked, we took on Marzanna's cultists and won. Now, we've got witches, nymphs, and you—all with powers. We'll be invincible once Wacław shows up."

If.

Kuba scratched his chin, where patches of an unshaved beard had grown. "You asked about how I got here. Honestly, I don't get it. I followed Wacław and the rest of the group for a couple weeks, but after the Battle of Kynnytsia, I went ahead of them to home, to Maja." His gaze dropped to the fire. "I've missed her so much… I wanted to stay forever, but something dark attacked me. When I fell, I woke alongside the Smorodina."

The flaming river… I shuddered at the thought of the river that priests claimed lay between Jawia and Nawia. "Father never spoke of souls being forced to Nawia faster. If only the same would work for Wacław." I sighed. "Something's happened. We're... connected... and he was in agony. He's fine now, I think, but I'm worried about him."

"What if he doesn't come?" Kuba asked, looking to Ivan with his leg shaking. "The plan—"

"Has options," Ivan interrupted. "The presence of Wacław would simplify the escape, as his power would help us in the air in our defense and during the assault on the Heart of Nawia, but Kyustendil may be enough. The Ascension must happen regardless of the boy's arrival."

"What about these people during my Ascension?" I asked. "Kyustendil said Weles's warriors will know where I am once the ritual starts."

"That is true. Those here will fight to defend you once Weles's forces arrive. All of them—both nymphs and living souls—belong back in Jawia. Only Vlatka, Kuba, and I have met death."

I stood as Sabina returned to the firelight, smiling with a bowl of soup. "Tomorrow is the last day of Kwiecień," I said. "Is that really enough time for two sets of Trials and the Ascension? It's one thing if I get caught here by Jaryło's return. But I *can't* let all these souls and nymphs die because I wasn't fast enough."

"We know the risks," Sabina said. "For once, I can say it's worth it."

Ivan nodded. "It is indeed a risk. Completing the Trials in such quick succession is unheard of, but so is a goddess living among mortals for her first sixteen years. We had hoped to allow you more time. Unfortunately, Weles discovering much of our plan has made things more difficult."

Kuba grinned at me. "Don't worry. You'll Ascend and Wacław will come. Then we'll storm the Heart and get out of here! I can't wait to see Maja again."

If we all make it. But I forced myself to return the smile. His optimism, though often foolish, was welcomed after all I'd seen. "Then it's settled," I said, finally taking the bowl from Sabina. Its warmth warded away the chill of the night, if only for a moment.

"I hope we can do it…" she said, shaking. "It's…"

"Gutsy." Kuba popped to his feet and rubbed his hands together. "I like gutsy."

Ivan sighed but nodded himself. "I believe this to be a heavy burden for you to bear in one day, Lady Otylia, but I trust in you."

"Don't," I muttered. "I've lived sixteen years, not thousands. I wish we had more time too, but Weles might be too powerful already. With Jaryło, we'll have no chance."

"Then I shall ensure our allies are prepared," Ivan said, rising and walking toward the other fires before stopping for a moment. "Tomorrow will be a long day. Gods save us all."

45

Wacław

Did Dariusz betray me too?

I GRITTED MY TEETH and glared down at the six guards before the eastern gate. In the end, it didn't matter what Dariusz had done. If Mieczysław knew the truth, soon, the whole tribe would. No sense hiding from it now. Mieczysław would threaten me anyway, and I didn't intend to go into his longhouse unarmed.

"If you know I'm a demon," I replied, letting a snarl creep into my voice, "then you know I don't need blades to be dangerous. Let me through. The danger to Dwie Rzeki is gone. My mother is safe."

He jabbed his spear at me. "Get off the horse!"

The winds snapped at my command, rushing around me and throwing the guards back a dozen strides in each direction. It drained what little remained of Kwiecień's usable *żityje* but was enough to avoid bloodshed. As much as I hated Mieczysław, he wasn't my enemy. At least, not for now.

Tanek huffed as I pushed him into a canter. We burst down the trail toward Dariusz's cottage, but when I arrived and threw open the door, it was empty. Even my body had been moved, and rage flooded through me as I mounted once again and galloped toward the village center. *You picked the wrong day to get in my way, Mieczysław.*

People scrambled out of the way as I rode past with Kwiecień drawn, the tip of its blade just inches from the dirt at my side. They probably thought me something from a nightmare. A rider with veins of black, my dark cloak flapping behind me and a bloodied blade in hand. Maybe they were right. Everywhere I went, death followed, and with the demon gaining strength within me, it would only get worse.

The winds rushed through the bones hanging from Perun's Oak upon my arrival. There was power in them that I'd never sensed before, ancient. If only Perun bothered to do anything with his strength.

A crowd had gathered in the longhouse already. They moved aside as I stormed in, ready for a fight. Some part of me wished to avoid one. The demon's will was stronger. It fed on my resentment for the warchief—I let it.

"Mieczysław!" I pointed my blade toward the high chief, who gripped a battle ax and stared down at my physical body, laid on the long table. "Give me my body."

Dariusz emerged from the crowd. The torchlight cast a shadow over his face as he hung his head. "I'm sorry, Wacław. He thought we were conspiring against him."

Mieczysław scowled at me. "*What* are you?" he roared.

"I am a płanetnik—a demon of the wind," I replied, spurring gasps from the people tucked against the longhouse walls. They watched me in horror, but I didn't care what they thought. The entire village had mocked me for years. All that mattered was that they saw the true threat. "Though you are free to despise me for my power, I slayed the beast haunting our lands and saved my mother. The wilkołak bore Marzanna's Frostmark, High Chief. She lives past the equinox, and if you want our tribe to survive her wrath, you'll listen to me."

"Idiocy!" he shouted over the crowd's murmurs. "Jaryło has banished Marzanna as he always does."

I advanced without sheathing my blade. "You have no idea what I've seen. Marzanna has slaughtered innocent women and children, cut down our warriors and destroyed our chance to ally with the clans. She has captured Dziewanna and seeks to conquer Jawia. It was her curse that killed my father, but this is just the beginning."

Dariusz stepped to my side, his arms folded within his wide sleeves. "The boy speaks the truth, my high chief. The gods warn of such things, and the unfamiliar frost must have been her doing."

"You believe the lies of a demon?" Mieczysław shouted.

"*I* killed the wilkołak," I growled. The torches flickered around me as the winds swept through the hall. "I've fought every minute of the last two moons to protect our tribe. What have *you* done but march us into a useless war?"

Mieczysław slammed the butt of his ax into the ground. "Quiet! It does not matter that you defeated the demon when it was just to recover your mother."

Footsteps approached from behind me. "You're being stupid," a voice snapped.

My jaw dropped as Narcyz limped on with Andrij's help. Behind, Ara and Zakir flanked Mom as Sosna yapped at my side. "What are you doing here?" I hissed.

"I tried keeping Narcyz back," Andrij replied. "When we heard the commotion at the gate, though, he insisted."

The ironsmith's son wore his signature furrowed brow. For once, it wasn't directed at me. "Half-Chief's all we've got," Narcyz continued. "He killed that stupid demon Marzanna sent, but you'd rather point fingers at him? Gods, that's idiotic."

"He may have needed a little help along the way," Ara said, stepping to my other side with Zakir in tow, "but we have faced the same horrors as Wacław. We've seen what Marzanna's Frostmarked are doing in the east." She looked to me, smirking. "Maybe, when the gods are against us, we need a demon to fight back."

Sosna curled around my shin as Mieczysław scoffed. "You speak highly of your friend, but sentiment does not rule the tribe. I will have you exiled, demon."

My chest ached as the cheers of support echoed through the hall. *Exile?* Such a punishment was what I'd sought to save Otylia from for four years. Now, I faced it myself.

Andrij shook his head. "You need allies against Marzanna. King Boz used a demon of his own to attack the clans and those rebelling against his rule. You see the cloak I bear: that of a commander from the Tribe of Astiw. I come here now bearing a message more dire than when I arrived two moons ago: Marzanna's Frostmarked Horde is coming, and the clans have fallen. From warrior to warrior, I know you need everyone you can get—especially someone as powerful as Wacław."

I offered Andrij a nod as the crowd broke into a frenzy. Both villagers and warriors alike roared about the implication of Boz turning against us and demons being used in battle. It was deafening, and I saw the terror in their eyes. No matter what Mieczysław decided, this would no longer be home.

"Silence!" Mieczysław swung his ax over his shoulder and stomped toward me. "War has begun with the Solgawi, Wacław," he grumbled. "What would you have me do? Turn our forces east to face the Astiwie and this so-called Horde? Run to the aid of nomadic raiders who demanded entry to our lands?"

I stood my ground as he stopped before me. Gods, he'd once been threatening. Though I was taller than most, he met my height and more. But compared to me now, he was nothing. "I would have you make peace with Solga," I replied, brow furrowed. "What you do with me doesn't matter. My journey remains the same whether you exile me or not. All I ask, though, is that you spare my friends of any judgement."

"You do not care for your own fate?"

"I've faced Death's grasp and lost many to him in the last two moons," I replied, running my fingers along my arm's blackened veins. "He's failed to take me away, but I must go to Nawia willingly to bring back Otylia from Weles's palace. The god holds her hostage."

He raised his brow. "Why bring back this girl when you yourself say war is coming?"

I paced around Mieczysław, speaking to both him and the crowd. My heart burned and my mind spun, but the tribe needed to hear my voice. If only once. "Marzanna survives because she has captured Dziewanna. Though we've so often forgotten the goddess of the wilds, she is crucial for spring's thaw, and without her opposition, Marzanna's power will only grow. Otylia is the sole szeptucha of Dziewanna. We have reason to believe she is our only hope to find the goddess and free her from Marzanna's grasp, but to do so, I must reach Nawia by the end of the Kwiecień moon." I stopped before Dariusz and bowed my head out of show more than actual respect. "The high priest has a way."

Dariusz nodded. "Living demons have returned, and Marzanna has survived the equinox. Such occurrences threaten more than just our tribe. They stir chaos, shaking the foundations of the Three Realms. Therefore, the boy *will* travel to Nawia, and he *will* return with my daughter in order to face Marzanna when the time comes. Exiling him will accomplish nothing."

"Enough!" Mieczysław declared, his chin jutting out as he circled back to his throne. "I have decided." The crowd watched him with eager eyes and debated among themselves until he raised his fist. "You selected me as your high chief to defend this tribe against all threats: foreign and not. Demons are dark beasts, and it matters not that the one before us is Jacek's son. As long as he is within our lands, Wacław taints the ground he walks upon and poisons the air he breaths."

His glare fell upon me. "Because of your efforts today, I will not have you killed, but Wacław Lubiewicz, you are banished from the Tribe of Krowik. When Dadźbóg rises tomorrow morn, you will be gone from our lands or I will slay you myself."

Instantly, shouts for me to leave filled the hall. Some people threw wooden totems as they called for the gods to cast me out. Amid it all, I stood with the gales rising around me.

Why did I expect anything more?

The Krowikie had despised me from the moment of my birth. Dariusz had wished me dead, Natasza exiled. They had mocked me as the Half-Chief. Nobody. A failure who would never inherit his father's lands or amount to anything more than a farm boy beyond the woods. For two moons I'd toiled to save them. I'd fought demons, slayed a god, and negotiated with distant clans to bring them hope. Instead of chasing Otylia as quickly as I could, I'd stayed with the clans. And in return, all I'd earned was more scorn.

I'd had enough.

"No," my voice replied. It was raspy, as if someone else spoke through me, but satisfaction met me with that defiance. Cursed or not, I had been granted a power greater than Mieczysław could ever wield. Why would I bow to him?

He raised his ax. "No? Would you rather us kill you and your poor mother? The old concubine birthed you, so—"

"Shut up!" I shouted, rising into the air with *żityje* pulsing at my fingertips.

Before me, *he* was nothing. Like Father had been, Mieczysław was a weak mortal clinging to a blade and throne as if they gave him power. But he knew nothing of power. He hadn't channeled lightning, danced among the clouds, or sent a dagger through a god's heart. *I* held the Moonblade of Kwiecień. *I* had freed Dwie Rzeki of Marzanna's demon. *I* had lost everything for my tribe.

The winds tore through the open doors. Within them, I felt the high chief's breaths, quick as I surged toward him until I reached my body. *Żityje* lurked within his soul, maintaining his feeble life. It was just beyond my grasp…

I closed my fist before me.

People screamed as I grabbed hold of the air within Mieczysław's lungs. His death would be painful. Suffocation was a slow process. For a ruthless warlord like him, though, it would be a fitting end.

"Wacław!" Mom called from behind me. "This isn't you! Stop this, please!"

My friends' voices cried out too, but they were nothing. Anger and resentment ruled my shattered heart. Words could not fix such pain so easily.

Mieczysław dropped, clutching his throat as the chorus of voices begged me to stop, for me to show Mieczysław the mercy he'd denied me. Even Sosna's yapping couldn't stop the pounding in my head, though, demanding that I take his life. The demon fed on what remained of Kwiecień's *żityje*, its power coursing through me like a flood. Powerful. Dominant. Wicked.

And it felt good.

That sensation overruled my fear and sorrow. I was the storm, the lightning, the winds. No longer were they simply at my command. They breathed *through* me as one, and I understood now the true lure of the demon's soul. I wasn't a god. I wasn't creation.

I was Death's blade.

A hand caught mine as a small voice whispered, "Waci?"

I caught my breath in a gasp. Noise broke through the barrier my mind had formed. Everywhere I looked, chaos surrounded me as the winds carried a swirling darkness and pushed back all who tried to approach. All but Nevenka.

My little sister stared up at me with her big eyes, probably completely unaware of what I'd been seconds from doing. The tears forming in her eyes exposed her fear regardless.

With a sharp breath, I brought my arms to my chest and silenced the winds. They obeyed in an instant, leaving us in silence as I dropped to my knees and wept. Pain flooded through me. All the rage and pain I'd channeled hadn't left. It lingered like a festering wound—one the demon within me had used against me. *How long can I resist its call?*

"I'm all right, Nevenka," I whispered. "Run back to Natasza."

She nodded rapidly before skipping across the clearing to her mother, who watched me with her typical harsh gaze. *Even with Father gone, I can't escape your scorn.*

A roar echoed from the throne. Taking a deep breath, I rose to meet the red-faced high chief, his back curled like a wolf ready to strike. He'd called me a threat to the tribe. And as I stood before him under the gaze of the villagers who'd watched me grow, I came to a painful conclusion.

He was right.

Behind me, Dariusz muttered a prayer in the old tongue as Mieczysław lumbered forward. Blood trickled from the chief's chin. His hair was mangled, his bear cloak torn, but when he spoke, his voice boomed, "Get out of my lands before I regret letting you live!"

"I'm sorry…" I mumbled, looking from him to Mom's shocked face before I raised my voice for all to hear, "I will leave before sunrise. I will go to Nawia and bring Otylia back to the realm of the living. And then, I will leave our lands forever. You never wanted me anyway, so perhaps it's best you will finally be rid of me."

The shouting continued as I lifted my body from the table and rushed through the doors with my friends in tow. I wanted to vomit, to run, but I was both too numb and exhausted to do either. So I walked. My legs went without direction, yet there was only one possible place to go: home. Not that it would be home much longer.

"Wacław, wait!" Dariusz's voice called out behind me. I paid him no heed.

Rain poured as I neared the eastern gate. There, the warriors parted for me, not daring to get in my way again. *Good.*

A hand fell upon my shoulder as I neared our house. "Wacław, we must speak."

"Leave me," I said flatly.

Dariusz furrowed his brow, his deep red robes drifting in the breeze. "There is much to mourn today, but if there is any hope of avenging the dead and saving our tribe, we must act swiftly. Otylia awaits."

"I know!" I shouted, dropping my body against a tree before spinning to face him with lightning cracking at my fingers. Another dose of hatred burned within me at the sight of him. Dariusz had driven Otylia from me almost as much as Father, and if he'd had his way, I would've been dead upon my birth.

He staggered back in shock as my friends arrived with Mom. "You must control the demon…"

"I know she's waiting," I muttered. "I've counted every minute that she's been in Nawia, away from me and in Weles's grasp. For a moon, I have wished to rescue her, but I couldn't. The Simukie and

Zurgowie needed me. Then our people needed me. And what do I have to show for the weeks wasted helping them? Nothing but slaughter and exile!"

I screamed, loosing my rage as it swept away my sorrow. The winds whipped around me in a vortex of darkness. Lightning struck in the distance. I feared the demon within me feeding on my anger, but even now, aware of its presence, I let it take over.

"It doesn't matter what I do!" I growled. "I'm a demon, and death follows me."

"Calm yourself!" Dariusz demanded, pushing against the winds. "Gods, boy, stop this!"

A blow struck the back of my head.

The storm broke as I dropped to my knees, stunned and disoriented. At once, my anger dissipated and left nothing but a void of sorrow, dragging me to its depths. *What have I done? Why do I keep losing control?*

Narcyz grabbed my tunic and yelled something. To me, though, the words were meaningless, and I just stared up at him as he shook me. "I'll send you to Oblivion, Half-Chief, if you don't say something! You sent another one of your dark storms flooding over us!"

Gasping, I dug my fingers into the dirt as the world rushed back to me. *Not again…* My gaze dropped to my hands: one Frostmarked, the other streaked with veins of black.

Mom knelt before me with tears in her eyes. The others stood behind her, wary. "Wašek, say something, please," she pleaded.

"I'm here…" I whispered, my voice weak.

"And you're done trying to kill us?" Narcyz muttered.

Ara jabbed him in the side. "He meant to ask if you're all right."

I shook my head, forcing myself to breathe as Andrij grabbed my forearm and pulled me to my feet. "No," I said. "The demon's growing stronger. It helped me kill Bidaês and save Mom, but now…" I shook my head.

"You gave us quite the scare," Andrij said as he clasped my shoulders. "Seems you did the same to your high chief."

Zakir bowed his head. "You took his punishment for us. I will not forget such a thing."

"Mieczysław won't either," Dariusz added. "You've made all of our lives more difficult if we are to stop Marzanna."

"It doesn't matter. I'm exiled anyway," I replied before taking a deep sigh. "I appreciate all of you for standing by my side against Mieczysław. It's good to know I'm not alone."

Ara pulled me into a forceful hug. "We've fought together this long. An idiot warlord wanting to exile you won't change that."

"She's right," Mom said, her voice somehow calm despite all she'd seen. "It's not your fault that they can't see how much we need your help. Otylia will show them. They cannot deny a goddess."

Dariusz stepped forward. Before, I'd missed the priest's weakness, but I saw it now in the way he hobbled and the frailness of his breaths. "Wacław, I fear what you will become after what I have just seen. However, you are my daughter's only hope, so I will tell you all I know about the way to Nawia: Zorza Wieczorna."

My heart raced at that. Finally, after a moon of searching, I had an answer. "Dadźbóg's daughter?" Zorza Wieczorna was the goddess of the evening. The legends claimed she guarded the evening gate her father's sun took into Nawia each day as her twin guarded the morning one.

"Yes, her gate into Weles's realm lies far to the west. I know little more of its location, but if you leave in the morning, you should be able to reach Nawia before the end of the Kwiecień moon. Well, that is if you manage to convince Zorza Wieczorna to let you through."

I looked to the west. Such a flight would take me to the end of Jawia, alone, and I had no idea what that meant. "How?"

He shook his head. "I do not know. The evening aurora rarely takes szeptuchy, and those she has rarely speak of their goddess's intentions."

"Then I will do what I have to." My hand drifted to Kwiecień's pommel at my back. "I won't fail now."

"Do not harm my daughter," he replied, turning away. "Bring her home, but then leave her. You cannot flee what the blood moon made you."

I met his gaze as the demon stirred within me, defiant. "Maybe not, but I can give it quite the chase."

46

Otylia

Two moons ago, they called me a witch. Now, I'm to Ascend as a true goddess. What will they say then?

DADŹBÓG'S SUNLIGHT APPEARED TOO EARLY the next morning, demanding I wake. Not that I'd slept well.

My arm still throbbed from Wacław's pain, as did my heart. I stared at the smoldering embers of the fire and tried to think of anything else. I couldn't. Seeing Kuba last night had made me realize how much I missed my friends after a moon in Nawia. Though I'd been isolated for years, losing them—losing Wacław—had left me empty. I needed them.

Despite my determination, the Ascension and remaining Trials scared me more than I was willing to admit. None of the Trials had been enjoyable so far, so if these were last…

What could be worse than facing Death?

I shuddered at the thought. Then, I decided I'd had enough fearing what was to come. Difficult or not, I would pass them and Ascend. Wacław would arrive, and when he did, we would help the souls and nymphs escape to Jawia. It *would* work.

The frigid air met my skin as I ripped away my blanket and stood. That lingering chill confused me. Dadźbóg should've warmed the realms enough, even without Dziewanna and Jaryło, yet it was only getting colder. *One problem at a time.*

I had enough to figure out without the sun god making things worse. It didn't matter if my breaths fogged the air. Surely, gods didn't worry about such minor inconveniences, so neither would I.

"Ah, Lady Otylia," Ivan said, once again in his bear form. "I am pleased to see you are awake. The morning is young, but if you are to complete the four Trials in time, then we must be swift." With a wave to Sabina, he continued, "Once you have eaten, we can begin with the first pair."

Will and Destiny.

Wacław's mention of destiny alongside the Lake of Reflection came back to me as Sabina rushed forward with a bowl. Mind adrift, I took it. "Mokosz's divination rituals only showed me what *could* happen," I said. "Her teachings said the future can be molded and changed."

"Who am I to doubt the Great Mother?" Ivan replied.

I shook my head, looking to the volcano at the island's center, high above us. With the daylight, the crater at its peak was visible now, where more of the jagged black rocks coated its rim. "Then how can there be destiny?"

"That is an eternal question, is it not?" He chuckled and nodded down the slope. On the other side of the island, the nymphs and souls he'd introduced last night were heading our way. "Perhaps the Trials shall bring answers. Eat quickly. Then, we climb."

"We're going up there?" I asked, pointing to the volcano. "Why?"

With another hearty laugh, he rose onto his hind legs. "There is great power in the volcano. According to Vlatka, it will help begin the Trial."

Sabina clapped as the others, led by a beaming Kuba and fluting Kyustendil, arrived. I ate three spoonfuls of Sabina's stew and rose to greet them. *Gods, I probably look like a bleary-eyed child.* I hadn't even thought of braiding my hair.

"Is the lady ready for the journey up to the peak?" Kyustendil asked, lowering his flute. His attire was far more elaborate than the others: an open midnight blue coat lined in fringes of white with buttons of gold. A thin cape of the same deep blue fluttered behind him as he bowed. "I have been looking forward to this moment for quite some time."

Arms folded, I raised my brow. "Well, I would *hate* to keep Lord Kyustendil waiting."

He leaped into the air, and a tune, light and sweet, flowed from his flute as he spun above us. When he landed, he brushed some imaginary dust off his immaculate clothes and smiled. "As you should. More than one king has discovered what my wrath entails, and perhaps quite a few will learn of your own soon enough."

I scoffed, but before I could reply, Ivan cleared his throat. "Let us begin, Lady Otylia."

There was no trail to the volcano's peak. Though the nymphs could fly, the rest of us carved our own switchbacks into the steep slope, steadily making our way up its side. Behind me, Kuba rambled to the souls about our battles with Marzanna's cultists and how I'd slain a rusałka. I doubted that was impressive to the souls, some who had spent hundreds of years among the odd sorcery and power of Nawia. Kuba didn't seem to care.

With the hood of my cloak raised to ward off the winds, I led the journey in silence. To Kyustendil, Vlatka, and Ivan, this was a day of celebration and victory after years of planning for my arrival. They, however, didn't have to face the Trials. They hadn't seen Mother's withered body beneath Marzanna's dragon or floated at Oblivion's edge while the one they loved suffered.

No, what lay ahead wasn't a celebration. It was the start of a war.

Steam became visible above the volcano's rim as a warmth struck my skin. I stopped in shock. *What is this place?*

The march halted behind me, but Ivan walked past, grinning. "Enjoy the warmth of the volcano, Lady Otylia," he said. "You have yet to see the heart of its power."

Brow raised, I followed as he turned away, not waiting for a reply.

When reached the peak minutes later, Ivan stopped just strides from the rim and let out a sigh. "Perhaps it was not the best choice to have such heavy fur here."

Sweat dripped down my face from both the climb and the sweltering heat that now washed over us in waves. For only a moment, I missed the chill. Beyond my exhaustion, though, I sensed the power radiating from the volcano. It pulsed like a heart, and *žityje* swelled near it.

"Come," Ivan said as the others formed a circle around the rim.

I looked back at Sabina, who smiled and squeezed my hand. "I believe in you," she said.

Everyone seems to… except me.

My eyes watered from the steam as I climbed to the rim, but I joined Ivan and stared into the pit below. A pool of thick red goo bubbled near the surface. "What is this?" I asked.

"Master Weles calls it lava," Ivan said. "The heart of the volcano."

"What does this have to do with the Trials?"

The stones crunched behind me. "You must jump," Vlatka said, taking my side. "The fifth and sixth Trials are linked, and to conquer them, you must enter the volcano. Will and Destiny will greet you."

I took a sharp breath and shot her a glare. "Why are all the Trials insane?"

"Not sure," she said with a shrug, "but I am glad you're the goddess and not me."

"Thanks…"

Around us, our allies joined hands and began to chant. Vlatka stepped back, leading them in the old tongue, and when Ivan did the same, I forced away my fear. This wasn't my choice anymore. It was duty. To escape and save Mother, I couldn't fail.

I pulled my boots free, never taking my gaze from the lava. *Gods, I miss home.* The chanting swelled around me as I stepped to the edge with each sharp stone jabbing into my feet. *Is this destiny?*

I leaped.

Pain replaced the world the second I struck the lava. Despite being liquid, it was nothing like water. It swallowed me slowly, its intense heat burning its way up my legs for an eternity.

Don't scream, I commanded myself. *They need to know you're strong, that you're the goddess that can save them.*

But I couldn't fight it. Nothing could compare to the agony, and my scream pierced the air until the lava filled my mouth and destroyed my throat. For the first time, I wished for death. I wished to be released from the pain. Destiny demanded otherwise.

The deep blue sky disappeared as I slipped beneath the surface. Darkness followed—flowing like the great Krowik River.

Time.

I spun, suddenly free from the lava's grip. Mokosz had showed me time's current during my divination rituals. The sensation was familiar, reassuring, but those rituals had shown a possible future, not the only one. *Then what is destiny?*

"Mokosz?" I called into the river. "Great Mother, give me your sight! Show me what is to come and what is done."

When no answer came, I gritted my teeth and closed my eyes. Before, Mokosz's presence had surrounded me during the rituals. As warm as Mother's embrace. But I was alone now, and the current pulled me away.

A stream of colors rushed by, swirling like visions of their own. They split around my outstretched fingers and spun in a rainbow that shattered the darkness. Awe filled me. I'd never seen such a display, but in a flash, it all disappeared.

Light of the purest white hung before me. The current forced me toward it at an alarming rate. I flailed, grasping for anything to hold, but there was nothing.

From the light's center, a woman dressed in white robes appeared. Her hair was wavy and long at first, but it shifted along with her clothes and skin faster than I could comprehend. Pale with long robes of gold one moment. An earthen, flawless tan clad in leather armor the next. She was chaos—ever-changing amid the constant purity surrounding her—and I found myself caught in wonder as time's flow pushed me faster.

"Destiny can swallow you, child," she said. Each syllable was a different pitch and each word another tone. "The gods must bend her."

A blast struck me from behind as the river became a flood, sending me past the woman and into the darkness once again. *Bend her? What is that supposed to mean?*

I needed to know more from the woman. Unfortunately, time thought otherwise. It was relentless and unyielding as it dragged me toward some swirling vision ahead. The details weren't visible, but I didn't care. This had to be the Trial of Will, and I would not surrender to Destiny's demands.

Mokosz's lessons flashed through my mind as I fought. No matter how strong the future's pull, it could be altered. I had always looked to her and Dziewanna to determine my fate. But now, it was my turn.

"*Vęžeši*!" I shouted in the old tongue. Bind.

Reaching back to the woman, I tied myself to her. *Žityje* drained from my soul with the channeling, but it took far less than most spells, and the tether held against the current. For now.

As time's power battered me, I focused on my knowledge of the old tongue. Father had taught me much, but each lesson in Nawia had taught me *intent* mattered more than the exact phrase. Neither Weles nor Tibês had needed words for their sorcery. I wasn't so skilled.

"*Velci*!" I called as a voice whispered the right word in my mind. Pull.

The tether ripped through the current with a brutal force, dragging me toward the woman's now distant light. My stomach flipped at the jolt. I shut my eyes while the ethereal world spun around me. *Just make it stop!*

Suddenly, it did.

I yelped as the tether snapped the other direction. The impact would surely leave a bruise on my ribs. But before I could even groan, I felt a hand on my shoulder.

"Rise, young Otylia, for you have defied Destiny's call."

Before me, the tall, glowing woman smiled. Her appearance had settled now: her hair the auburn of the autumn leaves and her skin darker than the people of eastern clans. The contrast was striking. Beautiful in her perfect uniqueness.

"Who are you?" I asked as I stood with her help. Time's rush still pulled against me, but the tether between us remained, holding against its weight.

"The mortals call me many names, but to you, I am both Will and Destiny."

I furrowed my brow. "How can you be both?"

The ends of her mouth flicked up. "The girl who wishes to be both szeptucha and goddess wonders how I can be both Will and Destiny? Ironic. Yet, one of these things is possible. The other… Well, I believe you are competent enough to understand."

"You aren't two different people, or things." I stepped forward, analyzing her face. "Will and Destiny are the same."

"In a way," she said. "Go on."

"Will shapes Destiny. Mokosz always said the future can change based on our actions, but how can that alter fate? The Sudiczki…"

Wagging her finger, she paced around me. The tether held tight and forced me to follow. "The three Sudiczki—those you call the givers of fate—weave a child's story into that of the Three Realms upon their birth. The first two of these grant positive fortunes that bind the child's soul to love, to passions, to joys, and to health."

"Like a tether," I whispered. *Wašek…* Our first *žityje* ritual had exchanged fragments of our souls, joining us. But *something* had connected us before. "Wacław and I were born on the same day—me only hours before him. Was the bond between us the work of the Sudiczki?"

"This was the gift of the first: A bond to join both demon and goddess. Destiny made it so, but the Will of one strong enough can shatter such a fate."

"Gods?"

Her eyes narrowed. "Though easier than for mortals or demons, such a feat is difficult for even gods. Your mother did so when she separated you from Weles, and Jacek did the same when he forced away the mother of his son."

I lost my breath and stepped away. "What are you saying?"

"The balance of Destiny is fragile, and Will in its essence can alter it for good or ill. The actions of both your parents and the boy's have shaken the roots of the future. Destiny bound you to Wacław upon your birth, not because he was to be rejected like you but because he was to be the one to unite the tribes: Krowik, Astiw, Solga. All within the arc of Perun's Crown were to follow the immortal king, and you were to be his queen."

"But Jacek cast him out," I muttered, cursing the dead chief. My head throbbed already, but there was no time to think what this meant for my relationship with Wacław.

Destiny nodded. "Your union was to mend the divide between gods and the unsettled dead, and the joining of the tribes would create a front against the great Frostmarked Horde that now ravages the land. The high chief's actions ruined my plan. Thus, the third of the Sudiczki…"

"The hag." What Mother had called her at least.

"That is one such name for her," Destiny said with a chuckle. "Insults do little to mask the ill omens she casts upon children, and you were no different."

"What did she say?" I asked, desperation creeping into my voice. Wherever this was going, I didn't like the sound of it, but I *needed* to know.

"Corruption was to be your end, and her promise has not been altered. Even when Destiny's call changes, the Sudiczki's decisions merely shift and take new forms." She held out an open hand to me. "Despite those shifts, your bond with Wacław remained, as did your fate to become a queen."

My breaths weakened as I remembered Wacław's blackened veins. "He's going to make me his queen and then kill me? Great…"

"This is the burden of Destiny and the strength of Will. They may clash, but one can never destroy the other."

"But what about the second Sudiczka?" I asked with a huff. "The first bound me to Wacław and the third marked my death, but what was the second's gift?"

Destiny smiled as a new force pulled against me. There were so many more questions I had. How had my fate been changed? Was

Wacław's demonic corruption truly inevitable? I clung to my tether with her, shouting against the current, "Please! I need to know what this means!"

"The second foresaw the force you will wield upon Ascension. A gift, yes, but I pity you for it."

"What force?" My voice trembled. "What do you mean?"

Destiny waved a hand, and the tether snapped. "Destiny's call tempts many gods, but your Trial is to leave without every answer you require. For not even the gods truly understand my desires."

"No!"

Her light faded. I reached out, trying to grab a hold of *something*, but the force ripped me away. I broke through the swirling colors along time's river. My mind tilted on the edge of consciousness.

Then the pain returned.

Part 4
Love & Loss

47

Wacław

Come morning, I leave this world and join Otylia in the next.

THE WARMTH RETURNED TO OUR HOUSE as Mom insisted on preparing us a meal. In mere hours, she had died, been brought back to life, and seen my demonic rage consume me, yet she went on like we had just returned from our journey as expected. I knew her too well. Soon, I would be leaving her again, and that was the last thing she wanted to confront.

In my soul-form, I sat on my bed alongside my sleeping body while my friends talked. Even Narcyz seemed in a better mood despite the bandages wrapped around his stomach. He'd refused to see his parents after seeing their support for my exile, so he rested on Mom's bed and occasionally shouted his ideas across the small room. I hadn't the energy to respond myself. Staring at my feet, I pondered the state of my soul.

The smell of Mom's stew brought me back to reality. She slid a bowl into my hands, her knowing gaze telling me to eat it whether I wanted to or not.

I gave her a small smile before she served the others. Somehow, Mom always knew what I needed, and after two moons of traveling, I needed a home-cooked meal more than I'd known. The venison mixed with grains filled more than my stomach. It warmed my soul.

"You don't look dead anymore, Half-Chief." Narcyz chuckled, leaning against the wall as he slurped loudly from his own bowl. "You know, besides the black veins."

I set aside my bowl. I'd finished it in less than a minute, and though I starved for more, my friends deserved their share. They had faced the same horrors as me. "Thanks, but you should rest. Otylia said wounds from a demon heal slower."

"I'll be fine," he muttered with a wince. Ara shot him a glare, and he grumbled before sitting down on Mom's bed. "I don't care what it takes. I'm going to kill Marzanna."

Sosna yapped and sat between us with what seemed to be the fox's equivalent of a smile. "Only if Sosna doesn't beat you to it," Ara said.

Andrij paced, and Mom cast him a worried glance as the stew grew cold in his grasp. "We must avenge what's happened to both of our tribes, but to do that, we need a plan."

"We have one," I said, pushing myself to my feet. "Zorza Wieczorna's gate will get me to Nawia. With Kwiecień ending tomorrow, I'll barely have time to make it, and I doubt I'll have enough *żityje* to bring anyone else."

"So," Narcyz quipped, "you're throwing us in the ditch and running off to your lover, eh?"

"I'm not throwing anyone anywhere." I sighed, my mind still spinning hours after the conflict at the longhouse. "The last thing I want is to fly into Nawia, alone, with no idea what I'm facing, but there is no real alternative."

Andrij stopped pacing, holding his arms behind his back as he stood up straight. "Then what do you want from us?"

"I ask nothing more of you. You saved my life, Andrij, and if that isn't enough, then nothing more could ever be." I scanned the room. "All of you have done so much for me. I just wish I could repay you."

"Stop acting as if you've done nothing for us," Ara replied.

"Have I? None of you would be in this situation if it wasn't for me."

"We'd be dead," Zakir said. He lingered near the stove, his fingers drifting along its surface as he spoke. "Your arrival ended my old life. It also gifted me a new one. If my grandfather is truly dead, then I am to be marzban. There has been so much loss, but in your tongue, I believe you would say I am blessed to travel by your side."

Stop saying that.

Though I cast my eyes to the dirt, Ara held my free arm, softer than I expected. "Our clans are shattered, but seeing you face Bidaês showed me that *something* could go right. I don't care if you're a demon. If I hadn't followed you east, I'd be lost too."

Every word felt like a punch to my gut. Just hours after seeing me at my darkest, they praised me for failure. *How can I deserve them?*

"Listen to your friends, Wašek," Mom said as she collected the bowls. "Dark or not, your power gives us hope against Marzanna. Few people have the chance to change the world for the better, and I know you will."

"My demonic soul took over in the longhouse," I said, meeting each of their gazes. "It fueled my anger, and when I could have quelled its fire, I surrendered to it. There's this power…" My body shook with anticipation of that feeling. "Nothing can match it. Honestly, I'm afraid of what could become of me, but more than that, there's this *need* to wield it again. That rage… Without it, I'm empty, numb."

Narcyz narrowed his eyes. "I know this doesn't help, but if you're corrupted and Otylia's our only hope. What if you destroy her?"

My heart stopped. He'd echoed my fears. With each day, the demon within me became stronger, and that fact choked me as I dropped onto the bed, trembling. "I don't know…"

I loved Otylia more than anything. For years, I'd loved her like the world itself, but it was more now. Kuba was gone. Mom had barely survived. Marzanna threatened everyone I'd ever loved, yet all I could think of was my Otylka. Not revenge. Not my family. Not the fate of Jawia or the Three Realms. Her. I needed her touch. I needed that unyielding look in her striking green eyes. I needed her scoff when I did something foolish. But most of all, I needed that feeling that came only with her—that no matter what happened, she'd be by my side until the end.

That desire was selfish. I knew it was; it didn't matter anymore. In two moons, I'd gained immortality and immense power, but in return, everything had fallen apart. Otylia was my only hope of finding a way forward.

"I doubt even you're strong enough to kill her if you tried," Ara said, offering a weak smile. She knelt next to Narcyz and laid a hand on his back before whispering something I couldn't hear.

After a moment, Narcyz raised his head with a new look of determination in his eyes. "I'll take your mark."

My jaw dropped. "You just said I'll destroy Otylia. Now, you want to take my mark?"

He stood and held out his arm. "I'd rather take your mark than the witch's, and you're gonna need to keep in touch with us while you're down under. This is strategy, nothing more."

What in Oblivion did she tell him?

"A commander's decision," Zakir said, almost to himself. "Brave."

"We'll need warriors who've seen what Marzanna can do," Narcyz replied before looking to me again. "Just get it over with before I change my mind."

So I did. As lightning snapped to my palm with a passion, I calmed the demon—for now. My hand met Narcyz's arm, but despite the pain, he didn't so much as wince. He clenched his jaw, never breaking my gaze. I saw something new in his eyes. Two moons ago, he'd despised me. Now, he looked at me like a brother, and I found myself thinking the same of him. I fought with him as often as I did my actual brothers. Unlike them, though, I trusted Narcyz with my life.

He flexed his forearm when I finished. The eclipsed moon stained his skin black, and a burn encircled the mark. "Make me regret this and I'll kill you."

"I would expect nothing less," I said. "Unfortunately, I think tomorrow will be the first and last time I ever see Nawia's paradise."

"But it will not be the end," Andrij insisted as he watched the setting sun. "When the day ends, the night is long, but in time, the light returns."

Narcyz scoffed. "You listen too much to priests."

With a chuckle, Andrij shook his head. "And you, my friend, listen too much to warriors. It seems we might need more of those after today, though. Since the Krowikie have marched against the Solgawi, I suggest you and I go west to meet them. Someone needs to figure out a way to end this war before it escalates. Might as well be us."

"It's a good idea," Narcyz said. "Gods know I'm not going to sit here and let Marzanna kill our tribe."

"Zakir and I will take Sosna and head east, then," Ara said, sweeping to the Simuk's side. "Our clans are out there, somewhere."

Mom stood among them, silent with tears welling in her eyes. I stepped to her and wrapped her in my arms without a word. For sixteen years, I'd never left home for more than a day or two, and nothing I said could heal the pain I knew she felt without me. "I'll come home, *matka*," I whispered, fighting my own sorrow. "I promise."

"I know you will." Her voice cracked through her sobs as she stepped away and raised her hand to my cheek. "Bring her home too. I want to see you happy… That's all I've ever wanted."

"Promise me you'll stay within the walls for now? Marzanna won't stop, not after all I've done."

Ara stepped to my side. "My family will have a spare bed without me here. They'll let you stay if I ask."

Mom pursed her lips, forcing back a smile as she nodded and took Ara's hands. "You are too kind. It has been sixteen years since I lived within Dwie Rzeki's walls, but with Jacek gone, maybe it's time."

"Thank you," I added to Ara before turning to meet the gaze of each person in the room. "All of you… In times as dark as these, you give me hope for the future."

Narcyz nodded. "We'll make sure Jawia keeps itself together while you're gone."

I offered him a smile. "Then I will bring back our goddess. One way or another, we will face every threat Marzanna has and rescue Dziewanna from her grasp. I cannot claim horrors like we've seen will not happen again, but without us, they will never cease."

As a silence came over us, only the stone stove's low crackle filled the room until Andrij held aloft the flaming feather of the firebird. "There's no one else to do it, so it has to be us. We're that light at the dawn. For now, we are few, but we've just begun. Together, we're going to end this winter, and when spring comes, it will be us who bask in its glory."

Agony consumed me that night, tormenting my physical body as I lay in my old bed alongside Sosna. From the moment I'd surrendered my soul-form, the aches of the fights had hit me, but this was far worse. A fire surged through my connection with Otylia. While she suffered, nothing else mattered.

I stifled my sobs while the others slept. Though Ara and Narcyz could've returned home, no one wanted to leave the group after what we'd seen. Mom rested in her bed while my friends filled the floor with their bedrolls. Despite the pain, I grinned at Zakir sleeping by Ara's side as Narcyz and Andrij slept with one hand on their weapons.

Is it the Trials? I tried to ask Otylia. Like usual, though, no reply came.

The searing pain escalated until it covered me from head to toe and my only defense was to hold my breath and stare at the ceiling. Closing my eyes would take away the only other sensation I had. With the stove's flickering casting shadows across the room, I imagined them to be warriors and creatures—just as I had for years as a dreamless child.

But the futile distraction couldn't match my pain, my fear. *I can't lose her too.*

I flung off my blanket and snuck to the door. Fire stung my feet with each step, but I gritted my teeth as Sosna followed me out of the warm cottage.

Outside, the trees creaked beneath the weight of the night gales and trickling rain. The winds weren't under my command while I was in my physical body, but I extended my arms, embracing their powers. Their cool touch against my skin tamed the flames for a moment, no more.

Those flashes were when I was connected most to Otylia. Be it pain, passion, or rage, the more intense her feelings, the closer I felt to her. In a way, even the worst of it was better than isolation. I knew that was childish, but I needed her. Even if all I experienced was her hurt.

When the agony slipped away, only my sorrow remained.

A shiver trickled down my spine with each drop of frigid rain that slipped beneath my tunic. The drizzle slowly soaked my hair, and it clung to my face as I sauntered to the pasture.

Cold. Dull.

The muck sloshed underfoot when I leaped the fence. My sore legs complained, but I hadn't the energy to care. I'd come far too close to losing Mom. She'd given everything to protect me as a baby, and now, I had saved her. What had it cost?

I stopped, staring at my boots. *What would Otylia say? Xobas?*

My breaths fogged the air as I flexed and clenched my hands. Otylia would've called those doubts foolish. Xobas would've told me to fight on for those who'd died, to rescue Otylia and do what must be done to stop Marzanna. *I miss them…*

A huff came from ahead, and I chuckled as Tanek dropped his head onto my shoulder. His weight threw me off balance. The distraction was welcomed, however, and I rubbed his neck. "I'm sorry to only stay a day," I whispered. "To swoop in on the winds and disappear as quick."

Carelessly, Tanek swung his neck, knocking me to the ground as he paced around the pasture. I winced and lay back in the mud. Mom would scold me for dirtying my tunic, but it didn't matter anymore. None of it did.

I cried for what felt like hours, my tears joining with the trickling rain. Every time I closed my eyes, I saw the life leaving Mom's eyes. The entire village screamed in my mind as Mieczysław commanded my exile. And the demon's rage… Gods, how close had I come to losing to its call forever?

A void engulfed my chest and sucked my heart dry. Soon, even my sorrow faded, and I just stared up at the clouded night sky.

What am I fighting for?

There had been a time the answer was obvious: my tribe and my family. Now, though, I'd been banished from my tribe, never to see my family again. I had done all I could to bring the clans to reinforce the Krowikie warriors. It hadn't been enough. Our alliance with the clans was doomed, and likely, so was our imminent defense against the Frostmarked Horde. As I lay in that pasture, I found myself not caring anymore.

To the tribe, I had become nothing more than a demon. It didn't matter that I had saved them from Eryk's blizzards and Bidaês's attacks. Only a few people remained who bothered to see beyond my blackened veins and Frostmarked palm, and wretched Mieczysław was high chief now.

All that mattered now were my family, friends, and the girl I couldn't get out of my mind. Those friends had fought and journeyed by my side. None of them deserved the suffering they had experienced over the past two moons, yet they refused to abandon me—even now. Despite my exile, I would do what I could to protect the innocents within the arc of Perun's Crown because I knew it was right. For those I loved, though, I would sacrifice everything.

A force snapped through the air.

The void in my chest vanished as I pushed myself to my feet, scanning the dark forest. Across the pasture, Tanek startled and trotted to my side. I wished I'd been in my soul-form. Without the winds, I drew Kwiecień and the Thunderstone dagger, ready for a strike.

This sensation, though… It was different. It felt *right*, as if part of my shattered soul had been pieced back together.

Softly, the force pulled me from the pasture and across the trail.

My legs, stumbling and heavy, followed until I reached the tree line, where a wet and matted Sosna waited. The cool winds blew through my overgrown hair. I closed my eyes, remembering my excitement four years before, when I'd followed Otylia into the woods at that exact spot.

A warmth rushed across my skin. *It's her…*

The feeling in my soul, the tether pulling me to the woods—it *had* to be Otylia guiding me. But how? Had she escaped Nawia?

Sosna yapped at me and took off. Despite the aches and fatigue holding me back, I sheathed my weapons and sprinted after her with my heart racing. I needed to see Otylia, to hold her in my arms and know that when all else crumbled around me, something was right in the Three Realms.

In the years since Otylia's first use of her goddess powers to save me, I had never returned to the place of the wolf attack. There had been too much pain. The path had been engraved in my mind, however, and with each stride, I left those regrets behind. Forever, they would linger with the remains of my old life.

The moon's faint glow split through the trees when I reached the clearing.

Once, Otylia had twirled and called for me to dance in that spot. It had been a few rare moments of pure joy before the wolves ruined everything.

Four years later, she now stood in that same place with a silent grin as Sosna ran to her side. She looked just like the girl I'd lost a moon before, wearing a simple dress of gray and a wide belt that hugged her torso. Now, though, her skin pulsed with an ethereal glow. No longer did a braid contain her hair, and it draped freely over her shoulders to her waist. And those eyes. Gods. They pierced my soul.

"It's reassuring to see you haven't changed," Otylia said, holding her hands before her. "Hesitant as always, my Wašek."

I rushed forward without a reply and took her in my arms. She smelled like a soft autumn rain shower—a pleasant release from the stench of blood, sweat, and death.

"I missed you too," she whispered. "I'm glad Sosna's kept you safe." The fox yapped at her name and rubbed her face against Otylia's leg. Otylia was tense, though, and she pulled away, meeting my gaze.

"How are you here?" I asked. "Did Mokosz—"

Her hands gripped mine, hard. "No, this wasn't the Great Mother's doing."

"Then how?" From both excitement and the run, my breaths were heavy, my voice weak. "Did you escape Nawia?"

"I wish I did…"

Her head dropped, and she held her hands to her chest. There was a fear in her eyes. Knowing her as I did, that was enough to scare me too. She paced away, the skirts of her dress drifting lightly behind her on the breeze.

When she stopped, still with her back to me, she continued, "The final Trials sent me here."

I stood in silence for a moment. Away from her, I felt cold, but following her didn't seem like the right choice. "The Trials of Ascension?" I asked. "If you're almost ready to Ascend, then you can escape Nawia. Dariusz told me a way to reach you. I'll pass through Zorza Wieczorna's evening gate tomorrow, and we can flee together!"

"It's not that simple," she replied, glancing over her shoulder.

"Nothing is anymore, but this one thing doesn't need to be." I stepped toward her. "Otylia, what's happened here… I need you. Bidaês killed Mom. Somehow, I channeled Kwiecień to bring her back, but the demon's growing stronger within me."

She turned to me with tears in her eyes. "You used a Moonblade? I don't know what this means, but I'm sorry, Wašek. I should've been there. Kuba warned me of evil here."

"Kuba?" My heart ached. "You've seen him?"

She nodded. "His soul followed you for a few weeks before coming to Dwie Rzeki. Apparently, when he arrived and saw Maja, some type of darkness drove him to Nawia before his forty days were up."

Suddenly, her voice cracked, and when she spun away again, I caught her arm. A cold armband made of wood and silver met my hand. "Otylka, what's wrong?" Tears stung my own eyes as I held her gaze. "Please, don't close yourself to me."

"I'm not!" she snapped. "I didn't want any of this. I didn't want to be a goddess. I didn't want to fall for a corrupted demon. I didn't want to be stuck in the underworld while everyone we know suffers."

I released her. "A demon…"

Scoffing, she rubbed her heal into the dirt. "You know what I meant."

"That you can't love me?" I growled. "That I'm some kind of inconvenience to the princess of Nawia?"

Silence hung between us. Those few strides felt like a mile as I studied her mournful face, and I cursed myself for yelling. Just a moment before, I'd told her to be open. Then I'd driven a blade into the gap.

"I'm sorry," I said, forcing down my anger. "This has been an awful day, but you didn't deserve that."

She looked to me as she clenched and unclenched her fists. "Tell me. What's Marzanna done?"

So I did. I told her everything that had happened since our meeting at the brink of Oblivion. It had been mere days, yet so much had changed. From channeling Kwiecień to wielding the dark winds in the longhouse and draining the trees near the Wyzra, I could hardly believe I'd done those things. Otylia had been thankful I hadn't changed. But I had. That frightened me.

By the end, I wanted to curl up in a ball beneath Otylia's heavy gaze. Her words had been passing, but they'd struck my fractured heart. To make things worse, the sentiment was right: I was a corrupted demon. My outbursts had proven that. When the demon's power attacked again, could I fight it with her by my side?

"You're right to be afraid," she said after a long silence, her voice hushed.

"About what?" I asked. "My soul?"

Taking my frostbitten hand, she traced the blackened veins up my arm. Her fingers shook. "Destiny herself told me your demonic soul will take you and then me. I thought we could choose our own path, but even gods can't outrun the Sudiczki."

The fates? I knew little of them besides the tales told to children. "Our choices are our own," I replied as I held her cheek in my free hand. "Neither Death nor Destiny can define who we are. This darkness within me… I will fight it, no matter what Marzanna believes. I promise, Otylka, that I would never do anything to hurt you."

"I know," she whispered as a tear slipped down her face, tracing the crescent scar. "And I love you for that."

"You… You love me?" Joy rose within me. I wept, holding my head to hers. "I feared you didn't, that this *thing* inside me would destroy whatever we have."

She trembled against me, her words rattled. "I do. I love you, Wašek. That's why the final Trials brought me here…"

Stepping away, she placed her hand against my chest, glowing as it rose and fell with my breaths. No, it hadn't been fear in her eyes but terror. The only time I'd seen her like this had been after Dziewanna had revealed the truth to her. She couldn't even meet my gaze.

"Love is what makes this so hard," she breathed.

"Tell me," I said as I laid my hand upon hers. "What do the Trials mean?"

She stared into the darkness, away from me. "We have a group of nymphs and souls seeking freedom from Weles. It's small, but when you arrive, we will lead them to the heart of Nawia and freedom. To succeed, however, I need to Ascend before Jaryło recovers."

Why won't you tell me? I wanted to comfort her, to tell her that it would be all right. By her shaking, though, she knew something I didn't. "Then we'll free them," I spoke softly and studied her. That crescent scar still graced her cheek, but now, it shone silver against her pale skin. When she finally looked at me, her green eyes split the night.

"You don't know what I'm asking you to do."

"Then tell me."

She took a sharp breath. "Your mortal soul must die if I'm to

Ascend."

My heart hammered my chest as I shuddered. "Why? What will that do to me?"

"We both know what it'll do." Still shaking, she pulled me so close I could feel her warm breaths against my neck. "These are the final Trials: Love and Loss. A god must fall in love—"

"And then kill the one they love," I finished. The realization shocked me. Though I knew my demonic soul would take over in time, for it to happen so soon…

"Most cheat the Trial," she continued, "granting their loved-one's soul a comfortable afterlife alongside them in Prawia or Nawia. But, obviously, we can't do that. Wašek, I won't force you into this."

"You don't have to."

Sliding her hands into mine, she stepped back. Tears coated her cheeks. "Why? Wašek, you'll lose your humanity…"

"That doesn't matter."

"Yes, it does!"

My fear faded as I ran my fingertips along her silver and wood armband. This *had* to happen. A determination as strong as iron filled my heart, and for once, I knew what to do. No hesitation. No regret. This was what I was to become, whether tonight or in a decade, and I wouldn't stand in the way of what Otylia must become too. In our souls, we were bound as demon and goddess. Our choices were ours. Nothing, though, could ever change *what* we were.

"I've seen the craving of demons and felt it in my soul," I said. "I've eaten the hearts of dead animals to absorb their *żityje*. It would have come slowly, but I'm making this choice. Destiny demands my human soul. Well, send her to Oblivion, I'll give it to you instead, Otylka."

She shook her head, but I held her waist as tears coated my cheeks, merging with the rain. "My tribe has banished me," I continued. "My hope of defeating the Frostmarked is crumbling. But I have you. Gods, I have *you*! Whether I'm mortal or demon doesn't matter anymore. The life I've known is destroyed, but I'm not finished. I will follow you to the depths of the Three Realms and against Marzanna's Frostmarked. I'll stand by you for eternity if that's what it takes, and I promise… I swear to you… I will send myself to Oblivion before I ever corrupt you."

Wrinkling her nose, she clenched her fists against her chest. I chuckled through my sobs. *Why can she be adorable even now?*

"Do what must be done," I said, raising her hand to my chest again. "Take my soul, and when the dawn comes, I will find you."

She furrowed her brow. "I know you're lying to make this easier. What's coming can't be defeated by you loving me. You'll have to constantly drain *żityje* from living things, or from me, and the power will tempt you."

"Then I'll take your mark," I insisted. "Once you Ascend, you'll have the power to claim demons, creatures, and people under your power. If I ever stray, that mark will let you end me."

"I don't want that power."

"And I don't want to be a demon."

She held my gaze, her eyes sharp, but I wouldn't back down. For us to defeat Marzanna and rescue the goddesses of spring, Otylia had to Ascend.

Her hand pressed against my chest. "I'm sorry."

The impact threw me across the clearing. I crashed into a tree, and my back spasmed as a haze clouded my vision.

"Wašek!" I heard Otylia cry.

When I opened my mouth to reply, no sound came. Sosna rushed to me, whimpering as I raised my hand and felt the winds at my fingers. *My soul-form.* A pain struck my heart, my vision clearing.

Otylia knelt with my physical body cradled in her arms. Beneath the moonlight, her glow seemed to fade as she wept. "I'm sorry…"

"Otylia!" My legs were weak and my mind spinning, but I stumbled toward her. "Otylka, it's okay."

She laid my body onto the ground before looking at me like a wounded animal. "I… I *felt* you die. It was like my soul had been torn from my body. How are you fine with that?"

Am I fine?

I closed my eyes and sensed the *žityje* within me. Unlike before, there was only one pool of it, and a pulse hammered my mind. The pain grew with every second. The winds escalated and screamed around me as voices hissed in my head. They begged to be released, to feed on my anger, my sorrow. I fought it at first, but it dragged me deeper. "Stop!" I shouted as I dropped to my knees, clutching my head.

Otylia called out for me. Her voice was distant, though, as the winds drowned out both light and sound.

"What's happening to me?" I yelled.

"It's your demonic soul!" she replied, her voice piercing the winds. "You need to control it. Don't let it use your emotions."

I dug my fingers into the earth. Each breath was a battle, every thought a war. *This* was the power that had lurked in my soul, waiting to be released. I'd believed I'd felt the worst of its attacks—how wrong I'd been. But it wasn't just a part of me now. My demonic soul was all that remained, and its power was mine.

The dark storm grew as anger swelled within me. It was intoxicating, wonderful. As the black veins devoured my skin, I drank of the demonic force. "You won't control me," I whispered, reaching for Mokosz and Dziewanna's amulets, still hanging at my collar. The Great Mother's was as warm as it had been when Mom had gifted it to me at our journey's beginning. She'd trusted the gods until the end. Could I?

"You won't control me!" I screamed.

I extended my arms, closing my fists and ordering the winds to calm. They did in an instant, and the voices died with their screams. *Žityje* fled me. I dropped to my knees once again, breathless.

When I raised my gaze, Otylia was gone. She'd completed the Trials, and all that lingered of her was that pain in her heart. "She loves me," I whispered to myself.

The words came out as little more than a sob, but they meant everything as Sosna nudged my side. Otylia loved me. Though it changed nothing of the suffering I'd endured, a part of me felt whole. What I would've done for another moment…

No more time to waste, I told myself. *You won't sleep tonight anyway. Refill your życie and go west. She's waiting.*

The forest pulsed around me as Sosna yapped and nudged my calf. Despite Dziewanna's capture, trees clung to life against Marzanna's chill. I closed my eyes and reached for it, taking much of the *życie* from each until my soul had been replenished. The forest would survive, weakened.

Once, I would've felt guilt for draining the woods that had offered our tribe shelter for hundreds of years. This clearing, though, had tried to take my life once. Four years later, it had succeeded, becoming not a place of freedom and adventure but one of death. Letting the trees surrounding it live at all was mercy.

I stepped to the center of the clearing, where my still warm body lay. *Some wander for forty days when they die. I'm trapped for eternity.*

Lightning snapped at my fingers as I knelt alongside the corpse. The winds hummed overhead, as if voicing their approval, and I drove my hand into its chest. Flesh burned, filling the air with a harsh scent as my body turned to ash and joined with the earth. When I pulled away, my mark remained singed in the dirt.

It would be all that remained of me in Dwie Rzeki.

48

Otylia

What monster have I created?

THE AIR STUNG MY SKIN as I burst from the waters, sputtering and gasping.

When the volcano had released me at the end of Destiny's Trial, Ivan had guided me to the furthest shores of the island. I didn't understand the significance of the locations, but he and Vlatka had insisted. So, I'd dove into the depths, somehow breaking through the orange tide's ability to hold me up.

Everything after had gone far worse.

Why couldn't I admit Destiny's truth to him? The Sudiczki had bound me to him from our births. Somehow, I'd admitted I loved him yet had failed to reveal that. Why?

I shook my head. It didn't matter why. I'd finished the Trials and could Ascend. Despite my emotions shifting like a spring storm, I actually felt *good* about telling Wacław I loved him. If only the shock of his human soul's death hadn't ruined it.

"Lady Otylia!" Sabina called out, flying over the waters and to me in the shallows. "Are you well?"

"Well?" I scoffed. "I had to kill Wacław. What do you think?"

She blushed, holding her hands before her. "My apologies… I meant…"

I shook my head. "It's fine. Let's get back to shore."

Undeterred by the water, she pulled me into the air until I could stand upon the surface. It made little sense to me that I could dive through the sea one minute and walk on it the next. *Nawia, the realm of chaos and change.* When even water didn't make sense, what was I supposed to do?

The gathered crowd cheered when I shivered and stepped onto the black rocks. They cut into my feet, but I barely noticed. I couldn't get the image of the life leaving Wacław's eyes out of my head. The pain…

He's alive, I reminded myself.

That wasn't enough. Yes, Wacław was alive, but there would be a cost to this—one we would both pay in time. When the force had thrown him into his soul-form, I'd seen the darkness consuming him. I cursed the ritual for tearing me away so soon.

"It is done?" Ivan asked, offering me a paw.

I didn't take it. "Yes."

"Hmm. Very well." He held his paws behind his back and led the way up the slope. "You have finished the Trials, Lady Otylia, and can now Ascend. Yet, I fear you mourn the boy's mortal soul."

"You should be more afraid if I didn't." I held my arm across my body, clutching the armband. "I hate that he just *let* me do it. Why didn't he fight?"

Kuba huffed from beside me. "Because he's Wacław. You really think he wouldn't sacrifice himself for his friends—for you?"

I shuddered at the thought of his offer to take my mark. He was my… whatever one called a goddess and a demon couple. Unlike most, I'd thought little of what I wanted a relationship to be like, but it wasn't that. Romance was foreign enough to me. Having the ability to manipulate him would only make it so much worse. Especially because I could *feel* everything he did.

Do most girls have to worry about their boys being demons who are destined to corrupt them? Or is that just me? Ara would've had a joke about that, but she was back in Dwie Rzeki. Suddenly, I felt selfish having not thought of her more often.

"He's suffered enough," I replied as my chest throbbed. The pain from our connection was still fresh, or had it never stopped? "His mother nearly died. I don't know how, but he channeled Kwiecień's power to save her. The Moonblades are said to only respond to a god's call."

"Why's that a problem?" Kuba asked.

Because the boy I love will kill me. Not willing to give the truth, I bit my cheek and turned away. "I don't know, but it probably has something to do with his demonic soul taking over."

He just shrugged. "Wacław's strong. He'd never do anything to hurt us."

With that, he joined the others near the base of the volcano. I watched him go before looking to the sun as it ascended into Jawia. The Kwiecień moon would end when it returned, and Wacław would arrive in our night with only a sliver of the crescent remaining. Then, it was a race to the Heart of Nawia before dawn.

So much in so little time.

I clenched my fists. Little time or not, we *would* escape. Nawia had trapped me within its shifting maze for too long. Until I returned to Jawia, I was useless to Mother. So be it if I was her only hope. I wouldn't fail.

49

Wacław

No demon has ever seen Nawia's paradise. None until today.

"You might be a demon, Half-Chief," Narcyz muttered, rubbing his eyes, "but I thought zmory were the nightmares."

It was at least two hours before dawn, but I couldn't wait any longer. Every minute spent in Jawia was one wasted helping Otylia escape. She had to be free from Weles's grasp, no matter how much agony consumed me.

"A couple hours of beauty sleep wouldn't have done much for you," Ara quipped. She lingered by the warmth of the stove in the cottage's corner as Mom nervously boiled water for a soup. "Besides, there's not many girls left to impress."

Andrij was already pacing, his blue Astiwie cloak sweeping behind him. "As fun as it is to discuss sleep, we should address the obvious problem…"

"Little late for that," Narcyz said.

Zakir stood in the corner, his hands clasped before him as the candlelight faltered at the tip of his nose. He hadn't stopped watching me since I'd woken him. "It was an inevitability. From what we've observed of other demons, and of my brother, the demonic soul is stronger."

"This means Otylia's ready to Ascend, then?" Ara asked.

I nodded from my seat along my bed's edge. My head still spun from my soul's death, but talking about plans was a welcomed distraction. "As far as I know, Love and Loss were the final trials. Now, I just need to get to Nawia and help protect her from Weles during the ritual."

"Leaving now is the best tactical decision," Andrij said. "The closer we get to the Maj moon, the closer Jaryło gets to a full recovery. That Moonblade will ruin everything, so I couldn't care less about you waking us early." He stopped before me and rested a hand on my shoulder. "You've given me a chance to truly do something *good* for once. I won't fail here. When you return, hopefully we will have brought the clans and your chiefs together."

"Pah!" Narcyz spat. "Our chiefs are like I was before. Nothing matters to them but the war with the Solgawi."

Ara smiled. "Like you *were*. Glad to see you've changed your mind about something."

He scowled. "There's nothing okay about any of this, but it's not like we have a choice. Otylia needed Half-Chief to 'die' to Ascend. And we need her to skewer Marzanna for trying to kill our tribe." He glanced in my direction. "I still think that demonic soul of yours is gonna get all of us in the end. Just make sure you get Marzanna first."

"That's my intention—except the killing you part of it," I replied as I examined my veins. "At this point, I doubt I'll ever get rid of these."

A *thud* came from the corner as Mom dropped the pot of water. She reached down to pick it up, but I got there first, setting it on the table with a reassuring smile. "It'll be okay, Mom. If everything goes right, I might not be gone for long."

With a shaky breath, she held her hand to the warm stone of the stove. "I worry for you."

"I know." I stepped toward her and held the Mothermark amulet she'd given me when we'd first left. "Through Mokosz, you're always with me."

Tears streamed down her face as she pulled me into a hug. I held her tight, hating that I had to leave so quickly, but Otylia needed me.

Andrij returned to his pacing. "We need to prove to the people that there *are* real threats out there. Especially if you're the kind of demon that's willing to help them, that creates quite the image of one who won't."

"And Otylia?" Ara asked, crossing her arms. "You want to just tell everyone she's a goddess?"

"When the day's up," I said as I stood at the room's center, "she'll have Ascended anyway. Marzanna already knows. She'll use it against us if we leave our allies in the dark—no matter how untrustworthy they are."

Andrij stopped with a sharp nod. "Then it's decided."

"Fine, *commander*," Narcyz quipped.

"We may not trust your high chief," Zakir said, stepping to Ara's side, "but we must prove ourselves to be trustworthy."

I offered him a smile. It felt good to smile, despite my aching soul. "Well said."

Everyone was quiet as we delayed my unavoidable departure. Saying goodbye to them after the journeys we'd taken was more difficult than I'd expected. I may have been the one with the powers, but I needed them as much as they needed me. Maybe more.

Andrij was the first to step to me, grabbing my forearm as I did the same to him. "I look forward to meeting this goddess of ours upon your return."

"Please," Ara said, her eyes showing her pain, "bring her back. Then you and I are going to talk about how to treat my best friend."

We both forced a laugh.

"That's more frightening than a zmora," I replied before looking to Zakir. "Marzban Zakir of Clan Simuk, I promise we will do what we can to find the remnants of your people. Thank you for being here to help mine."

With a slight bow, he recited a Simukie farewell in the clans' tongue, "May your ride be swift."

"And Narcyz," I continued, turning to face him. "Show the warriors how to be brave against Marzanna's beasts. They're going to need it."

He laughed and punched my shoulder. "Don't die—again. We'll need you around here, Wacław."

I raised my brow at his use of my name, but his stern gaze told me not to mention it. So, I gave a quick nod and grabbed my wool coat before patting Sosna's head. "Keep them safe and out of trouble. Narcyz, especially, could use help with the last bit."

The ball of fur nuzzled my hand and whimpered. Somehow, that struck my heart once more, but I swallowed my sobs. *You'll see them soon.*

When Mom embraced me one last time, though, I let a few stray tears out. Even with the demon's will driving me on toward Otylia, I clung to that moment with her. I knew how much she needed it. Mom was strong, but after Father's death, I was all she had left. I promised myself I'd never leave her.

"I love you, Wašek," she whispered. "Always remember that."

"I love you too, *matka*." I kissed her on the cheek before stepping into the open air.

Tanek huffed as I passed the pasture. I wished to take him with me, but no horse could reach evening gate in the west. Without a complete idea of how far that was, I didn't know if even *I* could. Still, I'd miss my old friend. Even if he was just a horse.

Arms extended, I called for the winds at the trail's edge. They swept under me, and seconds later, I soared above the trees.

Zorza Wieczorna, goddess of dusk, here I come.

The stars seemed no closer as I climbed. Each soul on Jawia offered a glimmer in the night sky, and I prayed to whatever gods would listen that Mom's would remain there for a long time. It was the least she deserved.

I flew faster, driven on by the sight of Otylia only hours before. Despite the awkward nature of the conversation, things felt *right* with her. She loved me, and I her. My yearning to reunite with her was stronger than my demonic cravings for power and my desire to avenge Mom combined. Marzanna could take everything from me. As long as Otylia lived, so did I.

Žityje burned within me with the speed, but my soul had never held so much of it. The forest's weakness would give me the strength to save it in the end. I hoped. Against Weles, I would need every bit of it.

Time seemed alien as I flew over the lands of the Solgawi. Soon, though, the first rays of Dadźbóg's light appeared on the horizon behind me.

I flipped around and watched the sunrise. Flying blind felt odd, but there was nothing for me to run into this high, and the beauty of the golds and reds cascading across the clouds was unmatched. A shiver ran down my spine as the world ascended from darkness. The winds sensed something, but when I spun, trying to figure out who or what the presence was, there was nothing. Just clouds and miles of air.

"You are oddly oblivious for a demon, child," a soft voice giggled from beside me.

I yelped, dropping straight down before catching myself on the winds. The figure was obvious now as I followed the voice.

A young woman with flowing golden hair crowned with blueberries danced on the gales. She wore a simple light blue dress of loose fabric. Unlike most dresses in our tribe, its skirt was split down the center, revealing the trousers she wore beneath. Her limbs seemed one with the air as they flowed into nothing near their ends.

"Who are you?" I asked.

Smirking, the woman glided beside me, always facing east. "I am the kindest of my brothers and sisters. When they come with storms, bitter cold, or striking heat, I bring the gentle rains and breezes of the west."

"Dogoda!" I exclaimed. Both Eryk and Cervenko had spoken of her as the most helpful of the winds, and our tribe honored her throughout the year for her help with the crops. "Cervenko said you would know more about the way to Nawia. Do you know where Zorza Wieczorna's evening gate is?"

"Oh, brother, why must your words be as wild as your spirit?" She shook her head. "Such a thing should never be told to a demon. Grandfather Strzybóg has his rules."

"Please, I must reach Nawia before the new moon! If I don't, you'll be helping Marzanna."

She raised her face to the sun, enjoying its warmth. "Marzanna has had quite the fascination with manipulating my brothers and I in recent moons. As have you, however."

My cheeks burned, and she giggled again, holding her hand to her mouth. "You are much different than the others like you," she said. "I see why our newest goddess chose you."

"How…"

"The winds know much," she interrupted. "Though we cannot hear all, among the eight of us, there are few secrets. Kyustendil, my northwestern brother, is a member of the party protecting Otylia in Nawia. He is an odd one, yet I believe his intentions are true with her."

I tried to imagine a wind trapped in Nawia. "How is Weles keeping him there?"

Sorrow crossed her face as she sighed. "Kyustendil has sought to escape through Zorza Poranna's morning gate many times, but Weles stopped him. The morning gate is the only path out of Nawia not under Weles's control, so he watches it closely. Well, not the *only* path. No one would dare take that, though."

"There's another way out?"

"You ask many questions." Glancing to each side, she held a finger to her lips. "I will answer. I should not do so, but I have watched you these past moons. Few demons would risk themselves for innocents as you have."

The screams of the dying echoed in my mind—first from Bustelintin, then from the clan. "Not that it mattered."

"It matters more than you know. That is not the topic, however…" She tapped her chin. "There are three connections between the lower and middle realms: the morning and evening gates, the roots of the World Tree, and the Way of Souls."

"Is that the path that dead souls follow?"

"Indeed. In Nawia's ever-changing landscape, though, it is hidden. Souls are meant to travel through it from Jawia, but never the other direction. There are many protections to ensure souls do not tarry or attempt to flee back to Jawia."

My eyes widened. Our plan was to take the roots of the World Tree, but even the priests knew little about this Way of Souls. "So, it *is* a route out of Nawia," I said. "For those desperate enough to do so."

Dogoda shrugged. "To attempt such an escape is an invitation to Oblivion. I will tell you no more about it, demon. Nawia is no place for you, and certainly, neither is the Way of Souls."

"But you will tell me the location of the evening gate?" I asked.

To that, she smiled and turned to face west. The sun shone on her golden hair as she pointed to the southwest. "Perun's Crown ends with Solga, but the sea is not for another thousand miles. A cluster of islands rests far from shore, encircling the gate from a distance. This is where you will find Zorza Wieczorna's gate. It is unlikely, though, that she will allow you to pass easily."

"Unfortunately, nothing has been easy in the past two moons." I sighed and looked over the Solgawi lands, continuing to stream past us as we flew. "Why would things change now?"

"This is why you are different, child," she said. "When most men in your position would seize kingdoms, lands, and power, you fight to protect. Do not stray from this path. I have chosen to assist you, and we gods do not appreciate being proven wrong."

I bowed my head. "I appreciate the help. I will do what I can to protect your wind from Marzanna and her demons."

Lying back, she began to fade with her face to the sky. "Let us hope it is enough."

Then she dissipated into a puff of fog.

I continued on, heading in the direction Dogoda had pointed. The sun had risen further during our conversation, and I felt time creeping on with it. It was impossible to know how far I'd flown in the few hours since I'd left. The Kingdom of Solga was hundreds of miles wide, but the mountains of Perun's Crown slowly neared. Their highest peaks split the clouds. From this far, though, they appeared as gray blades, stuck from the earth into the sky.

I'll make it. I have to.

50

Otylia

What is my role? Goddess of the earth, of isolation, of lies? Where among the Three Realms is mine?

Dadźbóg's light faded in the east as he rose through the morning gate into Jawia. Days were short in Nawia, and each of the Trials had taken multiple hours. Soon, night would spark Wacław's journey west.

Then I would Ascend.

While Ivan, Kuba, and Vlatka discussed with the others how to protect the island during my Ascension, I paced with Sabina. I hated relying on them. It was hard enough for me to admit I needed Wacław to defend me during the coming ritual. But knowing these people, most who were still little more than strangers, were risking everything for me was too much.

"Otylia," Sabina said, catching my arm. "Perhaps you should rest." She nodded her head to the rocks at my feet, where I'd worn a path a few inches deep.

I snapped around. "Fine…"

"By *fine*, you mean *not* fine, right?" She sighed and fluttered down next to me. "Nymphs have so much less sarcasm."

"Sarcasm's better than using all my *żityje* to take out my frustration," I muttered, fighting the smirk at her innocence. "The Trial forced me to admit to Wacław I loved him. Then it made me kill him…"

Giggling, Sabina grabbed my hands. "But he's not dead. He's coming here for you, and he loves you too!"

I pulled away. "You didn't have to watch his mortal body die at your hand. Unlike most girls, I don't dream of admitting love to a boy, but even I never wanted it to be like that. The betrayal on his face… Gods, I *used* him to Ascend. He'll be trapped as a demon forever because of me."

"Oh…"

"I'm not upset with you, Sabina." I took a deep breath and looked to the sky, as if searching for Wacław within it. "I feel like a fool for worrying about my relationship with him so much. We've barely been talking again for two moons—one of which I've been trapped here—but I panic whenever I think about him. We rely so much on each other now…"

She cocked her head, smiling. "I thought most couples rely on each other. Isn't that the point: to have love and support?"

I blushed. That just ignited my frustration even more. "What am I going to do?" I asked with a groan. "I should be with the others, preparing for the Ascension. Instead, I'm fawning like a child."

"Because you love him."

"What's your point?"

"Must that love be rational?"

Rational? Nothing about a goddess loving a demon was rational—nor was my obsession with those feelings. Sure, we were bonded, but was our relationship inevitable? And why did just the thought of being completely vulnerable with him stop my heart?

I'm doing it again…

The Ascension was far more important than mere feelings. It would grant me my role among the gods and nature. It would finally give me the power to escape Weles's realm and search for Mother. Why did none of that matter when I closed my eyes and let my thoughts wander?

"How can you trust someone with every part of you," I said, "knowing they could destroy you at any moment?"

The question wasn't directed toward Sabina. It had slipped from my lips as I stared at my arm, remembering Wacław's frostbite. Dark veins had consumed him the instant I killed his mortal soul. Would he surrender to the corruption and take me with him?

Sorrow filled Sabina's eyes as she rested a hand on my shoulder. "I know it's hard…"

"How could you?" I scoffed.

She recoiled, the emotional strife apparent on her face. "Because I surrendered to you," she whispered. "There's more than one type of love, Otylia, but they all bring hope."

"I… I don't know what to say to that." My chest ached as I looked at her. Sabina had sacrificed all she'd known to help me escape, but I'd never realized how exposed she'd made herself to *me.*

"You don't have to say anything. My faith is in you anyway. If that hurts me in the end, then it was worth it." She offered a weak smile. "Maybe, it's the same for you and Wacław."

I wrinkled my nose and shook my head at myself. *What kind of goddess can confront gods and demons with ease but falters at feelings and friends?* In the past moon, I'd passed the Trials, but none of them had tested my ability to care. "I'm sorry. You've deserved better than my bitterness."

With a bow, she replied, "I am simply a nymph. There's no reason to apologize to me."

"There is," I insisted. "I've been alone in Nawia until now, and all that time, it was you who cared for me. You're a good friend. I'm not."

"Well," she said shyly, "if Marzanna has proven anything, it's that even deities are imperfect. To me, though, you have been a wonderful first friend."

First. To be isolated in Nawia for years… I didn't envy her. In Dwie Rzeki, I'd had Mother and Wacław most of my life, and even when they were gone, Ara had found me. No, Sabina had suffered far more than me. Stolen from her home and family, she had never truly been free. I promised myself I'd change that.

"Once we escape," I said, "we'll find your home and your family. There is war coming, but I won't force you to come with me to fight it. I don't know what I'd do if I lost you."

Beaming, she squeezed my hand. "That's the closest I think you have ever been to truly opening up. I'll take it, and of course, I'm coming with you. Don't be silly."

"Don't you want to live a life for yourself? Weles has made you a servant."

"But I *choose* to serve you, my lady."

My skin crawled at the idea of having servants like Weles, but Sabina was being kind. Besides, having her with me would be far better than the banter of warriors. I curtsied. "Then you'll be alongside me, Lady Sabina, bravest among the forest nymphs."

As she giggled, Ivan approached. He was in his human form once again, but instead of royal robes, he wore the simple tunic of a warrior. A sword hung at his side and a circular wooden shield was strapped to his back.

"Lady Otylia," he began with a swift bow. "Our plan is prepared. If you have a moment, we would like to discuss it with you before we rest."

I returned the gesture and followed him to the fire. The sun disappeared as we walked, but I hardened myself against the fear of what lurked in the darkness. For now, this island was ours. Weles and his minions would come during the ritual, but we were safe until then.

The others sat, but my nerves forced me to stay on my feet, always shuffling. They talked of the defensive patterns around the island: which hills were the best to defend, where they would retreat to if a flank fell, and what would happen if Weles's warriors reached the volcano—the Ascension's location—before the ritual had finished. I knew little of military strategy, and my mind wandered the deeper they went into the details. The defense would go on without me anyway. Vlatka didn't know how long the Ascension would take, but both she and I would be useless until its completion.

One thing, however, was apparent: *We need Wašek.* There were far too few of our allies to hold against a significant force for long.

Our connection had been stronger ever since the final Trial, as if his mortal soul had dampened its strength. I felt the rapid beat of his heart, the straining of his muscles as he flew west, and the *żityje* bursting through him. Neither of us wanted to admit that his humanity had shackled his power as a płanetnik. But it had.

He's enjoying it.

A thrill rose within me as he charged with the winds. There was a desperation to reach me, yes, but beneath that was a rush that came from his new power. Raw. Visceral.

My own fear countered that exhilaration. Wacław would need to be at his strongest if we had a chance, but I didn't want him to lose his hesitance, that bit of him that cared for each word he spoke. The Three Realms held too many men who thought themselves to be the strongest warriors. They needed his tenderness. So did I.

That's the boy I fell in love with, I admitted to myself. *I love him for every way he's different than me. He's warm, empathetic, peace-seeking. When he takes his time to consider what's right, I act. I need him to slow me, to force me to see the moment I'm in. I need him to let me feel.*

"Is all to your satisfaction, Lady Otylia?" one of the male forest nymphs asked. He was dressed in a deep brown tunic of bark and leaves—green strewn over brown. It seemed bark was the nymphs' idea of armor.

"It is," I said, realizing I'd missed the last few minutes of the conversation. Why were they asking my opinion anyway? Ivan had won wars. Kuba and others had trained for battle. I was a sorceress of the woods, far from spears and shields.

Ivan waved a hand, which the others took as a signal of dismissal, before standing. Across the fire, the smoke grayed his pale face. "You have come far since I met you at the base of that tree," he said.

"The first Trial was startling," I said, remembering my long, bloody crawl. "If only Isolation had been the worst."

"Indeed."

I raised my brow. "That's it? No dose of wisdom or story to raise my weary spirits?"

The old king leaned his head back and stared into the starless sky.

"I am but a mortal man who has lived far too many years in both this realm and the one above. Some days, I wished to live long enough to see Prawia. Now, however, I have come to the realization that there is a place for the gods and another for man. You will be greater than I could ever dream of being, child."

"You said you were a king. What can be greater than that and defeating Koschei?"

"I reigned for many years, yet when my time came, my star dropped from Jawia's sky the same as any tribesman's." He raised his hand and dropped it, wiggling his fingers in the imitation of a falling star. "Your star shall shine until time's end."

Stepping around the fire with his hands clasped behind him, he continued, "Koschei the Deathless was a mighty foe, but he was just a sorcerer. Marzanna wields vast power. She influences men, demons, and even żmije to follow her—as you have seen."

"Mother is entrapped by one of her dragons," I said with a nod. "But I barely escaped, let alone doing any *real* damage to it."

He stopped alongside me and stared into the fire. In the few strides, he seemed to have aged a decade, his hair a deep gray and his skin wrinkled. "Ascension will not gift you mastery of your power nor the pure strength to defeat such a beast. This will come through experience." Turning to me, he sighed. "I know that will not please one as determined as you, but Ascension is the beginning of your journey as a goddess, not the end."

51

Wacław

Will I never have peace again?

FOR HOURS, THERE WAS NOTHING BUT THE ENDLESS SKY and the demon's hunger for *žityje*. It was hammer, striking a nail into my head over and over. My sanity slipped with each blow, and I pushed faster, desperate for it to end.

Then came Rolika.

Columns of smoke stretched to the sky ahead. Clustered, they turned the clear day into a haze. At their bases, a thousand fires burned within buildings of both stone and wood that were raised head's height above the ground.

The capital of the Kingdom of Solga spanned miles, engulfing the forests completely within the curve of the Avka River. I'd never seen anything like it. Among the Krowikie and Astiwie, villages wove with the forest. Clearings were only made at village centers and rarely for more than a hundred strides. This monstrosity was different, and the smoke was dense enough to make me cough as I flew over.

Why do the Solgawi live like this?

There had to be many thousands of people crammed between the tight trails and bridges that spanned between buildings. People clustered in those raised areas and shouted to each other. Their clothes were brightly colored and made of a multitude of fabrics. Many wore furs lining their tunics, and I blushed, realizing the women walked with their hair free from braids and headscarves.

Warriors clad in studded leather and iron armor led nearly-naked men to the west. Dozens of these groups headed the same direction. At my pace, I soon found why.

A giant wall of stone rose at the western edge of the city. Still obviously in progress, even the unfinished sections were far taller than the few remaining trees, and hundreds of these unclothed men hauled stones around the structure.

Screams echoed below me as I swooped down, invisible, to get a closer look. The warriors jabbed the workers who walked too slow with the blunt ends of spears. Those who fell too far behind received the sharp end instead.

My stomach churned, and I looked away, horrified. *What is this?*

No answers would come. I had already passed the wall, and soon, all that was visible of the city was the columns of smoke staining the sky. Disgust hung over me, not fading until I reached the mountains.

There had been few other signs of the Solgawi west of the Krowik River, but after seeing Rolika, I was relieved at that. The world beyond our lands was different than I'd expected. Frightening. What lay ahead was bad enough already without watching warriors torture other men.

Much of the western Solgawi hills were arid before giving way to the mountains. Near Rolika, though, vegetation fought for space. The trees were barren without Dziewanna—like in our lands—but they were tight together for as far as I could see. Patches of green spotted the ground where sunlight crept through the branches. *Does some of Dziewanna's power remain here? Jaryło's?*

Then came Perun's Crown's western edge. Like the mountains in the east, they devoured the land far to each side of me, but these were higher. Snow covered much of the alpine slopes. They broke up my path, forcing me to either side, and I was grateful for the distraction. Though the demonic whisper lingered, I drowned it out with my sweeps through the gorges.

Żityje seeped from me as I flew, slowly draining the reserve I'd built up. It was so difficult to measure. I'd never held this much—or used it for so long—but it *seemed* my soul-form could hold on better without my mortal soul. If the gate was where Dogoda had indicated, I would make it. Whether I would have enough strength left to fight Weles was another question entirely.

Cross that river when you reach it.

It took more focus to command the winds the further I went. My mind tired from the effort and the voice's constant pounding. I had to stay strong, to fight it. Otylia was relying on me, and surrendering to its will would mean breaking my promise to her. No, I wouldn't let it win.

West of Perun's Crown, I reached lands no Krowik had ever seen before. No known pass through this section of the mountain range existed except if you traveled far to the north. Not even Father had known the names of the tribes here.

Behind me, Dadźbóg had begun his descent. The air remained chill, even with his light, but I numbed myself to the cold. I'd reached the sea. Only the gate remained. I wondered how to convince the goddess of dusk until the deep blue ocean appeared ahead of me. I'd never seen so much water in my life. Part of me wished for land once again.

At the ocean's edge, I willed the winds to push me faster. They did, and with the speed, the air stung my cheeks. The gales whipped past me, deafening me to the world beyond their beat. For those few minutes, the demonic craving dulled as I let the thrill of flight fill me. Such a feeling was alien to nearly every human but me. I was grateful for the freedom in it.

Soon, land appeared in the distance. *The islands.*

I steadily descended as I approached. Varying in size, the islands ranged from ten strides wide to miles. Barren trees and shrubs covered some. Sands and short grasses others. All arced westward in rows, spiraling from a mass of fog ahead. *Almost there.* I pushed away my fatigue and charged on.

When I broke the rim of the fog, the winds wavered. A force

ahead pulled me. I tried to fly back, to regain control, but the force was stronger. It dragged me to the fog's depths.

I shivered within the fog. The air was dense and frigid. Even with my coat, it felt like I'd been dropped into the snow. As the time dragged on, I worried that Dadźbóg would catch up, that I'd be too late. There was nothing I could do, though, and each time I tried to reach for wind or storm, nothing answered.

Then the fog broke.

Below, the ocean spun into a crater with seemingly infinite depths. The pull originated from it, and this close, it was all engulfing. My chest heaved with each breath. My soul ached. No matter how hard I fought, I fell faster.

I screamed as I dropped toward the gate's center. This had been the goal all along. I'd traveled for weeks to find a way to Nawia, but now, all I felt was terror at the gate's maw.

But I didn't fall in. Instead, pain rushed through me as I slammed into an invisible barrier upon the gate's surface. Air fled my lungs, and I wheezed, holding my chest.

An elderly woman hovered above me, shaking her head. She donned a yellow kokoshnik crown and scarf, and her long white dress, adorned with an array of bright-colored trims, fractured the light. This halo encircled her, mesmerizing against the sea of fog.

"Get up, demon," she ordered as she landed upon the barrier alongside me.

With a groan, I pushed myself to my feet. "Zorza Wieczorna, I presume?" I asked.

She clicked her tongue. "That would be *Lady* Zorza Wieczorna to a creature as despicable as you."

"My apologies, my lady." I bowed. "It has been a long journey, but that is no excuse to disrespect a goddess. My name is Wacław Lubiewicz, *formerly* of the Tribe of Krowik." Anger rose within me at the reminder of my exile.

"The tribes used to give us such honor," she said, standing with her hands clasped behind her and her chin held high. "Few sacrifices are given to my sister and me now."

Turning her gaze to me again, she scoffed and swung her arm. "Stop bowing, child. You did not come here to hear me moan about how I have been reduced to the lowest of the gods. No, you came to defy nature itself!"

"That is one way to say that I would like to enter Nawia, yes."

"And why is that?"

I stepped toward her. "The fate of Jawia rests on me getting through the gate. Please, goddess."

"Pitiful." She waved her hand and the fog seemed to draw closer. "Demons are not meant for paradise. What hope do you believe Destiny has in you?"

"Marzanna." I gritted my teeth, desperation turning into anger. The winds hummed at my fingertips, distant. "She will conquer Jawia if I don't free Otylia from Weles's grasp. Otylia must Ascend, and she needs me to do so."

With another wave of her hand, a force struck my chest. I flew across the gate, sliding to the ocean's edge. She followed faster than I thought possible. Light strewn behind her as she wielded a staff of reddened fog. "You believe the daughter of Weles needs *your* help?"

Fury took over. I drew Kwiecień, and she pulled back as I shot to my feet.

"That blade… Moonstone, drained of its life force…" she hummed. "So it's true."

I shook my head. "What's true?"

The Zorza floated to me. Her expression softened, and light fluttered around her in the colors of dusk when she spoke, "There are things beyond your comprehension, child. The last time someone besides a god wielded a Moonblade… Father…" She caught herself before sighing deeply. "How did you come to hold Kwiecień?"

"When Jaryło took Otylia, I killed him with a dagger made of Thunderstone. The Moonblade slipped from his hand as he died. This was days before the beginning of the Kwiecień moon, so he couldn't heal with its power."

"You have slain a god?" Zorza Wieczorna clicked her tongue. "Who is Otylia to you? You say she is your hope against Marzanna, but I sense more to your story."

"I love her," I whispered before repeating it louder as I gripped Kwiecień's hilt. "I love her, and I'll do whatever it takes to free her from Weles."

"A demon in love with a goddess. Adorable." With a chuckle, she drove her staff into the gate. The fog spiraled around us, and beneath my feet, the gate shifted. "Go to her, Wacław Lubiewicz. The evening gate will take you where you wish within the western regions of Nawia. I fear, though, that your return will not be so simple."

As I opened my mouth to reply, the barrier gave way. I dropped into the gate's jaws as the fog gave way to an endless whirlpool. Forces battered me from each side, and despite the wind's aid, I couldn't find the air to breathe.

Darkness filled my vision. I didn't know who or what would greet me in Nawia, but I held the image of Otylia in the woods in my mind. *Take me to her,* I begged the gate. *Take me to the newest goddess.*

52

Otylia

When will he come?

FOR THE SECOND NIGHT IN A ROW, I DIDN'T SLEEP.

Dreariness was nothing compared to the worries that claimed both my heart and mind. I worried for Wacław, for Mother, for Ara, for Father, and even for that bastard Narcyz. I worried for the fate of my tribe and the eastern clans in the Horde's path. But most of all, I worried for myself.

Selfish as it was, I couldn't help but wonder what the Ascension would make of me. I'd seen the true form of Wacław's demonic soul. There was a power within it, but it frightened me. In a way, the trial of Loss had been his *Descension.* Would my Ascension be as terrifying?

I remembered my first encounters with Dziewanna and Mokosz. Despite being their chosen, I'd shaken, barely able to lay my eyes upon them. A goddess shouldn't have given me the same horror as a demon, yet each had.

Power intimidates, no matter its form.

Once, I'd thought I loved the fear my channeling caused. Stupid boys dared not drunkenly pursue me. The fickle girls kept their gossip away. Now, I wondered if I'd been the one afraid of *them.*

I groaned and rolled over on my bedroll to face the fire. It had weakened, but its flames crackled through the silence. There was a beauty in the endless motion—chaos, just like Nawia. Fire could offer saving warmth or devour miles of forests, as they had in the southern hills years before. *Are demons so different? Gods?*

The more I thought, the more I wondered the real difference between the two. Father would have scolded me for such a claim, but he hadn't seen the gods as I had. I'd live a moon within Weles's palace. I'd learned from the cattle god, heard his tales of great battles and Jawia's cycle of destruction. We condemned demons. Had they slaughtered as the gods had? Or did we simply fear the woken dead because they were what we *could* become? Ravenous. Desperate. Without the replenishing *żityje* of souls, either mortal or deity, were we reduced to nothing but the craving of that life force to survive?

Wacław is different, I told myself. *He does little for himself. Why would he ever surrender to that selfishness?*

Unless it wasn't selfish. We honored wolves and bears, both which killed to live. Even humans did, and our—*their*—little *żityje* would flicker and fade without food. Only gods could not take. Weles had made it clear we could only accept offerings.

Gods, I was more like Father than I wanted to admit. He would stay up late often with priests or even Mother discussing the Three Realms and the forces within. Most nights I would just try to sleep, but when I grew older, I would sit alongside the doorway and listen until my eyes closed. Mother had joked about discovering me resting against the wall. She'd carried me back to bed and sang me to sleep in the way only a mother could.

A pull came from my connection to Wacław.

I flung to my feet and shouted for Ivan and Kuba. They scrambled as I tore up the volcano's side, following the tether. *He made it! Thank the gods!* It was stupid to thank the very group I was to become a part of, but who else was there to thank?

Behind me, Ivan gathered the others, and Vlatka called after me. She would want to begin the ritual as soon as possible. But I didn't care. I needed to see Wacław.

My doubts melted away with each step. Every question, every

worry silenced. It was silly to act like every girl I'd cursed for years, but as I faced the Ascension, his presence calmed my soul.

The sky split above when I neared the volcano's peak.

A massive vortex swallowed the air, a bright burst of light devouring the darkness. Heart pounding, I charged on. It was him. It *had* to be.

"Lady Otylia!" Vlatka cried from behind me. "Lady Otylia, we must begin the Ascension!"

"I need to see him," I replied, not looking back as her footsteps approached.

Her hand closed around my arm and stopped me at the volcano's rim. "You will. I promise you that. But it will take time for him to pass through, and Weles will know what has happened. If we begin now, we may finish before he arrives."

I gritted my teeth but nodded. *Just the beginning…*

"Good," Vlatka said, joining me alongside the volcano. The winds escalated around us, blowing her free hair across her scarred face. "Close your eyes, and when I say so, step over the volcano. This time, you will not fall."

My body shivered. Anticipation swelled within me, both for the Ascension and Wacław's arrival. It was all happening so fast, but there was no other choice. I closed my eyes and reached for the power within the volcano.

The winds encircled me as Vlatka chanted in the old tongue. They stole her words and the shouts beyond. I felt the world drift and turn, my feet leaving the sharp rocks as the air thickened, burning like smoke amid a blaze.

Up I drifted. Through the haze and beyond, I obeyed Vlatka's demand as my nostrils burned and my eyes watered.

This realm, far from what I'd left, spun around me. It shifted with each moment. Smoke vanished. Tides of cool water came. Then sand, spiraling up my legs with the searing summer sun. And finally ash—cold and dead—its taste coating my tongue with each labored breath.

"Open your eyes," a voice said, through the rushing winds that deafened my ears. "Open your eyes and see."

I wheezed, coughing on the soot as I gazed upon the plains of despair. Thick, gray ash rained from the sky, blown about by the gales. It covered me to my knees and stretched for miles in every direction. From upon a cliff's edge, I could see smoldering fires burning ahead. Two rivers converged upon a razed village, their currents stained a deep red. I wept at the sight.

Dwie Rzeki…

All our tribe's lands lay in ruins before me. Impossibly far distances seemed within an arm's reach. It had all burned. Within the arc of Perun's Crown, ash replaced man.

"To become a god is to hold the world at your mercy," the voice continued, pounding and deep. "Some may destroy, others create, but this ritual is not about them…"

My gut turned as the world slipped away again. I fell, tumbling through an airless void until I crashed into the ground at the base of a willow. Its roots stretched far, and its leaves soaked in the light that encircled it from above.

"In a way," the voice said, "our roles choose us as much as we choose them. Your mother's spirit attached her to the wilds far before her Ascension. Your father's fascination with change and the secrets of the realms gifted him rule over many types of sorcery and the realm of chaos itself. So, too, have you found such a bond."

I shuddered on my knees, sensing Mother's presence within the willow. "How do I know what is my place? I've always served as a szeptucha."

"You are strong, little one." As the vision turned to black, the voice softened, "Though a dominant force when called upon, you choose to entrench yourself in the little you can control. Worshipping Dziewanna and Mokosz did not define you, but they anchored you in place, as did your sorrow for your mother's absence."

It hummed to itself, thinking before a *snap* tore through the void. "Yes… Those will do."

"What will?" I called out. "What choice do I have?"

A circle of light formed before me. I stepped upon it, and instantly, I sensed the presence of three powers surrounding me. Each pulsed with my heart as I closed my eyes.

"Call to them," the voice said. "If your soul joins with the force, then you shall be bound for eternity as one."

I exhaled a long breath, allowing each of the forces to flow over me. They approached the *żityje* in my soul and tugged. But there were too many to focus on. So I held out my hand and called to the first.

When I opened my eyes, I gasped at the object hovering above my palm. An orb of blue spun with streaks within it, flowing, ever-changing. Within it, I saw the Krowik and Wyzra rivers, their waters granting life to the forests and villages along their sides.

"The power of rivers," the voice said. "Many hold some sway over them, whether it be Weles, Dziewanna, or the spirits of each stream itself. None are their true protector, though."

I raised my hand to the orb. It was cool to the touch, and streams of its water trickled across my fingers. They ran down my wrists and arms, as if they flowed with my blood. Then they began to boil.

With a yelp, I jumped back as the rivers disappeared into a puff of vapor. All that remained were stinging lines of red across my skin. "That was unpleasant," I muttered.

The voice hummed again. "I had believed this to be the one due to your parents' sway over nature and the lowlands, but it seems such a force is not right for you." He—I assumed it was a he—sighed. "I should have known better than to assume you would accept something so connected to populations, so influenced by other gods. No, you would not accept such a thing."

"Accept?" I shook my head, holding my arm across my body. "I didn't do anything."

"Oh, but you did, little one."

I clenched my jaw at his lack of clarification, but before I could speak, a man appeared before me, clothed in robes of white with trim and jewels of gold. A red cape trailed him as he stepped upon the circle of light. His face was aged, his beard gray, and he looked upon me with gaze of a proud father as another force appeared in his hand. This orb did not spin or cast the vibrant blues of the first. Instead, it was deep gray wisps of light.

"Perhaps this…" he said quietly, as if deep in thought.

"Tell me who you are first." I pushed away his hand, softer than I wanted to. "You haven't even told me your name."

The man chuckled. "You may call me Rod, the first of the gods."

The first? "But Swaróg—"

"Crafted the upper realms from the World Egg at time's beginning, yes, but it was I that gave him the egg." He waved a dismissive hand. "You will learn in time, child, but you have an eternity for such things. For now, you must complete your Ascension. Your friends await your return."

There was so much I wanted to ask. For years, I'd thought Father had taught me most of the Three Realms' secrets. How wrong I'd been.

"Take it," he repeated, offering me the orb once again.

I did, and instantly groaned as it dragged me down.

What is this?

The orb's weight strained my muscles, but more than that, it dampened my soul. My heart slowed. My excitement faded. All that remained was dread and misery.

Memories flashed through my mind. That of Mother's death, her hand clasping mine as she took her last breath. Wacław turning away and leaving me to weep alone in the woods. Every time I'd been mocked and forgotten. Every time I'd wished for friends but denied myself the chance.

The orb dimmed in my hand, its few wisps of light vanishing.

"A shame," Rod sighed. "I thought you might—"

Light burst from the orb's center, piercing through the dense fog within. I'd aimlessly torn my thoughts from the worst of my life and focused on the best: Wacław's hand in mine. Our first kiss, then our second. Each moment with him in the woods. Each time I was free with him or Mother, feeling nature's embrace away from the judgements of the tribe. I remembered Ara's smile when we'd first met, how she'd accepted me without question. And Sabina… Gods, how she'd given me hope.

The white light was blinding now. I shaded my eyes with my free hand, but Rod's voice interfered, "Do not look away, Otylia. Gaze upon what you have done."

I held the orb closer as a new, vibrant force radiated from it, replacing the heaviness with excitement and joy. My heart raced with it. My mind cleared. I smiled and raised the orb in the darkness. "What did I just do?"

"Splendid!" he cheered. "Just splendid! It was a risk to attempt such a thing, but I had never expected *this*."

Something in me said I should be annoyed at his continued lack of response, but I couldn't. There was a warmth in the orb's force that released my anger. "This obviously isn't rivers."

"Indeed, it is not. This force is far more powerful—one sought by even your mother once." His smile spread, and he laughed in joy as he clapped his hands. "Otylia, daughter of Weles and Dziewanna, you are to be the goddess of endings. For though all things in the Three Realms are a cycle, there must be an end for them to begin anew."

"Endings?" I furrowed my brow as the ethereal light spiraled from the orb and wove across my arm. In its illusions, I saw roots covered in fungi and the moon in its crescent form. The designs changed so quickly I couldn't keep track. They were cold against my skin, and I shivered before cupping the orb in my hands, sensing its power flow through me.

A force ripped me from the black.

I fell into time's familiar current. It rushed past me with a visceral strength like in the Trial of Will and Destiny, but now, I controlled my movement within it. Rod floated alongside me, studying me silently as I raised my fingers toward the swirling colors that drifted past. Images formed in each. I could *sense* the people within them, their hopes and sorrows. They drew me in, and when my fingers struck one, it grabbed hold.

I tried to fight, but time's pull was too strong. Voices and images surrounded me in an endless stream for what could've been hours or seconds as I fell toward the vision. There were too many to make sense of it. I screamed for Rod to let me go, but the chorus grew louder and louder until I had to cover my ears. Even then, I couldn't hear myself think.

My feet struck earth, and I dropped to my knees, gasping for each breath. A vision took form around me. Its frigid air struck my skin, but I just dug my fingers into the dirt. *Whatever you're doing, Rod, stop it!* Mokosz had shown me plenty of visions before. Nothing had been like *that.*

A cough came from nearby.

I snapped my head up to see a room filled by only a simple bed. Moonlight slipped through patterned openings along the top of the wooden walls, barely enough to show the bed's frame. Without the cough, I would've thought myself alone. Another soon followed, weaker.

"Rod?" I asked, my shaky breaths fogging the air as I rose and slowly approached the bed. "This isn't funny."

Whoever lay on the bed didn't reply. I gritted my teeth, caught between fear and frustration. There had to be a reason for this, but what?

Curiosity pushed me onward until a figure became visible beneath a thin blanket. An old man. He lay on his back, staring up at the thatched roof, his brown eyes unblinking and his bearded chin of gray trembling with each forced breath. As I approached, I *saw* his little *żityje* drifting away in a white vapor. Death lingered near.

Yet he didn't fear. I sensed the peace within him—hope of what came next. Suddenly, the confusion of my fall made sense. The voices and images had told me his story. The last living member of his family, he had no lineage or loved-ones left in Jawia. Everyone he'd known had gone to paradise, and I remembered each of their faces as I sat alongside him, feeling completely unprepared for what came next.

Goddess of endings…

This man was ready to meet his family again in Nawia. Was it my responsibility to free him from his mortal life? I took a sharp breath and looked away. No. Marzanna was the goddess of death.

I yelped as a hand fell upon my shoulder, but Rod looked down at me with a fatherly smile. Gently, he sat me back down. "To pass on to Nawia like this is right, natural. You are not the goddess of death, Otylia; however, you will have the power to foresee the end of cycles. Yes, death is one such end, but not all are so painful."

Rod quieted as the man took another raspy breath. The aura of *życie* slowly faded around him, and I found myself sniffling with the memories of his life filling my mind. His death would be a natural one. That didn't remove the sorrow of watching him die alone.

Not alone.

"That's why I'm here," I said, mostly to myself.

"*Why* is up to you to decide," Rod replied. "Yet, I find it fitting for you to have this force as your own. For with the cycles of the Three Realms there comes suffering—when what *once* was must be molded into what *is* to be. You have felt such loss more than any new god before you, as you are the first to be raised as a mortal. You have endured the pains of life and lost those you love. Thus, armored against the darkness within the Three Realms, so too shall you guard those who mourn."

He rose. "Endings are often considered dark. Death. Night. These things can bring sorrow and danger. You can help mortals mourn and give them hope."

"What if I never stopped mourning?" My heart twinged at that admission. Knowing Mother was alive had changed everything, but even after seeing her in the żmij's grasp, some part of me still clung to her death. She'd left, only to leave a message *four years* later. I hated how much that hurt.

"Loss is the greatest Trial, little one. This is why it is the last."

Memories of Mother swelled in my mind, but I pushed them away, along with the tears that followed. I had to be strong for her. To prove I deserved to Ascend.

Rod approached, laying a hand upon my shoulder. "That pain you feel right now makes you strong. Like the lava you stepped into, its heat allowed you to mold yourself into who you are now."

"I didn't choose to be a goddess." I bit my cheek. "I didn't choose any of this! All of 'who I am' has been controlled by everyone else."

"No, Otylia. They can try to make you into *what* they want you to be, but only you can decide *who* you want to be."

Who do I want to be?

That question haunted me as I looked down at the dying man. Each moment for him was agony. He wanted his life to end, but why did I have to be the one to finish it?

I took his hand, my heart pounding. The man was barely lucid, but his fingers closed around mine. Weak, cold, they shook with just that little effort. "Your family awaits you," I said, remembering Father's words when he'd consoled the dying of Dwie Rzeki. "For forty days, your soul will be free to fly with the birds, run with the wolves, and swim with the fish. All of Jawia will be yours, and then, your ancestors will greet you in Nawia. I've seen it. Nothing in this realm can compare."

A tear slipped down my cheek as his grip loosened. With his breaths gone, the room dropped into a hollow silence. Empty.

Then a new presence ignited my senses. I took a shallow breath, staggering back as the man's soul emerged from his body. Other than the dull glow emanating from him, his appearance was unchanged. "Thank you," he said with a bow.

Before I could reply, the vision drifted, giving way once again to time's flow. Fear came with it. How could I face so many experiences like the one I'd just seen? The voices and images of that man's life dwelled within me now. Could I just forget, or was it my duty to hold onto those pieces?

A single white wisp floated before me now. I stepped away, fists clenched. "Why are you showing me these?"

Rod smiled as he ran his fingers through his beard. "The force of endings is one not easily explained. Upon your return to the Three Realms there will be much you must discover yourself, but it is my hope these visions may give you some understanding of your power." He nodded to the wisp, the only light in time's darkness. "I believe you will find the second to be kinder than the first."

I hesitated, but a force tugged on my soul. *Wašek's coming. Hurry!* Ivan's allies were probably fighting to protect me already. According to Vlatka, Weles could sense the Ascension's beginning, and they needed my help.

Light consumed me as my fingers broke through the vision. I braced for the swarm of memories that had come in the first, but instead, it was silent. Even the air felt light against my skin.

When the light faded, my boots landed among the damp ground of a swamp. The moonlight cast shadows over the swaying willows around as the familiar smell of rotten eggs met me along with an array of new senses. They were odd, similar to the bond I'd had with animals through Dziewanna, but now, I felt thousands of tiny ants and other creatures scurrying through the earth. There was another, though. Something pulsing in my mind like a beating heart.

Rod appeared beside me and stared up at the sky. "You feel its strength. Don't you, Otylia?"

"What is it?" I asked, forcing each breath as a warm breeze blew through my hair. "The ants and creatures I've felt before, but this…"

My voice faltered. The white orb appeared between us, its power flowing from cracks in its glass. I raised my fingers and gasped as its mist traced my skin. Mystical and cold, it spread up my arm to the rest of my body. The orb's power joined with the *życie* in my soul, and my skin glowed, enveloped by the white mist as the pulsing grew stronger in my mind.

"The time has finally come!" Rod exclaimed. "The moon has found a bond."

The moon?

I tried to force out a hundred questions, but the weaving mist stole my breath. Patterns formed in it unlike any I'd ever seen. Each clung to my skin as a feeling of completion rushed over me—as if for once, things were *right.* The sea of creatures became little more than distant whispers compared to the moon's pull, and I raised my gaze to it as light shot from my fingers. The ground fell away. No, I took flight with white streaks swirling in a vapor. They rose with me as my skin glowed and the mists took solid form.

"As the moon ends the day," Rod's voice called from below, "the smallest creatures of the earth complete the process of death, allowing new life to be formed. Both are essential cycles, and thus they are your realm to control."

His words seemed distant as I rose through the night. The mists molded my simple dress, transforming it into a sweeping gown, its layered skirts of white fluttering at my feet and embroidery of autumnal reds, oranges, and browns lining its sleeves and hem. Unlike my modest traveling dress, it left my shoulders and neck exposed with only a translucent shawl over them. At my back fluttered the cape of autumn leaves I'd worn during the Trial of Life.

I laughed and spun with the streaks, amazed at how the dress flowed with me. Slits upon its bottom formed wisps of their own as I flew. The trail of white light in my wake illuminated the night, and within me, the swelling power of the moon joined with my soul.

Maybe being a goddess isn't so *bad.*

Rod waited for me below, but I didn't want to descend. This flight was the thing of dreams and mothers' bedtime stories to children. It was freedom and grace—a grace I'd never experienced before.

I blushed at that thought. Though Wacław had claimed I was beautiful, I'd never believed it myself. I *felt* it in that moment. Like something had awoken within me, and for once, I was who I was meant to be.

When I returned to Rod's circle of light amid the swamp, he beamed with the giddiness of a child. "Oh, Otylia, you cannot know how long I have waited for there to be a deity of endings. There is little that surprises me anymore. You, my child, are quite the shock."

Humbled, I knelt at his feet as a tide of emotion rushed over me. Tears raced down my cheeks. Was it joy? Sorrow? I didn't know, but it poured out of me before the *true* eldest god.

"Such emotion!" he exclaimed. "Come, take my hand. I am no master to be bowed to."

I took his outstretched hand, standing as I wiped away the tears with my other. "I… I've never felt like this before."

"Yet, you shall have this power for eternity—for only time has no ending. Yes! Endings are yours to foresee, and if you have the will and the strength, yours to alter." He raised my chin. "Be wary, however, that you do not let your whims and fears divert Destiny's call. She is no fickle thing. Neither should you be."

I swallowed. It felt as if a mountain had been dropped on my shoulders. "How am I supposed to control that? I don't understand."

With his hands resting on mine, he gave a solemn smile. "This is a great responsibility. Your power, like any other, will take time to grow within you and longer to master. We have gone a millennium with no goddess to protect the natural cycles, but now, the force of endings has found its master. There is hope."

"How? What do I do?"

"All will come in time," Rod offered. "Time answers so many questions."

Panic struck my chest. I dropped to my knees once again, wheezing for each breath. "What… What's happening?"

"I believe your *other* bond has arrived," he said, his gaze knowing. "Even I do not know what is to come, but it does not take a god to know the demon boy will need your aid against Weles."

"You're okay with me defying him?" I asked.

Releasing my hands, he simply shrugged and stepped back as the vision dispersed around us. "Who am I to determine the fate of the realms? Even Destiny is beyond me. However, before you return, there is one last ending you must see."

The wind struck instantly. Rain whipped through the air as the deafening, violent gales sent me staggering. A dark cloud filled the air. I sensed the moon's power above, but the whirlwind blocked out all light but a golden glow twenty strides ahead.

"Kwiecień…" I whispered, recognizing the Moonblade's vibrant *żityje*.

My stomach turned as a piercing scream tore through the torrent. I hadn't recognized it with the winds' strength. Now, it pulled on my soul.

"Wašek!" I shouted, but my voice was carried away.

Another call echoed his name nearby. *Me?* The second voice had been mine, and I caught my breath as rays of light broke through the black. Blinding, brilliant, they filled my heart with hope against the encroaching dread. Rod seemed to be nowhere in this vision, so I stumbled toward the light, desperate for answers.

Then she emerged—*I* emerged.

My legs failed at the sight of the woman before me. Light refracted around her, forming shapes and symbols with every stride as her elegant dress of white streaked with black flowed behind. Her presence alone sent away the dark cloud, and her glare was enough to send a shiver down my spine. She rushed through the winds to Wacław, shouting his name.

When her light poured over him, my heart stopped. I felt his hate and rage as darkness covered him like a shroud, dimming even Kwiecień's glow beneath its weight. Wacław raised his gaze to the woman. His eyes were entirely black, and demonic blood drained from them, staining his face. If only the veins of black hadn't consumed him already.

Pain stabbed at my heart as the woman took his hand. Instantly, his anger dulled. They fell into each other's embrace, Wacław's darkness clashing with her light and forming a vortex that fed the growing storm.

I tried to move closer as they spoke, but the winds were too powerful. I dropped to my hands and knees just to stop them from carrying me away. Though the pair exchanged impassioned words from their expressions, none met my ear.

They raised their free hands palm to palm—hers turning a shimmering white as black veins entrapped his. Despite the pain, despite the panic, I sensed an acceptance between them. Power radiated from the connection. Raw and passionate, it burned my skin this close, and I screamed as a force threw me into the whirlwind.

Then the world went quiet.

Time's flow seemed to stop. I floated in its void once again, and Rod appeared again as I gasped for each breath, the vision's surge of emotions washing over me. *What was that?* Wacław had wielded storms before, but nothing like that. The violent rage within him frightened me to my core.

"What ending was that?" I spat at the first god, forcing each breath. "Mine? Wašek's? Why show me my death?"

"Hmm." He sighed as time's current returned. The wisps of visions floated past, but I ignored them, glaring only at the god. "Your fates are not so simple. What you have seen is indeed an end, yet what that end is, I know no more than you. This force will show you many such visions of others as well as yourself. It is up to you to decide what must be done with them."

"I don't understand!"

The god's form began to dissipate as he smiled. "You will in time."

Time's void slipped away. Moments later, the volcano's heat struck me as screams echoed across the island. My new powers burned within my soul as my moon dress swept around me. The ritual had taken much of my *žityje*, however, and I dropped into Vlatka's arms at the volcano's rim.

"You did it!" she yelped, stumbling as she lowered me to the ground. Images flashed through my mind when her skin touched mine, and I pulled away. *Rod, what have you done to me?*

Vlatka's excitement wasn't echoed by our allies. Everywhere I looked, sorcerers, nymphs, and warriors clashed across the moonlit isle. There was so much noise on top of my new senses striking me like a hot needle. Despite my mind spinning, though, it was obvious we were in full retreat.

"Wašek," I whispered. "Has he come?" With my exhaustion, he was our only hope until I found my bearings.

Lightning answered my call. I forced myself to stand. The winds battered my face and flung my white dress behind me. *He's here.*

Our tether was taut. It pulled me to him, and I didn't resist.

I evaded Vlatka's attempts to grab my hand and called the moon's strength to me. It was dim, weak upon the final day of its cycle, but its power infused with my will. As a figure appeared amid the torrent of light above, I took flight.

I'm coming.

53

Wacław

To paradise I fall.

FOR WHAT SEEMED AN ETERNITY, I DROPPED THROUGH THE GATE. The ocean pressed upon its sides for miles, but its invisible barrier held. Somehow.

Then it stopped.

The water disappeared without warning, and I found myself free-falling from a stream of blinding light. Here, night ruled the land. Or, more accurately, the seas.

Waters of a deep orange stretched in every direction, their waves crashing beneath me. It would've been the only sound if a battle hadn't raged on the island below.

Where are you?

My bond with Otylia drew me toward the dark island at full speed. A mountain rose at its center, and on its peak drummed a power unlike any I'd ever felt. With each moment I rushed downward, the winds swirled, asking to catch me. I refused.

It has to be her. It has to be.

I demanded the winds drive me *down.* Though hesitating, they followed my command. The world blurred as I extended my arm and called to Otylia.

From the mountain she rose with bands of white, red, and orange streaming from her fingers. With each breath, she illuminated the sky as each strand of her gown swept behind her in a dance of its own. Her hair flowed with the winds—black with a streak of white above her left ear. She was brilliant, alluring.

She was a goddess.

"Otylka!" I shouted, reaching for her. Despite my speed, I strained each muscle in my fingers, desperate to meet her.

"You came," she whispered, her voice slipping through the winds with ease. "Wašek."

We slowed as the distance closed between us. Our fingertips seemed to hover just inches apart for too long. At full stretch, our souls pulled us together, demanding we reunite. After crossing hundreds of miles and the boundary between realms, we finally had.

Our hands met. We floated on air, our eyes locked and our souls joined. From the moment we touched, the demon's voice silenced within me.

Below, spears crashed against shields and bolts of sorcery blew black rock into the sky. I numbed myself to it. I'd lost so much in the last moons, but for that single moment, I released the pain and regret choking me.

"You Ascended!" I beamed as we embraced. "Gods, maybe there *is* some hope."

"We need to help the others," she said, taking a sharp breath and pulling back with her green eyes narrowed.

My heart ached, but she was right. Those defending the island were struggling to hold back the tide of attackers, both winged and not. Kuba fought alongside one group of souls further down the slope. Weles's sorcerers lurked behind the front lines—their spells too powerful for mere warriors to resist.

I could sense the diminishing *žityje* within Otylia's soul. This close, our bond was stronger than ever. "You sure you have the strength for this?" I asked. "The ritual…"

"I'll be fine," she said with her fists clenched. Shock stirred within her, and I wished for the chance to know what she'd seen. "These powers are new to me, but I'll figure them out."

I drew Kwiecień, its blade now a dull gold. "Then let's show them Oblivion's fury. Stay with me. If you fall, I want to be there to cover you."

When she nodded, I dove toward the island, calling the gathering storm to my fingers. The lightning snapped and surged within me. It raced through my veins, brilliant blue clashing with black. I smirked and readied my strike.

Weles's sorcerers scattered at the sight of me, turning their staffs from the defending warriors and aimed up instead. Chants echoed. Iron clanged. Bolts of fire, ice, and forces I didn't know cracked toward me.

I met them.

Lightning struck me as the spells arrived, shredding their attacks to nothing. *Żityje* fled my soul, but I balled the lightning in my hand and dove to the ground.

The impact threw every attacker for a hundred strides. Sorcerers screamed. Warriors groaned.

"You're a sight for sore eyes," Kuba huffed with his spear and shield tight in hand. Sweat clung to his brow, but he grinned as he eyed the attackers.

"As are you, brother," I replied.

Beneath my feet, the black stones sparked, buzzing with the lightning's energy. I knelt and reached for it. I didn't know how or what it could do, but the lightning's echo within the stones answered my call. When the attackers recovered and charged from each side, I clenched my fist.

Burning flesh.

My stomach churned at the stench as a dozen of Weles's warriors and sorcerers collapsed, steam rising from their blackened, charred bodies. *What did I just do?* The thrill subsided. I shuddered at the horror I'd caused and the death the battle had wrought. *This shouldn't be fun…*

"Look out!"

Kuba's voice pulled me from my thoughts too late. A sharp pain struck my shoulder, burning a hole in my tunic. The power rushed through me again as I spun and met the gaze of the sorcerer who'd struck me.

"So, this is the demon boy," he said with a shake of his head. A raven skull rested upon it, and in the night, his black robes fluttered as if they were of the winds. "What a disappointment."

I groaned, but there was to time to check the wound. Fire arced from the sorcerer's hands.

Diving to the right, I dodged the attack and swung my free arm. Winds followed like an extended fist. The sorcerer cast a defensive spell, but the gales smashed through and bloodied his nose.

I grinned. Before I could advance, though, Otylia appeared next to me.

She panted as if she'd been locked in combat, yet her dress and skin were unmarked. I didn't question it. Jaryło had been the same after our fight with the wolf pack.

"Tibês is mine," she muttered, her gaze fixed on the Raven Wizard.

Wisps of white rose from her outstretched arms like a smoldering blaze. An elegant goddess one moment, a deadly force the next.

Without waiting for a reply, she rushed the Raven Wizard. I turned to cover her flank with Kuba.

The winds alerted me to four water nymphs swooping toward Otylia. They were quick, already closer to her, and together, they were conjuring a spell. I didn't want to find out what.

As Kuba held the ground with the other warriors, I bound after them on the gales. My strides struck the air as if it were stone, and when the nymphs slowed to release a tide of steaming water, I crashed into them.

They yelped as I slashed at the closest of them. Terror filled her eyes. I saw my dark reflection within them—black gusts encircling me and the shimmering Moonblade driving toward her heart. It struck, and she released one last breath as my momentum carried me into the remnants of their spell.

Fire! my mind told me. The boiling tide they'd summoned hovered before them like a wall of water, waiting to be pushed. I couldn't let them interfere with Otylia's fight.

But the pain. It seared my skin. Water rushed down my throat and choked me, forcing me to the ground, gasping and seizing.

I screamed at the burns consuming me, disfiguring my skin. As I fought to my knees, though, *žityje* poured from me, and my skin repaired itself before my eyes. The burns had vanished in seconds. Even the throbbing of my shoulder had dulled.

This'll be useful.

There was just one problem: Healing had taken nearly all of my remaining *žityje*.

I coughed and glared up at the nymphs, who dove at me. *At least I'm a good distraction.* Kwiecień hummed in my hand as I took a fighting stance and searched for options. The dead nymph lay just strides away. *Žityje* seeped from corpses quickly, so I needed to act quickly to take it. But my stomach turned at the thought of eating a person's heart—nymph or human. Every part of me hated what I had to do. I'd scorned Bidaês for consuming a warrior's heart just a week before. How could I claim to be better?

The nymphs were preparing another attack above. Seconds remained until their spell was ready to strike Otylia, and I sensed her own *žityje* depleting too.

She needs me.

I swallowed my stomach's objections and scrambled to the corpse, driving my dagger into her chest and tearing her heart free. Above, the water nymphs screeched at the sight. As I bit into the heart and drew the new *žityje* into my veins, they launched the boiling wave at me instead.

My senses sharpened instantly. Though I hated taking that lingering life force from the dead, I didn't have time to mourn what I was becoming. Survival came first.

Throwing out my arms, I split the wave before me with the winds. The slit was narrow, and as the water surged to each side, Weles's warriors cried out. They had been sneaking toward me. Only Kuba's few allies had kept them at bay.

I wanted to check on Otylia more than anything, but the nymphs weren't done. They flew at me from each side with blasts of water that zipped quick enough to do real damage. My patience was out. I launched into the air, dodging their strikes and ending above them with one bound. As my upward movement faltered, I flipped and summoned lightning.

The nearest nymph charged, sensing my fall as a weakness. He was wrong.

Without his ranged attacks to worry about, I sent a bolt at him. He tried to dodge, but even nymphs couldn't outpace lightning.

The others cried out at their comrade's fall before attacking with a new fury. Blasts of water, both boiling and not, struck my side and leg, but I gave them little attention. One hand gripped the dagger and the other lightning. When I fell between the flanking nymphs, I launched one in each direction.

My legs groaned when I hit the ground, but satisfaction swelled within me. I watched above as the two nymphs tumbled from the sky—one charred, one stabbed. The winds had guided the blade without my conscious direction. There was something incredibly pleasing about that.

After grabbing the Thunderstone dagger and taking the *żityje* from the hearts of three fallen nymphs, I took a deep breath and sensed my burgeoning strength. *I need to control it.* Drying blood clung to my chin and hands. I'd promised Otylia and myself I wouldn't surrender. But it was tempting…

Pain struck every bone in my body. Gasping, I dropped to a knee as a new voice pierced my mind, *"Wašek! Please, Wašek! He's come."*

Otylka!

Dread filled me as I spun to where she'd been fighting the Raven Wizard. A man stood before her, his hand clasping her throat as he held a warped wood staff to her chest. Snakes slithered beneath his robes of green and brown, seemingly *becoming* beings from the stones themselves. Upon his head, two cattle-like horns protruded through his scalp.

Weles.

54

Otylia

This is true power.

THERE WAS FREEDOM IN FLYING, in wielding the moon's pull. It came so simply.

I hadn't comprehended Wacław's joy when he'd talked about his connection with the winds. Now, however, with my gown sweeping behind me and the chill air blowing through my hair, I finally understood. There was nothing that could match the wonder of soaring among the clouds.

Nothing but the bond that pulled me to him.

Darkness rushed behind Wacław as he fell. Those horrid black veins covered his outstretched arm, but I fixed my gaze on his bright blue eyes. The desperation, the passion within them. Nothing could destroy that.

When we joined, I clung to him at first, but more images flashed through my mind. Horrid, vivid. I tore myself away, turning back to the battle raging below. *Why do you curse me?* Even with those visions threatening, my soul complained when his hands slipped from mine. I forced away the sorrow and yearning swarming within me. These new powers would need all my focus if I was going to figure out how to use them.

Wacław dropped to Kuba and drew the sorcerers' attacks while I flew to the side, searching for Ivan among the front lines.

Where are you?

The moon gifted me clearer sight, but the battle was hectic. Warriors clad in Weles's deep greens and browns streamed forward in great numbers as our allies fled. Among them, Ivan shouted and organized the souls' defense into a shield wall on a ridge. Above, our nymphs clashed with Weles's.

I dove behind the lines of Weles's warriors. They stumbled on the rocks, but I had no idea how my powers could help. Rod had shown me natural death and the moon. Neither seemed all that useful in combat. *Unless...*

Thousands of little creatures thrived beneath the sea of black shards, feasting upon plants that had thrived many years before. Their tiny senses met mine, and they crept up at my call. In seconds, the warriors screamed as the creatures streamed up their legs like an invisible army. Men collapsed into writhing masses, dropping their axes and spears. I held my hands to my mouth as the swarms stripped skin from bone until only blood remained.

Rod's warning flashed through my mind. The eldest god had showed me the destruction gods were capable of—and an ominous ending I was a part of. As I watched those creatures of decay, I realized for the first time how dangerous I was. Demons slaughtered innocents and craved *żityje.*

I could do worse.

Unnerved, I searched for Wacław. My attack had given Kuba and Ivan time to organize a stronger defense, but commanding the creatures had drained much of my *żityje.* Every second in flight made it worse.

Lightning raced across the stones not far away. Warriors fell, but the sorcerers channeled from a distance, encircling Wacław in their trap.

Fireballs and bolts of *żityje* streaked at me as I dove to Wacław's aid. He dodged with ease in the air. Flight was new to me, however, and I gritted my teeth when a spell struck my side. My focus slipped.

The wound stung. I dropped sloppily to the rocks, landing by Wacław and Kuba's line of warriors.

A nasty burn covered Wacław's shoulder as his power seemed to engulf the moonlight. Wielding the winds, he struck at a distant sorcerer. I clenched my fists at the sight of the man's raven-skull helm.

"Tibês is mine," I demanded. A need for revenge burned within me. For once, I let it roar.

Reluctant, Wacław nodded, or at least I thought I saw it out of the corner of my eye. I was already running.

The Raven Wizard swung his staff, his brow furrowed at my approach. Disdain filled his eyes. That feeling was mutual, and when he launched an array of spells at me, I released my anger.

The army of tiny creatures swarmed him as I dove past the first two of his bolts. But the third struck, loosening my grip. The creatures' fervor faded. When I fought to my feet, clutching my throbbing chest, Tibês grinned and took flight.

I grumbled to myself but followed. Airborne, I knew of no weapons except for a few old tongue spells. It didn't matter. I would find a way to punish him, no matter what.

Black wings lifted the wizard over the battle. His grin didn't fade, and he extended his staff as a harsh blue glowed at its end. "You are yet untrained," he sneered. "It is truly a shame."

The blue bolt shot from his staff.

"*Rìnoti*!" I shouted with my banded arm extended. Push.

Glyphs of the old tongue glowed upon my armband as a force shot from me. It crashed into the spell, shattering it into a thousand shards that colored the night. Then, I smirked and learned from the teacher.

"*Bǫdi*," I whispered. Be.

Tibês's smile faded as the spell shot from my hand. He raised a defensive shield, but I channeled another *bǫdi* spell, then another. My soul ached, parched for *žityje*. I ignored its cry. I *needed* to finish him. He'd betrayed me, abandoned me, mocked me.

Never again.

The last of the spells struck his chest. Growling, he tried to launch another bolt, but his body froze.

The paralysis drained my *žityje* with each second, so I wasted no time. As the cries and clamor of battle resounded below, I charged and shouted with all my strength, "*Svět!*"

Light.

Blinding light surged from my hands, forming a spear made of silver. It shone with the moon's power, and red stained the blade's tip as I drove it through Tibês's chest. *Bǫdi* held him in place, but I released it and savored his brutal scream.

The raven's wings crumpled as he fell. I watched with no regrets this time. Tibês had toyed with me, pretended to earn my trust just to trick me. No, this death was a just end.

My glory didn't last long. In the scuffle, I'd lost track of my final ounce of *žityje*, and it dissolved with my flight. I fell, clutching the spear and begging for the impact to be softer than I feared.

It wasn't.

Rocks sliced my cheek and cracked my bones when I struck. The spear slipped from my grasp. I whimpered, but no one heard me. Even Wacław was distracted, fighting off a gaggle of nymphs.

I should be dead. I knew it, yet my body disobeyed. Without *žityje*, my night vision failed, and what sight remained blurred as a figure loomed over me. *Weles.* My nose revealed the master of cattle—his damp, swampish smell suffocating me as a chorus of snakes hissed around us.

I heard Ivan cry out for me. It was distant, too far to be of any help. What help could a mortal soul be against Nawia's king anyway?

My tether to Wacław tightened as Weles reached down and gripped my throat, lifting me into the air. I called to him in my mind. Desperate, I screamed over and over in the breathless cry.

"Otylka!" he replied.

Blood pooled below me, dripping from my finger and chin. Part of me wished to slip from consciousness and leave this agony. But I clung to whatever kept me awake, glaring down at the god who'd claimed to be my father.

"You have no idea what you have wrought, child," he sneered with his staff to my chest. A power pulsed at its end, and when it touched, the moon's pulse faltered within me. "Goddess of endings. You've seen the visions already, haven't you? Do you fear your demon boy now?"

I couldn't speak. So, fighting the pain in my jaw, I spat in his face. It was petty, but it felt good. *I'm probably the first goddess to ever spit at a god.* Even Mother hadn't been *that* gutsy.

Around us, souls and nymphs on both sides fought on. From what I could tell, our interference had allowed our allies to counterattack, but we didn't need to control the island, just escape it. They should've taken the distraction as a chance to flee across the sea. *The fools won't abandon me.*

Weles dropped me into the rocks, sending a jolt through my body as he wiped the spit from his beard. In this form, he appeared as a man of middle age. Fitter and taller than his older one, he'd have been intimidating even if he weren't a god.

"I was right to delay your Trials," his voice boomed. "You are too young, too immature to wield such power. What was Ivan thinking? And how could Rod gift you such a force when you are ill prepared for—"

Hissing filled the air as Wacław dove for my dropped silver spear, grabbing it and taking flight in one swift motion. Displeased, the serpents covered me. I couldn't fight them. My body screamed with each movement.

Wacław rushed Weles with the black winds streaming at his back. The spear exposed the rage in his eyes. His fury for *me*.

But his target was no demon, no sorcerer. Weles was god of magic and master of deception. Such a charge could not surprise him.

The god's staff snapped around, summoning a glimmering shield. Wacław stabbed anyway.

No!

I wanted to scream for him to stop. To run. Wacław would never abandon me, but no demon could pierce Weles's defense.

Spear collided with shield in a brilliant explosion of light. Wacław tumbled, the spear flying from his hand as Weles's ward faltered. The god actually seemed surprised. He swung his staff and sent a blast at

Wacław.

I winced as the wave struck. Wacław cried out but dove to the side, his left arm hanging awkwardly at his side. His right moved swiftly, though, and something glimmered in his grasp.

The dagger!

As Weles channeled the rocks and entrapped Wacław's airborne legs, Wacław allowed himself to be pulled down. He tucked his head as he fell, blocking Weles's sight of the Thunderstone dagger until he hit the ground.

Then he struck.

The ground quaked as Weles released a deafening roar. Blood seeped from his abdomen, where Wacław pulled the blade free. Before Wacław could stab again, Weles slammed his cane into the ground.

A blast sent us flying, and my mind teetered on consciousness as we crashed into a ridge. *Stay awake,* I commanded myself. *For Wacław. For Sabina. For Ivan.*

But I was crippled, useless.

Minutes seemed to pass each time I blinked. The sounds of battle drew closer, and I felt a hand upon my cheek. *Wašek?* I asked through our connection.

"I'm here," he whispered. Were those tears? "It's going to all right. Kyustendil is leading a charge against Weles. Looks like they've bought us some time, so you just need to tell me how to give you my *žityje.*"

No, I replied. *I can't let you.*

"It's okay. It's okay." The shaking in his voice said otherwise. "I can take it from the hearts of the dead, and it should be able to heal you. At least, it did for me."

Blood. I have to drink your blood.

I wanted to vomit asking him. It was disgusting enough to take it from those choosing to worship me, but from the boy I loved? From a demon? Gods, our relationship was a disaster.

Wacław slid the dagger across his wrist without hesitation or hint of disdain. Instead, he held his arm over me, allowing the blood to trickle into my mouth. "Like this?" he asked.

I'm sorry, was all I could think to reply.

He surveyed the battle, looking anywhere but at me. Honestly, I couldn't blame him. It felt so *wrong* to take from him after he'd sacrificed his mortal soul for me. But he was Wacław. I'd seen the devotion in his eyes when he'd passed through the portal. He would've gone to Oblivion if I'd asked.

"Okay," he said after a minute, his voice softer than it should've been. "Kuba and your friends are fleeing across the water with Kyustendil. It's just us and one warrior left."

A warrior? I asked. *Who?*

"Elderly man with a golden cloak… Gods, how is he doing that?"

Ivan…

Wacław huffed, squeezing my hand with his non-bloodied one. "Whoever it is, he's holding his own against Weles. I don't understand how, but he fights like a hero from the legends." He glanced down at me, and though he tried to hide his unease, his honest eyes exposed him. "Is the blood working?"

It was. The process was slow—I'd broken more bones than I cared to count—but I could feel them healing. Soon, they were all mended. Though aches remained, I counted my blessing as my *żityje* finally started to replenish.

How are you? I asked. *Tell me if I'm taking too much.*

"I'm fine." He flashed a smile. "But we need to go soon if we're going to help the others break through the Heart of Nawia."

This was probably the majority of the force Weles was expecting to use, I replied. *Still, he could have more at the Heart.*

"We'll figure it out. Between a demon and goddess, I have to imagine not much can stand in our way."

You'd be surprised. My *żityje* had recovered to a level I would've been fine with as a szeptucha. I wasn't sure how much Wacław had, but our connection told me it wasn't too much more. *That's enough.*

His brow furrowed. "You sure?"

I snatched his arm and pulled it away. The blood coated my tongue, but I swallowed what remained. "What?" I quipped, finally able to speak. "You *like* letting me drink your blood?"

"You're sounding like Narcyz now," he replied as his wound healed. "See, told you."

"I'm glad being a complete demon has some advantages, but you can show off later. C'mon."

We ran across the island, past where Ivan fought with Weles. It really was a miraculous sight—a god's sorcery matching the hero's strength. *He's more than he let on.* The former king had revealed much about his life, but to face a god was no mortal feat.

Wacław tried to hold my hand as we ran, but I slowed, wishing to help Ivan. "We're no help to him," he said. "Weles almost killed us both."

"I know," I muttered, "but I hate leaving him."

We crested the next hill. Here, we could take flight, but I stopped and looked back. Ivan still sparred with the god, his motions slowed by the battle's wear. His gaze met mine. Though it may have been a trick of the moonlight, I chose to believe otherwise. "I'll miss you," I whispered, holding my free hand to my heart.

At full stride, we bounded into the sky. Our allies flew ahead, carried by Kyustendil's northwest wind. At least forty of them had fallen, but the rest continued fought on. Just over sixty nymphs and souls, most of whom would be free to return to Jawia and live for the first time—away from Weles's grasp. The palace was far. It would take some time for us to reach the Heart, and I could only hope Ivan managed to hold Weles until then.

Sorrow clenched my gut. I would truly miss Ivan's wisdom, his honor. There had been an aura about the man that had made me want to rise to the role I'd been given. No longer was I the witch in the woods, scorned by my village. I'd become a goddess, and I needed to act like one. I still didn't know *how.* He, at least, had given me a few steps in the right direction.

"I doubt this is the best time for this," Wacław said as we closed in on the rest of our group, "but you have no idea how happy I am to see you… you know… not in a vision."

Definitely not the time. Our bond pulsed so near to him, though, and his boyish enthusiasm was contagious. "You do realize I feel your emotions, right?"

"And I yours." He stared at me. Not ahead, not at the seas or back at the dead on the isle. His eyes never left me, and fear rose within my chest.

What do you sense in me? I wished to ask, but instead, I stayed silent. Becoming a goddess and escaping Nawia was enough to handle for one night. Love—and the visions that struck whenever his hand touched mine—could wait.

Wacław was disappointed at my lack of reply. I knew he was. If he could feel the storm within me, I hoped he'd understand what I failed to.

"I wish I'd grabbed that spear," I finally said as we reached our allies. They greeted us with smiles, but I kept my distance. The awe in their eyes was as dangerous as my power.

"It seemed bound to you," Wacław replied. "Maybe, you just need to call it again."

I extended my free arm before us, the silver and wood armband shining beneath my sleeve. Like my gown, it seemed to be enjoying my new power.

"*Svět*," I whispered.

Instantly, the spear's weight fell into my hand, its silver leaking light that streamed behind us. It felt good to know the weapon had claimed me. No Krowikie women were trained in warcraft, unlike the clans, but I'd always admired the art of fighting with a spear.

Wacław smiled. "It suits you. Brilliant and deadly sharp."

"Maybe you should wield it," I said. "It was quite the trick, using the spear to create an opening for your dagger."

"Xobas taught me it once." His head dropped, and for just for a moment, his grip loosened. "I can show you how to use it. Though, I assume being goddess of the moon is far more than a few basic spear lessons."

What I wouldn't give to see the world through his mind. I offered him a smile. "I'd like that. But what makes you think I'm goddess of the moon?"

"Mostly a guess. It seemed fitting based on the glow of that scar on your cheek."

Instinctively, I raised my hand to it. Since I'd shattered my mirror, I'd thought little of that crescent scar. I'd worn it with pride, but now, I worried how he saw me.

"Don't," he said, softly pulling my hand from the scar. "I like it. It's far better than an arm consumed by frostbite."

"Or veins running black," I said with my gaze narrowed.

His heart ached at that, but he hid it behind a smile. "The streak of white in your hair is quite rebellious too. I like it, especially without the braid."

I rolled my eyes. "At some point, I'm just going to assume you'll claim to like anything about me. Then I can't trust you."

"You're asking for an insult?"

"No, just honesty."

"Then I *honestly* fear you're a goddess, and I'm a demon who can never match you."

That didn't sit well with me. Each time I closed my eyes, I saw the violent gales swirling around Wacław and me. The flashes I'd seen in our few moments of contact had threatened to add to the vision, but I didn't want to see more. Rod had warned me of my power. It had been less than an hour—I'd felt enough to know he was right.

"Endings," I said absently as we flew through a cloud, its moisture sending a shiver down my spine. "I'm the goddess of endings. The moon is just part of it."

When I dropped my head, Wacław reached for my hand to comfort me, but I snatched it away. My heart raced. *Not again.* I couldn't take another horrific image just minutes after losing Ivan. *Will this happen when I touch anyone?*

Wacław held his hand to his chest as if I'd tried to stab it. "What's wrong? Aren't you happy to have Ascended?"

I bit my cheek and stared down at the massive trees below. Flight was dizzying, but seeing the ground calmed my stomach. "It's complicated. The things Rod showed me during the ritual… Everything ends eventually before beginning anew. There's good in that, but I see visions of what's to come. Mokosz's divination was only what *could* happen. My power seems to be woven with Destiny's, as if the endings were defined unless I say otherwise."

"I'm sorry," he said. "I can imagine what visions come with endings."

"Rod said there's more to ending's force. The moon ends the day and the creatures I can apparently command end the cycle of life through decay, but what else comes with this? I thought Ascending would bring answers." I shook my head, gripping my spear. "All I have is more questions."

"Then we'll find the answers in time. Together."

Wacław's voice was calm despite me pushing him away. Part of me wished he'd be angry at me, that he'd tell me I was stupid and that the key to my powers was obvious. But he just looked at me with those thoughtful eyes. *Why do you have to make staying away so difficult?*

55

Wacław

Defying Marzanna, Jaryło, and now Weles. Maybe I am a demon…

Our flight across Nawia was stunning. Even with only the fading moonlight to light the landscape, awe filled me with each new area.

We had passed trees that stretched hundreds of feet high, fields full of golden cattle, and cliffs of rock that dropped and rose with little cause. If we'd had more time, I would've spent days adventuring through each.

"We would've loved this as kids," I said, flying behind Otylia.

Otylia glanced back at me. Whatever power that allowed her to fly had nothing to do with the winds, and it was unsettling to the gales that she moved through them at ease. "Too bad Weles decided to lock me in his palace for the entire moon."

"Ironic to be trapped in a paradise and able to experience none of it," I replied. "Though, even my flight across Jawia made me realize how little I've seen of our own realm."

She smirked—the wicked kind that I'd dearly missed. "We're immortals. If we survive this, we'll see it all someday."

My soul began to throb as we neared a swampland. Kyustendil dove with our allies toward it, and a thrill rose within me. "This is it?" I called ahead.

"It better be," Kuba shouted. "My stomach is *not* meant for flying."

Otylia eyed me. "Weles's palace is within the swamp. How'd you know?"

"You don't feel it?" I replied.

She shook her head. "Ever since I Ascended, I have a hundred new senses swarming me. Which one are you talking about?"

"There's a pulse," I replied, pointing toward the center of the swamp. A mass of vines and trees spread within it, too dense to be natural. "It's calling me to it."

"It's the Heart!" Kyustendil exclaimed. "Our way to Jawia."

Wrinkling her nose, Otylia stared toward the Heart. I felt her unease through our connection. "What's wrong?" I asked.

"When I focus," she said, "I feel the Heart's presence too, but there's something else. The moon's end is near."

My breaths caught as I looked to the sky, where the moon hung in the east. Nights were long in Nawia, but Dadźbóg had only been a few hours behind me at most. When he passed through the gate, the new moon would start in Jawia.

The Maj moon.

"Jaryło's Moonblade will heal him soon," Otylia said. "My power is slipping. We need to hurry!"

We landed among the trees at a sprint, slipping through the muck. My legs throbbed. Though *żityje* had healed my injuries, much of the pain remained. I ran on anyway. We *needed* to reach the Heart before the sun's arrival.

"It's just ahead," Otylia breathed as a nymph flew alongside her. "But the inside is a maze."

"I know the way," the nymph replied, casting a nervous glance in my direction.

Otylia nodded. "Then Sabina will lead the way. Everyone else, be ready! Weles won't let us in easily."

Soon, a pair of wooden doors appeared. Vines stretched on each side of them, blocking all but the doorway as Otylia and Sabina pushed them open. Her anxiety rushed through our bond. Disdain.

Hatred. She'd been trapped for a moon within these walls, and knowing her, she wasn't looking forward to entering them again.

"Let's go," she muttered as Kyustendil and I flanked her. It was odd to stand alongside a wind who seemed so much like a man, but there was little time to wonder more about him. Otylia bounded through the open door with Sabina flying overhead.

Narrow halls of more vines followed, and I shuddered at the roots stretching above. Trees covered the entire palace, using it as their base. *I see why she felt trapped.*

The Heart's pull grew stronger as Sabina led us deep into the palace, each intersection of halls seemingly identical to the one before, yet the nymph showed little hesitation until we neared another pair of massive wooden doors. Gold patterns wound across its rim and handles. We'd seen hundreds of doors during the run, but only this one remained completely untouched by the vines.

"This is it!" Otylia said, stopping alongside Sabina.

Kyustendil smiled and strode forward with an open coat of deep blue draping from his shoulders. Though thin and frail-looking for a god, he held his chin high. "It's high time I get myself out of this realm." He looked to a short woman at his side. "Vlatka, may you do the honors?"

Vlatka furrowed her brow and extended her arms at her sides. *Žityje* snapped in her open hands. "I've waited a long time to do this."

Speaking in the old tongue, she brought her hands together and released a surge of power. The spell slammed into the doors with a *bang*, and they shattered instantly. Vlatka grinned cheekily and nodded to the gathered warriors and nymphs. "What are you waiting for? C'mon!"

Our allies cheered and charged toward the Heart, but I caught something strange out of the corner of my eye.

The vines *moved.* Otylia and Kuba had followed the leading pack. At first, I thought it a trick of my tired mind or of my demonic soul, taunting me as it had ever since I'd lost my mortal soul. Then the creaking became deafening.

Vines whipped through the opening, grabbing hold of the dozen of us yet to make it through the door. "Otylia!" I shouted as they dragged me to the ground.

Warriors cried out around me as Otylia turned in horror. Everywhere, vines twisted and snatched. They covered me, holding my arms and wrapping themselves around my neck. "Do something!" I shouted before they slid down my throat.

The sounds of battle echoed from the room ahead. Otylia glanced toward them before returning her gaze to me. *"I can't stop them!"* her panicked voice said through our connection.

With the vines choking me, I stared down the hall at her, desperate. *You can,* I replied. *I saw you wield the moon. These vines are nothing.*

She held her spear aloft, shouting in the old tongue. The vines closest to her loosened on the trapped warriors, but they clung to me until my vision disappeared. I heard Otylia's chanting and the battle beyond. They sounded distant as the vines pulled me down, breaking through the dirt as the earth itself swallowed me whole.

I wanted to fight, to break free. The winds whipped above. So near. But the palace rejected their power when I called it, and they scuttled away, hissing like Weles's snakes.

My hope ran out. Dirt surrounded me, filling my mouth and nose as I gasped for breath. We'd been so close. The Heart's power *pounded* in my soul. It tempted me like Marzanna's cruel wishes. And like her promises of power and glory, the Heart stole everything in return.

As my body went limp and the sounds of battle and weeping disappeared, I whispered one last prayer to Otylia through our bond, *Run, my love, my goddess. Be free from Weles, from Nawia and the Trials of Ascension. Bring Kuba home. Find Dziewanna. And never look back.*

56

Otylia

I'll never abandon you.

THOSE WORDS WERE ALL I COULD TELL WACŁAW as I sparred with the vines. They'd released most of the others but had torn him beneath the ground. I could feel his *żityje*. Though weak, he still lived.

But the sea of roots wouldn't *listen*. They were like insolent children, straying from my commands the moment I turned my attention to another. Controlling the creatures of decay on the island had been easy with such little to focus on. Here, there were hundreds of independent roots. Weles was too powerful. Even distant, his influence over the palace lingered everywhere, and his roots wouldn't release Wacław. They grew among the decay that I'd controlled before, but they were no longer my power to wield.

"Lady Otylia!"

Sabina's sweet voice rose my spirits as she swept toward me on her nymph wings. Her green dress hung tattered from her shoulders, but her eyes were narrow, bold. "The vines!" I yelled. "They won't listen to my commands."

"Weles is their master," she replied, landing beside me. "Only he commands them. Luckily, I'm a nymph."

Tiptoeing forward, she whispered in a tongue I'd never heard. It flowed like a calm melody and reminded me of Mother's lullabies.

She'd sing them the nights after Father had scolded me for escaping to the woods, weaving my hair in intricate patterns as she stroked my cheek. The strongest woman I'd ever met, yet so soft with me. I still remembered every word, even those she'd sung when I'd pretended to sleep with my head in her lap.

The vines retreated around Sabina, and soon, the last few warriors stumbled free. Those around Wacław wouldn't relent. Sabina's song rang through the hall and her tone sharpened—like a mother's last warning before she grabbed the broom.

Hold on, Wašek.

I held my breath. His heart beat alongside mine, but it slowed with every second. The vines had been willing to release the warriors. But a demon? The first to step foot in Nawia in known history? No, they wouldn't let him go easily.

Rising, I chanted in the old tongue. Like Sabina, I pled with the vines to listen. This seemed to use less *życie* than commands, but I needed to be careful. Wacław had saved me once. He'd lose too much blood if he tried again.

The seconds passed slowly. Each of our tuned heartbeats seemed a minute as Sabina continued her advance. "Rest, and be still," I sang to the roots, following close behind. "Your master will return soon."

As Sabina approached the place where Wacław had stood, the vines slowly pulled back, exposing his extended arms. She grabbed one and I the other. Seconds later, we dragged him, gasping, out of the dirt. Wacław collapsed into me. His breaths were forced, ragged as I cradled him against my chest. We'd been reunited just hours before. I would *not* lose him again.

"You have a bad habit of saving me," he said with something that sounded like a mix of a laugh and a cough.

"No, I failed." I looked to Sabina, hovering above us with that innocent smile of hers. "Luckily, my favorite nymph didn't. But we'll have time for introductions later. The moon is gone. I know it."

I helped Wacław stand before leading them through the shattered doors into the Heart's chamber. Dread weighed heavy on my shoulders at the sight of our allies. Pinned back and outnumbered, Kuba had organized the souls and Kyustendil the nymphs, but the former was just a boy, and the latter's power would be limited within the palace's walls.

My own powers were different here too. The moon's absence hadn't left me empty. Instead, my soul seemed to be *searching*, like a bird scanning the ground for a meal. Voices and visions tickled at the end of some sixth sense, luring me in, but I resisted their call. Based on the array of death filling the room, I didn't want to experience those endings.

I forced away my thoughts and focused on the battle beneath the World Tree. Our allies had sent an attack through the center, toward the bulbous roots that formed the Heart of Nawia. Unfortunately, that had just allowed the defenders to flank us on both sides.

"This was a terrible strategy," Wacław said with a shake of his head as he gripped his Moonblade. "Xobas would be ashamed."

"Blame Kuba," I replied.

"I usually do." He sighed, squeezing my hand, and I winced at the images of wind and flames that came with it. "You ready for this? No matter what, I'm not leaving unless you're free too."

When I nodded, we charged into battle, Wacław toward Kuba at the battle's core and me around the right side. The vines were everywhere here. Unlike the ones in the hall, however, Weles's presence didn't linger on them. Even he couldn't rule the World Tree.

I couldn't call those vines either, but where there was life, there was an end. Fungi coated the damp roots. The orb's light during my Ascension had shown them as part of my power—turning one life's end into another's beginning in the wilds. As I neared the warriors clashing with spears and axes, I spotted a patch of mold behind Weles's souls. Forest nymphs flew there too, launching attacks of their own. *Perfect targets.*

The mold released a flurry of spores at my command. It was something, but not nearly enough. I channeled my *życie* into them and demanded they multiply.

Suddenly, the air around the nymphs turned to a dark cloud of spores. They covered the nymphs and descended upon the warriors below.

"Oh, Oblivion," I muttered.

The spores fell toward our allies too. Above, the forest nymphs screamed as the mold consumed them. If I didn't act fast, our warriors would suffer the same.

Use the wind! Though it was weak here, the spores were light.

I turned to Wacław, but he drifted over Kuba's warriors, too engaged in the battle to leave. Kyustendil wasn't. He zipped above and sent blasts of wind at Weles's nymphs, who badly outnumbered our own.

"Kyustendil!" I shouted to him.

He snapped his gaze to me, an eccentric smile crossing his face as he raised his flute. Instead of blowing into it, he spun and whacked a male water nymph square on the chin. "Lady Otylia! I am rather occupied."

I pointed to the spores. They were accumulating on the souls, and some of the enemy warriors were already scrambling away, trying to brush them off. "Stop the spores from falling on our warriors," I called to him.

The god's eyes lit up. Of course, he would enjoy my trick with the mold. Streaking with Weles's nymphs close behind, he blew into his flute.

A barrier formed in the air between the lines of warriors. It blocked the spores, but Weles's men themselves broke through easily. They rushed forward with a new fury, desperate to escape the spores that consumed their comrades.

My heart raced. Screaming voices whipped past me with each death as I *felt* their lives end. Like a candle being extinguished, they were gone, and only I could see the lingering smoke. I hated battle. There was no thrill in these violent, unnatural deaths. It was events like this that created demons in the first place, breaking the natural cycle. Many of the corpses were our allies.

What is that? Another ten, twenty?

At this rate, less than half of those who'd honored me the night before would make it to the Heart. They deserved better.

Three forest nymphs swept toward me, singing a song like the one Sabina had earlier. Just harsher. The roots groaned beneath me. *How are they doing this?* Even I couldn't reach them here, but their song…

I dove to the side as the roots broke through the ground. They snapped at my legs, but I backed away, sweeping my spear. Even with its length and apparent weight, my moon dress moved with me easily as I fought. A bolt of light shot from the spear's end. I hadn't called its power, but *żityje* drained from me regardless as Kyustendil and Sabina arrived to scatter the nymphs.

These powers are going to take some getting used to. Channeling was hard enough. This *force*—as Rod had described it—had a will of its own. I was just its vessel.

"We're breaking through!" Wacław called through our connection.

He was right. The right flank, bolstered by my attacks against Weles's nymphs and souls, surged forward, routing the rest of the defenders on that side. The center pushed forward with the effort, and even the left had gained a stronger foothold.

We did it, I replied. *We're going to be free. I'm going to be free!*

As I rushed to Wacław, calling down more spores as I did, the remaining defenders crumbled. It had taken two gods, a demon, and an army of souls and nymphs, but we'd broken through. The Heart was just strides away from us.

Then a figure emerged from the Heart.

Loose, golden hair hung over Jaryło's broad shoulders. Six swords hung from his back—one of pure silver and five of Moonstone. The final Moonblade hummed in his hand, its green blade pulsing with bright white inscriptions upon its flat. Kwiecień's reign had ended.

Maj had come.

"You bastard!" I screamed before charging Jaryło.

The god of war and spring cut through warriors with ease. Vlatka leaped to the side, sending bolts of energy at his flank, but he spun quickly and kicked her chest. She collapsed with one sharp breath.

I gritted my teeth, but I sensed the life still within her. Jaryło wasn't finished either. With Wacław occupied against Weles's remaining nymphs and warriors, it was up to me to clear a path to the Heart. *Žityje* poured from me with each stride forward. It pooled in my hands as I gripped my spear and stabbed.

Jaryło didn't see me until too late. He raised Maj's blade in haste, barely catching the spear against the flat and deflecting the blow over his head. Light sparked from the contact between silver spear and Moonblade. It exposed the fury in his eyes and the curl of his lip.

"I thought you were smarter than this," he said.

I am.

Maj forced the sharp tip of my spear up, so I used it as a pivot. Ducking, I swung the spear's butt under the blade. Momentum guided me, and I dove at the god's legs before driving my spear through the gap between his blade and chest.

The dull end smashed his nose with a *crack* as my feet struck his shins. At once, blood streamed down his nose and he staggered back, creating an opening in his guard. *That felt good.*

Jaryło scoffed, wiping away the blood as Kyustendil dove from above. Somehow, he saw. He raised Maj, and with one mighty slash, sent the sword straight through Kyustendil's torso. Sabina screamed from somewhere behind as Kyustendil's smile faded. His flute slipped from his grasp, and his body struck the dirt in two parts. The cut was horrifically clean.

I wanted to scream too, to cry out for the god. But I felt cold, numb. Kyustendil had been exuberant and irritating. In the end, though, he'd fought by my side, and now he was dead—or at least as dead as a god could be.

Whenever you return, I promise I'll listen to your stupid songs.

Jaryło flexed his free arm, summoning his golden shield to it. Voices rushed by as Weles's final warriors died, but I glared at the god as Sabina landed at my side. "You thought you could *have* me?" I spat. "I'd rather waste away in Oblivion."

"Like your lover?" he quipped.

My tether to Wacław tightened. I didn't need to look to know he'd landed beside me, his heart racing. *Gods, he's angrier than I am.*

"You know he'll die," Jaryło continued. "One slip and his immortality fails, but you and I will carry on forever. We can defeat Marzanna and rule Jawia together as king and queen. Maybe, we can even accomplish what your mother could not: conquer Prawia."

Wacław tensed. He didn't look at me when he replied, "What in Weles are you taking about? You're the reason Marzanna is dark in the first place! Why would Otylia trust you?"

"She doesn't have to." Jaryło gripped Maj and stepped forward, still wearing that cocky grin. "But *she* is a goddess, capable of understanding what will happen to everyone here if she continues to fight." He turned his gaze to me. "Ivan, that blasted fool, is dead, and Father will return. There is no escape for your friends."

I scowled. He was right, of course. Our only hope of escape was through the winding roots that composed the Heart of Nawia, and he stood in the way. No warrior could defeat him. And with Maj in his grasp, Jaryło could just regenerate his *żityje.*

We were trapped.

Jaryło laughed as Sabina took my hand. "Your little rebellion was quite the sight, sister, but it's over now. You may have tricked me before and taken my sword—one he seems to have somehow tapped into—but this time will be different. Though I am not my father when it comes to tricks, I *am* a god of war."

Wacław stepped forward, his eyes narrow. *What are you doing?* He grinned. "And I'm a płanetnik. This palace of Weles's is impressive, but I've spent a lot of time in the forest. You know what wood *really* doesn't like?"

Then I felt it. *Żityje* poured from him. Far less than I could wield but enough to call a storm from nothing. I smirked at the sight of Weles's dead warriors surrounding us, many of their chests cut open. Wacław must've drained them throughout the battle. Once, that may have disgusted me, but survival was all that mattered now.

Lightning shot from him.

Jaryło charged with a shout as the bolts scattered in every direction, cracking into the World Tree and the walls of the chamber. The god's shield deflected most of the bolts, but one struck his cheek.

His skin charred. Rage consumed his gaze as flames spread throughout the room. Wacław used that aggression, diving to the side and raising Kwiecień.

Maj struck its sister blade in a brilliant light. The resulting blast tore across the room, flinging away souls and nymphs alike, but I held out my free hand, whispering, "*Rìnoti.*"

The power rushed around my shimmering shield like a river. The spell held, though, and Wacław shouted to me as he struggled to defend against the god. "Now, Otylia!"

I took a sharp breath and gripped my silver spear. It glowed with my passion, my hatred of Jaryło. He'd betrayed me. He'd stolen me from my realm and the people I loved. He'd delayed my quest to find Mother. And worst of all, he'd dared to *claim* me. I didn't care that he opposed Marzanna. Jaryło had turned her into a monster, and he deserved to suffer for the pain he'd caused Jawia as a result.

The voices around me grew deafening as I drove the spear into Jaryło's stomach. Smoke stung my eyes, and visions flashed within the haze, each life lost in the battle. I felt their sorrow and grief. I felt the pain of the blade striking them down. Warriors, nymphs, and then Kyustendil himself. Eternity came with his memories, too much to comprehend as I heard the winds through his ears. An ending for the god. Temporary, fleeting, but an ending nonetheless.

Amid it all, a louder scream pierced the noise. It came from above. Weeping, like a mother for her lost child. *The World Tree…*

The flames burned its roots along with Weles's palace. Such a blaze couldn't destroy the backbone of the Three Realms, but it felt pain nonetheless. I'd never considered the World Tree to have a spirit of its own. I sensed her now. Greater than any god or even Death himself, she'd lived since the realms' beginning, and she would remain until its end. I mourned her suffering.

"Let's go!" Kuba shouted to the others, tearing me back to reality after what had seemed like hours.

A staggering Vlatka led our remaining allies through the Heart, but shock paralyzed me. Despite the blaze and shouting of our allies, the battle's aftermath seemed like silence compared to what I'd just experienced. Tears streamed down my cheeks. I released the spear, impaled into the god of war as I dropped to my knees, shaking. It was too much. The visions, the death, and the World Tree's suffering. I'd felt all of it.

"Jaryło's not dead," Wacław said as he knelt before me. Determination filled his eyes, not the panic of the boy I'd known for so long. "You did it, but we need to get out of here now!"

I nodded absently. The World Tree still screamed around me, but I staggered to my feet with Wacław's help. *I'm sorry…*

With my arm over Wacław's shoulder and the flames closing in, we approached the Heart. I felt its pull now, calling me home. It felt like years since I'd left Jawia's forests and plains. So much had changed in the moon since, and I barely knew who I was anymore. But I had Ascended. Mother awaited me. I would free her, no matter the cost.

57

Otylia

Goodbye, Nawia. May I never see you again.

THE WORLD TWISTED AROUND US the moment we entered the winding roots of the Heart. Unlike my visions, though, there were no voices or images. We instead stepped into a world unlike any I knew.

Sand met me as I dropped, my breaths shallow and quick. *We made it. But where are we?*

The new moon cast little light over the landscape. Wacław was barely visible beside me, Kwiecień's glow dulled from his use of its power. Scrapes covered his arms and his chest beneath his ripped tunic, but he smiled as he drove the blade into the sand and leaned on it. "So, this is a desert."

"Apparently," I huffed. "Where are the others? Sabina? Kuba?"

He shook his head, sending his unusually long hair over his eyes. "The winds don't sense them anywhere. They made it through before us. Maybe the Heart sent them somewhere else?"

I clenched my jaw. Sabina had stayed by my side whenever I needed her in Nawia, and now, she was on her own in an unfamiliar realm. I hoped the others were with her. "We need to figure out where we are. Then, we need to find them."

"Then we better start walking. Calling that lightning storm used basically all my *żityje*."

"I'm drained too." I groaned and stood with his help, trying to keep my skin from touching his. *How do I tell him I can't touch him?* For now, it was incredibly annoying, but I feared what it would mean for our future. *Survive first,* I reminded myself. We were in the middle of nowhere with no water or food sources in sight.

So, we started walking. There were no obvious signs of life, but a distant voice came from the north. Though it spoke a tongue I'd never heard, I followed it up a steep dune. My legs ached with each stride. It had been far too long since I'd rested. In the middle of that desert, the cool sand covering me to my shins, I would settle for anything familiar. A house, trees, even dirt would do. But there was only sand.

Neither of us spoke for a long time. There was a simplicity in just walking side-by-side, too exhausted to do anything but continue on. Somehow, we'd escaped Weles and Jaryło. That fact hadn't settled within me yet. I didn't feel free, yet there was a calm within me. Was it Wacław or the silent pulse of the moon's power?

The force of endings had been so loud during the battle that I was content with the quiet. In time, I would figure out my new powers. I would become the goddess I needed to be in order to save Mother. For now, though, I let myself be glad Wacław was by my side.

He'd fought his way across Jawia and between the realms to find me. Why? Destiny had claimed the Sudiczki had bound us from birth, but there was something more. Wacław loved me, and I him. He was a demon, yes. But he cared. He was mine. Even if it was just for hours walking in a moonlit desert, something felt complete with him.

As we walked, the voice grew louder. Others joined it. A disjointed chorus, they filled the air as wisps floated by, carrying images with each. Hundreds of them. Death, birth, failure, redemption… I saw it all in the passing visions.

"A village must be close," I said, taking care not to touch any of the wisps.

Wacław let out a relieved sigh. "Thank the gods. I'm too drained to even search with the winds anymore. How far is it?"

Pulling my cloak of autumn leaves tighter around me, I continued north for a few more steps. A light flickered in the distance. It hung in the air, and when I squinted, releasing a small bit of *żityje* to help my night vision with the moon's power, I gasped. "It's a tower."

I charged on, my skirts flapping behind me on the breeze. That light had ignited a hope within me. We weren't alone. We'd find a place to rest before recovering and finding the others.

A wall of stone soon became visible. It stretched further than I could see in each direction, and more lights illuminated what seemed to be hundreds of buildings within. "We made it!" I exclaimed, stopping and looking back at Wacław.

He reached my side with raspy breaths. Sweat dripped from his brow despite the cold, and he held his hands on his knees as he looked ahead at the city. "Hopefully they're friendly. I love the dress, but you don't exactly look like an average traveler."

"You're right." I remembered Weles's changes of appearance. Had he been able to manipulate his body and clothes at will? He'd said that the gods represented how people saw their forces. What did that mean for me?

Eyes shut, I pictured myself wearing the bone-colored dress I'd left Dwie Rzeki in two moons ago. Amulets and woven hair. I added the silver fox pelt as well, its bond calling to me. *Żityje* trickled from my soul, but I had enough as I opened my eyes and watched the streaks of light circle me. They worked quickly. From my boots to the talismans lining my braid, I looked like Dziewanna's szeptucha again. *Why does that hurt so much?*

"Well, that works," Wacław chuckled.

I grinned and looked down at the familiar clothes. My long gown and armband were gone, but something was wrong. They still felt as if they were against my skin. I ran my fingers along the sleeves, and a ripple of light split around them.

"It's an illusion," I breathed. "Not exactly what I intended, but it'll have to work. It looks convincing, right?"

Wacław wasn't looking at me though. Panic struck his heart, flooding through our connection as he stepped back, his jaw ajar. "How?" He held up his Frostmarked hand. Marzanna's cross glowed brightly upon it. "Her Frostmarked are here," he muttered. "I've never sensed so many of them."

Surely enough, when we drew closer, the sand gave way to snow and our breaths fogged the air. Fear stopped me when we reached the skulls—impaled on the end of spears driven into the ground, there were hundreds of them. They lined the path to a gate in the stone wall. Above it hung a banner. Before, it must have held a tribe's emblem, but now, all that remained was a Frostmark drawn in blood.

"Marzanna conquered the desert," I said, shivering.

"No," Wacław replied, his eyes narrow as he examined the decapitated heads. Each bore a Frostmark. "She's enslaved it, and we're next."

END OF BOOK 2

A Word From The Author

I have to begin by saying that this has been the most fun book I have written so far. Switching between Wacław and Otylia's points-of-views in separate locations with their own stories for much of the book was a great challenge, and I hope you had as much fun reading this as I did writing it. Much of *A Dagger in the Winds* was building the elements of the world and introducing the character dynamics, so being able to capitalize on those in *The Trials of Ascension* was freeing. With Wacław and Otylia back together, I'm looking forward to showing you how their relationship and powers interact! We're just getting started.

If you have enjoyed reading this story, please take the time to post an honest review on whatever retailer you purchased this book from. Every review helps new readers discover the series.

To receive your free copy of *The Rider in the Night*—the prequel novella to The Frostmarked Chronicles—other side-novellas attached to the series, and exclusive first looks at upcoming books, join my newsletter at www.Brendan-Noble.com.

- Brendan

About the Author

Brendan Noble is a Polish and German-American author currently writing fantasy books based on Slavic mythology. He is fascinated with history, economics, and politics in both reality and fiction.

Brendan is a recent graduate in Economics from Hillsdale College in Michigan. In 2019, he moved from his hometown of Canton, Michigan to Rockford, Illinois when he married his wife, Andrea. Brendan began his writing career in November of 2018 with a challenge from his wife to complete NaNoWriMo (National Novel Writing Month) and has been an author ever since.

Outside of writing, Brendan is a data analyst and soccer referee. His top interests include German, Polish, and American soccer/football, Formula 1, analyzing political elections across the world, playing extremely nerdy strategy video games, exploring with his wife, and reading.

www.ingramcontent.com/pod-product-compliance
Lightning Source LLC
Chambersburg PA
CBHW020343310726
48979CB00015B/2489/J

* 9 7 8 1 7 3 3 0 4 2 5 3 6 *